PENGUIN BOOKS

MAN'S ESTATE

ANDRÉ MALRAUX

MAN'S ESTATE

Translated from the French by
ALASTAIR MACDONALD

PENGUIN BOOKS

Penguin Books Ltd, Harmondsworth, Middlesex, England
Penguin Books Australia Ltd, Ringwood, Victoria, Australia

—

La Condition humaine first published 1933
This translation first published by Methuen under the title
Storm in Shanghai 1934 and under the title *Man's Estate* 1948

—

Published by Hamish Hamilton 1968
First published in Penguin Books 1961
Reissued 1972

—

Made and printed in Great Britain by
Hunt Barnard Printing Ltd, Aylesbury
Set in Monotype Bembo

Part 1

12.30 A.M.

SHOULD Chen try lifting up the mosquito-net? Or should he strike through it? He felt desperate in his inability to decide. He knew he was strong really, but for the moment it was only a blank realization, powerless before that mass of white muslin which draped down from the ceiling over a body that was vaguer than a shadow; from which only a foot protruded, the foot of a sleeper, angular but still convincingly human flesh. What light there was came from the neighbouring building: a great rectangle of pale electric light, striped by the shadows of the window-bars, one of which cut across the bed just below the man's foot, as if to give it greater substance and reality. Four or five klaxons rasped out all together. Had he been discovered? If only he could fight, fight an enemy who was on his guard, who gave blow for blow – what a relief that would be!

The wave of noise receded: a traffic jam (so there still were traffic jams out there, in the real world . . .). Once more he was faced with the great shapeless splodge of muslin and the rectangle of light, fixed particles in a world grown timeless.

He kept telling himself that the man must die. It was foolish; for he knew that he was going to kill him. Whether he was caught or not, paid the penalty or not, mattered little. Nothing counted any more but that foot, this man whom his blow must paralyse before he could resist: there must be no resistance, or he would call out.

Chen's eyelids fluttered as he stood there, and the thought came to him, rose up till it sickened him, that he was not the

5

fighter he expected, but one performing a sacrifice. And to more than the gods of his own choosing. This was his offering to the Revolution, but in its train black horrors would rise from the abyss, till the crushing anguish of that night would pale into insignificance before them. 'Assassination isn't like ordinary killing: far from it. . . .' In his pockets his hands waited doubtfully; in the right he held a razor, closed; in the left a short dagger. He stuffed them in as far as possible, as though without that aid the darkness were insufficient to conceal his doings. The razor was safer, but Chen knew that he could never bring himself to use it: he was less revolted by the dagger. The back of the razor was digging into his clenched fingers, and he let go of it; the dagger lay naked in his pocket, without a sheath. He changed it over into his right hand, his left dropping down on to the woollen surface of his singlet, and clinging there. He raised his right arm a little, amazed that the silence remained unbroken around him, as if some catastrophe should have been precipitated by his gesture. But nothing happened, nothing at all: he was still in control.

That foot lay there like a sleeping animal. Was there a body on the end of it? 'Am I going crazy?' He must see that body. Have a look at it, look at its head; to do that he had to move into the light, let his squat shadow fall across the bed. How much resistance did flesh offer? Suddenly Chen jabbed the dagger into his left arm. He was almost beyond realizing that it was his arm, but the pain, the certainty of punishment if the sleeper should awake, brought him back to reality for a moment. Punishment was preferable to this atmosphere of insanity. He went closer. It was undoubtedly the man he had seen two hours earlier, with the light full on him. All at once the foot, which was almost touching Chen's trousers, turned round like a key in a lock; then went back to its old position, and was still again. Perhaps as he slept he could feel him there, though it didn't fully rouse him. . . . Chen shuddered: an insect was running over his skin. No; it was the blood which was

6

coming trickling out of his arm. The feeling of sea-sickness persisted.

One move and the man would have ceased to live. To kill him was nothing; it was touching him that was impossible. And the blow had to be delivered with the utmost precision. The sleeper, lying on his back in his European style of bed, wore only a short pair of pants; but his ribs were invisible under the loose flesh. Chen would have to take aim from the position of the man's nipples. He knew how difficult it is to strike directly downwards. He held the blade of the dagger up in the air, but the left breast was the farther from him; with the mesh of the mosquito-net in the way he would have to strike at arm's length – following a curve, like the swing in boxing. He altered the angle of the dagger, so that now the blade was horizontal. To touch this motionless body was as difficult as touching a corpse; possibly for the same reasons. As if invoked by the thought of a corpse, the man's breath rattled in his throat. Chen could not even draw back, his legs and arms had ceased to obey him. But the rattling noise became rhythmical: not a death-rattle, the man was snoring. At once he was alive again, vulnerable; and simultaneously Chen's sense of bafflement returned to him. The body slipped fractionally over to the right. Was he going to wake up at this point? With a blow hard enough to pierce a plank, Chen stopped him short, to the screech of slit muslin and a dull thud, commingled. Physically conscious to the tip of the steel blade, he felt the body jerk towards him, rebounding off the spring mattress. Furiously he stiffened his arm to hold it there; the legs swung up together to the chest, as if tied to it – then suddenly stretched out straight. He ought to strike again, but how was he to draw out the dagger? The body still lay on its side, unstably, and despite the convulsion that had just shaken it Chen had the impression of holding it down to the bed with his arm, on which he was still leaning the whole of his weight. Through the wide tear in the mosquito-net he could see the body quite clearly; the eyelids

7

were open – could he have woken then? – and the eyes them-selves showed white. Blood began to seep along the blade of the dagger, looking black in this unreal light. There seemed to be life in the very weight of this body, ready to fall to right or left. Chen could not let go of the dagger. Along its blade, up his stiffened arm, across his smarting shoulder, a sensation of the utmost horror found its way, from the body, deep into his chest; to his thumping heart, the only thing that moved in all the room. He stayed absolutely quiet; the blood which still flowed from his left arm seemed to belong to the dead man. For although there was no external change, he knew for certain that the man was dead. Scarcely breathing, he held this thing still on its side in the dim, unaltered light, in the emptiness of the room. There was nothing to indicate a struggle – not even the rent in the muslin, which seemed to have been split into two strips; only the silence and an overpowering tipsiness in which he clung to his weapon, foundering, far from the world of the living. His fingers clenched tighter and tighter, but the muscles of his arm relaxed and its whole length swung loose, like a rope. It was not fear that possessed him, it was a frightful and at the same time solemn sensation of panic such as he had not known since childhood; he was alone with death, alone in a place where no man was, feebly overcome at once by horror and by the taste of blood.

He managed to open his hand. The body rolled gently over on to its stomach; as the hilt stood crooked, a dark stain began to spread on the sheet, growing like a living thing. And next to it, becoming larger too as it became larger, he saw the shadow of two pointed ears.

The door was a good way off, the balcony closer; but it was from the balcony that shadows came. Although Chen did not believe in evil spirits he stood rooted where he was. Something miaowed; he gave a start. Half-way to deliverance, he now dared to look. A gutter cat glided in from the balcony on silent pads, its eyes fixed on him. A furious rage shook Chen as this shadow advanced towards him, anger not against the animal itself but against its presence here; nothing that had life ought to enter this strange region into which he himself had sunk; this thing that had observed him knife in hand barred the way of his return to reality. He opened the razor, took a step forward; the creature fled through the window. Chen dashed after it – and found himself face to face with Shanghai.

To his tortured mind the night seemed to froth up into an enormous swirl of black smoke, full of sparks; then, as his breathing came more smoothly, it took shape, and through the rifts in the clouds stars clicked into place, dragging him back as he met the colder outdoor air, to all the ordered universe that they implied. A siren droned up the scale, then gave way to utter peace. Down below, right down, in the lights of midnight which the glistening tarmac and the pale lines of rails threw back through a yellow fog, throbbed the world which does not kill. There were millions of lives in that world, and each one had cast him out: but what did their puny outlawry avail against the relief he felt that death was leaving him, the feeling that it welled out from him in long gushes, like that man's blood? All those shadows, flickering or still, went to make up Life; like the river, like the sea that was too far off to be visible – the sea. . . . At last he breathed as deep a breath as he could take, and as his chest expanded he felt with immeasurable relief that Life had received him again – relief that was near to tears, that was almost as shattering as all that he had just passed through. 'Best get out of this . . .' He remained, watching the cars go by, and the people moving quickly past in the lighted street underneath; like a blind man who sees again, like a starving man eating. Greedily, madly he wanted Life; he would have liked to touch those bodies. The screech of a siren split the air, on the far side of the river: the night-shift coming off duty at the Arsenal. If the Workers were stupid enough to go and turn out arms that were destined to kill the men who fought for them – then let them! Was that brightly lit town to be held for ever by her military dictator, be farmed out for ever, like so much livestock, to War Lords and Western commerce? His murderous deed was worth many days' output from the arsenals of China. The approaching attempt to place Shanghai in the hands of the Revolutionaries would not have two hundred rifles behind it. If the short carbines (almost three hundred in number) which the dead entrepreneur had just arranged to sell to the Government were thrown in too, the chances of the rebels would be doubled, for their first step would be to seize the arms of the police for their own troops. But during the last ten minutes, Chen had not once thought about that.

And he hadn't got the paper yet – the paper for which he had killed that man. He went back, as though he were going back to prison. The clothes were hanging at the foot of the bed, beneath the netting. He went through the pockets. A handkerchief, some cigarettes. . . . No wallet. The room looked just the same: mosquito-net, white walls, clear-cut rectangle of light; so murder doesn't make any difference to things. . . . He felt under the pillow, shutting his eyes. The wallet was there, very small, hardly bigger than a little note-case. Distraught (was it fear or shame?), for the sensation of the head gently pressing down the pillow was horribly eerie, he reopened his eyes: there was no blood on the bolster, and the man didn't look in the least dead. For a moment he almost thought he would have to kill him again. But a glance at the staring eyes and the blood on the sheets reassured him. He drew back into the light, to examine the wallet: the light came from a restaurant, full of people gambling. He found the paper, put it back in the wallet, then almost ran across the room, locked the door, and put the key in his pocket. A corridor of the hotel – he tried to walk slower – with no lift there at the end. Should he ring? He walked down. Down below, where the dancing went on, and the bar and billiard-rooms were to be found, ten or a dozen people stood waiting for the lift, which was coming down. He mingled with them. 'The little piece in red is an absolute peach!' said the man next to him, in English. He was Burmese or Siamese by the look of him, and rather drunk. Chen wanted both to strike him, to make him hold his tongue, and to embrace him because he was alive. He mumbled an incoherent answer; the other man leered at him, and tapped him on the shoulder. 'He thinks I'm drunk too. . . . ' But the man was starting to speak again. 'I don't know foreign languages,' said Chen, in Pekinese. The other man said no more, but gazed with interest at this young man who wore a neat woollen sweater, but no collar. Chen was opposite the mirror inside the lift. His face showed no signs of the murder. . . . There was nothing but fatigue in his face: the features were unchanged, more Mongolian than Chinese: strongly marked cheekbones, nose very flattened, but with a slight ridge like a beak; even his massive shoulders and thick, dominating lips betrayed nothing untoward; only his arm, sticky when he bent it, and hot. . . . The lift stopped. He got out with the others.

1.30 A.M.

He bought a bottle of mineral water, and called a taxi: a closed one, in which he washed his arm and bound it up with a handkerchief. A faint gleam came from the deserted tramlines and the puddles left by the showers of the afternoon. It was a reflection of the glow in the sky. Without knowing why, Chen looked up at it: how much nearer he had been to it a moment before, when he had first noticed the stars! As his exaltation diminished and he came gradually back to ordinary life, they seemed to become more and more remote.

At the end of the street were machine-guns, almost as grey as the puddles, and a bright barrier of bayonets, carried by silent shadows. It was the picket which showed where the French Concession began. The taxi went no farther. Chen showed his faked passport, passing himself off as an electrician at work in the Concession. The official just glanced at it ('It certainly doesn't show what I've just done'), and let him pass. In front of him rose up the Avenue des Deux-Républiques, which marked the boundary of the Chinese town. Alone in the silence. Laden with all the noises of the largest town in China, waves of sound came rumbling up and died away, like vibrations coming from the depths of the earth, to lose themselves at the bottom of a well: the noises of men in arms, and the last fretful tossings of a multitude which has no wish to sleep. But men were far away; the world made no contact here. There was only the night, and Chen gave himself up to it instinctively, as if to a sudden offer of friendship. Murder was quite in keeping with that restless world of the night; a world in which men played no part, a timeless world. Would there ever be another dawn? Would those crumbling tiles ever see the light again, or all those passages in whose depths lanterns gave a glimpse of windowless walls, mazes of telegraph wires? Murder had absorbed him into a world of its own, and he found it as hard to escape from it as from the heat itself. There was no sign of life. Not the least movement, no noise anywhere near; not even the cries of hawkers, not even the barking of stray dogs.

At last he came to a miserable little shop: *Lou You Shen and Hemmelrich, gramophones.* He must come back to reality now. ... He waited for a few minutes, but something of the spell still remained. Then he knocked on one of the shutters. The door opened almost at once. The place was full of gramophone records, carefully arranged, so that it looked like a sort of little library: beyond, in the back part of the shop, large and bare, sat four men in shirt-sleeves. The lamp swayed as the door was shut: the faces disappeared, appeared again: on the left Lou You Shen, completely rotund; then Hemmelrich, a battered hulk of a boxer, with shaven head, broken nose, and sagging shoulders. Behind, in the shadow, Katow. On the right, Kyo Gisors; as the lamp swung over his head it showed up his mouth in strong relief, drooping at the corners like a Japanese print: when it swung away the shadows shifted, and the face which had looked half-caste became almost European. The lamp grew gradually steadier, and Kyo's two faces reappeared one after the other, less and less dissimilar.

Desperately anxious for information, they all looked at Chen with pathetic earnestness, but no one spoke. He looked down at the stones in the floor, spattered with sunflower seeds chewed and expectorated. He could give these men information, but he could never put into words all that was in his mind. The way the body had resisted the knife obsessed him, it was so unlike his own arm: surprise had given it impetus at the last moment, or the weapon would not have gone in very far. 'I should never have thought it would be so hard.'

'It's all right,' he said.

In the room, face to face with the body, once full realization had come to him, he had been quite certain: he had *felt* Death.

He held out the order for the delivery of the arms. It was very long-winded. Kyo started to read it.

'Yes, but . . .'

They all waited. Kyo showed no impatience or irritation; he hadn't moved; perhaps he looked just a little tense. But every one knew that he had discovered something which shook him to the core. At last he got the words out.

'They haven't been paid for. *Payable on Delivery*.'

Chen felt a sudden rage, as if he had stupidly let some one steal something from him. He had been convinced that that piece of paper was the one he was looking for, but had had no time to read it. In any case, he couldn't have done anything about it. He took the wallet out of his pocket and gave it to Kyo: some photos and receipts; nothing else.

'I think we'll be able to fix it up with one of the Shock Sections,' said Kyo.

'As long as we can manage to climb on board,' answered Katow, 'it'll be all right.'

Silence. Their presence was breaking down Chen's ghastly feeling of isolation. It yielded gently, like an uprooted plant which still clings to the ground with a few slender threads. And as he gradually drew nearer to them it seemed to him that he suddenly knew them for the first time – as he had known his sister after his first visit to a brothel. They had the feeling of strain which comes to gamblers at the end of a night's play.

'Did it go well?' asked Katow, at last putting down his record and moving into the light.

Chen looked at that honest, comic, Russian face, but did not answer: those mocking little eyes and upturned nose, which even that light could not make impressive. *He* knew what death meant, if the other didn't. Katow got up; he went and looked at the cricket asleep in its tiny cage; Chen might have reasons for his silence. Chen was watching the light swinging; it relieved the strain. The cricket had been woken up by his arrival, and its shrill chirping joined in, as the swaying shadow wobbled to a standstill.

The memory of the hardness of that body haunted him; he felt an urge to press his arm hard up against the first thing he came across. Speech would shatter the intimacy of his communion with death.

'What time did you leave the hotel?' asked Kyo.

'Twenty minutes ago'

Kyo looked at his watch: twenty to one.

'Good. Let's get things settled here, and move on.'

'I want to see your father, Kyo.'

'You know that it is probably arranged for tomorrow?'

'All the better.'

They all knew what *it* meant: the arrival of the revolutionary troops at the railway termini, which was to be the signal for the rising.

'All the better,' said Chen again. Like all violent sensations murder and danger left a void behind them: he burned to experience them anew.

'Still – I want to see him.'

'Go along there tonight: he never goes to sleep before dawn.'

'I'll go about four o'clock.'

Whenever he sought support and sympathy, Chen instinctively went to old Gisors. He knew that he made a very painful impression on Katow by doing so – the more so because it had nothing to do with conceit. He knew it, but it had no effect on him. Kyo was one of the organizers of the revolt, a man trusted by the inner council; Chen no less; but he would never take life in cold blood. Katow was nearer to him, Katow who had been condemned to five years' penal servitude in 1905 when a medical student, for having attempted to blow up the prison gates at Odessa. Still ...

The Russian was eating little sugar sweets, one after another, without taking his eyes off Chen; and Chen had a sudden feeling of greed. Now that he had killed a man, he had the right to feel anything he wanted. The right. Even if the feeling was a childish one. He put out his spade-like hand. Katow thought that he wanted to leave, and gave it a shake. Chen stood up. Perhaps it was just as well: he couldn't do anything more; Kyo had all the information – it was for him to act on it. As far as he, Chen, was concerned, he knew well enough what he wanted now. He went to the door, but came back again.

'Pass me some of the sweets.'

Katow gave him the bag. He wanted to divide them; no paper. He poured them out into the palm of his hand, crammed them into his mouth and went out munching.

'It must have been a pretty tricky business,' said Katow.

He had been a refugee in Switzerland from 1905 till 1912, when he returned secretly to Russia, and though he spoke French without any trace of a Russian accent, his vowels were blurred at times, as if by way of compensation for the precise articulation which became necessary when he talked Chinese. When he stood almost underneath the lamp like that, the light hardly touched his face. Kyo liked him best that way: the whimsical, ingenuous expression which Katow's small eyes and even more his upturned nose gave him struck him all the more forcibly because it differed so completely from his own features: it often irritated him.

'Let's get it over,' he said. 'Have you got the records, Lou?'

Wreathed in smiles, bobbing up and down in his anxiety to please, Lou You Shen submitted two records to Katow for examination, then placed one on each gramophone. It was essential to start them off together.

'One, two, three,' counted Kyo.

The scratching of the first record rendered the other one inaudible; suddenly it stopped – and they heard: send. Then it went on again. Another word came through: thirty. More scratching. Then: men. Scratching.

'Excellent,' said Kyo. He stopped them, then started off the first record alone. Scratch, silence, scratch. Stop.

'Good. Label that as a dud.'

Now the other one: Third lesson. To run, to walk, to go, to come, to send, to receive. One, two, three, four, five, six, seven, eight, nine, ten, twenty, thirty, forty, fifty, sixty, one hundred. I saw the men running. There are twenty women here. Thirty . . .

Those imitation language-records were excellent: the counterfeit label was beautifully done. Kyo was worried though:

'Didn't my voice record well?'

'Excellently, splendidly.'

Lou began to smile; Hemmelrich didn't seem to be taking any notice. From upstairs came the cries of a child in pain.

Kyo couldn't make it out:

'Then why has it been changed?'

'It hasn't been changed,' said Lou. 'It's your own. Hardly any one recognizes his own voice, you know, when he hears it for the first time.'

'Does the gramophone distort it?'

'It's not that, for there's never any difficulty about recognizing other people's voices. You see, we just aren't used to hearing our own voices. . . .'

Lou was experiencing to the full the delight of the Chinaman in explaining to a person of intelligence something of which he was previously unaware.

'The same thing applies to our own language . . .'

'Right. Is it still the plan to come and fetch them tonight?'

'The boats leave at dawn tomorrow for Hankow.'

The records which made the scratching noise were sent off by one boat: the talking ones by another. The latter were in either French or English, according to whether the local Mission was Catholic or Protestant. The revolutionaries sometimes used genuine language-records, sometimes those of their own recording.

'At dawn,' thought Kyo. 'A lot's got to happen before then. . . .' He stood up.

'We need volunteers, for the arms. And if possible a few Europeans.'

Hemmelrich came up to him. Upstairs the child was crying again.

'There's the kid's answering you himself,' said Hemmelrich. 'Is that enough? What the blazing hell would you do yourself with the kid just about to kick the bucket and the old girl lying moaning up there – not making too much noise about it, in case she disturbs us. . . .'

There was something like hatred in his voice, according well enough with the broken nose and sunken eyes, reduced to two black daubs by the light coming straight down from above.

'There's a job for everybody,' Kyo answered. 'The records are essential, too. Katow and I can manage. Let's go and collect some of our men: we can find out incidentally whether the attack is to come off tomorrow or not, and I . . .'

'They may run across the body at the hotel,' said Katow.

'Not before dawn. Chen locked the door. There's no night-watchman.'

'Perhaps the agent had arranged to meet him?'

'At this time of night? Unlikely. Whatever happens, the vital thing is to see that that boat is moved to another anchorage. They'll waste at least three hours looking for her then, if they do try and start anything. She's right out by the harbour-bar.'

'Where are you going to shift her to?'

'Inside the harbour. Not alongside the quay, naturally. There are hundreds of ships there. Three hours lost, at least. At least.'

'The captain will wonder what's up.'

Katow's face rarely gave any clue to his feelings: his whimsical expression never deserted him. His voice alone reflected his uneasiness just then; but the impression was all the stronger.

'I know a man who specializes in the arms traffic,' said Kyo. 'The captain won't suspect him. We haven't much money, but we can make it worth his while. . . . I imagine we're agreed on the best way to go to work: we use the paper to get us on board, and after that we'll take things as they come?'

Katow shrugged his shoulders, as though it wasn't much use arguing. He put on his pea-jacket, which he always left open at the neck, and handed Kyo a coat which was hanging from a chair: they both shook Hemmelrich warmly by the hand. Pity would only have increased his humiliation. They went out.

They left the avenue at once, and entered the Chinese quarter.

Heavy banks of clouds hung low overhead, drifting less densely in places, but for the moment hiding the stars from view, save for glimpses through the rifts here and there.

The shifting clouds made the darkness like a living thing, fading and deepening, as though at times huge shadows were arriving and the night grew darker at their bidding. Katow and Kyo were wearing light rubber-soled shoes, and it was only when they slipped on the mud that their steps became audible: over by the Concessions – the enemy – a dull glow lowered over the house-tops.

Slowly a long siren-note swelled until it filled the wind which wafted across the faint hum coming from the besieged city, almost silent now, and the hooting of the picket-boats as they returned to the men-of-war. Wafted it across, and bore it away past the wretched electric lamps which glimmered down the side streets and the alleys which engulfed them: all around them crumbling walls stood out from the waste of shadow, laid bare in all their blotchy nakedness by that merciless un-wavering light, which seemed unearthly in its unrelieved drab-ness. Those walls hid half a million men: hands from the spinning-mills, men who work sixteen hours a day from early childhood, ulcerous, twisted, famine-stricken. The coverings which protected the bulbs lost their clear outline, and in a few minutes rain, rain as it only falls in China, raging, slashing down, took possession of the town.

'A good quarter,' thought Kyo. For more than a month he had gone from one meeting to another, organizing the rising, oblivious of the existence of streets: what was mud to him beside his plans?

The scrabbling of the myriads for their daily bread was giving place to another, a more vital energy. The Concessions, the rich quarters of the town, with rain-washed palings guard-ing the streets which gave access to them, no longer existed save as a menace, a barrier, long windowless prison walls; but in these nauseous slums, which provided the largest muster of Shock Troops, throbbed the pulse of a vast and vigilant horde. As he turned out of a narrow passage he suddenly found him-self looking down one of the main streets, wide and well-lit. Despite the rain beating down, which half obscured its out-lines, he never for a moment saw it save as something flat which would have to be attacked in the face of rifles and machine-guns, firing horizontally. After the failure of the February insurrections, the central committee of the Communist Party had instructed Kyo to set about the coordination of the revolutionary forces. In each of those silent streets where the downpour was blotting out the outlines of the houses, the number of combatants had been doubled. The rain smelt of smoke. Kyo had asked for the numbers to be raised from two thousand to five, and it had taken the military staff less than a month to do so. But they hadn't got two hundred rifles among them (and there were three hundred carbines there for the taking on board the *Shan-Tung* as she rocked up and down in the estuary). Kyo had divided up the fighting-men into a hundred and ninety-two detachments of about twenty-five men, all provided with leaders: only the leaders were armed.

They went past a garage full of old lorries converted into omnibuses. All the garages were 'listed'. The heads of the military department had constituted a General Staff: the Party Assembly had elected a Central Committee; once the insurrection began they would have to be kept in touch with the Shock Sections. Kyo had organized a liaison detachment of a hundred cyclists for a start; directly the first shots were fired, eight Sections were to take possession of the garages and seize the motor-cars. The leaders of these sections had already visited the garages and would make no mistakes. All the other section-leaders had spent ten days now studying the districts in which they were going to operate. How many visitors, that very day, had made their way into the principal buildings, asked to see a friend whom nobody knew, chatted and suggested tea before they went away? How many workmen, notwithstanding the torrential rain, were repairing roofs? All the vantage-points were known as far as street-fighting was concerned; the best points to fire from, marked in red on the plans, at the Shock-Section headquarters. Kyo knew enough about the underground preparations for the rising to feel fairly confident about the details of which he was ignorant. Something far bigger than himself was rising from the great tattered flanks of the town, from Chapei and Pootung, covered with factories and misery; something that would galvanize into activity the giant nerve-centres of the city. That judgement-night was quickened by an unseen host.

'Tomorrow?' said Kyo.

Katow hesitated, stopped swinging his huge hands. No, the question was not addressed to him. Nor indeed to anyone.

They walked in silence. The shower was giving place to a steady drizzle: the rapping of the rain on the roofs grew fainter, and the darkness of the street was filled with the gurgle of water running away. Their faces relaxed: they saw the street now with the eyes of reality – long, black, expressionless; and it seemed to Kyo as though he was re-experiencing something which had long lain buried in his memory, so strong had been his obsession.

'Where do you suppose Chen has got to?' he asked. 'He said he wouldn't go to my father till about four o'clock. Would he be asleep?'

There was an incredulous admiration behind the question.

'Don't know. . . . In a brothel, perhaps. . . . He doesn't get drunk. . . .'

They came to a shop: SHIA, LAMPSELLER. Like everywhere else, the shutters were up. The door was opened. A ghastly looking little Chinaman confronted them, dimly shown up by the light behind him. A halo of light surrounded his head, and his slightest movement sent an oily streak darting across his huge pimple-studded nose. Innumerable hurricane-lamps hung on the walls, the flames of two lanterns on the counter striking a reflection in them, until they were lost in the gloom, far away in the invisible depths of the shop.

'Well?' said Kyo.

Shia looked at him, and rubbed his hands obsequiously. He turned round without a word, walked a step or two, and rummaged in some hiding-place or other. His nails scratched against a tin in a way that set Katow's teeth on edge: but he was back almost at once, his braces flapping loose. . . . Kyo read the paper which he had unearthed, his head almost touching one of the lamps, with the light coming up from underneath. It was a report from the combatant detachment operating with the railwaymen. The reinforcements for the defence of Shanghai against the revolutionaries were being drawn from Nankin: the railwaymen had gone on strike: the white guards and the Government soldiers were compelling those whom they caught to drive the troop-trains, under penalty of death.

'One of the men arrested has derailed the train he was driving,' read the Chinaman. 'Killed. Three other troop-trains were derailed yesterday owing to the track having been removed.'

'Issue orders for extension of "sabotage" policy to all sections, and have notes inserted concerning the quickest way of effecting repairs,' said Kyo.

'The White Guards shoot anybody caught doing wilful damage. . . .'

'The Committee know that. We'll shoot back. Another thing: any munition trains?'

'No.'

'Is it known when our men reach Cheng Chow?'

'I haven't had the midnight report yet. The man from the Central Office thinks it'll be either tonight or tomorrow. . . .'

So the revolution would begin on the next day or the day after. They would have to await instructions from Headquarters. Kyo was thirsty. They went out.

They weren't far from the point where they would have to leave each other. Again there came the sound of a ship's siren; three short blasts, then one long one. The noise seemed to expand in waves through the drenched night: at last it died down again, with the suddenness of a rocket. 'Would they be getting anxious on board the *Shan-Tung?*' Absurd. The

22

captain didn't expect any one till eight o'clock. They started off again, all their movements inextricably linked to that boat over there in the cold greenish water, with its cases full of arms. It had stopped raining.

'As long as I can find that chap, it's all right,' said Kyo. 'All the same, I should feel happier if the *Shan-Tung* changed her moorings.'

Their ways lay separately now: they arranged where to meet again, and parted. Katow was going to fetch the men.

Kyo finally reached the iron-barred gate which bounded the Concessions. Two Annamese troopers and a sergeant from the Colonial army came and examined his papers. He had his French passport. As a temptation to the guards, hopeful Chinamen had stuck little pies all over the barbs of the wire. ('Good way of poisoning a station, if need be,' thought Kyo.) The sergeant gave him back his passport. He soon found a taxi and gave the driver the address of the Black Cat.

As they drove along, at full speed, they came across several patrols of European volunteers. 'The troops of eight nations keep watch here,' said the newspapers. It didn't matter much. The Kuomintang had no intention of attacking the Concessions. Empty avenues, little hawkers creeping by like ghosts, their stock-in-trade swinging from their shoulders. . . . The taxi stopped in front of a minute garden, the entrance to which was lit up by the words: Black Cat. As he went past the cloak-room, Kyo looked at the time: two o'clock. 'It's a good thing any kind of clothes will do here.' Beneath his dark grey sports coat, of fluffy wool, he was wearing a sweater.

The jazz was inconceivably irritating. It had been going on since five o'clock, proffering not so much cheerfulness as a frenzied intoxication to which couples gave themselves up a little doubtfully. Suddenly it stopped, and the crowd broke up. The patrons of the establishment collected at the far end of the room, and the dancing-partners sat round the sides. Chinese women sheathed in worked silk, Russians and half-castes; one ticket for each dance, or each conversation. An old man who might almost have been an English clergyman remained standing in the middle of the floor, completely bewildered, flapping his arms up and down like a penguin. For the first time in his life, at the age of fifty-two, he had failed to come home one night, and his dread of his wife was such that he had never since dared to return. For eight months now he had been spending his nights in the night-clubs, unable to get any washing done, and going to the Chinese shirt-makers to change his underwear, between two screens. Business men faced with bankruptcy proceedings, dancing-girls and harlots, all who felt themselves in danger – in fact almost everybody – kept their eyes fixed on that apparition, as if it had some strange power to save them from being engulfed in the abyss. At dawn they would go to bed, in a state of utter exhaustion – just when the executioner would be on his way through the Chinese quarter. That hour reminded one inevitably of the severed heads lying in the cages, lying there with their hair soaked by the rain, before even it was quite light.

'Like monkeys, my dear girl. They'll be dressed up like monkeys!'

The facetious tone of voice, every modulation of which recalled Punchinello, seemed to come from a pillar. Its muffled malevolence was appropriate enough in those surroundings, froze out a kind of zone of silence, within the noise of clinking glasses, up above the harassed cleric. Kyo saw the man he was looking for.

As he moved round the pillar, he caught sight of him among the crowd at the end of the room, where the tables left vacant by the dancing-girls were placed in varying degrees of obscurity.

Amid a confused mass of backs and throats and silky chiffon, a Punchinello, thin and humpless, but looking very like what his voice had suggested, was illustrating his powers as a comedian for the benefit of a Russian girl and a Philippine half-caste seated at his table. He stood there with his elbows glued to his sides and his hands waving expressively, bringing every muscle of his unbelievably aquiline face into play; hampered by the unyielding square of black silk which covered his right eye, which had presumably suffered an injury.

Whatever he was wearing – tonight he was in evening clothes – Baron Clappique looked as if he were in disguise. Kyo had decided not to speak to him there, to wait until he went out.

'Precisely, my dear girl, precisely! Chang Kai Shek will come in here with his revolutionaries and cry – quite in the classic style, I tell you, as though it were a city that he was capturing: "Let these merchants be clothed as monkeys, and these soldiers in leopard skins" (as if they had sat on newly painted benches!).'

'Like the last prince of the Leang dynasty, precisely like the prince, my dear girl, let us board the imperial junks, let us gaze upon our subjects arrayed, to serve our pleasure, each in the hue appropriate to his calling; blue, red, green, complete with pig-tails and top-knots; not a word, dear girl, not a word, I tell you.'

Then, growing confidential:

'All music shall be forbidden except Chinese bells.'

'And what'll *you* find to do?'

He whimpered: 'Can't you guess, dear girl, do you mean to say you can't guess? I shall be Court astrologer, and one night when I am drunk – can it be tonight? – I shall meet my death digging for the moon in a pond!'

Measuring his words:

'... like the poet Tu Fu, whose works most unquestionably enchant – not a word, I'm quite sure I'm right – your leisure hours. And then ...'

The hooting of a siren filled the room: one of the men-of-war. Immediately the cymbals joined in with an impetuous crash, and the dancing began again. The baron had sat down. Kyo threaded his way through the tables and the couples, till

25

he reached an empty place just behind him. The noise of the music had drowned everything else: but now that he was close to Clappique he could hear his own voice again. The baron was fiddling about with the Philippine, but continued to address his remarks to the thin-faced Russian girl, all eyes.

' . . . the awful thing, dear girl, is that there's no imagination left in the world. Now and again . . . '

With fore-finger upraised:

' . . . a European statesman sends his wife a little parcel; she opens it – not a word . . . '

The finger laid across his lips:

' . . . and there's her lover's head inside. Still a subject of conversation three years later.'

Maudlin: 'A shocking business, dear girl!'

'Look at me. Do you see my head? That's what twenty years of congenital imagination have done. It might almost be syphilis – Sh!'

Forceful:

'Waiter! Champagne for these two ladies, and for me . . . '

Confidential once more:

' . . . a s-small Martini . . . '

Severely:

' . . . very dry.'

('At the very best, I've still got an hour in hand, with police like these,' thought Kyo. But is this going on much longer?)

The Philippine was laughing, or pretending to. The Russian was making prodigious efforts to understand. Clappique went on gesticulating, his finger almost possessed of a separate identity; now stiff and commanding, now beckoning appealingly. But Kyo hardly listened to him: the heat was sapping all his energy, and in the process a vague anxiety which till then had lain concealed, grew into a feeling of intense strain: that record, and not recognizing his own voice at Hemmelrich's just now. It produced the same perplexed uneasiness as the sight of his tonsils had done, when, as a child, they had been removed by the surgeon. But his thoughts defied further analysis.

'. . . in short,' squeaked the baron, blinking with his uncovered eye as he turned towards the Russian, 'he had a castle in North Hungary.'

'Are you Hungarian?'

'Not the least. I'm French. (And it leaves me completely cold, dear girl, com-plete-ly.) But my mother was Hungarian.'

'Well then, my old grandfather lived in a castle there, with large rooms – *very* large – ancestors buried underneath, and fir-trees all round; lots of f-firs. A widower. He lived alone with an e-norm-ous hunting-horn hanging over the chimney. Along comes a circus. With a female rider. Pretty . . .'

Magisterial:

'I repeat: pretty.'

Winking again:

'He abducts her – easy enough – Takes her into one of the large rooms . . .'

Commanding attention, hand upraised:

'Not a word! She lives there. Stays on there. Has a boring time of it. You, too, little girl' – he tickled the Philippine – 'but bear up. . . . Besides, he didn't make any attempt to amuse her: he used to spend half the afternoon having his finger-nails and toe-nails attended to by his barber (he still had a barber attached to the castle), while his secretary, the son of a filthy serf, read to him, aloud – over and over again – the family history. Delightful pastime, dear girl, a perfect life! In any case, he was generally drunk. She . . .'

'Did she fall for the secretary?' asked the Russian girl.

'She's splendid, this little girl, simply splendid! Dear girl, you're splendid. Remarkable insight!'

He kissed her hand.

'. . . but she slept with the chiropodist, not having your appreciation of culture. Then it dawned on her that the old grandfather was beating her. Not a word, it's no use: hence a separation.

'Well, he feels he's been jilted, wanders through his huge rooms, fuming with rage (with the ancestors there underneath all the time), vowing vengeance on the two culprits who had dared to make him a laughing-stock, while they were cuckolding him for all they were worth in a little inn (*à la Gogol*) in the country town, with a chipped water-jug in the bedroom and carriages in the courtyard. He takes down the e-nor-mous hunting-horn, fails to get any response out of it, and sends out his bailiff to call the peasantry to arms. (They still owed him homage in those days.) He arms them: five shot-guns, two pistols. Not enough to go round, dear girl.

'Then they ransack the castle: all those poor wretches marching off – just imagine it, just im-a-gine it, I tell you! Armed with foils, arquebusses, flintlocks, Heavens knows what! Rapiers and curious-looking sabres, with grandpa leading the way, off to the country town: crime pursued by vengeance. The news of their arrival spreads. The local ranger arrives, accompanied by the police.'

'Magnificent spectacle.'

' – and then?'

'Nothing. They were relieved of their weapons. Grandfather succeeded in reaching the town all the same, but the guilty pair had fled from the Gogolesque inn, as quick as they could go, in one of the dusty carriages. He replaced the circus-rider by a peasant girl, the chiropodist by another chiropodist, and got drunk with the secretary. From time to time he would work on one of his l-little wills . . .'

'Whom did he leave his money to?'

'A matter of no importance, dear girl. But, when he died . . .'

With wide-open eyes:

' . . . everything came out, all the fantastic ideas he had had, getting people to scratch his feet for him and read him

28

chronicles, when his quarterings went to his head! His instructions were obeyed: he was buried beneath the chapel, in an immense vault, upright upon his horse, killed to keep him company, like Attila's charger.'

The jazz ceased its raucous wail. Clappique went on, much less like Punchinello now, as though the silence had a damping effect upon his clowning:

'When Attila died, they set him on his horse, prancing high above the Danube. The setting sun threw such a giant shadow across the plain that the horsemen fled in terror, like dust before the wind.'

His thoughts were beginning to wander, under the influence of alcohol and the sudden quiet; were straying far afield. Kyo knew exactly what he wanted him to do, but he only knew him very slightly, though his father was better acquainted; in these surroundings he scarcely recognized him. He listened impatiently (directly there was a free table in front of the baron, he would go and sit there and sign to him to leave; he didn't want to address him openly), but not without curiosity. The Russian girl was talking now, a slow husky croaking; almost delirious from lack of sleep.

'My great-grandfather had a fine estate too . . . We left because of the Communists, you see. So as to retain some privacy, some respect; and here we are two at a table and four in a room together! Four in one room . . . and the rent has to be paid. As for being respected. . . . If only drink didn't make me ill! . . .'

Clappique looked at her glass: she had scarcely drunk anything. The Philippine, on the other hand . . . Half-drunk, she was luxuriating in the fumes that smouldered inside her, like a cat basking in front of the fire. No good taking any notice of that. He looked at the Russian again:

'I suppose you've no money?'

She shrugged her shoulders. He called the waiter, paid the bill with a hundred-dollar note. He took ten dollars from the change which was brought, and gave the woman what remained.

She looked at him with haggard intensity.

'All right.'

She started to get up.

'No,' he said.

He looked at her pathetically, like a friendly dog.

'No. You don't feel much like it tonight.' He was holding her hand. She looked at him again:

'Thank you.'

She hesitated:

'Still . . . if you'd enjoy it . . .'

'I should enjoy it much more some time when I've no money.'

He became Punchinello again:

'That'll be soon enough.'

He drew her hands together, kissed them several times. Kyo, who had already paid his bill, overtook him in the empty passage.

'Let's go out together, shall we?'

Clappique looked at him, recognized him.

'You here? Can't be true! But . . .'

The babble closed for a moment, as the forefinger was raised:

'You're living too fast, my young f-friend!'

'That's all right.'

Already they were outside. Although the rain had stopped, the air felt as wet as if there was water hanging suspended in it. They walked a few paces across the gravel in the garden.

'In the harbour,' said Kyo, 'there is a boat with a cargo of arms . . .'

Clappique had stopped. Kyo had walked on a step, and had to turn back: the baron's face was scarcely visible, but the huge cat, dazzlingly bright, the sign of the Black Cat, surrounded him like a halo.

'The *Shan-Tung*,' he said.

The darkness, and the position in which he was standing – with his back to the light – sufficiently concealed his expression; and he said nothing further.

'The Government have made an offer,' Kyo went on, 'of thirty dollars per gun. They haven't received a reply yet. Now I have got some one prepared to pay thirty-five dollars, plus three dollars commission. For immediate delivery, in the port. Wherever the captain pleases, as long as it's in the port. He can leave his anchorage at once. We'll take delivery tonight, and have the money ready. His agent has agreed: here's the contract.'

He handed him the paper and lit his cigarette-lighter, shielding it with his hand.

'He's trying to do the other buyer down,' thought Clappique, as he looked at the contract. . . . ' "Goods in Piece . . . ," and clear five dollars per gun out of it. It's clear enough. Well, what the devil do I care about that? I shall get three.'

'That's all right,' he said aloud. 'You'll leave me the contract, I suppose?'

'Yes. You know the captain?'

'There are others I know better, old chap, but I think I can say that I know him.'

'He might get suspicious (especially away down the river there). Sometimes the Government requisition arms without payment, don't they?'

'Don't you believe it!'

Punchinello again. But Kyo waited for him to continue: what force would the captain have at his command, to prevent their men (instead of the Government) from seizing the arms? Clappique went on, less stridently:

'These orders come from one of the official contractors. I know him.'

Mockingly:

'He's a traitor . . .'

31

The voice sounded very odd in the darkness, with no facial expression to render it convincing. As if he were ordering a cocktail:

'A thorough-going traitor, as treacherous as they make them! This is all arranged through a Legation which . . . Not a word! I'll see what I can do. But first of all it's going to cost me a prodigious amount in taxis: the boat's a long way off. I've got . . .'

He fumbled in his pocket, and produced a single note, turning round so as to let the light from the sign fall on it. 'Ten dollars, old chap! That won't do. I shall probably be buying some of your uncle Kama's pictures for Ferral, before long, but in the meantime . . .'

'Will fifty do you?'

'That's ample.'

Kyo gave them to him.

'You'll let me know at my house directly it's settled.'

'Right.'

'In an hour's time?'

'More, I expect. But as soon as I can.'

And in the same tone of voice in which the Russian had said 'If only drink didn't make me ill . . .' in almost the very same voice, as though the same feeling of despair has overtaken all the occupants of that place:

'This is a serious business.'

Off he went, with hunched back, nose pointing towards the ground, bare head, and his hands in the pockets of his dinner-jacket.

Kyo called a taxi and drove right to the end of the Concession, where the first small street of the Chinese quarter began; it was there that he had arranged to meet Katow.

Katow went down passages, through little doors, till, ten minutes after leaving Kyo, he came to a bare white room, brightly lit with hurricane-lamps. There was no window. Beneath the arm of the Chinaman who opened the door for him, he could see five heads: looking up at him as they leant over the table, gazing at that tall form which every Shock Section knew: legs widespread, arms swinging loose, blouse unbuttoned at the neck, nose in the air, tousled hair. They were examining various types of hand-grenades. It was a *tchon*, one of the units into which were divided the combatant sections which he and Kyo had organized in Shanghai for the Party.

'How many men have enrolled?' he asked in Chinese.

'A hundred and thirty-eight,' answered the youngest of the Chinese, a young man with a small head, very prominent Adam's apple, and sloping shoulders; dressed as a workman.

'I abs'lutely must have twelve men at my disposal for tonight.'

'Abs'lutely' formed part of Katow's vocabulary in every language.

'When?'

'Now.'

'Here?'

'No: in front of the Yen-Tang dock.'

The Chinaman gave some orders: one of the men went out.

'They will be there before two o'clock,' said the leader.

His hollow cheeks and great gaunt body gave an impression of weakness; but the resolute tone of voice, and taut facial muscles denoted nerves under iron control.

'How about the arms drill?' asked Katow.

'It's all right as far as the grenades are concerned. All the comrades know how to use our type now. As to the revolvers – the Nagans and the Mausers anyway – that's all right too. I make them practise with empty cartridges, but they ought to do some actual firing, even if it's only blank. . . . We've been offered the loan of a cellar which is abs'lutely safe.'

In each of the forty rooms where the revolution was being organized, the same problem confronted them.

'No ammunition. Perhaps it'll come through: for the present, that's all we can say. What about rifles?'

'They're all right too. It's the machine-guns which I'm worried about, unless we can get a little practice with blank.'

His Adam's apple rose and fell under the skin every time he spoke. He went on:

'But isn't there any chance of getting hold of a few more arms? Only seven rifles, thirteen revolvers, and forty-two live grenades! Half the men don't possess firearms at all.'

'We'll go and get them from those who do. Perhaps we shall soon have revolvers now. If things start tomorrow, how many men in your section won't know how to use their weapons?'

The man thought for a moment. He seemed engrossed, concentrating. 'An intellectual,' thought Katow.

'After we've relieved the police of their rifles?'

'Abs'lutely.'

'More than half.'

'What about the grenades?'

'They all know how to use them; and very well too. I've got thirty men here who lost relatives in the February executions. Unless. . . . '

He paused, finishing the sentence with a vague gesture. A deformed hand, but a sensitive one.

'Unless?'

'Unless those swine use tanks against us.'

The six men looked at Katow.

'That doesn't matter,' he answered. 'You take the grenades, tie them together in bundles of six, and bloody well chuck them under the tank; anything over four will send it sky-high. If the worst comes to the worst, you can dig trenches in one direction anyway. Have you got any tools?'

'Very few. But I know where to get some more.'

'Get hold of some bicycles too: directly things start the sections must all have some means of keeping in touch, apart from Headquarters.'

'You're sure that'll do the trick with the tanks?'

34

'Abs'lutely! But don't worry: the tanks won't leave the front. If they do, I'll bring a special squad along. Just leave that particular business to me.'

'Suppose we're taken by surprise?'

'You can see tanks coming a mile off: we've got scouts on the look-out. Take a bundle of grenades yourself, and give one to each of the three or four men you can most rely on.'

Everybody in the section knew how, when Katow was sentenced to one of the less drastic penal settlements after the Odessa affair, he had asked to be allowed to accompany the miserable wretches who were sent to the lead-mines, to teach them. They trusted him, but they were not entirely reassured. They were not afraid of rifles or machine-guns, but they *were* afraid of tanks; they felt quite helpless in front of them. Even in that room full of volunteers, who had all, almost without exception, had to submit to the execution of those near and dear to them, the prestige of the tank exercised a diabolical fascination.

'Don't you worry about the tanks coming, we shall be there if they do,' Katow went on.

How could he go away leaving things as uncertain as that? That afternoon, he had inspected some fifteen sections or so, but he had seen no signs of fear. The men he was dealing with now were no less brave than the others, but they saw things more clearly. He knew that he was powerless to free them from their fear; that with the exception of the picked men under his own command, none of the revolutionary troops would face the tanks. The tanks would probably be unable to leave the front; but if they did reach the town, it would be impossible, in the parts where so many small streets intersected, to stop them all by digging trenches.

'It's absolutely certain the tanks won't leave the front,' he said.

'How are we to tie the bombs together?' the youngest Chinaman asked him.

Katow showed him. The feeling of tension diminished a little, as though his demonstration were a safeguard against future emergencies. Katow saw his opportunity and left them, by no means reassured. Half the men wouldn't know how to use their arms. At least he could rely on his Shock Sections, whose duty it would be to disarm the police. Tomorrow. But what of the day after? The army was advancing, was getting nearer every hour. Perhaps the last station had already been captured. When Kyo came back, they would probably be able to find out from one of the Intelligence Bureaux. The lampseller had heard nothing since ten o'clock.

He waited some time in that little street, walking up and down all the time: at last Kyo arrived. They told each other what they had been doing; then set off again through the mud, in their heavy rubber-soled shoes: Kyo small and lithe as a Japanese cat, Katow swinging his shoulders, thinking of the troops getting nearer; their rifles glistening in the rain, advancing through the intense darkness, while Shanghai glowed dully like a coal. Kyo, also, wanted to know whether that advance had been checked.

The little street along which they were walking, the first that one came to in the Chinese quarter, was very close to the European houses, and was occupied by dealers in livestock. All the shops were closed: there was not an animal to be seen, or a sound to break the silence, save for the hooting of the sirens and the raindrops which still dripped from the roofs into the puddles below. The animals were asleep. They knocked at a shop door, and went in: a dealer in live fishes. A candle stuck in a photophore provided the only illumination, reflected as a feeble glimmer by a row of luminous jars ranged in line as if by Ali Baba himself; in which slept, unseen, the famous Chinese carp.

'Tomorrow?' asked Kyo.

'Tomorrow; one o'clock.'

At the back of the room, behind a counter, something vaguely human lay curled up asleep, its crooked arm serving as a pillow. It had scarcely raised its head when answering. That shop was one of the eighty-four depots of the Kuomintang, by means of which news was transmitted.

'Is that official?'

'Yes. The army is at Cheng Chow. General strike at midday.'

The gloom remained unchanged. The shop-keeper dozing at the bottom of his cell made no movement, but the gleaming surface of the jars began to quiver gently: smooth black ripples rose silently to the surface and expanded. The sound of voices was awakening the fish. Once more the note of a siren blared out and faded away into the distance.

They left the place and continued their walk. Still the Avenue des Deux-Républiques.

A taxi. The cab started off at breakneck speed. Katow, who was sitting on the left, leant forward and looked closely at the driver.

'He's crazy for his dope. Pity: abs'lutely insist on not being killed before tomorrow evening. Steady, old chap!'

'So Clappique is going to see about getting the boat,' said Kyo. 'The comrades at the Government clothing stores can provide us with police-uniforms.'

'No need. I've got fifteen at least at the depot.'

'We'll take your twelve men with us in the launch.'

'You'd be better left out of it.'

Kyo looked at him without saying anything.

'It's not all that risky, but it's not all plain sailing by any means. D'you get me? It's more dangerous than driving with this Goddam fool who's just starting to speed again. And it's not the right moment for you to do yourself in.'

'Nor you either.'

'That's not the same. I can be replaced, now, don't you see. . . . I'd prefer you to look after the lorry, see that it's waiting for us, and that the arms go to the right places.'

He paused, ill at ease, his hand on his chest.

'Must let him think it over,' he thought.

Kyo said nothing. The taxi still went rushing along between streaks of light only half-visible through the fog. There was no doubt that he was of more use than Katow: Headquarters were acquainted with every detail of his plans, but only as so many figures, while for him they were the breath of life. The town was in his blood – its weak points were so many wounds. Not one of his comrades reacted as swiftly and accurately as himself.

'All right,' he said.

More and more lights. . . . Again, the armoured lorries from the Concessions; then once more darkness.

The taxi stopped. Kyo got out.

'I'm going to get our new suitings,' said Katow; 'I'll send and fetch you when everything is ready.'

Kyo lived with his father in a one-storey Chinese house; it had four wings to it and a garden in the middle. He went through the first of them, crossed the garden, and entered the hall. The white walls were covered with Song paintings and blue Chardin phoenixes; at the back was a Buddha of the Wei dynasty, almost Roman in style. Tidy-looking divans and an opium table. Behind Kyo were the windows, bare like windows in a studio. His father appeared, having heard him come in: he had been suffering from insomnia for years, and welcomed gladly anything that served to enliven the hours of wakefulness that now invariably preceded the few hours of sleep which came to him with the dawn.

'Good evening, father. Chen is coming to see you.'

'Good.'

Kyo hadn't the same cast of features as his father: it seemed as though his mother's Japanese blood had been endowed with just sufficient strength to temper slightly the monastic asceticism of old Gisors' mask-like face – rendered even more mask-like that night by his camelhair dressing-gown – to remodel the lineaments of the son in the form of a Samurai.

'Has something happened to him?'

38

'Yes.'

No further question. They both sat down. Kyo wasn't sleepy. He recounted the Clappique episode – but said nothing about the arms. Not that he was in the least distrustful of his father; but his desire to retain complete control of his destiny was too strong for him to acquaint any one else with more than the bare outline of his doings. The old Professor of Sociology, expelled from Pekin University by Chang Tso Lin on account of the principles he expounded, had created the most effective revolutionary centre in Northern China; but he took no active part himself. Whenever Kyo arrived there, he noticed to his distress that his will-power turned to mere cerebration; his interest narrowed from events to individuals. And because his father, who knew Clappique well, was listening to him, he now found the baron more mysterious than when he had actually been talking to him.

'In the end he touched me for fifty dollars.'

'He doesn't want it for himself, Kyo.'

'But I've just seen him spend a hundred dollars. People who live in the clouds are always rather upsetting.'

He wanted to know how far he could go on using Clappique. His father, as ever, was trying to analyse the essential roots of the man's character. But the roots of a man's character rarely provide an immediate motive for action, and Kyo thought of his pistols.

'If he likes feeling rich so much, why doesn't he try to get rich?'

'He used to be the best-known antique dealer in Shanghai.'

'But why does he spend all his money in one night, unless to give himself the illusion of wealth?'

Gisors blinked and shook back his longish white hair; his voice was that of an old man, but if the tone was thin the words flowed evenly and steadily:

'Living in the clouds is a way of denying life, isn't it? Denying, not forgetting. You must see that it's no good looking at the affair from a purely reasonable point of view.'

He thrust his hand forward vaguely; his gestures were constrained, unexpansive, straight in front of him; the movements with which he completed a sentence seemed not so much to dismiss as to grasp hold of something.

'It looks very much as if he had been trying to convince himself last night that though he had lived for two hours like a rich man, there is really no such thing as riches. Because in that case there is no such thing as poverty either. And that is the vitally important thing. Nothing exists: it is all a dream. And remember that alcohol gives it substance.'

Gisors smiled. His smiling lips, drooping at the corners, already a little worn, were a subtler guide to his character than the words he spoke. For twenty years now he had pleaded the cause of his fellow-men, devoting all his energies to earning the love of humanity by his advocacy, and they were grateful to him for his sympathy, never suspecting that it had its origin in opium. The Buddhist patience with which he was credited was, in fact, the fatalism of a drug-addict.

'It's impossible to go on living without any confidence in life,' answered Kyo.

'It is a poor way of living, but it satisfies him.'

'He's really been forced into it.'

'The forcing is done in his case by the antique-dealing, perhaps by drugs and the arms-traffic too. In cooperation with the police, whom he doubtless detests, but who join in that little game in return for a reasonable rake-off. It didn't matter much: the police knew perfectly well that the Communists hadn't sufficient money to buy arms from the gun-runners.'

'You can tell what any man is like from what makes him suffer,' said Kyo. 'What is it in his case?'

'His sufferings are of no importance, they don't mean anything now, don't you see; they go no deeper than his cunning or his high spirits. He has no depth of any kind, and perhaps that is the best description of him, for it is unusual. He tries hard to fill the gap, but he would have to be a much stronger person for that to do much good. Unless you are really intimate with a man, Kyo, you have to think hard to tell what he is going to do. Now in Clappique's case . . .'

He pointed to the aquarium, where the black carp, soft and jagged like oriflammes, drifted up and down.

'There you see. . . . He drinks, but it is opium he was cut out for: one can choose the wrong vice just like the wrong anything else: lots of men never pick on the one which would set them right. A pity, for he is by no means a nonentity. But all this is hardly of interest to you just now.'

It was true. Kyo might not be thinking about his actual plans that night, but his thoughts certainly remained concentrated on himself. The heat was gradually taking hold of him, as it had at the Black Cat a little earlier: the memory of the record began to haunt him once more, and that tingling sensation which utter weariness produces to come creeping up his legs. He recounted his feeling of astonishment on listening to the record, but gave the impression that he was referring to one of the voice-recordings which could be made in English shops. Gisors sat there listening, stroking his angular chin with his left hand: he had very beautiful, delicate hands. His head was thrust forward: his hair had fallen over his eyes, despite the height of his forehead. He jerked it back with a shake of his head, but his thoughts were still remote:

'I have at times found myself in front of a mirror, un-expectedly, and not known who I was. . . .'

He was gently rubbing his thumb against the fingers of his right hand, as if it were a match to set the tinder of his memory alight. He was talking to himself, following a train of thought which took no account of his son.

'There's probably a physiological explanation: we hear other people's voices through our ears.'

'And our own?'

'Through our throat: stop your ears and you will hear your own voice. Opium, too, belongs to a world which we can't hear with our ears. . . .'

Kyo got up. His father scarcely noticed him.

'I must go out again in a moment.'

'Can I help at all about Clappique?'

'No: it's all right, thanks. Good night.'

'Good night.'

*

In an attempt to diminish his fatigue, Kyo passed the time of waiting lying down. He lay quite still, in the dark. It wasn't that his thoughts were on the rising; it was the rising itself which, as vital a part of as many brains as the sleep which held so many others, crushed him beneath a load of torturing suspense. Less than four hundred rifles all told. Victory – or execution, ingeniously protracted. Tomorrow. No; in a moment's time. It was a question of speed: of disarming the entire police force and arming the Shock Sections with their five hundred Mausers before the Government troops from the armoured train could intervene. The great mass of the population was ready. Half of the police were in so abjectedly miserable a condition that they would probably go over to the rebels. There remained the other half. But the revolt was timed to begin at one – which meant that the general strike would begin at noon – and arms would have to be found for the majority of the Shock Sections before five o'clock. 'Soviet China,' he thought. Recognition as human beings for those one loved. And the Russian Soviet Union had reached a total of six hundred millions. Success, or failure? The fate of the world was hanging in the balance there that night. Unless the Kuomintang, once Shanghai was captured, were to try and crush their Communist allies. . . . He started; the garden door was opening. Then he remembered. His wife? He heard someone shut the house-door. May came in. Her blue leather cloak, of an almost military cut, increased the latent masculinity of her walk and features. She had the wide mouth, short nose and prominent cheekbones of the north German type to which she belonged.

'Is it really starting soon now, Kyo?'

'Yes.'

She was a doctor in one of the Chinese hospitals, but she had come from the women's revolutionary association, whose secret hospital she looked after:

'It's always the same thing; I've just left a girl of eighteen who tried to commit suicide with a razor-blade in the marriage palanquin. She'd been forced into marrying some plausible brute or other. They brought her in with her red bridal dress all soaked with blood. Her mother came in afterwards, a wizened little shadow of a woman, sobbing away. Naturally enough. When I told her the girl wasn't going to die, she said: "Poor kid! She was nearly lucky, all the same!" Luck.... That word tells one more than all our talk about the position of women here.'

She was of German origin, but born in Shanghai; a doctor of the Universities of Heidelberg and Paris; and spoke French without any accent. She threw her beret on to the bed. Her wavy hair was caught back behind her head, to save trouble in arranging it. He found it wildly attractive. Her bold forehead also had something masculine about it, but directly she stopped talking she became more feminine (Kyo kept his eyes fixed on her), partly because her features softened and her will relaxed, partly because fatigue smoothed them out and partly because she had no beret. It was the sensual mouth and large, limpid eyes which lent animation to her face; eyes which were so clear that their deep, penetrating gaze seemed to come not so much from the pupil as to be a reflection cast by the forehead above their oval sockets.

Attracted by the light, a white Pekinese came trotting in. She called to him, wearily.

'Little curly pup: little hairy, woolly one!'

43

She caught hold of him with her left hand and lifted him up to her face, stroking him.

'Rabbit,' she said, smiling, 'little bunny-rabbit. . . . '

'He looks like you,' said Kyo.

'Yes, doesn't he?'

She looked at the mirror and saw that white head close against her own, and the little paws together underneath. It was her strongly marked Nordic cheekbones which produced the absurd similarity. Though she could scarcely be called pretty, he called to mind (amending them), the words of Othello:

O my sweet warrior . . .

She put the dog down, and got up. Her cloak hung half-open, uncovering her chest and revealing the contour of her high round breasts, which reminded one of her cheekbones. Kyo told her what he had been doing that night.

'At the hospital this evening,' she answered, 'we had about thirty young women belonging to the Propaganda service, who had managed to evade the White troops. . . . Wounded. We're getting more and more of them. They say the army is quite near; and that they've had a lot of casualties. . . . '

'Half those who are wounded will die too. . . . Pain can only be justified as an alternative to death, but actually death almost always follows in the end.'

May thought for a moment.

'Yes,' she said at last. 'And yet, perhaps that is a man's way of looking at it. For me, for women, pain is oddly enough associated more with life than death. . . . Because they bear children perhaps. . . . '

Then, after further reflection:

'The more wounded there are, the nearer we get to the Revolution, the more people sleep with each other.'

'Clearly.'

44

'There's something I ought to tell you, which you may not like very much. . . .'

Supporting his head on his elbow, he looked up at her inquiringly. She had brains and courage, but often lacked tact.

'I slept with Langlen this afternoon.'

He shrugged his shoulders, as much as to say 'That's your own affair'; but it was an uneasy movement, and, like the tense expression on his face, belied his indifference. She looked at him, desperately tired, her cheekbones sharply defined by the light coming down from above. He, too, looked at her, but her eyes were in the shadow, expressionless, and he said nothing. He wondered what gave her face its voluptuous quality: whether it was that the violence of the contrast between those clouded eyes and expansive lips, and her features, made her all the more feminine. . . . She sat down on the bed and took his hand. He was on the point of withdrawing it, then yielded. But she felt the impulse:

'Has that upset you?'

'I told you that you were free to do as you liked. . . . Don't let's discuss it any further,' he added bitterly.

The puppy jumped on to the bed. He took his hand away, perhaps in order to stroke it.

'You are free,' he repeated. 'That's the only thing that matters.'

'Still, I *had* to tell you about it. If only for my own peace of mind.'

'Yes.'

That it had been her duty to tell him, they neither of them doubted for a moment. He felt a sudden desire to get up: lying down like that, with her sitting on the bed, as if he were an invalid and she the nurse. . . . But what could he do? It was all so hopeless. . . . He continued to look at her, however, and realized that, though she still had the power to hurt him, for months now it had made no difference whether he looked at her or not. She didn't seem real to him any more. At times, just a fleeting impression. That intense love which bound them together – as the illness of a child might have done – bound them often almost more tightly than they could endure; their feeling of complete union, both in life and death: the physical compact which they had made with each other: all that faded away before the inevitable corruption of those features with which he had sated himself while they were yet pure. 'Am I less in love with her than I imagine?' he wondered. No. Even at that moment, he knew that in the event of her death all that he hoped for from the cause he served would die too, and that he would serve it despairingly, like a dead man. But all that availed nothing against the desecration in that face of something which lay at the very root of their intimacy; shrouded in obscurity, now, buried in the ground. He remembered a friend who had watched the mental death of the woman he loved, through months of paralysis, and it seemed to him that he saw May dying in the same way, saw the visible symbol of his happiness fantastically vanishing like a cloud merging into the greyness of its background. It was as if she suffered two deaths: one the work of nature, the other of her confession.

She got up, and walked over to the window; steadily, despite her fatigue. She decided, half fearfully, half on account of rather artificial feelings of guilt, to make no more mention of what she had just said, since he did not refer to it. She wanted to escape from that conversation, but realized that they would find escape impossible, and tried to express her affection by talking of trifles, instinctively calling to her aid the nature which he loved; opposite the window, one of the Mars trees had opened out during the night: the light from the room showed up its leaves, still a little crinkled, delicately green against the dark background.

'He's been hiding his leaves in his trunk during the daytime,' she said, 'and he's bringing them out at night now that no one can see.'

She seemed to be talking to herself, but Kyo was hardly likely to fail to catch her meaning.

'You might have chosen some other day,' he muttered by way of answer.

He was looking at his reflection in the mirror now, saw himself leaning on his elbow – a face that seemed pure Japanese peering out from the white sheets. 'If only I wasn't a half-caste.' He strove desperately to repulse the bitter and unworthy thoughts which crowded into his mind in justification of his anger, adding fresh fuel to it. And he looked at her, kept his eyes fixed on her, as though, by the very brutality of his gaze, he could compel that face to regain its former animation.

'But, Kyo, today is just the one day when it didn't matter . . . and . . .'

She nearly added: 'he wanted to so badly.' With death confronting them it had so little importance. . . . But all she said was:

' . . . I may die tomorrow, too. . . .'

All the better. Kyo felt pain in its most degrading form; pain which his self-respect dare not admit. In point of fact she was free to sleep with whoever she wished. What then was the cause of his suffering for which he could find no justification, but which held him in such complete subjection?

'When you realized that . . . that you meant a good deal to me, Kyo, you once asked me – only half-seriously perhaps – if I thought that I'd come to a prison camp with you, and I said that I couldn't tell – that the difficult part would probably be seeing it through when I got there. But you took that to mean that I would, because I meant a lot to you, too. Why should things be any different now?'

'It would take a very special type of person to do that. Katow would go, even without being deeply in love. He'd go because it fits in with his views on life and his place in the world. People don't go to penal servitude for the sake of a human relationship.'

47

'What a masculine way of looking at it, Kyo. . . . '

He pondered.

'Still,' he said, 'to have some one to love who will do that for you, or rather, to be loved by them – love can't go any further. It's pretty crazy to question their behaviour after that. Even if they do it from a sense of duty. . . . '

'It's not that,' she said slowly. 'A sense of duty would never be anything like enough in my case.'

'But your love' (he, too, spoke slowly) 'didn't prevent you sleeping with that man, even though you realized – you've just said so – that it would . . . upset me?'

'Kyo, I'm going to tell you something strange, but true. Until five minutes ago, I thought you wouldn't mind. Perhaps it suited me to think so. There are some things people ask of one, above all when death is as near as this (it's other people's death that I've had to face till now, Kyo . . .) which have no connexion with love. . . . '

Jealousy there was, notwithstanding; all the less clearly perceived in that the desire which she awoke in him was based upon affection. His eyes closed, and, still leaning on his elbow, he set himself the painful task of understanding. He could hear nothing but May's laboured breathing and the scratching of the puppy's paws. The principal cause of his suffering (he would inevitably find others: he could feel them lying in ambush, like his comrades who still waited behind their closed doors) lay in his idea that that man who had just slept with May ('I can't after all call him her lover') despised her. The man in question was an old friend of hers, whom he hardly knew; but he knew well enough the contempt in which women were ultimately held by almost all men. 'The idea that having slept with her, as a result of having slept with her, he may be thinking: "That little tart"; I could kill him for that. Are we always only jealous of what we imagine the other person is thinking? Men are pretty hopeless creatures. . . . ' As far as May was concerned, sexual relations implied no kind of contract. That

48

ought to be made clear to this man. If he slept with her, well and good; but don't let him start thinking he possessed her. ('This is becoming pitiable. . . . ') But that was something out of his control – and he knew that, in any case, it wasn't the vital thing. The vital thing, the thing which was torturing him almost beyond endurance, was the barrier which had suddenly cut him off from her: it wasn't hatred which had done it, though there was hatred in him: it wasn't jealousy (or perhaps that was just what jealousy was?): it was a feeling to which he could give no name, as destructive as Time or Death: he could not recapture her. He had reopened his eyes; was it really human, that athletic body, strangely familiar, that meaningless profile? A long slit of an eye, reaching to the temple, thrust in between the bold forehead and the cheekbone . . . did it belong to that concubine? Didn't it also belong to the woman who had strengthened him in his moments of weakness, of pain and petulance, the woman who had helped him to nurse his wounded comrades and watched with him over his dead friends. . . . The sweetness of her voice still haunted him. . . . One's memories are not so easily expelled. Once more, though, that body was beginning to take on the intensely mysterious quality which a sudden metamorphosis produces – was becoming dumb, blind, lunatic. And it was a woman. Not a variation of the male. Something else. . . .

She was completely lost to him. And perhaps, as a result of that, he felt a frantic, blinding urge for close contact with her, whatever it might entail: fear, cries, blows. He got up and approached her. He knew that he was completely unstrung, that tomorrow what he was feeling then would very likely seem completely incomprehensible, but it was as if he saw her dying there in front of him; and, seeing her die, felt irresistibly drawn towards her: the desire to touch, to run his hands over her, to hold back some one who was leaving him, to link himself securely to her. She looked at him with intense uneasiness, as he stood there close beside her. Then, in a flash, he realized what it was he wanted; to possess her, to make that a means of escape from the nightmare dread of losing her for ever. Could intimacy be more complete than in that moment when every muscle strained to bind their bodies to each other?

Suddenly she turned round: the bell had rung. Too soon for Katow. Had the rising been discovered? All that they had been saying, all that had passed between them, all their passion and their rancour, suffered instant and ruthless eclipse. There came another ring. He took his revolver from under the pillow, went through the garden in his pyjamas and opened the door: it wasn't Katow, it was Clappique, still in evening clothes. They remained in the garden.

'Well?'

'Before anything else, let me give you back your papers: here they are. Everything is all right. The boat has moved. It's going to anchor off the French Consulate. Almost on the other side of the river.'

'Any trouble?'

'Not a word. Implicit confidence – always have had. Can't see how it could have been managed otherwise. In these matters, young man, confidence is greatest when it least appears so. . . .'

'Meaning?'

Clappique lit a cigarette. All Kyo saw was a black silk cravat and the vague outline of a face above it. He went to fetch his wallet. . . . May was waiting – came back again and paid him the commission as arranged. The baron stuffed the notes in his pocket without counting them.

'An act of kindness brings good fortune,' he said. 'Old chap, the tale of my deeds tonight is an extra-ord-inarily moral tale: it begins with charity and ends with prosperity. Not a word.'

His forefinger upraised, he bent close to Kyo's ear and whispered: 'Love from Fantômas'; turned round, and was gone.

As if afraid to go inside again, Kyo watched him depart, his dinner-jacket rubbing along the white wall. 'He certainly looks it, dressed like that.'

Kyo heard a cough and recognized it instantly, for he was expecting it: Katow. There was no time to waste, that night.

Perhaps so as to be less easily seen, he was walking in the middle of the road. Kyo imagined rather than distinguished his pea-jacket: somewhere up above in the darkness, a nose protruded. . . . More clearly than anything, he imagined the swinging movement of those hands. He walked towards him.

'Well?' he asked, as he had asked Clappique.

'It's all right. What about the boat?'

'Opposite the French Consulate. A long way out. In half an hour's time.'

'The launch and the men are within four hundred yards of there. Let's go.'

'What about the clothes?'

'Don't you worry. They're fixed up all right, every man of 'em.'

He went inside and was dressed in a moment: trousers and singlet. Light canvas shoes (he might have to do some climbing). He was ready. May offered him her lips. In his heart Kyo wanted to kiss her; not her mouth, though – as if there alone bitterness still lingered. He kissed her at last, clumsily. She looked at him sadly, with listless eyes which suddenly filled with animation as the muscles regained control. He left her.

Once more he and Katow were walking side by side. But he could not put her out of his mind. Only a moment ago she seemed like some one blind or demented. 'I don't understand her. It's only my love for her which helps me to understand her. I only understand her from that point of view. The extent to which a person belongs to one is the extent to which one has changed them, as my father says. . . . And what then?' As his reasoning grew more and more introspective, so the street grew darker and darker, until even the insulators on the telegraph wires no longer appeared any lighter than the sky

51

above them. His anguish of mind was undiminished and he remembered the incident of the gramophone records: 'We hear other people's voices with our ears, our own through our throat.' Yes. The sound of one's life, too, comes to one through the throat; and other people's? . . . The thing that predominated was isolation, securely entrenched as the background to the ephemeral millions who moved in front of it, just as real Night, real primeval Night, loomed behind the covering of darkness which hung low and dense over the watchful waste of city, pregnant with the ferment of unfulfilled hopes. '*To me myself*, what does my life mean to *me*? The cosmos expressing itself in an identity, an idiotic identity: a concentration of forces in the prevailing nebulousness. For others, it's what I've done that counts.' Only May judged him other than by his actions: only in him did anything more than the record of her life awaken interest. The fierce embrace with which love seeks to break down isolation brought no comfort to his ordinary self: it was the unbalanced side of him which profited, the unspeakable monstrosity, dear above all else, which self-analysis evokes and which man cherishes in his heart. Since the death of his mother, May was the only person in the world who saw him not as Kyo Gisors but as the partner in a most intimate companionship. 'A mutual, triumphant, chosen companionship,' he thought, finding the night curiously sympathetic to his thoughts, as if they were for ever divorced from daylight now. 'What have other men in common with me? Just so many entities who look at me and criticize. My real fellow-creatures love me unreflectingly, love me in spite of everything, love me so that no corruption, vileness or betrayal has any power to alter it: love me for myself and not for what I have done or will do; whose love for me goes as far as my own – embracing suicide. . . . With her alone do I share a love like that, whatever batterings it may have undergone, as others share the sickness of their children, their risk of death. . . . ' It certainly wasn't a feeling of happiness, it was something primeval, in tune with the darkness, which set him tingling till he stood there locked in an embrace, as if his cheek were laid against another – the only part of him which was stronger than death.

On the roof-tops, vague shapes were already at their posts.

Gisors crumpled up the ragged scrap of paper on which Chen had written his name, and put it in his pocket. He was impatient to see his old pupil again. He cast another glance at the man with whom he was conversing, an aged Chinaman, who said in English, as he moved towards the door with little pattering steps, and forefinger poised: 'That women remain in complete subjection is a fit and proper state of affairs; likewise the existence of extra-marital sexual relationships and the practice of prostitution. I shall continue to publish my articles. It is the fact that our ancestors held that point of view which made possible the creation of these fine paintings of which we are so proud.' He glanced sideways at the blue phoenix, without turning his head at all, as though he were ogling it. 'Woman is subject to man as man is subject to the state: and the service of man is the less exacting. Do we live for ourselves? We are of no account. We live for the state now and for the glorious company of the dead through the countless years to come. . . . '

Was he going at last? He had something of the fascination of the mentally disordered, this man who remained shackled to his past, even at the present day (didn't the warship's sirens already make the night sufficiently hideous . . . ?), with China deluged in blood before his eyes, like one of his bronzes during the sacrificial rites. Glorious company! Innumerable skeletons in embroidered robes, lost in the mists of time as they sat in moribund conclave: before him, Chen, the two hundred thousand hands in the cotton-mills (no embroidered robes there), the prodigious multitude of coolies. The subjection of women? Every evening, May had a tale to tell of a bride driven to self-destruction. . . . The old man departed, forefinger upraised: 'The glorious company, Mr Gisors! . . .', with a final bob by way of leave-taking.

As soon as he heard the door shut, Gisors went to call Chen, and returned with him to the phoenix-room. Chen started walking up and down. Every time he passed in front of the divan on which he was sitting, his profile reminded Gisors of an Egyptian bronze falcon of which Kyo had kept a photograph out of friendship for Chen, 'because of the likeness'. It was true, despite the seeming benevolence of those thick lips. 'Perhaps a falcon tamed by St Francis of Assisi would be a better description,' he thought.

Chen stopped in front of him.

'It is I who killed Tang Yen Ta,' he said.

Gisors seemed to be looking at him with something like affection. He despised affection; but it frightened him. With his head sunk between his shoulders, hanging forward as he walked, and his curved beak of a nose, he looked more like a falcon than ever, in spite of his thickset figure: even in his narrow, almost lashless eyes, he resembled a bird.

'Is that what you wanted to talk to me about?'

'Yes.'

'Does Kyo know about it?'

'Yes.'

Gisors thought for a minute. Without appearing to have already come to the conventional conclusions, he could scarcely do otherwise than give his approval. But it was not without difficulty that he did so. 'I'm getting old,' he thought.

Chen ceased his walking up and down.

'I'm unbelievably lonely,' he said, looking hard at Gisors.

Gisors was perturbed. That Chen should come to him in his need seemed natural enough: for years he had been his mentor, with all that the term implies in China – on a slightly lower footing than his father, of more account than his mother. Now that they were both dead, Gisors was probably the only man who was really important to him. What he failed to understand was why Chen, who had presumably seen some of the terrorists since the crime, as he had just been seeing Kyo again, should seem so out of touch with them.

'What about the others?' he asked.

Chen thought of them as he had seen them, in the back of the gramophone-shop, now plunged in darkness, now with the light upon them, according to the swinging of the lamp; and the cricket chirping all the time.

'They don't know.'

'That it's you who did it?'

'Yes, they know that: that's not the thing.'

He was silent again. Gisors refrained from questioning him. At last Chen went on:

'. . . that it's the first time.'

It suddenly seemed to Gisors that he understood: Chen perceived his impression.

'Na-oo. You don't understand. . . .'

His French accent combined curiously a guttural pronunciation of the one-syllable nasal words, with certain of Kyo's peculiarities which he had adopted. He had instinctively stretched out his right arm along his side: once again he felt the resistance of the mattress-springs as his knife struck the body. That didn't mean anything. It wouldn't be the last time. But in the meantime he wanted to get his mind away from it. Kyo was the only person, Chen knew, for whom Gisors felt that profound affection which does away with the necessity for all explanation. How could he make himself understood?

'You haven't ever killed anybody, have you?'

'You know that well enough.'

It appeared evident enough to Chen, but today his mind refused to accept evidence. Gisors suddenly seemed to him to lack something. He looked up. The old man was staring at

55

him, his white hair seeming longer than ever as he threw his head back, surprised at his lack of animation as he talked. His wound was responsible. Chen had said nothing about it, and it didn't really hurt him; only worried him a little: (a friend from a hospital had dressed it for him). As always when he was thinking about something, Gisors rolled a non-existent cigarette between his fingers.

'Perhaps . . .'

He stopped, his bright eyes looking straight ahead out of that mask-like face that resembled a shaven Knight Templar. Chen was waiting. Gisors went on, almost savagely:

'I shouldn't have thought the mere memory of a murder was enough to upset you so.'

'It's clear that he doesn't know what he's talking about,' Chen forced himself to think. But Gisors' thrust had gone home. He sat down. Then, looking at his feet:

'Na-oo,' he said, 'I shouldn't have thought so either. It's not just the memory of it that's really worrying me. I should like to know what it is.'

Had he come there just to find out that?

'The first woman you slept with was a prostitute, I suppose?' Gisors asked him.

'I am Chinese,' Chen answered bitterly.

'No,' thought Gisors. Except, possibly, as far as sex was concerned, Chen was not Chinese. The migrants of all nationalities, who thronged Shanghai, had shown Gisors how national man remains even in the nature of his attempts to shake off his nationality; but Chen no longer belonged to China, even in the manner of his renunciation: complete liberty of thought had given him complete freedom.

'What were your feelings afterwards?' asked Gisors.

Chen clenched his fingers.

'Pride.'

'At being a man?'

'At not being a woman.'

56

There was no bitterness in his voice now, but a curious contempt.

'I think what you mean is,' he continued, 'that I must have felt . . . cut off?'

Gisors refrained from answering.

'Yes. Terribly. And you are right to bring women into it. One may feel great contempt for the man one kills. But less than for other people.'

'For those who do not kill?'

'For those who do not kill: the uninitiated!'

He began walking up and down again. The ejaculation of the last two words seemed to take a weight off his mind, and a silence followed, which grew more and more intense: Gisors was feeling now, not without distress, the isolation of which Chen spoke. He suddenly remembered Chen telling him of his horror of blood-sports.

'The sight of the blood didn't disgust you?'

'Yes. But there was more than disgust to it.'

He had moved away from Gisors as he said that. Suddenly he swung round, and looking at the phoenix, straight at it, but speaking as though he had been looking into Gisor's eyes, he asked:

'Well? I know how to treat women when they develop proprietary ideas: live with them. Does that apply to death?'

Then still more bitterly, but still looking at the phoenix:

'Is that a kind of mating too?'

Gisors always felt a desire to extricate those who conversed with him: his mind worked like that, sympathetically: and he had a real feeling of affection for Chen. But he was beginning to see the situation more clearly. This young man was finding life too dull in the Shock Sections; he was becoming fascinated with the idea of terrorism. Still rolling his imaginary cigarette, with his head hanging forward as though he were looking at the carpet, and a lock of white hair flapping against his thin nose, he said as unconcernedly as he could manage:

'You have an idea that you won't ever get out of this. . . .'
Then his control broke down and he mumbled on:

' . . . and it's the horror of that feeling that sends you to me for protection.'

Silence.

'Not horror,' muttered Chen at last. 'Isn't it destiny?'

Renewed silence. Gisors felt incapable of movement, felt the impossibility of taking his hand, as he had done in former times. At last he made up his mind, and said wearily, as though his distress had all at once become something permanent, inescapable:

'Think of it like that, then, and act upon it, wherever the thought leads you. And if you wish for real union . . .'

'I shall soon be killed.'

'Isn't that what he wants, more than anything else,' Gisors wondered. He has no desire for fame or happiness. Well-fitted to achieve victory, but not to live on when he has won it, what else can he be heading for? Death has doubtless for him the significance which others attach to life. Death in the noblest possible form. He is ambitious, comprehensibly enough; but sufficiently remote from his fellows, or sufficiently disordered, to despise all the hoped-for achievements of his ambition, if not the quality itself.

'If your intention is a kind of communion with this . . . destiny, there is but one practical road to follow: to sublimate it.'

'Who would be worthy to do that?' asked Chen, still between clenched teeth.

The atmosphere was growing more and more oppressive, as if their allusions to violent death were on the point of evoking the reality. Gisors felt unable to say anything more: to utter one word that would not sound false, indelicate, obtuse.

'Thank you,' said Chen. He bowed to him, inclining his whole body, in the Chinese fashion (that had never been his habit; it was as though he were loth to touch him), and then withdrew.

Gisors sat down again, beginning once more to roll his non-existent cigarette. For the first time he found himself confronted not with a struggle of distant forces, but with actual blood. And, as ever, he thought of Kyo. The highly charged atmosphere which surrounded Chen would have been intolerable to Kyo. Yet, was he sure of that? Chen also had loathed the hunting of animals, had been revolted by the sight of blood – before. When it came to fundamentals like that, what did he know of his son? On occasions when his love was powerless to intervene, and he had no past memories to help him in his analysis, he knew that his understanding of Kyo was at an end. He was seized with an overwhelming desire to see him again – like the desire that comes to look yet once more upon the dead. He knew that he had gone.

Where? Chen's presence still filled the room. Chen had plunged into the world of murder now, and would never escape from it: he had answered the call of terrorism – doggedly – as he would have entered prison. Before ten years were out, he would be caught – tortured or executed; till then, he would live the life of a fanatic, in the world of vigorous action and sudden death. He had lived for his ideals; now he was going to die for them.

That was what Gisors found it so hard to bear. Let Kyo plan death, well and good: that was his office. And if it were not, it made no difference: Kyo's deeds were their own justification. But he was horrified by this sudden realization of the inevitably fatal consequences of murder, of its toxic effect, all the more terrible because it had not yet developed very far. He felt the inadequacy of his response to Chen's appeal for help; the isolation which surrounds murder, and the gulf which was widening between himself and Kyo as a result of the stresses and strains which it sets up. For the first time, the words which he had so often repeated to himself: 'The human being defies knowledge,' became associated in his mind with the image of his son. Did he really know Chen? Memories seemed to him too flimsy for adequate understanding of a man. First of all there had been Chen's early education, religious in character. And when he had first begun to take an interest in him, he had found himself faced with a covertly insolent young orphan (his parents had been killed at the sack of Kalgan) fresh from the Lutheran College, where Chen had been the pupil of a tuberculous intellectual who had entered the ministry late in life: who was striving patiently, at the age of fifty, to overlay with Christian charity the fundamental instability of his faith. Obsessed, like St Augustine, by the unworthiness of physical things, the vileness of the body which hindered his communion with Christ – by his horror of the ceremonial-governed Chinese civilization which surrounded him and rendered the calls of genuine pity all the more insistent – the heart-searching of this pastor had led him at length to an interpretation of Luther which he communicated to Gisors now and then: 'There is no life save in God: but such, through sin, has been man's fall, such his irremediable defilement, that communion with the Godhead has become, as it were, sacrilege. And so came Christ, and his eternal expiation by crucifixion.' There remained Grace, that is to say boundless love, or fear, according to the strength or weakness of hope; and that fear was sin in a new form. There remained Christian charity too; but there were depths of affliction in the face of which charity was of no avail.

The pastor had taken a liking to Chen. He never suspected that the uncle of Chen's who had charge of him had only sent him to the missionaries so that he might learn English and French, and had warned him against their teaching, above all against the idea of hell, which revolted his Confucian principles. It was neither Satan nor Jehovah with whom the child was faced, but Christ – the example of the pastor had taught him that conversion invariably means conversion to mysticism – and he gave himself up to love with the same earnestness with which he approached everything else. But he felt sufficient reverence for his master – the one respect in which China had deeply influenced him – to perceive the pastor's agony of mind more clearly than the love which he expounded, and to see in it a hell more dreadful and more convincing than the hell against which his suspicions had been aroused.

His uncle reappeared. Profoundly shocked by the changes in his nephew, he was none the less scrupulous in his protestations of satisfaction, sending little trees of jade and crystal to the Principal, the pastor, and some of the others; a week later, Chen returned to his house, and the following week he sent him to Pekin University.

Still rolling his cigarette between his knees, and with half-open mouth and bewildered expression, denoting thought, Gisors tried to remember what the youth had been like then. But how difficult it was to separate him, to disentangle him, from what he had become. 'The religious side of him impresses me, because it is something Kyo has never had, and because any radical differences between the two make my mind easier. . . . Why do I have the feeling that I know him better than my own son?' It was because he saw much more clearly in his case the changes which his influence had wrought; that fundamental remodelling which he had achieved, was something quite definite; he could see where it began and ended, and nothing revealed itself to him so clearly in a person as something for which he was himself responsible. His very first impressions of Chen had convinced him that he was a young man whose ideals only retained their effectiveness when translated immediately into some practical form. The idea of good works did not enter into his philosophy, and a religious life could thus offer him nothing save contemplation or introspection; but he hated contemplation, and yearned for a life of service of the very kind from which his lack of charity cut him off. It was thus vital to his development that he should shake himself free from his Christian principles. (From what he had learned in semi-confidence it appeared that experiences with prostitutes and fellow-students had enabled Chen to overcome the one weakness which it had always been beyond the power of his will to control – masturbation; and therewith the mental anguish and the feeling of defilement which it had always brought in its train.) And when his new master had sought not to destroy Christianity by reasoned argument, but to replace it by other hierarchies of equal omnipotence, Chen's faith had dwindled steadily and unemotionally away, as sand trickles through the fingers. It had detached him from China, accustoming him to withdraw from the world instead of submitting to its influences, and Gisors had taught him to think of that period of his life as no more than a cultivation of his sense of the heroic; how shall the soul justify itself, if neither God nor Christ exist?

In this, Gisors saw that he had something in common with his son. Though indifferent to Christianity, Kyo too had learnt, from his Japanese education (he had lived in Japan from the time he was eight until he was seventeen), that ideas must not remain just intellectual concepts, but demand expression in life. Kyo had chosen action, gravely and deliberately, as others choose a military career or the sea; he had left his father, and gone to Canton and Tientsin, to live as the manual labourers and the rickshaw-coolies lived, and to help to organize the unions. Then Chen's uncle was held as a hostage after the fall of Swatow, and executed because he couldn't pay his ransom; and there he was, at the age of twenty-four, with no money and a string of unmarketable diplomas; face to face with China. He had been a lorry-driver on the northern routes as long as the excitement lasted there; then a chemist's assistant, and then nothing at all. Everything combined to drive him into politics; the hope of bettering the world, the chance of food, however frugal (he had naturally ascetic tendencies, perhaps due to pride), vengeance on all that he hated, and fulfilment of his ideals. They gave a meaning to his loneliness. But

Kyo's case was much less complicated. For him, a sense of the heroic had meant the imposition of a code rather than proved a method of interpreting life. Not that it caused him any uneasiness. His life had a meaning, and he knew what it was: to restore their personal dignity to every one of those whom hunger was destroying, before his eyes, like an insidious plague. Those were the people he belonged to; their enemies were his enemies. Despised by white men and still more by white women, as a half-caste, a mongrel, Kyo had made no attempt to win their sympathy: he had sought, and found, his own people. 'No dignity, no real existence is possible for a man who works twelve hours a day and still has no notion of what his work means.' Work must be made to mean something in cases like that, must achieve honourable status. It was only in moments of seclusion that Kyo began to consider his own personal problems.

Gisors knew all that. 'And yet, if Kyo came in like Chen just now, and said: "It's I who killed Tang Yen Ta," – if he said that, I should think: "I knew it." All his potentialities, his tendencies, strike so resounding an echo in me that whatever he said to me, I should think: "I knew it. . . . " ' He looked out of the window into the imperturbable stillness of the night. 'But if I really knew, with more than this vague and terrible half-knowledge, I should save him.' A painful realization, which he was far from accepting. What confidence had he in his reasoning?

Since Kyo's departure, his mind had steadily refused to attempt to criticize his son's activities, plans which had as yet scarcely begun to develop, somewhere away (often, for months on end, he didn't know exactly where) in central China or the southern provinces. The students rightly felt, when in difficulties, that his mind was there with all its ardour and analytical power, ready to come to the rescue. But the explanation was not, as those imbeciles thought at Pekin, that he enjoyed a vicarious participation in activities in which his age forbade him to play a practical part, but simply that each crisis, so similar to the last, recalled to him the perils of his own son. When he demonstrated to his students, who almost all came from the lower middle class, that they had no choice but to give their allegiance either to the military dictators or to the proletariat, he told those who had already chosen: 'Marxism isn't a doctrine, it's a form of will power. For the proletariat and its supporters – for you – it means the determination to know yourselves, to appreciate all that it can do for you, and to make it your watchword in the hour of triumph. It is not for the justice of its arguments that Marxism should appeal to you, but as the one road to victory which involves no forfeiture of self-respect.' And when he said that, it was Kyo whom he addressed, Kyo whom he defended. And even if Kyo's nature was too uncompromisingly impersonal for him to be in any way connected with the masses of white flowers with which, according to Chinese custom, the students were wont to deck his room after those lectures, at least he knew that the hands which now offered him camelias were at the same time being trained to violence, that on the morrow his own son would find renewed confidence in their grasp. That explained why strength of character attracted him, and why he had liked Chen so much. But when he took a liking to Chen, had he foreseen that night when the young man would come to him through the rain and say, almost before the blood had ceased to flow: 'It was more than a feeling of disgust . . .'

He got up, and bent down to open the drawer in the little table where he kept his opium things, neatly arranged on a tray, with a collection of tiny cactus underneath. Under the tray was a photo: Kyo. He took it out and looked at it, but his thoughts were vague, overshadowed by the knowledge that in the world which he was about to enter, all identity was submerged: that even Kyo's actual presence there, for which he had been longing a few minutes previously, would have made no difference, but rendered his feeling of separation all

64

the more agonizing; would have been as unsubstantial as reunion in a dream with a friend who has long been dead. He still held the photo in his fingers: it was warm, like a hand. He dropped it back into the drawer, pulled out the tray, switched off the electric light and lit the lamp.

Two pipes. In former days, as soon as his craving began to be satisfied, he saw people's good points, and the world appeared as a place of infinite possibilities. Now optimism found no place in his musings: he was sixty years of age, and too many of his memories ended in the grave. The purity of his feeling for Chinese art, for those bluish paintings which his lamp scarcely showed up, for all the subtle Chinese civilization which surrounded him, all this had brought him such keen enjoyment thirty years ago. But now, like his optimism, it was only a frail veneer, and underneath, like dogs which grow restless as the hour of awakening approaches, his agony of mind and his morbid fear of death stirred fitfully.

For all that, his thoughts still roamed the world, observing men, with an earnestness which age had not diminished. That in each one of us, and above all in himself, there was a degree of paranoia, he had long been convinced. Time was when – at one stage of his development – he had seen himself in a heroic light. No. This energy of his, this fervent imagination which worked like a leaven in him (if I were to go mad, he used to think, that alone would survive . . .) was capable of as many transmutations as light. Like Kyo, and for almost the same reasons, he thought of the gramophone-records, which the latter had told him about; and his thoughts were almost the same, for had not Kyo's mental processes evolved from his own? Just as Kyo had failed to recognize his own voice because the sound came to him through his throat, in the same way Gisors' consciousness of himself was presumably of a fundamentally different character from his perception of other people, because it was the product of an altogether different mechanism. It was nothing to do with his senses. He felt himself forcing a way (and his consciousness didn't belong there) into a territory which was peculiarly his own, agonizingly entering into the isolation of a forbidden area where he would for ever remain alone. For a moment, it seemed as though it was THAT which was appointed to survive.... His hands trembled slightly as they kneaded another pellet. Even his love for Kyo couldn't deliver him from that final utter loneliness. But if other people failed him as a refuge, he could still make his own escape: there was still opium.

Five pellets. For years now he had stopped there; not without difficulty, at times not without distress. He scraped the bowl of his pipe; the shadow of his hand darted from wall to ceiling. He pushed the lamp a few inches further away; the shadow lost its sharp outline. Other things, too, began to grow blurred; they kept their formal shape, but were no longer separate entities reaching out to him, deep down in that world he knew so well, where all distinctions merged into the all-pervading sense of well-being. A world which was truer than reality because it changed less, was more uniform; as staunch as any friendship, always waiting there with its sympathy: outward forms, memories, ideas, they were all slipping slowly down towards that ubiquitous freedom. He remembered one September afternoon when the sky had been of an exquisite greyness which turned the waters of a lake to milk beneath the vast expanse of silken water-lilies which covered it; and as he looked from the mouldering cornices of a deserted pavilion to the splendid desolation of that vista the whole world seemed draped in a kind of ritual gloom. With his bell beside him, a Buddhist priest was leaning on the balustrade of the pavilion. He had left his sanctuary behind him, allowing dust to corrupt the scent of the sweet-smelling wood which smouldered there. Some peasants glided noiselessly by, gathering seeds from the water-lilies. Near where the flowers ended, the rudder of their boat set up two tiny ripples, which expanded till they merged placidly into the grey water. They were like so many expanding rings in his own head now, which somehow contained all the world's afflictions, but afflictions which had lost their sting, transmuted by the opium into something quite impersonal. With eyes closed, and vast unmoving wings bearing him up, Gisors mused upon his loneliness: it was a feeling of isolation which had something divine in it, but which included also that reassuring wave which gently smoothed away all ideas of mortality as its circles grew wider and were absorbed.

4.30 A.M.

Already dressed as Government soldiers, with capes on their backs, the men went down one by one into the big launch which lay rocking to the movement of the river.

'Two of the sailors are in with us. We must ask them. They ought to know where the arms are,' said Kyo to Katow. Except for the boots Katow looked much the same in uniform. His soldier's blouse was just as badly buttoned as the other one. But the cap was new, and he wasn't used to a cap; it made him look ridiculous, stuck squarely on his head. 'That's an odd combination, a Chinese officer's cap and a nose like that!' thought Kyo. It was dark. . . .

'Put up your hood,' was all he said, though.

The launch swung slowly out from the quay-side, and then made off into the night. She soon disappeared behind a junk. The beams of the cruiser's searchlights came swooping down out of the sky upon all the confusion in the port below, stabbing through each other like swords.

In the bows, Katow did not take his eyes off the *Shan-Tung*; he could see her slowly getting nearer. He was very close to the water, and the stench of stagnant water, fish, and smoke from the harbour caught him, gradually eclipsing the reek of coal from the jetty. At once the picture which an approaching

67

fight always called up in him surged up overwhelmingly. On the Lithuanian front, his battalion had been captured by the Whites. Their arms gone, the men stood lined up on the vast snowy plain that was scarcely visible in the greenish light of the dawn. 'Communists stand out!' They knew that it meant death. Two-thirds of the battalion had stepped forward. 'Take off your tunics. Dig the trench.' They had dug. Slowly, for the ground was frozen. To right and left of them the White guards stood waiting, impatient and ill at ease, with a revolver in each hand, for spades might be used as weapons. The centre was left empty for the machine-guns trained upon the prisoners. The silence was immeasurable; it had the immensity of the snow which stretched as far as the eye could see. There was only the noise the frozen clods made as they hit the ground. Crisp thuds that came quicker and quicker. Even with death before them, the men were hurrying – to get warm. Several had begun to sneeze. 'That'll do. Stop!' They turned round. Behind them, beyond their comrades, were massed old men, women, and children from the village; but scantily clothed, wrapped in blankets. Gathered there to profit by the lesson. Many shook their heads, as if they were making every effort to look away, but were spellbound in their anguish. 'Take off your trousers!' For uniforms were rare. Many hesitated, on account of the women. 'Take off your trousers!' Wounds had appeared, one by one, bound up with rags; the machine-guns had shot very low and almost all of them were hit in the legs. Many folded their trousers, though their great-coats had been thrown aside anyhow. They were lined up once more, at the edge of the trench this time, facing the machine-guns, white against the snow; flesh and shirts. As the cold pierced them they sneezed incessantly, one after another, and those sneezes were so intensely human beside the grimness of that dawn, that instead of firing the machine-gunners had waited – waited till Life be more discreet. They had made up their minds in the end. On the following evening, the Reds recaptured the village; seventeen whom the shots had failed to finish were saved; Katow among them. Silhouetted against the snow, almost transparently bright in the eerie light of the dawn; convulsed with sneezes; so many shapes, they faced the machine-guns. And those shapes were there with him in the rain that night in China, in the shadow of the *Shan-Tung*.

The launch was moving steadily forward: there was enough of a swell to make the squat and hazy outline of the big ship appear to move up and down with the river; she had scarcely any lights, and was visible only as a still darker mass against the dull sky. The *Shan-Tung* was sure to be guarded. A cruiser's searchlight found the launch, watched her for a moment, then left her. They had moved in a wide circle, and came upon the big boat from behind, ending up slightly to her right, as if they had been making for the boat next to her. All the men were wearing sailors' duffle-coats over their uniform, with the hoods down. By order of the port authorities, every ship had her accommodation-ladder lowered. Katow looked at the *Shan-Tung's* through the glasses which his coat concealed. It came to an end a yard above the water, feebly lit by three lamps. If the captain asked for money, which they had not got, before allowing them to go on board, the men would have to jump out of the picket-boat one by one; it would be difficult to keep it under the ladder. Everything would depend upon that little slanting gangway. If they tried to pull it up from above, he could fire on those working the tackle; under the pulleys there, nothing would give any protection. But the ship would prepare itself against attack.

The picket swung round at right-angles, and bore down upon the *Shan-Tung*. The current, powerful at that time of day, caught her broadside-on; the big boat very high in front of them now (they were standing up) seemed to rush off at full speed into the night, like a ghost ship. The engineer got his engines going at their maximum; the *Shang-Tung* seemed to slow down, stand still, go backwards. They approached the ladder. Katow caught hold as they went past, heaved himself up, and stood on the steps.

'The pass?' asked the watch on the gangway.

Katow gave it him. The man handed it on, and remained at his post, revolver in hand. So the captain had to check his own permit. Probably that was it, as that was what he had done when Clappique had given it to him. Still . . . At the foot of the ladder, the picket rose and fell with the river, black against it.

The messenger returned: 'You can come on board.' Katow did not move; one of his men (the one who wore lieutenant's stripes, and the only one who spoke English) left the picket and went up after the sailor who had brought the message, who led him to the captain.

The latter was awaiting him in his cabin, behind his desk. He was a close-cropped Norwegian with pimply cheeks. The messenger went out.

'We've come to get the arms,' said the lieutenant in English.

The captain looked at him in amazement, but did not answer. The generals had always paid for the arms. The sale had all been arranged secretly by a consular attaché, even including the dispatch of Tang Yen Ta as agent; and it had been for a fair price. If they started breaking their contracts with the 'runners', who would continue to supply them? Still, as it was only the Shanghai government which he was dealing with, he might make an attempt to save his guns.

'Well – Here is the key.'

He felt calmly in the inside pocket of his jacket, then suddenly pulled out his revolver – on a level with the lieutenant's chest, from which only the table separated him. At the same moment, he heard behind him: 'Hands up.' Katow had him covered from the open window of the corridor. The captain was completely at sea now, for this one was a white; but for the moment there was nothing for it but to give in. His life was more important than the cases of arms. 'That's knocked the bottom out of this trip,' he thought. He would see if the crew could help him out. He laid down his revolver, which was taken charge of by the lieutenant.

Katow came in and searched him. He had no other weapons.

'No good at all having all those guns on board and only carrying one yourself,' he said in English. Six of his men came in behind him, silently, one by one. Katow's heavy tread, his stalwart appearance, upturned nose, and fair hair; all looked Russian. Or perhaps Scotch? But that accent . . .

'You're not an official, are you?'

'Mind your own business.'

The mate was brought in, efficiently trussed, surprised in his sleep. The men tied up the captain. Two of them remained behind to guard him. The others went below with Katow. The Communists in the crew showed them where the arms were hidden; the only precaution taken by the Macao importers had been to write 'Goods in piece' upon the cases. The removal began. It was easy with the gangway lowered, as they were small cases. When the last one was in the launch, Katow went and put the wireless out of action, then paid the captain a visit.

'Don't be in too much of a hurry to get ashore, or I may say you'll be getting yourself into something you won't fancy. Good evening.'

Pure brag, but the ropes cutting into the prisoners' arms lent colour to it.

Accompanied by the two sailors who had given them the information, the revolutionaries went back to the launch, which drew away from the gangway and made for the quay; in a straight line this time. As they tossed about in the swell, the men changed their clothes; delighted with their success, but still uneasy. Until they reached the shore, they were still in danger. There a lorry awaited them, with Kyo sitting beside the driver.

'Well?'

'It went fine. Child's play.'

As soon as everything was on board the lorry started off,

carrying Kyo, Katow, and four men, one of whom was still wearing uniform. The rest dispersed.

They lumbered their way through the Chinese quarter, with a rumbling that every jolt turned into a devastating tinpot rattling; at the sides, near the open frame-work, petrol cans were ranged. They stopped at every *tchon* of importance: shop, cellar, apartment. A case was put down, with a note of Kyo's calculations on the side, to regulate the distribution of the arms, some of which were to be sent to the smaller 'centres'. The lorry barely took five minutes over it. But there were more than twenty posts to be visited.

Treachery was all they had to fear now: that noisy lorry, driven by a man in Government uniform, aroused no suspicions. They ran into a patrol. 'I might be a milkman going on his round,' thought Kyo.

Dawn was breaking.

Part 2

'It looks bad,' thought Ferral, as he drove along the quay. (His car was the only Voisin in Shanghai; as President of the French Chamber of Commerce he could scarcely use an American one.) On the right a row of banners hung down, covered with such inscriptions as: *Strike for a twelve-hour day, No more work for children under eight,* and underneath were workers from the cotton-mills, in their thousands; standing, squatting, lying on the pavement in an uneasy mass. He passed a group of women, clustered beneath a banner which read: *Seats for women workers.* Even the arsenal was empty; the munition workers were on strike. On the left, thousands of watermen squatted along the river-bank, waiting. Their blue clothes were in tatters, and they had no banners. The mob of demonstrators stretched away into the distance. Towards the quay, till it was lost in the depths of the long straight streets; on the river-side, swarming over the wharfs, till it was impossible to see where the water began. The car left the quay and turned into the Avenue des Deux-Républiques. It was scarcely possible to make any further progress. He was completely hemmed in by the surging mass of humanity, which swarmed from every street, to find sanctuary in the French Concession. Like one racehorse over-taking another, by a head, a neck, by half a length, so the crowd was surely but steadily gaining ground upon the motor-car. Wheelbarrows, with babies' heads sticking out between the bowls which filled them; Pekinese wagons, rickshaws, shaggy ponies, handcarts; lorries carrying sixty people on board; enormous mattresses with the entire contents of a house piled on top of them, one mass of projecting table-legs; gigantic figures stretching a protecting arm (with a blackbird in a cage

73

dangling at the end of it) over little women with children clustered thick upon their backs. . . . At last the driver managed to turn aside into streets where the noise of his klaxon sufficed to keep a few yards in front of the car clear of the mob with which they too were choked. He arrived at the huge buildings which housed the French police.

Ferral almost ran up the steps. Despite the way his hair was brushed back over his head, his brightly coloured suit, almost flashy, and his grey silk shirt, his face still retained traces of the 1900 period when he had been young. He laughed at people 'who masquerade as captains of industry', and made that sufficient justification for himself masquerading as a diplomat. All he lacked was the traditional monocle. His drooping moustache, turning grey now, seemed to accentuate the sagging at the corners of his mouth, and gave his profile a subtly brutal expression: the face derived its strength from the combination of beaky nose and unbelievably prominent chin (badly shaved this morning), which produced an almost nutcracker effect. There was a strike at the water-works, and it was difficult to work up a lather with the chalky water which the coolies brought. He was saluted on all sides as he went in.

Martial, the commissioner of police, was in his office, and behind him stood a Chinese subordinate of gigantic size, asking:

'Is that all, sir?'

'Try and break up their organizations, too,' answered the commissioner, without turning round. 'And in future don't behave with quite such crass stupidity. If you got what you deserved it'd be a kick up the backside: half your men are stinking rotten double-crossers! I don't pay you to look after twisters who are afraid to show themselves in their true revolutionary colours. The police force isn't an alibi-factory. You bloody well get rid of all the men who are up to tricks with the Kuomintang; this is the last time I'm telling you that! And listen to what I'm saying, instead of gaping at me! If I knew as little about what was going on inside my men's heads as you

74

do about what your lot are up to, there'd be a fine sort of a mess . . . '

'But . . . '

'That's settled then. All arranged. Don't want to hear any more. Get to hell out of here and the quicker the better. Good morning, Mr Ferral.'

He had just turned round: his face had a military appearance, his broad, regular, rather characterless features seeming of less importance than his shoulders.

'Good morning, Martial. Well?'

'The Government are finding they require thousands of men just to protect the railway-line, so you can imagine that even a police force like ours has its work cut out to make a whole country toe the line. The only thing the Government can rely on is the armoured train, with its white instructors. That's worth taking into account.'

'Even there it's a case of a small minority struggling with a mass of "nit-wits". Still, you're right about that.'

'It all depends on the front. Here, they're going to start a revolution. They may find they get it in the neck, for they're practically unarmed.'

Ferral could only listen and await events, which was just what he hated doing. Nothing definite had been achieved, as yet, by the negotiations which those who, like himself and certain of the Consulates, controlled English and Japanese interests, had begun with the swarm of representatives who filled the hotels in the Concessions. That afternoon, perhaps . . .

With Shanghai in the hands of the revolutionary army the Kuomintang would have to decide definitely between democracy and communism. Democracies are always good customers, and privileges could still be obtained without necessarily having recourse to an actual legal agreement. But if the city were organized on Soviet lines, on the other hand, the Franco-Asiatic Consortium would break down, and French trade with Shanghai would be at an end. Ferral thought the

Powers would abandon their nationals, as England had done at Hankow. His immediate object was to prevent the town being captured before the army arrived, for in that event the Communists would be in sole control.

'How many troops are there, Martial, besides the armoured train?'

'Two thousand police and one brigade of infantry, Mr Ferral.'

'And how many revolutionaries who can do more than make speeches?'

'Armed, barely two or three hundred. . . . And the others can't matter very much, I suppose. There's no military service here, so they don't know how to use a rifle; don't forget that. In February there must have been two or three thousand of those enthusiasts, if one includes the Communists. There are probably a few more of them now.'

'How many will desert when it comes to the point?' Martial went on. 'It's an interesting question, Mr Ferral, but we can't get very much further without some knowledge of the reactions of its leaders. About the men's point of view, I already know something. You see, the Chinese . . .'

Ferral was looking at the chief of police in a way which never failed to reduce him to silence. His expression was not so much contemptuous or exasperated, as analytical. He didn't actually say, in his grating and rather mechanical voice: 'Have you nearly finished?' but that was the impression he conveyed. Ferral couldn't stand hearing Martial attribute to his own perspicacity things which his spies had discovered for him.

If Martial had dared, he would have answered: 'What business is it of yours anyway?' He was completely under the thumb of Ferral, and his relations with him were based upon orders which he had no option but to obey; as a man, too, he felt his own inferiority. But he could not endure this insolent indifference, this method of reducing him to the condition of a machine, by denying his existence directly he attempted to voice any individual opinions instead of merely transmitting information. The delegates with whom he negotiated had told him of the impression Ferral had made upon the Parliamentary Committees when he was still in power. Those very qualities which gave such strength and lucidity to his speeches were so abused by him in council that his colleagues came to hate him more and more every year: he had a technique all his own for pushing them completely into the background. On precisely those occasions when a Jaurès or a Briand would have shown perhaps even more deference to their personal feeling than they merited, making them believe that he was appealing to them individually – trying to convince them, to enable them to find some common ground in their experience of men and affairs – Ferral would confront them with an imposing array of facts, and conclude by saying: 'In view of which circumstances, gentlemen, it would be absurd *on the face of it* . . .' He would get his way by force, or be broken in the attempt. 'It was just the same now,' Martial reflected.

'Heard anything from Hankow?' asked Ferral.

'We've had news tonight. There are two hundred and twenty thousand unemployed, enough to form another Red army.'

For weeks past, the goods of three of the companies which Ferral controlled had lain rotting beside those magnificent wharfs: the coolies refused to move them.

'How are things going between the Communists and Chang Kai Shek?'

'Here is his last speech,' answered Martial. 'But for my part, I've no great faith in speeches. . . .'

'I have. In this one, anyway. Though perhaps. . . .'

The telephone rang. Martial took up the receiver.

'It's for you, Mr Ferral.'

Ferral sat down on the table.

'Hullo? Yes.'

' . . .'

'He's giving you rope to hang yourself with. He's opposed to intervention, we all know that. The only question is whether it would be best to accuse him of homosexuality or of taking bribes.'

'. . .'

'Naturally I'm not suggesting that there's any truth in either charge. And what's more, a colleague of mine should know me better than to imagine that I would tax a man with a sexual abnormality which he really possessed. Do you take me for a moralist? Good-bye.'

Martial didn't dare ask any questions. That Ferral should keep him in the dark with regard to his plans, and not tell him what his conferences with all the most prominent members of the international Chamber of Commerce and the leaders of the big Chinese commercial combines were likely to lead to, appeared to him both insulting and short-sighted. Nevertheless, if it is irksome to a commissioner of police not to know where he stands, it is preferable to losing his job altogether. Now Ferral, born as it were with the Republic as his sponsor, full of early memories of Renan, Berthelot, Victor Hugo, as so many kindly old gentlemen; the son of a great consulting lawyer; Professor of History at twenty-seven years of age; editor at twenty-nine of the first really comprehensive history of France; a deputy while still a very young man (seizing his chance in an age which allowed Poincaré and Barthou to rise to Cabinet rank before the age of forty); president of the Franco-Asiatic League; this man Ferral possessed a degree of power and prestige in Shanghai, despite his political eclipse, at least equal to the French Consul-General, whom he numbered, moreover, among his friends. The commissioner accordingly maintained a respectful cordiality. He handed him the speech:

In five months, for a total expenditure of eighteen million piastres, I have captured six provinces. Let those who are dissatisfied seek, if they please, another leader who spends as little and who accomplishes as much . . .

'Clearly, the financial problem would be solved by the capture of Shanghai,' said Ferral. 'The customs would give him several million piastres a month, just about enough to balance the deficit on the army.'

'Yes. But they say that the commissars have had orders from Moscow to arrange that their own troops are defeated outside Shanghai. And in that case the revolt might go badly.'

'Why have they had orders like that?'

'So as to defeat Chang Kai Shek, ruin his reputation, and put a Communist general in his place who would then get the credit for taking Shanghai. It's pretty certain that the Shanghai offensive has been undertaken without the consent of the Hankow Party Executive. It also appears that the Red general staff are opposed to this plan. ....'

Ferral was interested, but unconvinced. He went on reading the speech.

'*Though deserted by the majority of its members, the Hankow Central Executive Committee nevertheless regards itself, in this incomplete state, as the authority in supreme control of the Kuomintang party. I know that Sun Yat Sen has allowed communists to become affiliated to the Party. I have at no time opposed them, and frequently I have admired their spirit. Of late, however, they have no longer been content with a subordinate position; they are presuming to direct affairs, and to impose their violent and over-bearing counsels upon the party. I give them warning of my disapproval of these inordinate pretensions, which have no foundation in the agreement concluded at the time of their admission. ...*'

It began to look as though Chang Kai Shek might be of some use. The government in power was built upon the flimsiest foundations: brute force (which would be shattered by the defeat of its army), and the fears which the communists of the revolutionary army inspired among the bourgeois. Very few men had anything to gain by its survival. Chang had a victorious army and the entire lower middle class behind him.

'Nothing else?' he inquired.

'Nothing, Mr Ferral.'

'Thank you.'

On his way downstairs he met a vision of dark brown loveliness: a mask of godlike serenity, clothed in a dashing tailormade. It was a Russian from the Caucasus, who was reputed to act as Martial's mistress on occasions. 'I'd give a lot to see you between the sheets,' he thought.

'Excuse me.'

He bowed as he passed her, got into his car, and plunged into the crowd once more, against the current this time. The klaxon screeched, but was powerless to stem the exodus, utterly ineffective against the primordial seething wave of humanity which an invasion sets in motion. Little street-traders, looking like so many weighing-machines, with their two scales hanging loose and the pivots oscillating wildly; caravans, vinaigrettes worthy of the Tang Emperors, invalids, cages; Ferral breasted the current, peered at by each panic-stricken eye in turn. If his parasite life had to be concluded, what better setting could there be than that uproar, that frenzied despair which battered against the windows of his car? Just as a wound would have led him to reflect on the meaning of his life, so the threatened miscarriage of his plans led him to ponder over them and showed him in the process where their weakness lay. This outbreak had caught him unawares: these Chinese enterprises of his had been forced upon him by the need for finding new outlets for his Indo-Chinese goods. He was playing a waiting game: he was watching developments in France. And he couldn't go on waiting much longer.

His principal handicap lay in the absence of any real government. Undertakings of that magnitude demanded the co-operation of the state. Ever since his youth while still a deputy, he had been president of the Electrical Energy and Appliances Company, which manufactured all the electrical material for the French Government: afterwards he had organized the reconstruction of Buenos Aires harbour – he had always had that behind him.

Possessing that honesty, based on pride, which scorns bribes and carries out orders, he had looked to the Asiatic colonies for the money which he needed to restore his fallen fortunes: for he wished not so much to play a new game as to change the rules of the old.

Making use of his brother's enormous personal influence, still more important than his post as Comptroller-General of the Exchequer; installed at the head of one of the powerful French financial groups, Ferral had induced the Indo-Chinese Government – even his opponents were not averse from providing him with means to leave France – to contract for an expenditure of four hundred million francs on public works. The Republic could not but allow the brother of one of her most eminent officials to execute this work of civilization. And to the astonishment of a country where shady combines of every kind are taken for granted, it was excellently carried out. Ferral knew how to get things done. A benefit is never conferred in vain: the syndicate proceeded to industrialize Indo-China. There gradually appeared: two banks, dealing with real estate and farming. Four marketing boards; rubber, cotton, sugar, and tropical cultures in general – controlling the whole business of the transition from raw material to finished products. Three mining companies; gold, phosphates, coal and a subsidiary salt-mining enterprise. Five industrial companies; light and power, electricity, glass, paper, and printing. Three transport companies: barges, tugs, and trams. The Public Works Corporation presided over them, queen of the numerous products of all this exertion, competition and printer's ink; mother or midwife to almost every one of these sister companies, linked in incestuous alliance for their benefit. And it was they who managed to secure the construction rights of the Central-Annamese railway, whose line traversed a suspiciously larger proportion of the concessions of the Ferral group. 'That went pretty well,' the vice-chairman of the board of directors would say to Ferral, too busy to answer him, stowing away his millions, climbing up the ladder which would place Paris within his grasp.

Even with the drafts of new Chinese flotations in his pockets, his thoughts remained centred on Paris. To come back to France rich enough to buy up the Agence Havas, or at least to negotiate with them; to take up politics again, advance cautiously to ministerial rank, and then play off the combined forces of the ministry and a public opinion bribed to follow their lead, against the Parliament. That was power. But his dreams had receded into the background: the ramifications of his Indo-Chinese undertakings had involved the whole of the Ferral group in the commercial exploitation of the Yang-Tse basin. And now Chang Kai Shek was marching on Shanghai with the revolutionary army, and the mob was surging more and more closely around the windows of his car. Every single one of the companies which the Franco-Asiatic Consortium owned or controlled in China had been adversely affected: shipbuilding at Hong Kong by the insecurity of navigation; all the others – public works, constructions and electrical enterprises, insurance, banking – by the war and the menace of communism. Such goods as they imported remained in their warehouses in Hong Kong and Shanghai; their exports in Hankow, sometimes in storage, sometimes lying on the quay-side.

The car stopped. The silence – a Chinese crowd is usually the noisiest in the world – portended some immense catastrophe. A gun fired. Could the revolutionary army be so near? No: it was the gun which was fired at midday. The crowd cleared a little, but the car did not move. He seized the speaking-tube. No answer: chauffeur and footman had both disappeared.

He sat there in the car, quite still, overcome with amazement, while the crowd pressed past outside. A shopkeeper came out of a shop close by, carrying an enormous shutter across his shoulder; he turned round, only just missing the windows of the car: he was shutting his shop. All around, shopkeepers and workmen were pouring out, with shutters covered with characters upon their shoulders: the general strike was beginning. This wasn't like the Hong Kong strike, developing gradually, with a kind of tragic intensity: there was a military precision about it. As far as he could see, not a shop remained open. Better move on, and not waste any time about it. He got out, and called a rickshaw. The coolie didn't answer: he was running for shelter at top speed, almost alone in the road, with the deserted car. The crowd had surged back on to the pavements. 'They're afraid of machine-guns,' thought Ferral. The children stopped playing and dashed off on to the welter of scurrying legs which engulfed the pavements. The silence palpitated with life, remote and yet imminent; a forest teeming with insect-life. A ship's siren shrilled out. Ferral was walking in the direction of his house as fast as he could go, his hands in his pockets, and chin and shoulders thrust forward. Two sirens took up simultaneously, an octave higher, the note which had just died away as if the silence were concealing some vast animal which in this way gave warning of its approach. The whole town was on the watch.

1 P.M.

'Five to,' said Chen.

The men of his section were waiting. They were all hands from the spinning-mills, dressed in coarse blue cloth: he wore the same. All were shaven, lean and vigorous. Before ever Chen had made his choice, Death had thinned them out. Two of them were holding rifles under their arms, with the barrels pointing towards the ground. Seven of them carried revolvers from the *Shan-Tung*; one, a bomb; a few others had bombs concealed in their pockets. About thirty had knives, bludgeons, and bayonets; eight or nine were unarmed, and were squatting down beside a heap of rags, petrol cans, and coils of wire. A young man was taking some large, broad-headed nails out of a sack and looking at them carefully, as if they were so much seed: 'They ought to be big enough to do the trick. . . . ' The Cour des Miracles,* but energized with hatred.

He didn't belong with them. Despite the murder, despite the fact that he was there. If he died today, he would die alone. Their course was clear enough; they were fighting for bread to live on and for recognition as human beings. As for him . . . apart from their sufferings for the common cause, he was quite unable even to talk to them. But he realized that the coming hostilities would forge the strongest possible of bonds between them.

They stood up, packs on their backs, petrol-tins in their hands, and wire under their arms. It wasn't raining yet; the gloom of that empty street, as a dog sprang across it in two bounds, as though some instinct had warned it of what was about to take place, was as profound as the silence. Five shots rang out in a neighbouring street: three together, then one, then still another. 'It's begun,' said Chen. There was silence once more, but it didn't seem the same. The noise of horses' hoofs broke into it, and held the ear, getting nearer and nearer. And like a flash of lightning splitting the sky in two after a long drawn-out peal of thunder (though they still saw nothing) there was a sudden uproar in the street; confused shouting, shots, the neighing of frenzied horses; crashing falls: then, as the commotion subsided, snuffed out remorsely by that impregnable silence, came a howl like a dog mortally injured – a piercing howl that was suddenly cut short: a man's throat had been cut.

They went off at the double, and after a moment reached a more important street. All the shops were closed. On the

*A sanctuary for beggars and outlaws in Paris during the Middle Ages.

ground lay three bodies; overhead, up above a maze of telegraph wires, clouds of black smoke were sweeping across the sky; right at the end of the street, twenty or thirty cavalry hovered restlessly (there were very few cavalry in Shanghai), but did not notice the rebels pressed tight against the wall with their weapons, watching the nervous prancing of the horses. Chen saw that to attack them was out of the question: his men were too poorly armed. They turned off to the right, and at length reached the police station. The sentries calmly followed Chen in. The men were playing cards, their rifles and Mausers on the racks. The sergeant in command of them opened a window and shouted into the dark yard below:

'You will all bear witness to the violence which is being done to us. We are being illegally compelled to yield to force!'

He was about to shut the window, when Chen interposed and looked out: the yard was empty. Prestige was saved, however: the dramatic gesture had been made just at the right moment. Chen understood his compatriots well, and knew that the very fact of his staging an incident like that meant that he wouldn't take any further action. He divided the arms among his men. The rebels departed, all armed this time: there was no object in occupying a small police station from which the teeth had been drawn. The policemen hesitated. Three of them got up and attempted to follow them. (There might be some loot going.) Chen had some difficulty in getting rid of them. The others picked up the cards and continued their game.

'If they win,' said one of them, 'perhaps we shall get our pay this month?'

'Perhaps . . .' replied the sergeant, and dealt the cards.

'But if they're beaten, perhaps we'll be accused of treachery?'

'What could we have done? We yielded to force. We are all witnesses that there was no treachery.'

They pondered over the situation, their heads sunk between their shoulders, like cormorants in the throes of unaccustomed mental activity.

'We aren't responsible,' one of them said. Everybody agreed with him. But they got up and went and finished their game in a shop near by, the owner not daring to protest. A pile of uniforms remained in sole occupation of the police station.

*

Chen made his way to one of the central stations, feeling light-headed and at the same time mistrustful. 'It's going all right,' he thought, 'but these fellows are almost as wretched as we are.' The White Russians, on the other hand, and the soldiers in the armoured train would certainly fight. The officers too. He could hear distant explosions, deadened by the lowering clouds, setting the air throbbing in the centre of the city.

At a crossing, the men, all armed now, even those who were carrying petrol-cans, hesitated for an instant, looking all round. The funnels of the cruisers and the liners (unable to unload) were sending great volumes of smoke obliquely upwards, which the heavy wind drove in the direction of the rebels line of advance, as if the sky were taking part in the insurrection. The new station was an old red brick mansion with one upper storey; on each side of the door was a sentry, with fixed bayonet. Chen knew that the special police had been on the watch for three days, and the men were exhausted by the need for continual alertness. Here there were officers, some fifty policemen, well paid and armed with Mausers, and ten soldiers. Chen had stopped at the street-corner: 'I must keep alive,' he felt, 'alive at all costs, for at least a week.' The arms would no doubt be in the racks on the ground floor; in the room on the right, the guard-room which led to an officer's room: Chen and two of his men had made their way into it several times during the week. He chose ten men without guns, made them hide revolvers in their blouses, and went forward with them. Once they passed the corner, the sentries had them in full view, but their suspicions had been aroused so often that they were now no longer suspicious. Delegations of workmen

86

had kept coming to interview the officer in charge, usually to bring him offerings of money, a business which required the presence of numerous witnesses as a safeguard.

'Lieutenant Shuei Toun?' Chen said. As eight of his men went in, the last two slipped between the sentries and the wall, as if pushed aside by the rush of people coming in; and the moment the first lot were inside the passage, the sentries felt revolvers pressed against their ribs. They let themselves be disarmed – they were paid better than the other wretches, but not well enough to make them risk their lives. They were then taken along the wall by four of Chen's men who had not joined the first group and who pretended they were just passing along the street. Nothing could be seen from the windows.

From the passage Chen saw the racks packed with guns. In the guard-room there were only six police armed with automatics, and these were shut up in holsters round their waists. He threw himself in front of the racks, levelling his revolver at the police. If they had shown any resolution, the attack would have failed. Well as he knew the disposition of the place, Chen had not had time to tell each of his men which particular policeman he was to hold up; and one or two of them had a chance to fire. But they all put their hands up. In an instant they were disarmed. A new group of Chen's men came in. A new distribution of arms began.

'At the moment,' Chen thought, 'all over the city two hundred sections are taking the same action. If they are as lucky as we have been . . . ' He had hardly taken the third rifle when he heard someone running quickly up the staircase. He went to the door, and as he reached it, a shot rang out from the floor above. But there was no one at the top of the stairs afterwards. One of the officers had seen the rebels as he came down, fired, and at once retreated upstairs again.

The fight was going to begin.

The stairs were commanded by a door in the middle of the landing. Should he send up a man to negotiate in the regular

Oriental way? Chen debated the Chinese common sense which was inherent in him. But an attempt to take the stairs by assault would be sheer suicide: no doubt the police above had hand-grenades. The instructions of the military committee, passed on by Kyo to the different sections, were to set fire to such stations as showed resistance, and then to occupy the surrounding houses and summon help from the special squads. It was the only thing to do now.

'Set fire!'

The men with the cans tried to pour the petrol out in a stream, like water from a bucket, but only miserable jets came from the narrow openings. They had to let it flow slowly over the furniture, and down the walls. Chen looked through the window: opposite, there were closed shops, with barred windows which commanded the way out; above, the rotten warped roofs of Chinese houses and the infinite peace of a grey sky, no longer striped with smoke; a sky which seemed to nestle down over the empty street in a way that was friendly. How absurd fighting was; what, after all, was comparable to life? He pulled himself together just in time to see the panes and framework of the window tumble to pieces, the tinkling of the breaking glass mingling with a burst of rifle-fire. They were being shot at from outside.

A second volley. They were now caught in a room soaked with petrol, between the policemen (on the alert, and in possession of the upper floor), and their new enemies whom they could not see. Chen's men were lying flat on their stomachs, and the prisoners were tied up in a corner. If a bomb exploded, they would be roasted alive. One of the men on the floor gave a gurgle, pointing to a sharp-shooter on a roof outside; and on the extreme left of the window some more irregulars slid cautiously into the field of vision, working their way along sideways. They were some of the rebels' own men.

'Those idiots have started firing without sending out a scout,' thought Chen. He had the blue flag of the Kuomintang in his pocket. He took it out, and dashed into the passage. At the very same instant he received a prodigious thump in the small of the back; tremendously violent, yet muffled, and accompanied by a crash which seemed to split him in two. He threw his arms right back in an effort to steady himself, and found himself on the ground, considerably dazed. Not a sound: then, something metallic fell to the floor, and groans mingled with the smoke which came out into the passage. He picked himself up: he was unwounded. He half closed the door, which had been opened by the unaccountable explosion, leaving himself room to stick the flag out, with his left arm: he half expected to get a bullet through his hand. Not a bit of it: there were cries of joy. The smoke which was slowly emerging from the window prevented him from seeing the rebels on the left: but from the right voices called out to him.

A second explosion nearly knocked him over again. The policemen besieged upstairs were throwing down hand-grenades from the windows (how was it they could open their windows without being shot at from the street?) The first one, the one which had knocked him down, had burst in front of the house, and the splinters had come in through the open door and the shattered window just as if it had exploded inside the guard-room; terrified by the explosion, those of his men who hadn't been killed had jumped out, inadequately screened by the smoke. Under the fire of the policemen from the windows, two of them had been bowled over like rabbits in the middle of the street, all curled up; one of the others looked as though his nose was bleeding, his face a red smear of blood. The irregulars had recognized their friends all right; but the gesture made by those who called to Chen had told the police-officers that some-one was coming out, and they had thrown their second bomb. It had burst in the street, to the left of Chen: the wall had protected him.

He looked through into the guard-room from the passage. The smoke was eddying slowly down from the ceiling. There were bodies on the floor: the room was filled with groans coming from the ground; little yelping noises. In the corner, one of the prisoners who had had a leg torn off, was screaming to his companions to cease fire. His panting cries seemed to blow a hole in the smoke, which none the less continued its convolutions, despite that writhing agony: like destiny in a visible form. That man who lay screaming there, with his leg torn off, couldn't be *tied up*; it was impossible. But mightn't another bomb explode at any moment? 'It's nothing to do with me,' thought Chen, 'he's an enemy.' But imagine having a stump of mangled flesh down one's trouser, instead of a leg, and being trussed up all the time! It was something much stronger than pity which he felt; it was as though he himself was tied up there. 'If the bomb bursts outside, I shall fling myself flat on my face; if it comes in here, I shall have to throw it back immediately. Not one chance in ten of getting away with it. What the hell is all that to do with me? What the bloody hell?' Being killed didn't really matter; what he dreaded was being wounded in the stomach. But even that was easier to bear than having to look at the agony of that creature tied up there, a human being powerless to alleviate his suffering. Unable to prevent himself, he went towards the man with a knife in his hand, to release him. The prisoner thought he was going to kill him, and tried to scream louder; but his voice went out of control, became a whistling noise. Choking with horror, Chen felt the clothes clinging to his left hand, drenched with sticky blood; but he couldn't take his eyes off the broken window through which the bomb might be thrown in. At last he got hold of the cords, slipped the knife underneath and cut. The cries had ceased; the man was either dead or unconscious. Still looking at the shattered ruins of the window, Chen went back into the passage. Suddenly things smelt different, and he realized that the groans of the wounded had changed their note, too – had become screams: it seemed that he hadn't really heard them until now. Inside the room, the petrol-soaked wreckage had been ignited by the bombs, and was beginning to burn.

There was no water. Before the rebels could capture the station, the wounded (the prisoners didn't count any more, he only thought of his own men) would be charred corpses. . . . Escape, escape! But before he did anything definite, he must stop and think: then he must act as definitely as possible. He was shuddering, in an uncomfortable desire to escape, but his brain was working fairly clearly: he would have to make for the shelter of the porch on the left. He opened the door with his right hand, and signalled for silence with his left. He was out of sight of the enemy upstairs; only the behaviour of the rebels might have given him away. He felt the eyes of his companions concentrated on that open door, where his stocky figure stood outlined in its blue blouse, against the dark background of the passage. He began to edge towards the left, pressed tight against the wall, with his arms crossed in front of him and a revolver in his right hand. Moving slowly along, he looked up at the windows above him; one of them was guarded by a bullet-proof screen which projected like a kind of shutter. It was useless for the rebels to fire at the windows: the bombs were thrown from behind its protection. 'If they try again, I'm bound to see the bomb and probably the man's arm,' thought Chen, creeping along all the time. 'If I see it I must jump on to it and throw it as far away as possible. . . .' He continued his crab-like progress. 'I shan't be able to throw it far enough; unless I'm under cover, I shall get a handful of splinters in my guts. . . .' He kept moving. He realized from the strong smell of burning, and the sudden absence of support behind him (he didn't turn round) that he was passing in front of the ground-floor window. 'If I can catch the bomb I'll throw it into the guard-room before it bursts. With a thick wall behind me, once I'm past the window, I shall be all right.' What did it matter that the guard-room wasn't empty, that the man whom he had just set free was in there – and his own wounded comrades. He didn't look at the rebels, even when the smoke cleared for a moment, for he dared not take his eyes off the shutter; but all the time he could feel them watching for him, and though their firing at the windows undoubtedly harassed the policemen, he was amazed that they didn't realize that something was going on. He suddenly thought that they might be short of bombs, and be waiting for a good chance to throw one; immediately, as though the idea had sprung into their minds at the same time, a head appeared under the shutter: his comrades couldn't see it, but he could. Frantically, abandoning his tightrope walking attitude, he took aim and fired, then leapt forward and dashed for his porch. A volley of shots came from the windows, and a bomb exploded on the very spot where he had just been standing: he had failed to hit the policeman, but had made him hesitate before exposing the hand in which he held the bomb, fearing a second bullet. Chen had felt something hit his left arm: only a rush of air, but the wound which he had made with the dagger before killing Tang Yen Ta was sensitive. It began bleeding, though not really painful. He wrapped a handkerchief round it and drew the dressing tighter, then rejoined his comrades by way of the yards at the side of the station.

The leaders of the attack were clustered together in a dark alley.

'You didn't think of sending out scouts, I suppose!'

The *tchon* commander, a big clean-shaven Chinaman, whose sleeves were too short, looked at the dark figure approaching him, and slowly raised his eyebrows with a resigned expression.

'I told them to telephone,' he answered simply. 'We are waiting now for an armoured lorry.'

'How have things gone with the other sections?'

'We have captured half the police stations.'

'Not more?'

'That's a very good start.'

All those bursts of firing in the distance came from their comrades converging on the Northern Station.

Chen was breathing heavily, as though he had just come out of the water on a windy day. He leant back against the wall which was sheltering them all, and gradually got his breath back, thinking of the prisoner whose bonds he had cut. 'I should have left the fellow alone. Why go and cut him loose, when it couldn't make any difference to things?' Would he still be upset, even now, by the sight of that man straining at his cords, with his leg torn off? His wound made him think of Tang Yen Ta. How idiotically he had been behaving all that last night and morning! Nothing was simpler than killing.

Within the police station, the wreckage went on burning, the wounded went on screaming as the flames got nearer; their ceaseless cries rang through that narrow passage, sounding all the nearer because the explosions, the sirens, and all the sounds of fighting came from so far away, lost in the stricken air. A distant noise of rattling iron drew nearer and nearer until it was close upon them: the lorry was arriving. It had been fitted with armour during the night, very badly: all the plates wanted tightening up. The clatter ceased as the brakes were applied, and the cries became audible again.

Chen, the only one of them who had been inside the station, explained the situation to the leader of the reinforcements. He was an ex-cadet from Whampoo. Chen would have preferred to have one of Katow's sections instead of his party of earnest young citizens. He looked at his dead comrades, doubled-up there in the middle of the street, and realized that even if there was a gap which he couldn't quite bridge between himself and his men, it was nothing like his downright hatred of the middle-class Chinese: for what they were worth, his aspirations were embodied in the proletariat.

The officer knew his job.

'The lorry won't be any use,' he said, 'it hasn't even got a roof. They've only to throw a bomb inside and the whole thing will be blown to bits; but I've brought some bombs for us to use too.'

Some of Chen's men had had bombs with them, but they were in the guard-room – dead? And the second section had been unable to obtain any.

'Let's try and get at them from above.'

'Good plan,' said Chen.

The officer gave him an angry look: he hadn't asked his opinion. But he didn't say anything. They both surveyed the scene of operations: thick-set, blue-bloused Chen, and the other man looking like a soldier even in civilian clothes, with stiff wiry hair, moustache clipped short, and his loose tunic held in place by his revolver-belt. On the right-hand side of the door the flames were all the time getting nearer to his comrades, sending out puffs of smoke with the regularity of a machine; as persistent as the cries, which were becoming so monotonous that only their appallingly sinister character prevented them from losing their significance. On the left, nothing. The upstairs windows were screened. The attackers still fired occasional shots at one of the windows, and some more débris would be added to the remnants of plaster, and the splintered brickwork and mouldings which were piled deep on the pavement; from which came an occasional glint of glass, despite the dullness of the day. They had ceased firing inside the station, except when one of the rebels broke cover.

'How are the other sections doing?' Chen asked again.

'Almost all the stations are in our possession. The main one was captured by a surprise attack at half-past one: it provided us with eight hundred rifles. We are already able to send reinforcements to the points which still hold out against us: you are the third lot we've sent help to. They aren't getting any reinforcements through now, on the other hand. The barracks, the southern station, and the arsenal have all been blockaded. But the job must be finished off: we need every possible man for the attack on them. And there will still be the armoured train.'

The thought of two hundred sections all working in conjunction with his own left Chen both excited and worried. Despite the sounds of firing which the breeze wafted towards them from all over the town, he still regarded the scene of violence with which he was in actual contact as something quite apart.

A man took a bicycle out of the lorry, and rode away. Chen recognized him as he sprang into the saddle: Ma, one of the principal agitators. He was going to make his report to the military authorities. A typesetter, who for twelve years had been devoting his life to founding printers' Trade Unions, in the hope of bringing the entire trade into the system, all over China. Sought by the police, condemned to death, escaping, continuing his work of organization. There were cries of joy: at the same time as Chen, the men had recognized him and were cheering him. He looked at them. The world which they were preparing together involved not only the destruction of the social system of their enemies, but the end of his own life too. What would he do in the factory of the future? Stand and look at them all in their blue overalls?

The officer distributed bombs, and ten men went off over the house-tops to take up a position on the roof of the station. Their plan was to employ the same tactics as the policemen, and throw the bombs in through the windows. The windows controlled the street, but not the roof, and only one of them was protected by a shutter. The rebels advanced from roof to roof, sharply outlined against the sky. The police still went on firing occasionally. As though the dying men alone sensed their approach, the cries suddenly changed their character, became groans. They could hardly be heard. They were the strangled cries of men whose voices were failing them. The silhouetted figures reached the summit of the sloping roof of the station, and gradually worked their way down; Chen couldn't see

95

them so well, now that they no longer stood out against the sky. A guttural wail like a woman in labour was echoed for a moment by the groans; then they stopped.

In spite of the noise, the sudden cessation of the cries gave the impression of a deathly silence. Had the flames reached them? Chen and the officer looked at each other, closing their eyes so as to hear better. Nothing. As they opened them again, each saw the same questioning look in the other's face.

Clinging on to the ornamental roofing for support, one of the men stretched his free arm out over the street and hurled his bomb at the upstairs window which he overhung: too low. It burst on the pavement. He threw another: it fell inside the room with the wounded in it. A chorus of cries arose from the window through which it had gone; not the same cries as before, but the staccato shrieks of mortal agony, the reawakening of a capacity for suffering which had not quite reached its limits. He threw his third bomb, and once more missed the window.

He was one of the men who had come with the lorry. He had jerked backwards with some skill, so as to avoid the splinters. He leant forward again, with a fourth bomb ready poised. Behind him, one of Chen's men was crawling down. His arm never descended: his whole body was swept clean away, as if by an enormous boulder. A sharp detonation rang out on the pavement below; even through the smoke, a stain of blood a yard wide could be seen on the wall. The smoke cleared; the wall was spattered all over with blood and flesh. The man above had lost his balance and tumbled headlong down the roof, wrenching the other from his hold. They had both fallen on their own bombs, the safety-catches of which had been released.

On the other side of the roof, on the left, men from both contingents – bourgeois Kuomintang and Communist workers – were cautiously getting into position. They had stopped still when the fall occurred: now they were coming on down again.

Too many people had been tortured in the suppression of the February rising for there to be any lack of men who would stick at nothing. Some more were arriving on the right. 'Hold on to each other!' Chen shouted from below. Some of the rebels near the station took up the cry. The men took each other by the hand, the topmost one linking his left arm tightly round a secure looking piece of ornamentation. They started throwing the bombs once more. The beleaguered policemen were unable to retaliate. Within five minutes, three of them penetrated the windows at which they were aimed: another blew away the bullet-proof shutter. Only the windows in the middle remained intact. 'The middle ones,' shouted the cadet. Chen looked at him. There was a man to whom leadership gave all the pleasure of an ideal sport. He hardly bothered to keep under cover. He was undoubtedly brave, but he didn't possess the confidence of his men. Chen felt a bond between himself and his men, but an inadequate one. Quite inadequate.

He left the cadet and crossed the street at a place where he was out of range of the men besieged in the station. He made his way up to the roof. The man who was clinging on up at the top was beginning to weaken: he took his place. Even there, with his wounded arm encircling the cement and plaster decoration, and his right hand grasping the next man in the human chain, he still had that feeling of isolation. The weight of three men slipping was dragging at his arm, transfixing his chest like a metal bar. The bombs were bursting inside the station, which had ceased fire. 'We are protected by the attics,' he thought, 'but not for very much longer. The roof will go.' Despite their nearness to death, despite the weight of his comrades, which was almost pulling him in two, he didn't belong with them. 'Doesn't even blood mean anything?'

The cadet down below looked at him uncomprehendingly. One of the men perched behind him offered to take his place.

'All right. I'll do some throwing myself.'

He transferred the chain of bodies. His wrenched muscles

were yielding to an unfathomable despair. His owl-like face with its delicate eyes was tense, quite rigid; he was amazed to feel a tear trickling down his nose. 'Nerves,' he thought. He pulled a bomb out of his pocket, and began to climb down, clinging on to the arms of the men who formed the chain. But the ornamental work which supported the chain ended at the side of the roof. From there, it was almost impossible to reach the middle window. When he got to the bottom of the roof, Chen let go the arm of the man who was throwing the bombs; hung on to his leg, then on to the gutter, and then lowered himself down the pipe which ran down the building. He wasn't close enough to the window to touch it, but he was near enough to throw his bomb. His comrades kept absolutely still. A projection above the ground floor enabled him to rest for a minute. His wound hurt surprisingly little. Holding on by his left hand to one of the fixtures which kept the gutter in place, he balanced his first bomb in his hand: 'If it falls into the street beneath me, I'm done for.' He threw it, as hard as his position allowed: it penetrated and burst inside.

The firing was starting again down below.

The door of the station was still open, and the policemen, driven from the last room, were coming pouring out, firing wildly, in a mad panic-stricken rush. From roofs, porches, windows, the rebels were shooting them down. One after another the bodies were falling, in a thick cluster near the door, then more and more widely scattered.

The firing ceased. Chen climbed down, still hanging on to his gutter: he couldn't see his feet, and landed on top of a body.

The cadet went into the police station. He followed him, taking the bomb which he hadn't thrown out of his pocket. Every step he took reminded him more forcibly that the cries of the wounded had ceased. In the guard-room, nothing but corpses. The wounded were charred to a cinder. On the upper floor, more dead, and a few wounded.

'Now for the Southern Station,' said the officer. 'We'd better take all the rifles: they'll be needed by some of the other sections.'

The arms were loaded into the lorry; when they had all reassembled, the men hoisted themselves on to it also, standing up, packed together, sitting on the bonnet, clinging to the footboards, hanging on to the back. Those who were left over went off down one of the side streets, at a jog-trot. The huge bloodstain which remained on the wall seemed a strange phenomenon in the middle of the deserted street: the lorry was disappearing round a corner, bristling with armed men, rattling away, towards the Southern Station and the barracks.

It soon had to stop; the road was blocked by four dead horses and three dead men, their weapons already gone. It was the cavalry Chen had seen early that morning: the first armoured car had arrived just at the right time. On the ground, some broken windows, and the sole spectator an old Chinaman with a pointed beard, groaning to himself. He spoke out as Chen approached:

'This is a sad business! Four! Four of them!'

'Only three,' said Chen.

'Four, I fear.'

Chen had another look: there were only three bodies, one on its side, as if brought down on the run, and two face downwards. There they lay, the houses surrounding them seeming as though they were dead too, under that leaden sky.

'I am talking of the horses,' said the old man, cringingly. (Chen had a revolver in his hand.)

'And I of the men. Did one of the horses belong to you?'

They had probably been requisitioned that morning.

'No. But I used to be a coachman. I've had a lot to do with animals. Four of them killed! And for no reason at all!'

The driver broke in:

'For no reason at all?'

'Come on. We've no time to waste,' said Chen.

Assisted by two of the men, he moved the horses out of the

way. The lorry went on. Chen looked back from the end of the street, from his place on one of the footboards: the old coachman was still with the bodies, and still groaning no doubt, a black figure against the grey street.

'*The Southern Station has fallen.*'

Ferral replaced the receiver. While he was making appointments (some of the Chamber of International Commerce were against all intervention, but he controlled the biggest paper in Shanghai) the news of the rising was growing more and more alarming. He had wanted to be alone when he telephoned. He returned to his studio, where Martial had just arrived, and was discussing matters with Chang Kai Shek's representative: the latter had refused to meet the chief of police either at the police headquarters or at his own home. Even before he opened the door Ferral heard through the firing:

'Let me tell you that I represent French interests in this . . . '

'But what help can *I* guarantee?' answered the Chinaman with elaborate carelessness. 'The Consul-General himself tells me to await definite instructions from you. You know our country and its inhabitants so well.'

The telephone rang.

'*The Municipal buildings have fallen,*' said Martial. Then, in a different tone of voice:

'It is possible that I am not without a certain psychological experience of this country, and of men in general. Psychology and action are my trade; and on what . . . '

'But these people are as dangerous to your country as to mine, a menace to the peace of civilization. What if they take refuge in the Concession as they've done before now? The international police . . . '

'Now we're getting to it,' thought Ferral, as he came in. He wants to know whether Martial would let the Communist leaders take refuge with us, in the event of trouble between us and him.

' . . . have promised us all possible cooperation. What course will the French police adopt?'

'We'll fix up something. But remember this: no hanky-panky with white women, apart from the Russians. I have very definite orders on that point. But I'm speaking confidentially, mind: nothing official. Nothing official.'

The studio was a modern one; on the walls were some Picassos of the rose period, and an erotic drawing by Fragonard. As they conversed the two men stood one on each side of a huge black stone Kwannyn, of the Tang dynasty, bought on the advice of Clappique and which Gisors believed to be a fake. The Chinaman, a young colonel with a hooked nose, in civilian clothes, all buttoned up, was looking at Martial and smiling, his head tilted back.

'On behalf of my party I thank you. . . . The Communists are treacherous dogs: they betray even us, their faithful allies. It has been agreed that we should work together, and that the solution of social problems should be left until China is a united whole. But already they bring them up. They are not respecting our agreement. It's not China they are working for, but the Soviets. Our soldiers have died for China, not for the Soviets. The Communists stick at nothing. And that is why I must ask you, sir, if the French police would see any objection to making provisions for the general's personal safety.'

It was clear that he had made the same request to the international police.

'Not the least,' answered Martial. 'Send me your chief of police. Is it still König?'

'Yes. Tell me, sir, have you studied Roman history?'

'Most certainly.'

'At evening classes,' thought Ferral.

The telephone again. Martial took up the receiver.

'*The bridges are captured*,' he said as he put it down. 'In another quarter of an hour they'll be in control of the entire city.'

'In my opinion,' the Chinaman went on, as though he hadn't heard, 'it was moral corruption that caused the collapse of the Roman Empire. Don't you think that prostitution really well organized, organized on Western lines, like the police force, might sufficiently demoralize the men in control of Hankow, who are hardly as formidable a proposition as the leaders of the Roman Empire?'

'It's certainly an idea . . . but I doubt if it's practicable. It would need extremely careful working out . . .'

'Europeans never see the points of similarity between China and their own countries.'

Silence. Ferral was enjoying himself. The Chinaman intrigued him: that head thrown back almost disdainfully, and at the same time, that constraint . . . Hankow engulfed by trainloads of harlots . . . He reflected. And he knows the Communists, and undeniably is not entirely ignorant of political economy. Most peculiar! . . . As likely as not Soviets were already being formed in the town, and the man was dreaming about the subtle lessons to be learned from Imperial Rome. 'Gisors is right, they are always producing these damfool theories.'

Still another ring on the telephone.

'*The barracks are surrounded*,' said Martial. 'The Government aren't getting any more reinforcements through.'

'What about the Northern Station?' asked Ferral.

'Still holding out.'

'Then the Government can order troops back from the front?'

'It is possible, sir,' said the Chinaman. 'They are withdrawing troops and tanks to Nankin. They can send some here. And the armoured train can still put up serious resistance.'

'Yes, round about the station and the train they'll hold out,' answered Martial. 'The situation is continually changing as plans are altered after each new capture: there must be Russians or Europeans behind the rising; revolutionary employees from all departments of the Government are advising the rebels. There is a military staff at the head of everything. The entire police force has been disarmed now. The Reds have points where they concentrate, from which troops are dispatched against the barracks.'

'The Chinese have a genius for organization,' said the officer.

'How is Chang Kai Shek protected?'

'His car is always preceded by another one containing his bodyguard. And we have our spies.'

At last Ferral understood the reason for that disdainful carriage of the head, which was beginning to annoy him (at first it had seemed as though the officer was looking at his erotic drawing, over Martial's head): a leucoma in his right eye compelled him to look at things from above.

'Not good enough,' answered Martial. 'That must be seen to. The sooner the better. Now I must get along: we've got the job of electing an Executive Committee to take over the government. That's a thing I may be able to help with. Got to appoint a prefect as well, and that really matters . . .'

Ferral and the officer were left alone.

'May we then count on your support from now onwards, sir?' said the Chinaman, his head still tilted back.

'Liou Ti Yu is waiting,' he answered.

Chief of the Shanghai Bankers' Association, honorary president of the Chinese Chamber of Commerce, connected with all the masters of the guilds, Liou Ti Yu could operate even more effectively in the Chinese quarter of the city, partly in rebel hands by now, no doubt, than Ferral could in the concessions. The officer bowed and withdrew. Ferral went up to the first floor. Ensconced at a modern desk decorated all over with carvings in the style of the great days of China, Liou Ti Yu sat waiting, dressed in a white linen costume over a singlet as white as his short bristly hair; without a collar, and with his hands clinging to the shining tubular arms of his chair.

His whole face seemed concentrated in the mouth and the jaw: a virile old frog.

Ferral remained standing.

'You are determined to suppress the Communists.' There was no question in his voice; it was simply a statement of a fact. 'So are we, obviously.' He began to walk up and down, shoulders thrust forward. 'Chang Kai Shek is prepared to break with them.'

Ferral had never seen a Chinaman show any signs of mistrust. Did this man believe him? He offered him a box of cigarettes. Ever since he had resolved to stop smoking that box had lain open on his desk, as if continually looking at it were a method of increasing his strength of character, and confirming him in his decision.

'Help must be given to Chang Kai Shek. That concerns you vitally. The present state of affairs cannot possibly continue. In the country districts, where they are free from the influence of the army, the Communists are beginning to organize Unions among the peasants. The first thing that they will do will be to decree the invalidity of loans (Ferral carefully avoided the word usury). An enormous proportion of your capital is invested in land, your bank deposits are secured more by mortgages than anything else. A Soviet peasantry . . .

'The Communists will not dare to set up Soviets in China.'

'Don't let us quibble, Mr Liou. Whether Unions or Soviets, the Communist organizations are going to nationalize the land, and make advances on credit illegal. Those two measures destroy the entire basis of the system by which you have received loans from abroad. More than a thousand million francs if you include my Japanese and American friends. To guarantee that sum with all trade at a standstill is out of the question. And even apart from our own credit system, those decrees will be sufficient to make every single bank in China close its doors. That's obvious.'

'The Kuomintang will not allow it.'

'There's no such thing as the Kuomintang. There are the Blues and the Reds. They have managed to avoid quarrelling, up to the present, because Chang Kai Shek hadn't any money. But once Shanghai is captured – tomorrow – Chang Kai Shek will almost be able to pay his army out of the customs. Not quite. He's relying on us. The Communists have been preaching the taking over of land everywhere. It appears that they are trying to postpone it, but it's too late. The peasants have been listening to their speeches, but they aren't members of their party. They'll take matters into their own hands.'

'Nothing except force can hold the peasants back. That's what I told the British Consul-General.'

It seemed to Ferral that the other man was copying his own tone of voice, and he felt that he was winning him over.

'They have already tried taking over land. Chang Kai Shek is determined not to allow it. He has given orders that no land belonging to officers or officers' relations is to be interfered with. That will ...'

'We are all officers' relations,' Liou smiled. 'Is there a single property in China whose owner isn't related to an officer? ...'

Ferral knew all about the ramifications of kinship in China.

The telephone rang again.

'*They are besieging the arsenal,*' said Ferral. 'All the Government buildings are captured. The revolutionary army will be in Shanghai tomorrow. This has got to be decided *now*. Let me make myself clear. Numerous landowners have been expropriated, as a result of Communist propaganda; Chang Kai Shek must either accept the situation, or have those who seized land shot. The Reds in control of Hankow would never permit that.'

'They will try to gain time.'

'You know what happened to the shares of English companies after the fall of the English concession in Hankow. You know what your own situation will be, when every owner of land, of whatever kind, has been legally deprived of it. Chang Kai Shek realizes this and says that he has no alternative but to break with them *now*. Will you help him, yes or no?'

Liou spat, his head sunk between his shoulders. He closed his eyes, then opened them again and looked at Ferral with the puckered brow which the old usurer assumes, wherever you encounter him:

'How much?'

'Fifty million dollars.'

He spat again:

'All for us?'

'Yes.'

He closed his eyes again. Every few minutes, the sound of the armoured train firing burst through the sharp crackle of rifle-fire.

If Liou's friends decided to act, a stiff fight was in prospect; if they couldn't make up their minds, it would probably mean the triumph of Communism in China. 'One of those crises when the destiny of the world hangs in the balance . . .' thought Ferral with a mixture of pride and indifference. His eyes never left Liou's face. The old man's eyes were closed, he might almost have been asleep; but the blue veins on the backs of his hands stood out like cords, throbbing like arteries. 'I must find a more personal argument as well,' thought Ferral.

'Chang Kai Shek,' he said, 'cannot allow his officers to be stripped of their possessions. And the Communists are determined to assassinate him. He knows it.'

The rumour had been current for some days, but Ferral did not altogether credit it.

'How much time have we got?' asked Liou. And then straightway, with one eye closed and the other open, at once foxy and shame-faced:

'How do you know that he won't just take the money and not keep his word?'

'There is *our* money too, to be taken into account, and in any case it isn't a question of keeping his word. *He has no alternative.* Just look at it this way. It's not your money that is going to make him suppress the Communists: he is bound to try and suppress the Communists anyway; and you are financing the job.'

'I will talk to my friends.'

Ferral knew how these things were arranged in China, and the importance of the actual speaker at a ceremony.

'What advice will you give them?'

'Chang Kai Shek may be beaten by the Hankow people. There are two hundred thousand unemployed in the city.'

'Without our help his defeat is certain.'

'Fifty million. . . . That . . . is a great deal.' At last he looked Ferral squarely in the face.

'Less than a Communist Government would exact from you.'

The telephone.

'*The armoured train has been cut off*,' Ferral continued. 'The Government can't bring back troops from the front now, even if they want to.'

He held out his hand.

Liou shook it, and left the room. Ferral looked out of the vast window at the clouds that streaked the sky, and then saw the car going away, the noise of the engine momentarily imposing itself upon the firing. Even if he came out on top, his enterprises were in a condition which might well compel him to ask the French Government for help; help which it so often refused, which had just been refused to the Industrial Bank of China: but just now he was one of the men in whose hands lay the fate of Shanghai. Every economic force and almost every diplomatic one was working to his advantage: Liou would pay up. The armoured train still went on firing. Yes, for the first time, he was fighting against a properly organized opposition. He would have liked to meet the men at its head. And to have them shot, too.

The strife-ridden evening was deepening into night. Lights began to shine from the ground floors of the houses, and the giant river, invisible, to waft away on its bosom such dwindled vitality as the city still possessed. It had come from Hankow, that river. Liou was right, and Ferral knew it: that was where the danger lay. That was where the Red army was being formed. That was where the Communists really were in control. Ever since the revolutionaries had hurled the northern army back like a train ploughing its way through the snow, all the left-wing elements had been dreaming of the Promised Land: before ever they were captured the glaucous shadows of those arsenals and foundries had been the inspiration of the Revolution: now they were in her possession, and all the foot-sore wretches who merged into the sticky fog as the lanterns grew more and more numerous were also moving in the same direction as the river, as if they too had all come from Hankow, crushed with hopeless misery; grim portents driven thither by the lowering night.

Eleven o'clock. Liou's departure was followed by a stream of callers, before and after dinner; masters of guilds, bankers, directors of insurance and river transport companies, big importers, owners of cotton-mills. All were to some extent dependent upon the Ferral group or one of the foreign groups which had become bound up politically with the Franco-Asiatic Consortium: Ferral was not counting on Liou alone. Shanghai was the living heart of China, palpitating with her life blood; from the remotest country districts – the majority of the landowners were dependent upon the banks – blood vessels flowed like canals in the direction of the capital where the destiny of China was being shaped. The firing went on all the time. Patience was necessary.

Valerie was in bed in the next room. Although she had been

his mistress for a week now, he had never pretended to love her; she would have smiled, and entered into the spirit of the game with assumed innocence. She had never said anything to him either, perhaps for the same reason. The obstacles which confronted him at every turn led him to find relief in deliberate sexual excitement, rather than love. He knew that he was no longer young, and tried to persuade himself that his legendary reputation made up for the fact. He was Ferral, and he understood women. Understood them so well, in fact, that he did not believe a word of what he heard about them. He remembered one of his friends, an intelligent invalid, of whose numerous mistresses he had often been envious. One day when he had asked Valerie how she explained it, she had said: 'There is nothing more attractive in a man than a combination of strength and weakness.' Convinced that no one holds the key which explains his own life, he had been more impressed by that remark than by everything which she had told him about herself. She didn't see everything from a financial point of view, this rich dressmaker; not yet, anyway. She maintained that many women derived their erotic excitement from uncovering their nakedness in the presence of the man of their choice, and were incapable of more than one satisfactory orgasm. Was she thinking of herself? Yet it was the third time she had slept with him. He sensed a pride in her equal to his own. 'Men have their travels, women their lovers,' she had said to him the evening before. Did she get satisfaction, like so many other women, from the contrast between his normal toughness and the unfailing consideration which he showed when he was with her? He was aware that his pride was at stake – the foundation on which his life was built. A situation not altogether free from danger in the case of a woman who could say: 'No man is qualified to talk about women, my dear, because there isn't a man who realizes that each new cosmetic, each new dress, each new lover suggests a new mentality . . .' – all this with the appropriate smile.

He went into her room. She was lying with her hair pillowed upon the roundest of arms, and smiled up at him. Her smile filled him with the vivid yet carefree feeling of animation which pleasure brings. When at rest Valerie's face wore an expression of tender sadness, and Ferral remembered how when he had seen her for the first time he had said that she looked demurely perplexed – as befitted the softness of her grey eyes. But directly the coquette in her appeared, the smile which arched her lips, more at the corners than in the middle, seemed unexpectedly in keeping with her short wavy hair and hardened eyes, giving her something of the indescribable appearance of a cat sexually aroused, despite the delicate regularity of her features. Ferral loved animals, like all people whose pride is too great to adapt itself to their fellows: especially cats.

He kissed her gently. She yielded her lips. Out of desire or fear of sentimentality? He considered the question as he undressed in the bathroom. The light-bulb was broken, and the things on the dressing-table looked faintly red in the glow of the burning buildings. He looked out of the window: in the avenue outside, a mass of people thronging past, like myriads of fish working to and fro in the ripples of a black stream; it suddenly seemed to him that the soul of the crowd had fled, as the power of thought leaves the mind in a dream, and that it was burning feverishly in the thick strong flames which were lighting up the outlines of the houses.

When he came back, she was dozing and the smile had gone. Used though he was to that change of expression, yet once more it jerked him back uncomfortably into reality. It was surely the love of the woman who smiled which he wanted. This other woman was like a stranger, separating them. The armoured train was firing at intervals of a minute or two, as if in celebration of something: it was still in the hands of the government, together with the barracks, the arsenal, and the Russian church.

'My dear,' she asked, 'have you seen M. de Clappique again?'

All the French colony in Shanghai knew Clappique. Valerie had met him at a dinner party two days before: she was delighted by his fantasies.

'Yes. I've asked him to buy me some Kama wash-drawings.'

'Are there any to be had in the antique shops?'

'Certainly. But Kama is on his way back from Europe; he'll be passing through here in about a fortnight's time. Clappique was tired, and only produced two good stories: one about a Chinese thief, who was acquitted because of the extraordinary acrobatic skill he showed in effecting an entrance into the pawnbroker's which he was burgling, and this one: Mr Illustrious Virtue had been breeding rabbits for twenty years. His house was on one side of the Excise Offices and his hutches on the other. The customs officers were once more replaced by a new lot, and forgot to warn their successors that he went through every day. Along he came, with a basket full of grass under his arm. "Hey, there! Let's have a look at that basket!" Underneath the grass, watches, chains, electric lamps, photographic apparatus. – "Is that what you feed your rabbits on?" – "Yes, sir. And (glowering in the direction of the animals in question), and if they don't like that, then they can go hungry until tomorrow. . . ." '

'Oh! I see!' she said, 'a scientific story; now I understand everything. That's where all the little toy bells and drums made like rabbits come from, all those nice little animal objects which are so happy in fairy tales and so miserable in nurseries. . . . How shamefully unfairly they treated poor Mr Virtue. I foresee vigorous protests in the revolutionary papers, for you can be quite sure that's what the rabbits really eat.'

'Have you read *Alice in Wonderland*, darling?' He despised women enough to call them darling, though he couldn't do without them.

'What a question! I know it by heart.'

'Your smile reminds me of the Cheshire cat which never materialized, and of which all that was visible was a ravishing smile floating in the air. Why does the female mind always want to go beyond its proper province?'

'What is its province, my dear?'

'Charm and sympathy, clearly.'

She thought for a minute.

'That's the name men give to intellectual servitude. You credit a woman with intelligence in proportion to your success with her. It's so soothing, so flattering. . . .'

'Submission for a woman, and possession for a man; those are the only two ways in which human beings can make experience significant. . . .'

'My dear, don't you think that women hardly ever give themselves really, and that men don't really possess anything? It's a game: "I believe that I possess her, therefore she believes that she is possessed." But is she, though? You'll think this very bad of me, but isn't it a case of the story of the cork which thought itself so much more important than the bottle?'

Plain-dealing with a woman excited Ferral, but plain-speaking irritated him. He felt eager to reawaken the only feeling which gave him power over a woman; shame, gratitude for shame undergone. If she didn't guess the reason, she was conscious of a slight coolness between them, just as she sensed elsewhere in her body his increasing physical desire for her. The idea that she could satisfy him when and how she pleased amused her, and she gazed at him with parted lips (since he liked her smile), alluringly; quite certain that like almost every other man, he would interpret her desire to seduce him as voluptousness.

He got into bed beside her. His caresses brought a tense expression into Valerie's face, that he tried to smooth away. Her other expression had aroused such emotion in him that he longed for the moment when sexual emotion would bring it back, feeling as if he were destroying a mask, and that her profoundest, most secret depths were rightly what he preferred in her: he had always slept with her in the dark. But no sooner had he gently slipped his hand between her legs than she turned out the light. He put it on again.

He had groped silently for the switch, and she thought he had touched it accidentally; she turned it off again. He at once put it on. Her nerves were easily strained, and she felt at the same time angered and on the point of tears: but she looked him in the face. He had moved the bulb away, and she was sure that it was from the transformation of her features under the influence of passion that he awaited his keenest enjoyment. She knew that it was only really in the first stage of a liaison that she was entirely dominated by her sexual appetite; and when taken by surprise. When she failed to find the bulb, the warm current which she knew so well flowed up through her body to her nipples, up to her lips, which the look in Ferral's face told her were swelling imperceptibly. She abandoned herself to it, clasped her legs and arms around him and drew him towards her, his slow throbbing stabs dragging her far away from the shore on which she knew that she would be stranded later, determined never to forgive his behaviour.

*

Valerie was asleep. Her regular breathing and relaxed muscles gently swelled out her lips and imprinted on them the ineffable satisfaction which comes with sexual gratification. 'A human being,' thought Ferral, 'an individual life isolated and unique, like my own. . . .' He put himself in her place, imagining how it would feel to be in her body, experiencing in her stead that satisfaction; he imagined himself humiliated by that passive libido, by a woman's limitations. 'This is absurd; her sexual feelings seem as active to her as mine do to me, neither more nor less. She feels desire, sadness, pride all concentrating in her in an inevitable sequence. . . . Of course she does.' But not just then: sleep and the memories which lay upon her lips left her senses utterly satiated, as if she had renounced her freedom of will and action and become a mere vehicle for expressing gratitude for the conquest of her person. The tense silence of the Chinese night, smelling of camphor and leaves, spreading its somnolent veil far out to sea, held him in its timeless grasp: not a siren was calling; not a shot was being fired. She carried nothing away into her slumbers; no memories or hopes which he could never share: she was merely the node which enabled his pleasure to complete the circuit. She had never lived: she had never been young.

Guns again: the armoured train was reopening fire.

4 P.M. NEXT DAY

Kyo was watching the armoured train from a clockmaker's shop which had been fitted out as a depôt. The revolutionaries had blown up the line for two hundred yards in front and behind it, and demolished the level crossing. Of the train which blocked the street – motionless, a dead thing – Kyo could only see two carriages: one closed in like a truck containing livestock, the other looking squat and crushed, as if by a heavy petrol tank, with a small gun protruding from its turret. No men: neither the defenders shut up inside, hiding behind tightly closed shutters, nor those attacking them, secreted in the houses which controlled the railway track. In Kyo's rear, over by the Russian church and the Commercial Printing Works, the firing was continuous. The soldiers who were ready to surrender were already out of it; the others were about to meet their fate. All the rebel detachments were armed now; the Government troops had broken and were flying headlong towards Nankin, through the wind and the rain, by way of such trains as had not been completely wrecked, and roads that were no better than quagmires. The Kuomintang army would reach Shanghai within the next few hours; runners were arriving with dispatches every few minutes.

Chen came in, still dressed as a workman; sat down beside Kyo, and looked at the train. His men were on guard behind one of the barricades, a hundred yards away, but they were not supposed to be taking part in the attack.

The gun on the train was moving. Wisps of smoke like very low clouds, the dying spasm of the fire which had been burning, drifted past in front of it.

'I don't think they can have much ammunition left,' said Chen.

The barrel of the gun coming out of the turret looked like a telescope being projected from an observatory, and moved with a sort of cautious agility; despite the armour which shielded it, the circumspection with which it moved made it seem fragile.

'Directly our own guns are there . . .' said Kyo.

The one they were looking at stopped moving, and fired. In reply, a volley of shots rapped against the armour-plating. A break appeared in the grey and white clouds just above the train. A runner brought Kyo some documents.

'We haven't got a majority in the committee,' said the latter.

The delegates who had secretly been called together by the Kuomintang, before the rising, had elected a central committee of twenty-six, including fifteen Communists; but this committee had just elected in its turn the Executive Committee which was to organize the municipal government. It was there that the real power lay; and it was there that the Communists were no longer in a majority.

A second dispatch runner came in, in uniform, and stood waiting on the threshold.

'The arsenal has fallen.'

'What about the tanks?' asked Kyo.

'Gone to Nankin.'

'Are you from the army?'

He was from the First Division, the one which contained the largest number of Communists. Kyo asked him some questions. The man was embittered: they thought that the International didn't seem to be making much headway. Everything was done to favour the bourgeois who supported the Kuomintang: the soldiers' relations, almost all peasants, were compelled to shoulder the really heavy burden of subscribing funds for the war, whereas only moderate demands were made upon the bourgeoisie. If they tried to seize any land, orders came from above forbidding them to do so. The capture of Shanghai was going to change all that, according to the Communist soldiers, but the messenger himself wasn't so sure about it. He had only had one side of the position explained to him, and his arguments were poor arguments, but ones which lent themselves readily to improvement. There was going to be a Red Guard, and a Workers' Militia at Shanghai, answered Kyo; there were more than two hundred thousand unemployed in Hankow. Every minute or two they both stopped and listened.

'Hankow,' said the man, 'I know all about Hankow; there's . . .'

Their deep-sounding voices seemed to hang in the atmosphere around them, unable to escape through the quivering air which felt as though it too was waiting for a gun to fire. They both thought about Hankow, 'the most industrialized city in the whole of China'. A new Red army was being organized down there; even at that very moment there were detachments of workers down there, learning to handle a rifle. . . .

With legs spread wide apart, hands on his knees, and open mouth, Chen sat there looking at the runners, without saying a word.

'Everything will depend on who is made Prefect of Shanghai,' Kyo went on. 'If he's one of us, the majority isn't going to matter much. If he's from the Right . . .'

Chen looked at the time. In the clockmaker's shop there were at least thirty clocks, some wound, some run down, pointing to different times. Suddenly volleys of firing crashed out in a continuous flow. Chen couldn't bring himself to look outside: he was unable to tear his eyes away from that mass of clocks which ticked away in perfect order, quite unmindful of the revolution which raged outside. The departure of the runners broke the spell; he decided finally to consult his own watch.

'Four o'clock. It should be possible to find out . . .'

He manipulated the field telephone, then banged down the receiver in a fury, and turned to Kyo:

'The Prefect is from the Right.'

'First gain converts for the revolution, then widen its scope . . .' said Kyo, more in the tone of a question than an answer. 'The policy of the International seems to be to leave the power here in the hands of the bourgeois. For the time being . . . we shall be cheated. I have spoken to messengers from the front; all working-class movements are to be suppressed in that area. Chang Kai Shek has had strikers shot down, after the merest show of conciliation.'

A ray of sun came through. In the sky, the blue patch was getting bigger. Despite the bursts of firing, the armoured train looked deserted in that light. It fired again. Kyo and Chen were paying less attention to it now; perhaps the enemy was somewhere nearer at hand. Very uneasy, Kyo vaguely scanned the pavement, sparkling in the sunlight which for the moment lit it up. A huge shadow fell across it. He looked up: Katow.

'Within a fortnight,' he went on, 'the Kuomintang Government will be putting a ban upon our assault troops. I have just heard some Blue officers, sent back from the front to reconnoitre the position, cunningly insinuating that the arms would be better in their keeping than in ours. Disarm the Workers' Guard, and they have police, committee, Prefect, army and arms behind them. And much good we shall have got from the rising. We must break away from the Kuomintang, isolate the Communist Party, and if possible manoeuvre it into power. It's not a question of intrigue, of so many pawns on a chessboard, but of thinking seriously of the welfare of the proletariat. What sort of a lead are we to give them?'

Chen was looking at his delicately formed, if dirty, feet, bare in his sabots.

'The workers *are right* to go on strike. And we order them to go back to work. The peasants want to seize the land. They are right too, and we refuse to allow it.'

His accent was curious; he emphasized all the short words.

'Our programme is much the same as that of the Blues,' Kyo continued, 'only it makes rather more promises. But the Blues keep their promises to the bourgeois, and we don't keep ours to the workers.'

'That's enough,' said Chen, without even looking up. 'The first thing is to kill Chang Kai Shek.'

Katow listened in silence.

'It's no good thinking of that yet,' he said at last. 'At present, it is our own comrades who are being killed. Yes. And in any case, Kyo, I'm not at all sure that I agree with you. At the beginning of the revolution, when I was still a revolutionary-socialist, we were all opposed to Lenin's tactics in Ukraine. Antonov, the local commissar, had arrested the mine-owners and awarded them a little matter of ten years' penal servitude for *sabotage*. Without trial. On his own responsibility as commissar of the Tcheka, Lenin congratulated him; we all protested. They certainly did sweat their labourers, the mine-owners, and several of us had felt like condemned criminals when we went down the mines; that's why we thought they ought to treat them particularly justly, by way of an example. But if we had set them free, the proletariat simply wouldn't have understood. Lenin was right. Justice was on our side, but expediency was with Lenin. And we were also opposed to the special powers which the Tcheka exercised. We must take care. The present plan of campaign is a good one: win converts for the revolution, then widen its scope later. Lenin didn't start right away by saying: "Supreme power for the Soviets."'

'But he never in his life said: "Let us exalt the Menchevicks." Under no circumstances must we be forced into giving up our arms to the Blues. None whatever. For that means the collapse of the revolution, with no alternative left but . . .'

A Kuomintang officer entered, small, stiff, almost Japanese. They saluted each other.

'In half an hour's time the army will be here,' he said. 'We are short of rifles. How many can you let us have?'

Chen began walking up and down. Katow waited.

'The Workers' Militia still need their arms,' said Kyo.

'My request is made with the authority of the Government of Hankow,' replied the officer.

Kyo and Chen smiled.

'I shall be only too pleased for you to get it confirmed,' he went on.

Kyo manipulated the telephone.

'Even if the order . . .' Chen burst out in a cold fury.

'That'll do!' shouted Kyo.

He was listening. Katow seized the other receiver. They hung up.

'Very well,' said Kyo. 'But the men are still at their posts.'

'The artillery will soon be there,' said the officer. 'We'll clear up this business quickly enough . . .'

He pointed to the armoured train, waiting there in the sunlight, completely ineffective.

'. . ourselves. Can you deliver rifles to the troops tomorrow evening? We are in urgent need of them. Nankin is our next objective, and we are going straight on.'

'I doubt if it will be possible to recover more than half of the rifles.'

'Why?'

'Some of the Communists will refuse to give them up'

'Even under orders from Hankow?'

'Even under orders from Moscow. At least, not for the moment.'

They could feel the officer's exasperation, though he gave no sign of it.

'See what you can do,' he said. 'I'll send some one round, about seven o'clock.'

He went out.

'Are you in favour of giving up the rifles?' Kyo asked Katow.

'I'm trying to get the position clear. The first essential is to go to Hankow, you know. What does the International want? First to make use of the Kuomintang army to bring about the union of China. Then, by means of propaganda and so on, to extend the work of the revolution, which should of its own accord transform itself from a democratic revolution into a socialist one.'

'Chang Kai Shek must be killed,' said Chen.

'Chang Kai Shek won't allow us within striking range now,' replied Kyo. 'He dare not. The only way he can maintain himself in power is by filling his treasury from the customs and the contributions of the bourgeoisie; and the bourgeoisie won't make payments for no reason at all: he will have to present them with a few gutted Communists in return for their money.'

'That's absolute nonsense,' said Chen.

'For God's sake shut up,' said Katow. 'Do you really think you can't try and kill Chang Kai Shek without the sanction of the Central Committee, or rather the representative of the International?'

A distant rumble broke into the silence every now and then.

'Will you go to Hankow?' Chen asked Kyo.

'Sure.'

Chen was walking up and down the room, underneath the pendulums of all the alarm-clocks and cuckoo-clocks, which ticked away steadily.

'It's very simple, what I said,' he went on at last. 'It's essential. The only thing to be done. Warn the others.'

'Can't you wait a bit?'

Kyo knew that if, instead of answering, Chen hesitated, it wasn't because Katow's arguments had convinced him. It was because the present programme of the International completely failed to satisfy the deep-rooted passion which had made a revolutionary of him; if, for the sake of discipline, he were to accept them, he would be condemned to inactivity. Kyo looked across, underneath the clocks, at his disgruntled comrade, who had sacrificed both himself and others in the cause of the revolution, and whom the revolution seemed about to relegate to his original loneliness, alone with his memories of assassinations. At once both on his side and against him, he could no longer either make real contact with him, or cut himself altogether clear. They were comrades in arms, and when he looked at that armoured train and thought that perhaps they would attack it together the possibility of a break between them shocked him in the same way as the thought of an impending attack of epilepsy or madness in one of his friends, at a moment when he was in complete possession of his faculties.

Chen had started walking about again; he shook his head as if by way of protest, and said at length: 'All right'; shrugging his shoulders, as though his reply were merely intended to humour some childish whim of Kyo's.

The rumbling noise came back, louder, but still so indistinct that they had to listen very carefully in order to distinguish its cause. It seemed to rise out of the ground.

'No,' said Kyo, 'those are shouts.'

They got nearer, and grew more distinct.

'Can they be capturing the Russian church?' asked Katow.

There were a lot of Government troops entrenched there. But the shouts seemed to be coming towards the centre of the city, from the suburbs. Louder and louder. It was impossible to catch any words. Katow glanced at the armoured train: nothing there.

'Are reinforcements arriving?'

The shouting, still unintelligible, came nearer and nearer, as if some news of vital importance were being passed along from one crowd to another. But another noise struggled to make itself heard, succeeded, and at last grew distinct: the regular tramp of marching men was shaking the ground.

'The army,' said Katow. 'Our lot.'

He was probably right. The shouts were shouts of welcome, though it was impossible as yet to distinguish them from cries of fear; what Kyo had heard was the mob who had been driven from their homes by the flood. The ringing footsteps became a shuffle, then recommenced: the soldiers had stopped and were going off in another direction.

'They've been warned about the armoured train,' said Kyo.

Those inside the train probably could not hear the shouting as well as they could, but doubtless heard the tramp of footsteps much more clearly, owing to the vibrations set up in the armour plating. A prodigious uproar took all three by surprise; every gun, every machine gun, every rifle on the train was firing. Katow had served in an armoured train in Siberia; despite himself, his imagination reconstructed all too clearly the dying agonies of this one. The officers had given the command to go on firing until further orders. What could they do in their turrets, with a telephone in one hand and a revolver in the other? There wasn't a soldier, probably, who didn't guess the meaning of that rhythmic tread. Were they preparing to die altogether, or to hurl themselves at each others throats in that enormous submarine which would never come to the surface?

The train itself appeared panic-stricken. Firing continuously from every aperture, shaking itself violently in its frenzy, it seemed to be trying to wrench itself from the rails, as if the hopeless rage of the men whom it sheltered had infected the armour which imprisoned them, so that it, too, was struggling for freedom. What fascinated Katow in this hell let loose was not the drunken stupor which was overtaking the men inside, but the shuddering of the rails which held all these screaming wretches fast, like a strait-jacket: he stuck his arm out in front of him, in order to reassure himself that he was not paralysed. Thirty seconds later the din ceased. Through the dull vibrations of the marching feet and the ticking of all the clocks in the shop, a creaking of massive metal made itself heard: the artillery of the revolutionary army.

Behind each sheet of armour, a soldier was listening to that noise as if it were the voice of death itself.

Part 3

HANKOW was very close now: sampans covered almost the entire surface of the river. The chimneys of the arsenal gradually stood out from a hill behind, nearly obscured by the smoke which poured from them; at last the town appeared, in the bluish light of that spring evening, with its colonnaded banks just visible through the gaps in the sharp black foreground provided by the European men-of-war. For six days Kyo had been working up the river, without any news from Shanghai.

Low down on the waterline, a foreign launch whistled. Kyo's papers were in order, and he was well used to these hide-and-seek situations. He went up into the bows, by way of precaution.

'What do they want?' he asked a mechanic.

'They want to know if we have any rice or coal on board. It's not allowed.'

'By what authority?'

'It's a put-up job. If we are carrying coal, they don't say anything, but they arrange to have the ship unloaded at the port. No chance of getting any fresh provisions into the town.'

Over there, chimneys, cranes, storage-tanks: the allies of the revolution. But Shanghai had shown Kyo what a busy port was like. The port in front of him was full of nothing but junks and destroyers. He picked up his glasses: one cargo-boat, two, three. A few others. . . . The boat he was on was drawing in to the shore, over by Ou Chang: he would have to take the ferry in order to get to Hankow.

He left the boat. On the quay an officer stood watching the landing.

'Why are there so few boats?' asked Kyo.

'The shipping companies have sent them all away: they're afraid of their being commandeered.'

In Shanghai everybody imagined that they had already been commandeered long ago.

'When does the ferry leave?'

'Every half-hour.'

He had twenty minutes to wait. He walked around aimlessly. The petrol-lamps were lighting up inside the shops; here and there the outlines of trees and gables showed up against the sky in the west, where a curious light lingered, seeming to rise spontaneously from the velvet sky and fade away high up in the heavens, into the profound peace of the night. Despite the soldiers and the Workers' Unions, at the backs of dirty little shops, doctors with painted toads hanging up outside, herbalists and dealers in hideous little curiosities, public letter-writers, sorcerers, astrologers, and fortune-tellers; all continued to follow their fantastic callings in that confused light which hid the bloodstains from view. Shadows seemed to be absorbed by the ground rather than to stand out against it; bathed in a bluish, phosphorescent haze, the last reflections of the historic events which were being enacted that evening, somewhere very far away; of which no more than a mere glow survived to light up the earth around, glimmering feebly beneath a huge arch surmounted by a pagoda, preyed upon by ivy which was already black with grime. Beyond was a battalion of soldiers, merging into the banks of mist which filled the night down at the water-level. Kyo went down there, too, as far as a yard full of enormous blocks of stone: taken from the walls, razed to the ground in token of the liberation of China. The ferry-boat was quite near.

Still a quarter of an hour on the water, watching the evening fade over the city. At last, Hankow.

There were rickshaws waiting on the quay, but Kyo was too worried to be able to sit still. He preferred to walk: the British Concession, abandoned back in January, the great international banks, closed, but not yet in hostile hands. . . . 'Nerves play curious tricks: the pounding of one's heart shows how unevenly one is breathing, as if one were actually breathing with the heart. . . .' He was allowing them to get the better of him. At a street corner, through a gap in a big garden full of trees in flower, appeared the chimneys of the European factories, grey in the evening fog. No smoke. Out of all those which he could see, only the arsenal was working: could the Red Army be relied on, at any rate? He didn't dare to run now. Unless things in Hankow had gone the way every one expected, it meant death for all his comrades in Shanghai. And for May. For himself, too.

At last, the International Delegation.

The whole building was lit up. Kyo knew that right up at the top Borodin was working; on the ground floor, the printing-presses were going at full pressure, making a noise like a giant ventilator which had something wrong with it.

A guard peered at Kyo, dressed in a grey singlet with a large collar. Thinking that he was Japanese, he was already pointing to the orderly who was supposed to guide strangers, when he caught sight of the papers which Kyo was holding out; at once he led him through the crowded entrance to the part of the building occupied by the International Commission which had been appointed from Shanghai. All that Kyo knew about the secretary who received him was that he had organized the first risings in Finland: one of the Party, who introduced himself as he stretched out his hand over the desk: Vologuin. He looked more like a plump middle-aged woman than a man; was that due to the delicate curves of his highly coloured features, slightly Levantine in spite of the very light complexion, or to the long greyish curls, supposed to be trained back over the head, but falling down over his cheeks like the two halves of a parting?

'We're losing grip of things at Shanghai,' said Kyo. His words surprised him: his thoughts were running away with him. Still, they conveyed his meaning: unless Hankow could bring the detachments the help they needed, it was suicide to give up their rifles.

Vologuin stuffed his hands up the sleeves of his khaki uniform, and leant forward, squashed down into his little armchair.

'Again!' he muttered.

'First of all, what's happening here?'

'Go on: in what way are we losing grip at Shanghai?'

'But why on earth aren't the factories working?'

'Wait: which lot are complaining?'

'The Shock Sections. The terrorists, too.'

'Terrorists don't matter a damn. The others . . .' He looked at Kyo: 'What do they want?'

'To leave the Kuomintang. To organize an independent Communist party. To put power into the hands of the Unions. And above all, to keep their arms. That, above everything.'

'Always the same thing.'

Vologuin got up and looked out of the window towards the river and the hills, without the slightest expression of emotion on his face: a fixed stare like that of a sleep-walker was the only sign of life upon his rigid features. He was short, and his fat back, as fat as his stomach, gave him almost the appearance of a hunchback.

'Listen to me. Supposing that we do leave the Kuomintang. What are we going to put in its place?'

'We'll start with a militia for each Trade Union, and for each Syndicate.'

'How will we arm them? Here the arsenal is in the hands of the generals. Chang Kai Shek controls the Shanghai one. And we are cut off from Mongolia, so we can't get any from Russia.'

'We've captured the Shanghai arsenal.'

'With the revolutionary army at your back. Not safe in front, remember. Whom are we going to arm here? Ten thousand workers or thereabouts. In addition to the Communist nucleus in the 'Iron Army': another ten thousand. Ten rounds each! Against them, more than seventy-five thousand men here alone. Not to mention . . . Chang Kai Shek and the others. They'd be only too pleased to form an alliance against us, on the first sign of our adopting a genuinely Communist programme. And how are we going to keep the supply of munitions going?'

'Aren't there foundries – factories?'

'No more raw material is coming through.'

Standing motionless in front of the window, his profile hidden by the locks of hair, while the night deepened, Vologuin went on:

'Hankow is not the "workers'" capital, it's the capital of the unemployed. There are no arms: perhaps that's all to the good. There are times when I think: if we gave them rifles, they would fire on us. And yet, there are all those who work for fifteen hours a day without insisting on their rights, because the revolution is in danger. . . .'

Kyo was falling into a day-dream, deeper and deeper.

'It's not we who are in control,' Vologuin continued, 'it's the so-called Left Wing Kuomintang generals. They wouldn't accept the Soviet system any more than Chang Kai Shek accepts them. That's certain. We can make use of them, but that is all. Taking great precautions . . .'

'If Hankow were no more than the bloodstained scene of events which had no real significance . . .' Kyo's mind boggled at the thought. 'I must see Possoz on my way out,' he said to himself. He was the only member of the party, in Hankow, in whom he had confidence. 'I must see Possoz . . .'

'. . . You don't need to look so . . . so prostrated,' said Vologuin. 'If the impression has got around that Hankow is Communist, so much the better. It reflects credit on our methods of propaganda. But it is no reason for its being true.'

'What is the present plan of campaign here?'

'To strengthen the Communist element in the Iron Army. We can throw our weight on to one side of the scales or the other, but we aren't really strong enough to stand alone. The generals who are fighting against us here hate the Soviets and Communism just as much as Chang Kai Shek. I know it, I see signs of it every day. The least suggestion of an attempt to put Communism into practice, and we shall have them at our throats. And very likely push them into an alliance with Chang. The only thing we can do is to make use of them in order to smash Chang. And then Feng Yu Shiang afterwards, if necessary. In the same way, after all, as we have made use of Chang to smash up the generals who have fought against us up to the present. Propaganda is swelling our numbers just as effectively as victory is swelling theirs. We are keeping pace with them. That's why it is so important to play for time. The revolution cannot, ultimately, retain its democratic form. Its very nature means that it is bound to develop into socialism. It must be allowed to take its course. It must be brought to term, and not aborted.'

'Yes. But Marxism contains both the idea of inevitability and a worship of the power of the will. And whenever I see the first being allowed to predominate over the second, I am uneasy.'

'At the moment a genuinely Communist programme would immediately bring all the generals into line against us: two hundred thousand men against twenty thousand. That is why you must come to an agreement with Chang Kai Shek in Shanghai. If it is quite impossible, then give up the rifles.'

'On that basis, it was a mistake ever to attempt the October revolution: what were the numbers of the Bolsheviks?'

'By making "peace" our watchword, we got the support of the masses.'

'There are other watchwords.'

'They are premature. What are they, pray?'

'Immediate and total suppression of farm rents and interest-bearing loans. The agrarian revolution without any syndicates, and without any qualifications.'

The six days which he had spent making his way up the river had confirmed Kyo's opinion: in those mud towns which had existed at the river-junctions from time immemorial, the poor were as likely to throw in their lot with the peasants as with the city workers.

'The peasant always waits for a lead,' said Vologuin. 'Whether it is the worker or the bourgeoisie, he waits for a lead.'

'No. A peasant movement only *lasts* when it attaches itself to the town; unaided, a peasant rising becomes a mere *jacquerie* – that is clear. But there's no question of separating the peasants from the proletariat: the abolition of loans is a battle-cry, and the only one which might make them fight.'

'In fact, peasant ownership of the land,' said Vologuin.

'More definite than that; there are many very poor peasants who own their land, but who are sweated by money-lenders. It is well known. But at Shanghai we must start the Trades Union guards training as quickly as possible. And not let them disarm under any pretext. Show them off as an argument when it comes to dealing with Chang Kai Shek.'

'Directly that plan becomes known, we shall be annihilated'.

'So we will anyway, in that case. The Communist policy develops, even when we leave it to itself. A few speeches and the peasants want the land, but it will take more than speeches to choke them off again. Either we must agree to help Chang Kai Shek in the work of repression (how does that strike you – definitely compromise ourselves?), or they will be forced to crush us out of existence, whether they want to or not.'

'Every one in Moscow agrees that it will be necessary to break with them in the end. But not just yet.'

'Well then, if it's mainly a question of bluff, stick to the arms. Giving them up means betraying our comrades.'

'If they follow instructions, Chang won't make any definite move.'

'Whether they follow them or not, it won't make any difference to the situation. The Committee, Katow, and myself have organized the Workers' Guard. If you try to disband it, the Shanghai proletariat will all imagine it is a case of treachery.'

'Then let them give up their arms.'

'Workers' Unions spring up everywhere of their own accord in the poor districts. Are you going to forbid all attempts at organization in the name of the International Committee?'

Vologuin had gone back to the window. His head fell forward on to his chest, giving him a double chin. Night was falling, and stars were beginning to show dimly.

'Breaking with them means certain defeat. Moscow won't stand for our leaving the Kuomintang at this stage. And the Chinese Communist party is even more in favour of co-operation than Moscow.'

'Moscow knows that; the order to give up arms was circulated the day before yesterday.'

Overcome with amazement, Kyo said nothing for a moment. Then:

'And have they done so?'

'Barely half of them . . .'

Two days ago, while he was pondering over the situation, or sleeping on the boat. . . . He, too, realized that Moscow would stick to the same policy. And his realization of the position suddenly invested Chen's scheme with a vague importance.

'Another thing – though perhaps it's nothing new really: Chen Ta Eul, of Shanghai, wishes to kill Chang.'

'Ah! I see now.'

'What?'

'He sent word through to ask if he could see me when you arrived.'

He picked up a message lying on the table. It occurred to

Kyo that his hands were like those of a priest. 'Why didn't he have him shown up at once?' he wondered.

'... A serious matter. ... (Vologuin was reading the message.) They all say : a serious matter....'

'Is he here?'

'Wasn't he supposed to be coming? They're all alike. They're always changing their minds. He has been here, well, for two or three hours: your boat was very behind time.'

He telephoned for Chen. He didn't like interviews with terrorists, whom he considered narrow-minded, overbearing, and entirely lacking in political judgement.

'Things looked even blacker at Leningrad,' he said, 'with Youdenitch outside the city, and yet it all turned out all right in the end.'

Chen entered, also wearing a sweater, walked past Kyo, and sat down opposite Vologuin. The noise of the printing-machines alone disturbed the silence. Framed in the great window which rose up in front of the desk, the profiles of the two men stood out, quite distinct from each other, against the brightness of the night. Chen sat there motionless, with his elbows on the desk and his chin between his hands; dogged and tense. 'Some people are so utterly walled-up that they hardly come into the category of human beings,' thought Kyo as he looked at him. 'Is that because normally common weaknesses form a connecting-link ...?' As soon as he had recovered from his surprise, it seemed inevitable that Chen should be there, that he should have come to confirm his decision (for he did not suppose that he intended to discuss the matter) in person. As remote from him as the confines of that star-spangled night allowed, Vologuin was waiting too, standing there with his hair tumbling over his face and his fat hands folded across his chest.

'Did he tell you?' asked Chen, indicating Kyo with a jerk of his head.

'You know how acts of terrorism are regarded by the International,' answered Vologuin. 'Well, I needn't waste my time emphasizing that.'

'The case in point is a special one. Chang Kai Shek is the only man who is both strong and popular enough to keep the bourgeoisie united against us. Do you deny the necessity of his death, yes or no?'

He was still in exactly the same position, with his elbows resting on the desk, and his chin resting on his hands. Despite Chen's having come to see them there, Kyo knew that the discussion could never really be anything but fruitless as far as he was concerned. His instincts found satisfaction in nothing except destruction.

'The International must oppose this scheme.' Vologuin spoke as if he was in a court of law. 'But even from your own point of view . . . ' Still Chen didn't move. ' . . . Well, is this a good moment that you have chosen?'

'Do you prefer to wait until Chang has murdered all our comrades?'

'He will issue decrees and do nothing more. His son is in Moscow, don't forget. And then some of the Russian officers from Gallen didn't manage to get away from his headquarters. They will be tortured if he is killed. Neither Gallen nor the Red General Staff will allow it. . . .'

'So the question has been discussed even here,' thought Kyo. There was something curiously futile and unreal about this discussion, which worried him: he thought Vologuin seemed vastly more effective when he was ordering the giving up of the arms than when he was talking of the murder of Chang Kai Shek.

'If the Russian officers are tortured,' said Chen, 'that's that. So shall I be. That's beside the point. Millions of Chinese are well worth fifteen Russian officers. Very well then. And Chang will abandon his son.'

'What do you know about it?'

'Or you? And I doubt if you'd even have the guts to kill him.'

'It's fairly certain that he doesn't love his son as much as himself,' said Kyo. 'And unless he makes an attempt to crush us he is doomed. Unless he puts some check on the activities of the peasants, his own officers will desert him. So I'm afraid he will abandon the boy, after extracting a few promises from European consuls or some other farcical procedure. And the whole of the lower bourgeois class, whose sympathies you're trying to enlist, Vologuin, will declare for him the very moment he succeeds in disarming us: they will throw in their lot with the strongest side. I know them.'

'Not necessarily. And there's not only Shanghai to be considered.'

'You say that you're threatened with famine here. Where will you get supplies from if we lose Shanghai? Feng Yu Shiang stands between you and Mongolia, and if we are smashed up he'll betray you. Nothing up the Yang-Tse, then, and nothing from Russia. Do you think the peasants to whom you promised the Kuomintang · programme (reduction of farm-rents by twenty-five per cent; that's good, isn't it, by twenty-five per cent), do you think they'll be prepared to starve to death so that the Red Army can fill its stomach? You will be putting yourself more into the power of the Kuomintang than ever. As to forcing the issue with Chang now at once, by introducing a real revolutionary policy and relying on the peasantry and the Shanghai workers for support – it's risky, but it's not out of the question: the first division are Communist almost to a man, including the general; and they'll fight on our side. Then you say that we've kept back half the rifles. In any case, not having a try at it means just waiting like cattle in a stock-yard.'

'We didn't make the Kuomintang: it already existed. And for the time being it is stronger than we are. If we are to get control of it we must strike at the heart of it and bring all the

Communist influences in our power to bear upon the general rank-and-file. The vast majority of its members are extremists.'

'You know as well as I do that in a democracy numbers count for nothing against a powerful executive.'

'We will show that it is possible to make use of the Kuomintang – by doing so. Not by just talking. We have been making use of them continuously for ten years now. Every month, every day.'

'Only when you have accepted their ideals; not once when there's been a question of them accepting yours. You have put them in the way of presents which they were only too desperately eager to accept: officers, volunteers, money, propaganda. Soviets in the army, and peasant unions, are a very different matter.'

'What about the exclusion of anti-Communist elements?'

'Chang Kai Shek wasn't in possession of Shanghai then.'

'In less than a month we shall have induced the Kuomintang Executive to outlaw him.'

'After he has smashed us. What the hell does it matter to the Kuomintang generals whether the militant Communists are killed or not? All the better for them if they are! Don't you think, truly, that the Chinese Communist party, and possibly Moscow too, become so obsessed by ideas of economic inevitability that they can't see this crisis developing right under their noses?'

'That's opportunism.'

'Maybe it is! According to your way of reckoning Lenin ought not to have made the division of land part of his policy (that was much less a Bolshevik idea than a Revolutionary Socialist one, and *they* weren't exactly blasted to hell as a result of it). The division of the land meant the institution of smallholdings; he should therefore have introduced not division but immediate collectivization of the land, *sovkhozes*. But as he was successful in the end, you realize that it was all a matter of tactics. You are gradually losing your power over the masses. . . .'

'Do you imagine that Lenin kept it, either, between February and October?'

'There were moments when he lost it. But he was never really out of their minds. Your policy isn't consistent. The threads don't intertwine, they run farther and farther away from each other. In order to exercise the control over the masses which you presume to do, you would need supreme power. And you haven't got it.'

'That's not the point,' said Chen.

He got up.

'You are powerless to check the peasant movement,' Kyo went on. 'Here are we, Communists, giving instructions to the masses that they can only regard as treacherous. Do you suppose they'll understand your order suspending operations?'

'Even if I were a coolie in the Shanghai docks, I should think that obedience to the party was after all the only logical attitude for a militant Communist. And that all the arms ought to be given up.'

Chen stood up again.

'One doesn't go and get killed to order. Or kill other people that way. Except in the case of cowards.'

Vologuin shrugged his shoulders.

'It is a mistake to consider assassination the principal agent of true political progress.'

Chen was on the way out.

'Immediately the Central Committee meets,' said Kyo, giving Vologuin his hand, 'I shall propose the immediate breaking-up of the land and the cancellation of debts.'

'The Committee won't pass that,' replied Vologuin, smiling for the first time.

Chen's stumpy figure was waiting in the dark outside. Kyo joined him, after finding out the address of his friend Possoz: he was in charge of the docks.

'Listen . . .' said Chen.

The ground acting as a conductor, the vibrations of the printing-machines, regular, controlled, like those of a ship's engines, were running right through them: the windows of the delegation stood out in the sleeping town, all brightly lit, with the black outlines of figures showing through. They walked away, twin shadows preceding them: both were the same height, and the collars of their sweaters protruded in the same way. The sinister-looking straw huts of which they caught glimpses through the maze of streets, merged into the almost awe-inspiring colour of the night, smelling of fish and burnt fat. Kyo couldn't get rid of the jarring sensation communicated to his muscles by the machines, through the ground – as if those machines, whose nature was to produce truth, had in him encountered all the hesitations and assertions of Vologuin. All the time, on his way up the river, he had felt how scanty his information was, and how difficult it would be to know on what to base his plans if he once broke away from the policy of blind adherence to the instructions of the International. But the International was making a mistake. It was impossible to play a waiting game any longer. Communist propaganda had burst upon the masses like a flood, gone straight to their heart as only their predestined gospel could have done. However much caution Moscow might display, the leaven would continue to work; Chang knew it and from now on had no alternative but to beat the Communists down. That one thing was absolutely certain. Perhaps the revolution might have been handled differently; but it was too late. The Communist peasantry would seize the land, the Communist workers would demand new conditions of labour, the Communist soldiers would refuse to fight any more except for objects of which they knew and approved, whether Moscow liked it or not. Let Moscow, let the hostile capitals of Europe reconcile their conflicting passions and endeavour to shape their destiny, the destiny of the West. The revolution had gone to term: it must be delivered now, or perish. Kyo felt at once both the nearness of Chen as a comrade, there beside him in the night, and a great sense of dependence; the anguish of only being a man, of only being himself; he remembered nights like this when he had seen Chinese Mohammedans bend prostrate amid the scent of sun-scorched lavender which filled the steppe, and heard their wailing songs, the songs which for thousands of years have seared deep into the soul of suffering man who knows that death awaits him at the last. What had he come to Hankow for? To tell the International the facts about the situation in Shanghai. And the International had their own views about it – quite as definite as his own. What had impressed him far more than Vologuin's arguments was the silence of the factories, the agony of a moribund town; decked in the gorgeous trappings of a revolution, but moribund for all that. A corpse, which might be bequeathed for dismemberment to the next rising, instead of being allowed slowly to decompose, a sink of intrigue. Their lives were probably all forfeit: the essential thing was that they should not die in vain. He was certain that at that moment Chen too felt drawn to him, that they were fellow-prisoners. Chen spoke:

'Can't tell. . . . If it's a question of killing Chang Kai Shek, I can see my way. And I suppose it's the same with Vologuin; only in his case, instead of being murder, it's obedience. A life like ours must have something solid behind it. And there's no doubt executing orders does the same thing for him as killing does for me. There must be something that is definite and secure. There absolutely must.'

He was silent.

'Do you dream much?' he continued.

'No. Or if I do I don't remember much about it.'

'I have dreams almost every night. Then there are daydreams too. Sometimes when I let myself go, I see the shadow of a cat on the ground: more terrifying than anything real. But the dreams are the worst of all.'

'Worse than *anything* real, no matter what? . . .'

'I'm not the sort of person who gets conscience-stricken. The difficult part of murder isn't the actual killing. It's keeping a tight hold over oneself: rising above . . . what one is going through just then.'

Was there bitterness behind his words? The tone of his voice gave little indication, and Kyo couldn't see his face. In the empty streets outside, the faint hum of a distant car died away in a gust of wind which left a scent of orchards behind it, to mingle with the camphor-laden air of the night.

'. . . If that were all . . . But that's not the worst. It's the Creatures.'

Chen repeated:

'Creatures. . . . Octopuses, especially. They keep coming into my mind.'

Despite the vastness of the night around them, Kyo felt as near him as if they were shut in a room together.

'How long has it been going on?'

'A long time. As long as I can remember. It hasn't come so often just lately. And I don't remember anything else. Only . . . that. I hate remembering, as a rule. I can't cope with it: my life isn't over, it's still going on now.'

Silence.

'The one thing I dread—dread—is going to sleep. And I go to sleep every day.'

Two o'clock struck. Somewhere there in the night an argument was going on; a high-pitched, staccato, Chinese argument.

'Or going mad. Those tentacles, night and day, all one's life long. . . . And lunatics never commit suicide, so they say. . . . Never.'

'Does killing alter the dreams?'

'I don't think so. I will tell you after . . . Chang.'

Kyo had definitely come to realize that he was risking his own life, was living among men who knew that their lives were in danger every day: courage held no surprises for him. But it was the first time that he had seen death fascinate a man, as it fascinated this friend of his, scarcely visible in the darkness, who spoke so abstractedly; as though his words had been inspired by the same strange nocturnal force as his own anguish of mind, by the compelling intimacy of their uneasiness, of the silence, and of fatigue. . . . But his voice had a different note in it now.

'Does the thought of that . . . worry you?'

'No. I feel a kind of . . .'

He hesitated.

'I'm trying to find a stronger word than joy. There isn't one. Even in Chinese. A kind of . . . utter relief. A sort of . . . what does one call it? of . . . I don't know. There's only one thing which goes deeper still. Takes man further from himself, nearer to . . . Do you know what opium is like?'

'Not really.'

'Then it's difficult to explain what I mean. Nearer to . . . ecstasy. Yes. But heavier. Deep. Not light and soaring. An ecstasy which . . . plumbs the depths.

'And there's an idea which gives you that feeling?'

'Yes: my own death.'

Still that far-away voice. 'He'll commit suicide,' thought Kyo. He had listened often enough to his father to know that a man who seeks the absolute with such unremitting zeal will only find it in a form of sensationalism. Thirst for the absolute, thirst after immortality, and so fear of death: by rights Chen should have been a coward; but like all mystics, he felt that the absolute was only to be attained through the moment. Whence, probably, his disdain for everything which did not lead directly to the moment when he would enter into breathless communion with himself. From that human frame which Kyo could not even see, emanated a blind force which held it in thrall; the raw material of inevitability. There was a touch of insanity in that comrade of his, silent now, brooding upon the horrors of his nightmare, but there was something divine also, something of the mysticism which is always present in the supernatural. Perhaps he was going to kill Chang first and himself afterwards. Trying in the dark to visualize that pointed face with the full lips, Kyo felt that he too was a prey to the same elemental distress which drove Chen on towards the writhing tentacles of his dreams and to his death.

'My father thinks,' said Kyo slowly, 'that anguish of mind lies at the very root of human nature; that man is conscious of his destiny, and that all fears arise from this, even the fear of death . . . but that opium provides a means of escape, and that that is its justification.'

'Fear is waiting there inside all the time. It's only a question of looking deep enough: fortunately, action is a counter-stimulant. If Moscow support me, well and good; if they don't, the simplest thing is not to know anything about it. I am leaving here. Do you mean to stay on?'

'Before anything else I want to see Possoz. But you won't be able to leave: your papers aren't endorsed.'

'I shall get away all right.'

'How?'

'I don't know. But I shall . . . I'm sure of it. *It was ordained* that I should kill Tang Yen Ta, and *it is ordained* that I shall go now. Of course I shall.'

Kyo certainly felt that Chen's will played a very small part in deciding the issue. If, somewhere, there was such a thing as Destiny, surely it was close beside him there that night.

'Do you think it really matters whether it's you or someone else who organizes the plot against Chang?'

'No. . . . All the same, I wouldn't allow any one else to do it.'

'Because you couldn't rely on them?'

'Because I dislike the idea of *my* women receiving kisses from others.'

The phrase brought back with a jolt Kyo's previous distress:

he felt a sudden breach between them. They had reached the river. Chen cut a small skiff adrift, and moved out into the stream. Kyo lost sight of him almost immediately, but he could still hear the regular plop of the oars, still loud enough to drown the gentle swish of the water against the river-bank. He had known many terrorists. They took things very much for granted. They were all members of a group: murderous insects, living tightly bound together into a tragic fellowship. But Chen . . . Still musing as he walked along, Kyo made for the buildings which housed the officials in charge of the port. 'His boat will be stopped on the way out . . .' He arrived at a large structure guarded by soldiers, almost empty by comparison with that which housed the International. In the corridors, more soldiers were sleeping or playing cards. He found his friend without difficulty. With a round head like an apple, a face covered with red pimples, grey moustache reminiscent of a French bourgeois, and dressed in civilian khaki, Possoz was a working-man, an anarchist-syndicalist member of the Chaux-de-Fonds party, who had gone to Russia after the war, and turned bolshevik. Kyo had known him in Pekin, and trusted him. They shook hands calmly: in Hankow, even a visitor from the dead would have received the most matter-of-fact reception.

'The dockers are there,' a soldier was saying.

'Send them in.'

The soldier went out. Possoz turned to Kyo:

'You observe that I've damn all to do, my boy. We were expecting to have three hundred ships through the port: there aren't ten. . . .'

Beneath the open windows the port lay asleep; no sirens, nothing save the continuous rippling of the water against the embankments and the piles of the wharfs. A bright but pale-coloured light swept across the walls of the room: the search-lights from the gunboats in the distance had played momentarily upon that part of the river. A noise of footsteps.

Possoz drew his revolver from its holster, and placed it on his desk.

'They attacked the Red Guard with iron bars,' he said to Kyo.

'The Red Guard are armed.'

'The danger wasn't that the guards would get roughly handled, but that they might go over on to their side.'

The searchlight returned, threw their shadows into gigantic relief on the white wall behind them, then swung back into the night, just as the dockers entered the room; four, five, six, seven. In blue overalls, one of them bare down to the waist. Handcuffed. Different types of faces, not easy to see in the dim light; but with fierce hatred apparent in every one of them. Beside them, two Chinese guards, with Nagau pistols on their hips. The dockers stood there as if glued together into a solid mass. There was hatred there, but fear too.

'The Red Guards are workers,' said Possoz in Chinese.

Silence.

'If they act as guards, it's for the sake of the revolution, not because they've anything to gain themselves.'

'And to get something to eat,' said one of the dockers.

'It is fair enough that the rations go to the men who fight. What do you suggest doing with them? Playing cards for them?'

'Giving them to every one.'

'Already there aren't enough to go round. The Government have resolved to show the utmost consideration to the proletariat, even when they forget themselves. If Red Guards were to be killed right and left, the city would fall into the hands of the generals and the foreigners, as before; come now, don't pretend you don't see that. Well, then? Is that what you want?'

'We got enough to eat before, anyway.'

'No,' said Kyo to the labourers, 'you didn't get enough to eat before. I know, I've worked in the docks. And it was as near the starvation borderline as a man can go.'

143

Their eyes widened; the whites grew a fraction more visible, in the dim light. They were trying to get a better view of this strange being with the Japanese appearance, dressed in a sweater, who talked with a northern accent, and who made out that he had been a coolie.

'We want definite promises,' replied one of them in a low voice.

'Yes,' said another. 'Our principal rights are the right to go on strike and the right to starve to death. My brother is in the army. Why were those who demanded the formation of soldiers' unions expelled from his division?'

They were growing more excited.

'Do you imagine that the Russian revolution was accomplished in a day?' Possoz asked them.

'The Russians arranged things as they thought best.'

It was useless to continue the discussion: the only object was to discover the seriousness of the riot.

'The use of violence against the Red Guard is an offence against the revolution, punishable with the death penalty, as you well know.'

A pause.

'If you were released, what would you do?'

They looked at each other; it was too dark to see the expression on their faces. Despite the pistols and the handcuffs, Kyo could feel the imminence of that typically Chinese readiness to strike a bargain, which he had so often encountered during the revolution.

'And given work?' asked one of the prisoners.

'When there's any to be had.'

'Well in the *meantime*, if the Red Guard prevents us from getting food to eat, we'll attack the Red Guard. I haven't eaten anything for three days. Absolutely nothing.'

'Is it true that there's food in prison?' asked one of them who hadn't yet spoken.

'You will soon see.'

Possoz said no more, but rang the bell, and the guards removed the prisoners.

'That's just what is so exasperating,' he continued, speaking French now; 'they are beginning to get the idea that prison means having every conceivable delicacy crammed down their throats.'

'Why didn't you make a bit more of an effort to make them see reason, since you had had them brought up?'

Possoz shrugged his shoulders wearily.

'I have them sent up, my dear boy, because I go on hoping that they'll say something else. And yet they aren't all like that, there are the ones who do their fifteen or sixteen hours a day without a murmur, and who will go on doing them until we are really secure, come what may . . .'

Possoz smiled, and beneath the wall of ragged moustache his teeth gleamed in the dim light, like the eyes of the dock-hands just before.

'You are lucky to have teeth like that after the kind of life one lives up-country.'

'Lucky! Not a bit of it. They're a set that I had made in Chang-Cha. The revolution doesn't seem to have put an end to decent dentistry. And how about you? Are you a delegate? What the deuce are you doing here, anyway?'

Kyo explained, without mentioning Chen. Possoz listened, growing more and more uneasy.

'That's all likely enough, my dear boy, and all the more unfortunate. I've had to do with watch-making for fifteen years, and I know the trickiness of a mechanism in which all the parts are intimately related. If one has no faith in the International, one shouldn't be a member of the Party.'

'Half the International are in favour of our forming Soviets.'

'We've been following a more or less consistent policy hitherto; we ought to stick to it.'

'And give up our rifles! A policy which obliges us to fire upon the proletariat *must* be a bad one. Whenever land is seized by the peasants now, the generals arrange that a certain number of Communist troops are involved in the repression. Tell me frankly, would you obey an order to fire on the peasants?'

'My dear boy, there are times when one's ideals must take second place: I should fire over their heads, and that's probably what actually happens. I would rather the question didn't arise. But that's not the real point.'

'You don't understand. It's like seeing some one in the act of taking aim at you while we carry on a theoretical discussion about the danger of revolver bullets . . . There is no alternative for Chang Kai Shek but our annihilation. And it will soon be the same with the generals here, our "allies"! And they will be absolutely right. We shall put our heads in the noose, every one of us, without even saving the good name of the party; leading the way to the brothel, day after day, with a swarm of generals in our wake; as if that were our headquarters . . .'

'If every one behaves just as he pleases, that's the end of the whole blasted business. If the International win, there will be cries of: Bravo! and they'll certainly be deserved. But if we put a spoke in the wheel, they will quite certainly come to grief, and the essential thing is that they should win. . . . As to Communists being ordered to fire on the peasants, I know that's what one hears; but are you sure of it, really positively? You haven't ever *seen* it happen, and after all – I'm not suggesting for a moment that you've deliberately invented it, but all the same . . . – it fits in pretty well with your argument. . . .'

'It's quite enough that the story exists. This isn't the moment for elaborate inquisitions.'

What was the good of arguing? It wasn't Possoz whom Kyo wanted to convince, but his comrades in Shanghai; and they probably were convinced by now, just as his own decisions had been confirmed by this visit to Hankow, by the scene which he had just witnessed. He had only one desire now; to get away.

A Chinese non-commissioned officer entered, his features

looking as if they had been pulled out lengthwise, and his body bent slightly forwards, like those ivory carvings whose lines follow the curve of the tusks from which they were cut.

'A man has been caught trying to escape down the river.'

Kyo hardly dared to breathe.

'He makes out that he has your permission to leave Hankow. He's a merchant.'

Kyo breathed again.

'Haven't given any one permission,' said Possoz. 'None of my business. Send him to the police.'

When rich men were arrested they would pour out their woes to some official or other: sometimes they managed to see him in private, and offered him money. It was more sensible than allowing oneself to be shot without attempting to do anything at all.

'Wait!'

Possoz pulled out a list from his blotting-pad, and murmured some names.

'All right. He's down there anyway. He was already on the list. Let the police deal with him!'

The sergeant left the room. The list, a page torn from a note-book, still lay on the blotting-paper. Kyo's thoughts were still for Chen.

'That's the list of "wanted" people,' said Possoz, who saw that Kyo was still gazing at the paper. 'The latest additions are sent by telephone, before boats leave — when they are just leaving. . . .'

'May I see?'

Possoz handed it to him: fourteen names. Chen's name was not among them. Vologuin must surely have realized that he would try and leave Hankow as soon as possible. And it would have been no more than reasonable to circulate his description as that of some one likely to leave, just on the off chance. 'The International don't wish to incur the responsibility of killing Chang Kai Shek themselves,' thought Kyo; 'but I daresay they wouldn't regard his death as an absolute catastrophe, all the same. . . . Is that why Vologuin's answers seemed so vague? . . .' He handed back the list.

'I shall get away,' Chen had said. It was easy to explain his eagerness to go, but the explanation wasn't a very satisfactory one. Chen's unexpected arrival, Vologuin's secretiveness, the list, all that Kyo understood; but every movement Chen made was hurrying him once more down the road that led to murder, so that the finger of destiny seemed to be apparent in everything with which he came into contact. There were moths fluttering around the little lamp. 'Perhaps Chen is a moth himself, diffusing the very light which will scorch his flimsy wings. . . . Perhaps all mankind . . .' Are we incapable of seeing our own destiny? Wasn't he like a moth himself, in his eagerness to get back to Shanghai, to help the sections to carry on at all costs? The sergeant returned, and he seized the opportunity to leave.

Outside, the night was as calm as ever. Not a siren blew, nothing but the lapping of the water. Along the embankment, beside the street-lamps humming with insects, coolies lay sleeping in attitudes which suggested a visitation of the plague. Here and there, on the pavements, little red notices were scribbled, round like the lids of drains; all were composed of the same character; the one word *Hunger*. As with Chen a moment earlier, he was conscious that throughout all China, and away to the West until half Europe was included, the night was filled with men in a dilemma similar to his own, torn between obedience to discipline and the slaughter of their comrades. Those dockers who protested did not understand. But even though they saw the position clearly, how should they choose the finer course, in this town which to Western eyes held the key to the fate of four hundred million souls (maybe his own among them), and which slept beside the river the troubled sleep of a starving man – wallowing in its helplessness, its misery and its bitterness?

Part 4

12.30 P.M.

CLAPPIQUE was sitting in the almost deserted bar of the little Grosvenor Hotel – with its polished walnut, bottles, nickel, flags – spinning an ash-tray on his outstretched forefinger. Count Chpilewski entered; he had been waiting for him. Clappique crumpled up a piece of paper on which he had been amusing himself by making each of his friends an imaginary present.

'H-how are things going, old chap, in that sunny little village of yours? Well?'

'Hardly. But they'll be better at the end of the month. I'm getting rid of some of my produce. Only to Europeans, naturally.'

Despite the unpretentious white clothes he wore, Chpilewski's hooked nose and bald forehead combined with the grey hair, brushed well back, and the prominent cheekbones, to give him the appearance of an eagle in disguise. The monocle increased the fantastic resemblance.

'As you will realize, my dear friend, somewhere about twenty thousand francs is what I need, and the trouble is where to find them. With that amount, one can make quite a respectable position for oneself in the provision trade.'

'That's the sort of thing I like to hear! You want a l-little place, no, a *respectable* place in the provision trade? Excellent. . . .'

'I never knew you were so . . . narrow-minded.'

Clappique looked at the eagle out of the corner of his eye: not forgetting that he was an ex-sabre champion of the Cracow garrison.

'Narrow-minded! I'm one mass of unreasonable whims! Just imagine how I should spend that money, if I had it! I should follow the example of a Dutch civil servant from Sumatra, who used to sail past the Arabian coast every year, on his way home to his beloved tulips; and who got the idea into his head (this happened nearly seventy years ago, it's true) that he'd like to burgle the Mecca treasury. The spoils are prodigious, it appears, of the purest gold, and housed in huge black vaults, where the pilgrims are for ever adding to them. It's in just such a vault as that that I would like to live. . . . Well, finally our tulip-fancier comes into a legacy and goes off to the West Indies to raise a gang of ruffians for a surprise descent upon the town, providing them with the most up-to-date weapons; rifles which would fire two bullets, detachable bayonets, every kind of thing. Then takes them on board – just listen to this – and sets sail for the scene of operations. . . .'

He placed his finger on his lips, delighting in the Pole's curiosity, which was almost as keen as if he were himself about to take part in the expedition.

'Right! They mutiny, slit his throat with professional efficiency, and make use of the ship to do some rather more serious piracy elsewhere. That's a true story; and a moral one, what's more. But as I was saying, if you're counting on me for your twenty thousand shekels, you're absolutely crazy! Ask me to do some negotiating for you, or anything in that line, and I'm your man. Looking at it another way, since your damned police spies get a "rake-off" on every racket I've got a hand in, I'd rather you had the money than any one else. But as long as we're in this utter chaos, people take just no interest at all in opium and cocaine.'

The ash-tray began to revolve again.

'I'm telling you about it,' said Chpilewski, 'because if I want to succeed, I've obviously got to have a try with every one. I should certainly have done better to wait . . . anyway. But when I asked you to meet me here for a drink (which incidentally is not what it pretends to be), I wanted to do you a good turn. Here it is: Leave Shanghai tomorrow.'

'Ah! ah! ah!' said Clappique, his voice going up the scale. Like an echo came the sound of a motor-horn from the street, in a rising arpeggio. 'And for what reason?'

'For a very good reason. My police, as you say, do their work pretty well. You clear out.'

Clappique knew that he would have to give in. For a moment he wondered whether it might not be a trick to get the twenty thousand francs. No – the idea was absurd.

'And have I got to go tomorrow?'

His eyes wandered round the bar, and the cocktail-shakers and the bright nickel rail seemed like old friends.

'At the very latest. But you won't go. I see that. Well, I shall have warned you.'

Clappique felt vaguely grateful (vaguely, not so much because he mistrusted the advice as because he didn't understand it, didn't know what the danger could be).

'Perhaps he's going to pay some attention after all?' the Pole went on; he took him by the arm: 'You must leave. There's a little matter of a ship . . .'

'But I've had no hand in that!'

'You clear off.'

'Can you tell me if old Gisors is suspected?'

'I don't think so. But I'm not so sure about the young one.'

The Pole was certainly well informed. Clappique covered the other man's hand with his own.

'I'm really genuinely sorry I can't raise the money for your grocery business, old chap: it looks as though you are saving my life. . . . But I've still a few odds and ends left; two or three statues. Take them.'

'No. . . .'

'Why not?'

'No.'

'A little secret . . . ? I see. All the same, I should like to know why you won't take my statues.'

Chpilewski looked at him.

'After the way I've lived, how could I do this kind of . . . job, and not recoup myself occasionally?'

'Most jobs have their perquisites, I suppose.'

'Yes. For instance, you'd never imagine how badly the shops are looked after. . . .'

Clappique couldn't see what that had got to do with things, and nearly said so. But he had learnt by experience that remarks which follow up an idea in that particular way are always interesting. And he was desperately anxious to find some way of expressing his thanks to the other man, even if it was only by not interrupting him. Finally his apprehensions got the better of him:

'You mean that you watch the shops?'

He had always regarded the police as a sinister conglomerate of blackmailers and racketeers, a body whose main function was to levy a secret toll upon the opium trade and the gaming-houses. Any police officers with whom he had had dealings (and Chpilewski more than any of them), had always been as much accomplices as enemies. The giving of information to the police, on the other hand, was a thing he loathed and feared. But Chpilewski answered:

'Watch? Well, not exactly. In fact . . . rather the opposite.'

'How's that? You just all take what pickings you can get?'

'It only applies to toys. Nowadays I don't have enough money to buy toys for my little boy. It upsets me very much. All the more because as a matter of fact the only time I feel any affection for the lad is when I'm doing him some sort of . . . kindness. And I don't know any other way. It's very difficult.'

'Well then, why on earth don't you take my statues? Or even just a few of them?'

'Please, please. . . . Well, I go into the shops, and I say . . .'
He threw back his head, and screwed up the left side of his face,

around his monocle; all with the utmost seriousness. ' "I am an inventor. And of course I build to my own designs. I have come to look at your models." They let me have a look. Then I steal one; just one, never more. Sometimes they keep an eye on me, but not often.'

'What would you do if you were caught?'

He took out his pocket-book, and half-opened it. Clappique could see the police badge. He closed it again, with a vague gesture.

'I might have enough money, sometimes. . . . Or I might be thrown into the street. Anything is possible. . . .'

Clappique was amazed; he felt all of a sudden quite respectable and level-headed by comparison. Quite a new sensation, for he never ordinarily accepted responsibility for his actions.

'I must warn young Gisors,' he thought.

Chen was ahead of time, as he walked along the quay with a satchel under his arm, passing one after another the various Europeans whose faces he knew by sight. It was the time of day when they almost all went for a drink and a chat to the Shanghai Club or to the bars of the hotels close by. A hand was laid gently on his shoulder, from behind. He started, and his hand went to the inner pocket where his revolver was hidden.

'It's a very long time since we met, Chen. . . . If we're both walking this way . . .'

He turned round; it was Smithson, the minister, his first teacher. He recognized those fine features immediately; American, but with something of a Red Indian strain in them. And with the ravages of Time all too evident now.

'. . . shall we go together?'

'Yes.'

Chen preferred to walk accompanied by a white; it was safer, and it pleased his sense of irony. His satchel contained a bomb. He was quite conventionally dressed this morning, and it seemed to hamper even his thoughts: the presence of a companion completed the disguise. Finally, a superstitious fear of hurting the good man's feelings. Earlier in the morning he had counted the motors in the street, to find out (according to whether the result was odd or even) if he was going to succeed. It had come out right. He was angry with himself. Why not talk to Smithson, and work off his irritation?

The minister could see that something was wrong, but was at a loss for the reason.

'Aren't you well, Chen?'

'I'm all right.'

He still felt affection for his old teacher, but also a certain bitterness towards him.

The old man slipped his arm through his own.

'I pray for you every day, Chen. What have you found to replace the faith which you abandoned?'

He was looking at him with intense affection, but in no way paternally; as though he sought to approach him on equal terms. Chen hesitated.

'I'm not the sort of person who finds happiness.'

'There are other things than happiness, Chen. There is peace of mind.'

'No. Not for me.'

'For all. . . .'

The minister closed his eyes, and Chen felt as if he were holding the arm of a blind man.

'I don't seek peace of mind. I seek . . . the opposite.'

Smithson looked at him, without slackening his pace.

'Beware of pride.'

'What makes you suppose that I haven't found the faith I seek?'

'What political creed is really aware of the sufferings of the world?'

'Aware of them? I prefer to make some effort to diminish them. Your voice is full of . . . human kindness. I haven't much to say for the sort of kindness which comes from the contemplation of pain.'

'Are you sure that there is any other sort, Chen?'

'Wait: it's difficult to explain. . . . At any rate there's a form which isn't *only* based on that.'

'What political creed can destroy death?'

The words were spoken less as a question than as the sorrowful statement of a fact. Chen was reminded of his talk with Gisors, whom he had not seen since. Gisors had placed his intelligence at *his* disposal, and not just referred everything to God.

'I told you that it wasn't peace that I was looking for.'

'Peace . . .'

The minister was silent. They walked on.

'My poor boy,' he continued at last, 'none of us can appreciate the sufferings of others as we do our own.' His arm was pressing hard against Chen's. 'Don't you think that a truly religious life implies a new conversion every day?'

They were both looking at the pavement, their linked arms alone seeming to keep them in contact with each other. '. . . every day . . .' repeated the minister, with a sort of weary insistence, as though the words were no more than the echo of an obsession. Chen didn't answer. The man was expressing his profoundest convictions, and what he said was true. The minister put his ideas into practice; he was no mere windbag. Under his left arm, the satchel and the bomb; his right held tightly by the arm of his companion: '. . . a new conversion every day . . .' The essential intimacy of the confidence revealed the speaker in an unexpectedly pathetic light. With murder ahead of him, imminent, Chen's emotions were easily aroused.

'I shall pray to God every night, Chen, to deliver you from pride. (It is at night that prayer comes easiest.) God grant that the saving grace of humility may descend upon you. I see now where your salvation lies; your path was hidden from me, and now lies open.'

It was the vision of his suffering, and not his words, which had drawn Chen towards him. That last sentence – the manifest eagerness of the fisherman to land his catch – evoked an anger which gradually gained increasing control, without entirely eliminating a lingering feeling of pity. He had ceased to understand his emotions.

'Listen!' he said. 'In two hours' time I am going to kill a man.'

This time he looked the other man straight in the eyes. Half unconsciously he raised a trembling hand to his face, and clutched at the lapel of his neat new coat.

'Now do you see?'

No. He was alone again now; no one to help him now. His hand dropped from his own coat, and grabbed hold of the other man's collar, as if he were about to shake him. The minister laid his hand on top of it. They remained like that, in the middle of the pavement, quite still, as if about to wrestle with each other; a passer-by stopped. A white, who thought that a dispute was going on.

'It's a vile lie,' said the minister in an undertone.

Chen let his arm fall. He was beyond laughter.

'A lie!' he shouted to the man standing beside them, who shrugged his shoulders and went on. Chen turned on his heel and almost ran from the spot.

At last he found his two comrades, nearly a mile beyond. They looked convincing enough, with their cloven hats and workmen's clothes, chosen with a view to lessening the conspicuousness of the little bags they carried, one of which contained a bomb, and the other hand-grenades. Souen – of the aquiline Chinese type which resembles the Red Indian – was plunged in reflection, didn't seem to notice anything; Pei was looking amazingly young – Chen realized for the first time how extraordinarily young he looked. Perhaps the effect was increased by the horn-rimmed spectacles. They set out, and soon reached the Avenue des Deux-Républiques. All the shops were open; it was coming to life again.

To reach the avenue, Chang Kai Shek's car would come down a narrow street which ran in at right angles. It would slow up at the corner. They would have to keep a look out for it, and throw the bomb when it slowed down. It passed by every day between one o'clock and a quarter past: the general conformed to the European luncheon-hour. The man who kept watch on the side-street would therefore have to warn the other two directly he sighted the car. He would be able to take advantage of the fact that there was an antique dealer's shop right opposite the corner; unless it was in any way connected with the police. Chen proposed to do this job himself. He placed Pei in the avenue, just near where the car would finish turning the corner, before gathering speed again; Souen a little farther on. He himself would give the signal, and throw the first bomb. Unless the car stopped, whether it was hit or not, the two others would then throw their bombs in turn. If it stopped, they were to move nearer: the street was too narrow for it to be able to turn round. But there a hitch might occur: if the bomb missed the car, the guards standing on the running-board would open fire on any one who attempted to approach.

Chen thought it best for them to separate. There were sure to be police-spies in the crowd, all along the route followed by the car. Pei was going to make for a little Chinese bar, from which he could keep a look-out for Chen's signal; farther on, Souen would wait until he saw Pei come out. One of the three would possibly be killed; probably Chen. They didn't dare bid each other farewell. They parted without even a hand-shake.

Chen went into the antique shop and asked to see some of the little bronzes found in excavations. The dealer opened a drawer and took out an almost bewilderingly large handful of little boxes covered in violet satin, emptied them on to the table, so many little square shapes, and began to arrange them. He wasn't a native of Shanghai, but came from northern China or Turkestan. His thin but fluffy moustache and beard, and his slit eyes, were those of a low-caste Mohammedan; likewise his servile mouth. But not the unrelieved flatness of the features, which gave him the appearance of a goat with no bridge to its nose. Any one denouncing a man found with a bomb on the route taken by the general would receive a big reward and acquire considerable prestige among his fellows. And maybe this rich bourgeois was a supporter of Chang Kai Shek.

'Have you been long in Shanghai?' he asked Chen. Who could this strange customer be? His embarrassed, constrained manner and his lack of interest in the objects set out in front of him were disquieting. Perhaps the young man wasn't accustomed to wearing European clothes. He could not help liking Chen's large comfortable lips, in spite of his forbidding profile. Was he the son of some rich peasant in the interior? But the big farmers didn't collect old bronzes. Was he buying them for a European? He wasn't a servant or a dealer, and if he were a collector himself, he was displaying extraordinarily little enthusiasm for the specimens which were being shown to him: he seemed to be thinking of something else.

For Chen was already watching the street. He had a clear view of more than two hundred yards of road. For how long would he have the car in sight? But how could he work that out while this idiot seemed to be taking such an interest in him? He must answer him first. It was ridiculous to go on standing there without saying a word.

'I used to live up-country,' he said. 'I was driven from my home by the war.'

The other man hadn't finished questioning him. Chen felt that he regarded him with suspicion. The dealer began to wonder now whether he wasn't a thief who had come to explore the ground, with the intention of ransacking the shop during the next outbreak of disorder. But the youth didn't ask to see the best pieces. Only bronzes or foxes, and only moderately priced ones. The Japanese like foxes, but this customer wasn't Japanese. He would have to try a few more skilful questions.

'Perhaps you live somewhere in Hupei? Times are very hard in the central provinces, so they say.'

Chen wondered whether to pretend to be deaf. He didn't dare, for fear of appearing even more peculiar.

'I don't live there any more,' was all he said in reply. Even in Chinese, the tone of his voice and his mode of expression gave a certain effect of curtness; he said what he meant, bluntly, without the elaboration of conventional phraseology. It occurred to him to bargain.

'How much?' he asked, pointing at a buckle ornamented with a fox's head – a type which is frequently found in tombs.

'Fifteen dollars.'

'Eight seems a fair price to me. . . .'

'For a piece of that quality? How can you think so . . . ? When I paid ten for it. . . . Fix my profit yourself.'

Instead of answering, Chen was looking at Pei, who was sitting at a little table in his open bar, with the light playing on his spectacles; he probably couldn't see him inside, through the shop-window, but he would see him as he came out.

'I couldn't possibly pay more than nine,' he said at last, as if this were the conclusion to which his reflection had led him. 'And even then I should be going far beyond its value.'

There was a time-honoured ritual for this procedure, with which he was well acquainted.

'This is the first business I have done today,' answered the antique dealer. 'Maybe that I should submit to this small loss of a dollar, for the satisfactory conclusion of the first transaction embarked upon augurs well. . . .'

The street was empty. In the distance, a rickshaw was crossing it. Then another. Two men appeared. A dog. A bicycle.

The men turned off to the right; the rickshaw vanished. It was empty once more – except for the dog. . . .

'Wouldn't you give nine dollars and a half?'

'I wouldn't do it for any one else.'

Another porcelain fox. More bargaining. Chen aroused less suspicion now that he had made a purchase. He had a right to stop and think now: he was considering what price he should offer, what price would correspond accurately to the quality of the piece: he found that there was no interference this time with his honest calculations. 'The car comes down this street at twenty-five miles an hour, nearly half a mile in a minute. I shall have it in view for less than a minute. It's not very much. Pei mustn't take his eyes off this door. . . .' Not a car was passing outside. One or two bicycles. . . . He haggled for a jade belt buckle, refused the dealer's price, and said that he would continue the discussion later. One of the shop-assistants brought some tea. Chen bought a little crystal fox's head, for which the dealer only asked three dollars. The shopkeeper's mistrust had not, however, entirely disappeared.

'I have other pieces, extremely fine and genuine ones, including some very attractive foxes. But they are extremely valuable, and I don't keep them here in the shop. Perhaps we could arrange a meeting?'

Chen didn't say anything.

'I might even send one of my men to fetch them.'

'Valuable pieces don't interest me. I am unfortunately not sufficiently rich.'

So he wasn't a thief; he didn't even ask to see them. The dealer showed him the jade buckle again, handling it as if it were as fragile as a mummy; but despite the words of admiration which came one by one from his lips of gelatinous velvet, despite his covetous eyes, his customer remained aloof and indifferent. . . . It was he, nevertheless, who had chosen that particular buckle. Bargaining, like love, demands cooperation; the dealer might have been in bed with a plank of wood. What was the man buying things for? Suddenly he guessed: he was one of those unfortunate young men who are foolish enough to be seduced by the Japanese prostitutes in Chapei. They have an almost religious passion for foxes. His customer was buying these for some little waitress or pseudo geisha-girl; if he took so little interest in them, it was because he wasn't buying them for himself. (Chen was thinking all the time of the arrival of the car, and the promptness with which he would have to open his satchel, take out the bomb, and throw it.) But geisha-girls don't like the type of things that are excavated. . . . Perhaps they make an exception in the case of foxes? The young man had also bought both crystal and porcelain . . .

Some open, some closed, the minute boxes were spread out on the table. The two assistants were leaning beside them, watching. One of them, a mere boy, had his elbows on Chen's satchel; as he shifted about from one leg to the other, he was dragging it off the table. The bomb was in the right-hand pocket, an inch or two from the edge.

Chen stood rooted to the spot. At last he reached out and pulled the satchel towards him: too simple for words. None of those men had felt death there, or realized that they had been within a hair's-breadth of disaster. It was nothing; only a shop-assistant playing with a satchel and the owner removing it. . . . And suddenly, Chen seemed to find everything extraordinarily easy. Objects, even actions, did not exist any more: all were dreams which fettered him only while he allowed them to do so, and whose spell he could break at will. . . . At that moment, he heard the horn of a motor-car: Chang Kai Shek.

He grabbed the satchel as if it were a weapon, paid, threw the two tiny packages into his pocket, and went out.

The dealer pursued him, with the belt-buckle which he had rejected in his hand.

'Japanese ladies are particularly fond of that kind of jade.'

Was the imbecile going to cling to him for ever?

'I'll come back.'

What shop-keeper is deceived by that formula? The car was approaching, going much faster than usual, so it seemed to Chen, and preceded by the Ford which acted as a guard.

'Go away.'

The car came plunging towards them, bouncing in and out of the gutter, and jolting the two detectives who clung to the running-boards. The Ford passed him. Chen stood still, opened the satchel, and placed his hand on the bomb wrapped up in newspaper inside. The dealer smilingly slipped the buckle into the empty pocket of the satchel. It was the farthest away from him, and as he reached across he prevented Chen from using either of his arms.

'Make your own price.'

'Go away!'

The dealer gaped at Chen in utter amazement.

'Are you sure you aren't ill?' Chen's eyes had ceased to take anything in; he felt on the point of collapse. The car was right in front of him.

He hadn't been able to free himself in time. The dealer thought he was going to faint, and tried to support him. With one blow, Chen beat down the outstretched arms and went off up the street. The dealer stood there writhing with pain. Chen was almost running.

'My buckle!' cried the dealer. 'My buckle!'

It was still inside the satchel. Chen's mind had ceased to function. Every muscle and every nerve was strained, waiting for a crash that would fill the street and lose itself in the clouds that hung low over the town. Nothing came. The car had turned the corner, had probably even passed Souen by now. And that dolt was still there. There was no danger, for everything had failed. What had the others done? Chen began to run. 'Stop, thief!' shouted the dealer. Some shop-keepers appeared. Chen realized what it was all about. In his rage he felt an impulse to run off with the buckle, to throw it away, no matter where. But he was attracting attention. He hurled it straight at the dealer's face, then noticed that the satchel was still open. It had been open ever since the car had gone by, in full view of that imbecile and of any one who was passing, with the bomb showing quite plainly, not even protected by its wrapping, which had slipped out of place. He closed it carefully (it was all he could do to prevent himself from slamming down the fastening; he was struggling desperately to keep his nerves under control). The dealer was already on the way back to his shop, as fast as he could go. Chen went on.

'Well?' he said to Pei when they met.

'What about you?'

They looked at each other breathlessly, each waiting for the other to speak. As Souen approached, he saw them standing there, outlined against a blurred background of houses, hazy in the heat; quite still, struggling to reconcile the conflicting impulses which were passing through them. The light was very strong, despite the clouds, and showed up clearly Chen's good-humoured sparrowhawk profile, and the round bullet-head of Pei; seeming to single out those two, with their trembling hands, firmly planted there with their shadows shortened almost to invisibility at that time of day, amid the restless bustle of the pavement. All three were still carrying their satchels; it was unwise to stay there too long. The restaurants were dangerous. And they had done too much meeting and separating in that street already. Why? Nothing had happened. . . .

'Let's go to Hemmelrich,' said Chen at last.

They plunged into the side-streets.

'What went wrong?' asked Souen.

Chen explained. Pei had felt uneasy when he saw that Chen was not alone as he came out of the antique shop. He had taken up his position a few yards from the corner, ready to throw. The rule in Shanghai is to drive on the left. Usually the car turned very close in to the curb, and Pei had placed himself on the left-hand pavement, so as to be close when he threw. But the car was going fast; the Avenue des Deux-Républiques was almost empty of traffic for the moment. The driver had taken the corner very wide, going right over to the far pavement. And a rickshaw had come in between them.

'So much the worse for the rickshaw,' said Chen. 'There are thousands of other coolies whose lives depend upon the death of Chang Kai Shek.'

'It would have made me miss.'

Souen hadn't thrown his grenades because his comrades' failure to act had made him suppose that the general wasn't in the car.

They walked silently on, between walls which looked flat and colourless beneath that misty yellow sky, sharing their solitude with the refuse on the ground, and the telegraph wires overhead.

'The bombs are perfectly good,' said Chen in an undertone. 'We'll try again later.'

But his two companions had completely lost their nerve; would-be suicides who fail to achieve their object rarely make a second attempt. Their nerves had been keyed up almost to breaking-point, and the anti-climax was equally pronounced. Gradually, bewilderment gave place to despair.

'It's my fault,' said Souen.

Pei repeated:

'It's my fault.'

'That'll do,' said Chen, his patience at an end. He was thinking, as they dragged wearily along. They must find another method next time. That plan was a poor one, but it wasn't easy to improve upon it. He had imagined that. . . . They found themselves at Hemmelrich's.

From the back of his shop Hemmelrich heard a voice talking Chinese, and two others answering. Their seeming uneasiness had attacted his attention. 'Only yesterday,' he thought, 'I saw a couple of blokes hanging round here who looked as sour as if they'd got creeping piles, and who certainly weren't there for their amusement . . .' It was difficult to hear distinctly: the child upstairs was keeping up a steady wail. But the voices stopped and three short shadows striking across the pavement gave a clear indication that there were people there. The police? Hemmelrich got up and walked towards the door, thinking that his flat nose and sagging shoulders, the shoulders of a boxer who has reached the decrepit stage, would scarcely appear very formidable. His hand went to his pocket, but before it reached it he recognized Chen. He left the revolver where it was, and offered the other man his hand to shake instead.

'Let's go through to the back,' said Chen.

They all three filed past Hemmelrich. He looked closely at them as they went by. They were all carrying satchels, and there seemed to be an unnatural constraint about the way they carried them, tightly clasped under their arms.

'Listen,' said Chen, as soon as the door was closed, 'can we take cover here for a few hours? More important still, can our satchels stay here too?'

'Bombs?'

'Yes.'

'No.'

Upstairs, the child was still crying. When the pain was worst its cries became sobs, and at times it made a sort of clucking noise, as if it were trying to amuse itself. That was horrible. The records, the chairs and the cricket, all were so completely unchanged since the night when Chen had come there after the murder of Tang Yen Ta, that Hemmelrich and he were both reminded of it. He said nothing, but Hemmelrich guessed it.

'This isn't a time when I can have bombs here,' he went on. 'If they find bombs here, they'll kill them both, mother and child.'

'All right. We'll go to Shia.' Shia was the lampseller whom Kyo had visited on the evening before the rising. 'There's only the boy there at this time of day.'

'You understand, Chen: the kid's very bad, and his mother's feeling pretty sorry for herself. . . .'

He looked at Chen, and his hands were trembling.

'You've got no idea, Chen, you just can't imagine how lucky you are to be free! . . .'

'Yes, I can.'

The three Chinese went out.

'Oh, my God,' thought Hemmelrich, 'oh, Christ in Heaven, won't things ever be like that for me?' He was cursing quietly to himself, as if he had not the energy for anything more. Then he went slowly up to the room above. His woman was sitting there (she was Chinese), staring at the bed. She didn't turn round.

'The lady was nice today,' said the child; 'she hardly hurt at all. . . .'

'The lady' was May. Hemmelrich remembered what she had said: 'Mastoid . . . My poor fellow, it means breaking the bone . . .' That child, little more than a baby, had just sufficient life in its body to feel pain, and no more. He'd better put it to him. Put what to him? That it was a good plan to have the side of its head broken open? A better plan than dying, to be rewarded by an existence of the same rare utility as its father's? For twenty years he had been saying: 'Bloody marvellous to be young!' How long would it be now before he could say 'Bloody marvellous to be old!' and in these two phrases provide that unfortunate brat with a perfect summary of life? Last month the cat had dislocated a paw, and had to be held while the Chinese veterinary put it back, and the creature howled and struggled. It hadn't understood in the least; he felt that it thought it was being tortured. The cat wasn't like a child; it didn't say: 'He hardly hurt at all . . .' He went downstairs again. The stench of the corpses in the narrow streets outside, close by, was wafted in with a stray beam of sunlight. The dogs were probably already busy with them. 'It's a cheerful world,' he thought.

He couldn't forgive himself for his refusal. Like a man who has confessed secrets under torture, he knew that he would behave in the same way if it happened again, but he couldn't forgive himself for it. He had betrayed his youth, betrayed his aspirations and ideals. But what alternative had he? 'The essential thing was only to want what was within one's power . . .' He only wanted the impossible: to shelter Chen, and to accompany him when he went out. To go out. To requite by no matter what violence, to avenge with bombs the unspeakable horror of the existence which had poisoned him since the day of his birth, and which would poison his children in the same way. That was the worst part. His own suffering he could bear: he was used to it. . . . But not to see a child suffer. 'He has become very intelligent since he has been ill,' May had said. A curious sort of accident . . .

To go out with Chen, take one of the bombs hidden in the satchels, and throw it. There was some sense in that. In his present state it even seemed the only thing which had any sense in it. He was thirty-seven. Still another thirty-seven years to live, maybe. To live on what? On that wretched gramophone-record business (sale or return) which he shared with Lou You Shen, and which didn't provide either of them with a living. And when he was old . . . Thirty-seven. As far back as the memory carries, people say; there was no object in carrying his back: from start to finish, it was the same tale of misery.

He had been a bad pupil at school – absent every other day. His mother used to make him do her work for her, so as to be free to get drunk. Then ceaseless toil as a factory-hand. A thoroughly bad hat; in the army, always under detention. And then the war. Gassed. For whose sake, for whose benefit? For France? He wasn't French, he was just a poor devil. But the war had meant food, anyway. Then he'd been sent to Indo-China, and demobilized there. 'The climate is one unsuited to manual labour . . .' But it was suitable enough for the ravages of dysentery, especially in the case of a known *mauvais sujet*. He had messed things up properly in Shanghai. The bombs, merciful Heaven, give him the bombs!

He had his woman: she was the one thing life had given him. She had been sold for twelve dollars. Abandoned by her purchaser when she ceased to please him, she had come to him, terrified, in the hope of food and sleep. But at first she used to lie awake, expecting him to display the depravity which she had always been led to associate with Europeans. He had been good to her. Gradually recovering from her panic-stricken condition, she had nursed him when he had been ill, worked for him, and borne with his futile outbursts of hatred. She had attached herself to him with the devotion of a blind and miserably ill-treated dog, sensing that his own plight was very similar. And now there was the child. What had he to offer it? Just enough food to keep body and soul together. All that distinguished him from something completely inert was his power to inflict pain. There was more pain in the world than there were stars in the sky, but nothing to equal the pain which he could make that woman endure if he were to abandon her by dying. Like the starving Russian, living almost next door to him, who one day found life as a factory-hand a little more intolerable than he could bear, and committed suicide; and whose wife, mad with anger, had slapped the corpse which was leaving her to her fate; with four children crouching in the corners of the room, and one of them saying: 'Why are you fighting?' . . . It was he who kept the woman and the child alive. But what was that? Less than nothing. With a little money, with something to leave them, then he would have been free to kill himself. Not content with assaulting him, ever since he could remember, with a series of kicks up the backside, fate was now depriving him of his one chance of retaliation, this one means of asserting himself – his death. He shuddered as his nostrils caught the stench of corpses, wafted through the sunlit air with every gust of wind; shuddered involuntarily, though it was familiar enough, with the instinctive revolt of a living creature for decay. But he imbibed it greedily, at once nauseated and assuaged, obsessed by the memory of Chen, by the idea of a comrade *in extremis*, and trying to analyse – as if that could alter things – his subservience to something stronger than shame, friendship, and even what seemed to be his strongest impulses.

*

Once more Chen and his companions thought it best to leave the avenue. The police paid very little attention to the alleys and side-streets which were not on the route of the general. 'We must find another plan,' thought Chen, walking with bowed head and watching his very creditable shoes plodding forward one after the other. Could they run into Chang Kai Shek's car with another one driven in the opposite direction? All cars were liable to be commandeered by the army. To try and use a legation-flag to protect their car was hazardous, for the police knew the chauffeurs who drove the ministerial cars. Could they block the road with a cart? Chang Kai Shek was always preceded by the Ford containing his body-guard. Any obstacle that looked suspicious would mean that the guards and the policemen on the running-boards would fire on whoever tried to approach. Chen suddenly realized that his companions were talking.

'Many of the generals will desert Chang Kai Shek if they see that there's a real danger of their being assassinated,' Pei was saying. 'We are the only ones who have any honour.'

'Yes,' said Souen, 'condemned men's sons are good material for terrorists.'

They both answered to that description.

'And as for the generals who stand their ground,' added Pei, 'even if it turns out that they unite China against us, they'll make a great nation out of her, for they will shed their own blood for her sake.'

'No!' said Chen and Souen, both together. They both real-

169

ized how large a proportion of nationalists the Communist ranks contained, especially among the intellectuals.

Pei used to write, in reviews which were speedily suppressed, stories full of resigned and philosophical bitterness. His last article had begun: 'Observing the financial plight of Imperialism, China humbly craves one final favour of this incubus: that the gold ring which it has driven through her nose may be replaced by a nickel one. . . .' He was also engaged upon the preparation of a sort of terrorist manifesto. For him, Communism alone was really capable of giving new life and vigour to China.

'It's not saving China that I am concerned about,' said Souen; 'it's saving my fellow-sufferers, with or without China. The poor. It's for their sake that I am prepared to die, to kill. For them alone. . . .'

It was Chen who answered:

'As long as we go on trying to find a way of throwing the bomb, we'll still be in a quandary. Too much chance of its going wrong. And something definite must be done today.'

'I can't see any other way of going about it that isn't equally difficult,' said Pei.

'There is a way.'

The low, heavy clouds were keeping pace with them overhead, moving forward with them in the yellowish light, uncertainly, and yet with a suggestion of power that was intensely ominous. Chen had closed his eyes; he could think better like that. But he walked on, and his comrades waited, watching that sweeping profile, which held to its course between the narrow walls no less steadily than usual.

'There is a way. And I think there's only one. Not to throw the bomb at all, but to throw oneself under the car with it.'

On they walked through the wilderness of backyards. No children played there now. They were all three thinking hard.

They were there. Shia's assistant led the way to the back of the shop. They stood quite still for a minute, with their satchels under their arms, surrounded by the lamps; then carefully put them down. Souen and Pei squatted down on the floor, in the Chinese manner.

'Why are you laughing, Chen?'

He wasn't laughing, he was smiling; quite gently, though to Pei's uneasy mind it seemed something very grim. To his amazement, a feeling of complete contentment was gaining possession of him. It was all becoming clear. His anguish of mind had vanished. He understood the distress which was seizing his comrades, despite their courage. However great the danger, to throw bombs was still adventure. But to make up one's mind definitely to die, that was something quite different; the opposite, maybe. He began to walk up and down the room. The back of the shop got no light except that which penetrated from the front part. When the sky was grey – as then – it was filled with a leaden gloom like that which precedes a storm. The light played upon the rotund, bulging hurricane-lamps, like so many rows of question marks hanging upside-down, shining out through the murky penumbra. The eyes of the others followed Chen's shadow uneasily as it passed over their heads, too vague to stand out very clearly.

'Kyo is right: the *hara-kiri* impulse is something that we entirely lack. But the Japanese who kills himself has a very fair chance of becoming a god, which leads to all kinds of half-baked nonsense. No. Man's blood is on his own hands – and there it ought to stay.'

'I prefer to try,' said Souen, '– to try and bring off several *coups*, rather than to make up my mind to confine myself to one because I shall be dead afterwards.'

There was an undercurrent in Chen's words, nevertheless (something in the tone of voice rather than in the meaning: when his emotions were aroused, and he made Chinese their vehicle, his voice throbbed with an extraordinary strength); an undercurrent which Souen strained his ears to catch, and which lured him to an unknown destination.

'It is for me to throw myself under the car,' replied Chen.

Without moving their heads, they followed him with their eyes as he came and went; *he* had ceased to look at *them*. He stumbled over one of the lamps placed on the ground, and steadied himself against the wall. The lamp fell over with a crash of breaking glass. But laughter seemed utterly inappropriate. As he stood up again his shadow was thrown into vague relief above their heads, against the top rows of lamps. Souen was beginning to understand what Chen expected of him: he was still on his guard, though, whether against himself or against what he seemed to see.

'What do you want?'

Chen realized that he didn't know. He felt himself struggling, not so much in order to explain, as to regain his concentration. At last:

'That it shouldn't be wasted.'

'You want Pei and I to promise to follow your example? Is that it?'

'It's not a promise that I'm waiting for. It's something more spontaneous.'

The reflections on the lamps were growing fainter. It was getting darker even in that windowless room: probably there were clouds coming up, outside. Chen was reminded of Gisors: 'When near to death an emotion of that intensity seeks expression, seeks proselytes.' Suddenly, he understood. Souen was beginning to understand too.

'You want to make a kind of religion out of terrorism?'

Chen's exaltation was growing. Words were hollow, ridiculous, quite inadequate to serve his purpose.

'Not a religion. The meaning of life. The . . .'

His hand clutched convulsively, kneading the air, and his thoughts seemed to strain for expression as if he were gasping for breath.

'Complete possession of oneself. Total. Absolute. The only possible key. No more searching, groping after ideals and oughts. This last hour I haven't felt anything of all that was on my mind. You hear that? Nothing.'

His exaltation was reaching such a point that his appeal was becoming no more than a description of his own state of mind.

'I am my own master. None of the qualms and conflict which normally unbalance me. But under control, held fast, held tight, like that hand holds the other' – he was gripping it with all his force – 'that doesn't do.'

He picked up one of the pieces of broken glass from the lamp. A broad triangular splinter, catching the light as he moved it. In a flash he had jabbed it into his leg. His words came jerkily, but the voice rang with an exultant confidence; it seemed that he made his infatuation do his bidding, rather than that he was a prey to it. There was no madness in him whatsoever. The two others could scarcely see him in the gloom, and yet he dominated the whole room. Souen began to be alarmed.

'I'm not as intelligent as you, Chen, but . . . it wouldn't suit me. I saw my father hung up by his hands and beaten across the stomach with a cane, to make him confess where his master had hidden the money which he hadn't got. I fight for the party, not for myself.'

'You couldn't serve the party better than by making up your mind to die. There's no one comparable in usefulness to the man who makes that decision. If we had made it, we should have got Chang Kai Shek just now. You know that.'

'I dare say it's necessary in your case. I don't know.' He was struggling desperately to get things clear. 'If I agreed with that, you see, I should feel that it wasn't the party that I was dying for, but . . .'

'But?'

The feeble afternoon light still lingered, as to be almost imperceptible, but never quite disappearing. Eternal.

'You.'

A strong smell of petrol reminded Chen of the cans used to fire the police station on the first day of the rising. But everything was fading into the past; even Souen, since he would not follow his lead. There was one desire, however, which he had no wish to stifle in his present mood – the organization of this band of avenging judges. The birth of this idea, like all births, racked him and exalted him at the same time: and was stronger than him. The presence of the others had become intolerable. He got up.

'You're a writer,' he said to Pei, 'you can explain.'

They took up their satchels again. Pei was wiping his glasses. Chen pulled up his trouser-leg and bandaged the wound in his thigh with a handkerchief, without washing it. (Why bother? It wouldn't have time to get infected.) They went out. 'How one's actions repeat themselves!' he said to himself, discomposed, thinking of the knife which he had stuck into his arm.

'I'll go off on my own,' he said. 'And there won't be any bungling tonight, either.'

'I shall try and organize something, all the same,' replied Souen.

'It will be too late.'

Outside the shop, Chen went off to the left. Pei began to follow him: Souen stood still. He went on. Pei still followed. Chen looked at him – spectacles in hand, very young; far more natural, that baby-face, without glasses in front of its eyes. He saw that he was crying to himself.

'Where are you going?'

'I'm coming with you.'

Chen stood still. He had always imagined that he took the same view as Souen. He pointed in his direction.

'I'll go with you,' replied Pei.

He was trying to say as little as possible; his voice sounded odd, and his Adam's apple worked up and down as he stifled his sobs.

'Prove it first.'

His fingers dug into Pei's arms.

'I want proof,' he repeated.

He moved away. Pei remained on the pavement, his mouth hanging open, still wiping his glasses, looking ridiculous. He could never have believed that it was possible to feel so lonely.

Clappique had expected to find Kyo at home, but he wasn't there. In the large room downstairs the carpet was strewn with drawings which were being collected by one of Gisors' disciples in a kimono. The old man himself was talking with his brother-in-law: Kama, the painter.

'Good afternoon, old chap. Marvellous to see you!'

He sat down, entirely at his ease.

'It's a pity your son isn't here.'

'Would you like to wait for him?'

'Let's try. I am quite unusually anxious to see him. What's that new little c-cactus, under the opium-table? Your collection is coming on. Charming, my dear fellow, charr-ming! I must buy one. Where did you find it?'

'It was given to me. It was sent to me only a couple of hours ago.'

Clappique was reading the Chinese characters traced on the flat stake which supported it. One large one: Faith; three little ones, and a signature: Chen Ta Eul.

'Chen Ta Eul . . . Chen . . . don't know him. Pity. There's a fellow who knows a good cactus when he sees one.'

He remembered that he had got to leave by the next day. He must find the money, and not worry about buying cactuses. No chance of selling any antiques quickly now that the town was under military occupation. His friends were poor. And Ferral never let people touch him for a loan on any pretext. He had authorized him to buy some of Kama's wash-drawings, when the Japanese artist arrived, but that only meant twenty or thirty dollars commission.

'Kyo should be here,' said Gisors. 'He had a lot of engagements today.'

'Maybe he'd do better to give them a miss,' growled Clappique.

He didn't dare say any more. He didn't know to what extent Gisors was aware of his son's activities. But the complete silence which greeted his remark was in the nature of a snub.

'It's a matter of great importance, I may say.'

'For me everything which concerns Kyo is important.'

'You can't suggest any way of earning or coming by four or five hundred dollars, immediately?'

Gisors smiled sadly. Clappique knew that he was a poor man; and his works of art, even if he had been prepared to sell them . . .

'Well, then, let's make sure of the pocket money,' thought the baron. He went over to the drawings that littered the divan. Though discriminating enough to avoid judging traditional Japanese art from the point of view of its relation to Picasso or Cézanne, he had no use for it at all just then; a hunted man does not greatly appreciate serenity. Lights buried in the mountains, village streets melting in the rain, cranes flapping their way over the snow – all that world where the road to happiness was paved with melancholy. Clappique visualized only too easily the paradise beyond the threshold of which he must not pass, and found the vision tantalizing.

'The loveliest woman in the world,' he said, 'naked, ardent; but wearing a chastity belt. Ferral's line, not mine.'

He picked out four of them, and the disciple took down the address.

'It is because you are thinking of *our* art,' said Gisors, 'which serves quite a different purpose.'

'Why do you paint, Kama San?'

The old teacher was also wearing a kimono. (Gisors was still in his dressing-gown; Clappique alone was wearing trousers.)

A highlight played across his bald head. He was looking at Clappique with curiosity.

The disciple laid the drawings aside, translated the question, and answered:

'The master says: "In the first place, for my wife, because I love her."'

'I don't mean for whom, but for what reason?'

'The master says that it is difficult to explain. He says: "When I went to Europe, I visited the museums. The more apples your artists paint, the more they are talked about. Even when they produce work which does not represent anything at all. For me, it is reality which counts."'

Kama added something. His expression was that of a benign old lady; almost imperceptibly, it grew even gentler.

'The master says: "That which we call art, would be a form of charity for you."'

A second disciple brought in little bowls of *saki* from the kitchen, then withdrew. Kama spoke again.

'The master says that if he were to cease to paint it would be as though blindness had come upon him. More than that, isolation.'

'One moment!' said the baron, one eye open and the other closed: finger levelled. 'If a doctor said to you: "You are suffering from an incurable disease, and you have only three months to live," would you still go on painting then?'

'The master says that if he knew that he was about to die, he thinks that he would paint better; but in the same manner.'

'Why better?' asked Gisors.

His thoughts were still with Kyo. Clappique's words as he came in were sufficient to make him uneasy: at a time like that, to remain unmoved amounted almost to an insult.

Kama answered. Gisors translated himself:

'There are two smiles – my wife's and my daughter's – which I should realize then that I should never see again, and I should come nearer to understanding grief. The world is like the characters of our alphabet. Just as the character does no more than portray the actual flower, so this drawing' – pointing to one of them – 'represents something else. Everything is a question of symbols. To progress from the symbol to the thing symbolized is to penetrate from the crust to the kernel, to approach God. He thinks that the approach of death ... Wait.'

He questioned Kama afresh, then resumed his translation:

'Yes, that's it. He thinks that the approach of death would infuse all he did with a new intensity, with such a feeling of sadness that the objects which he painted would all become living symbols, revealing their significance and their mystery to the understanding.'

Clappique experienced the intolerable sensation of suffering in the presence of some one who denies the existence of suffering. He was listening carefully, looking all the time at Kama's benignly ascetic face, while Gisors translated: standing there with his elbows pressed to his sides, and his hands joined. It only needed an expression of intelligence in the face for him to look like a dejected monkey, shivering in the cold.

'Maybe that's not the right way of putting the question,' said Gisors.

He added a few words in Japanese. Up to that point Kama had answered almost at once. This time he thought for a minute.

'What was the question that you asked him just now?' said Clappique, in an undertone.

'What he would do if the doctor told his wife she was going to die?'

'The master says he would not believe the doctor.'

The disciple from the kitchen reappeared, and removed the little bowls, on a tray. The European clothes, the smile, the gestures, which his state of ecstasy exaggerated, even the deference; everything about him seemed strange, even to Gisors. Kama muttered something, which the other disciple didn't translate.

'In Japan the young disciples never drink wine,' said Gisors. 'He is upset because this young man is drunk.'

His eyes grew vacant; the outer door opened. Steps sounded. But it wasn't Kyo. His eyes focused again, meeting Kama's firmly.

'And if she were dead?'

Would he have pursued the conversation with a European? Perhaps not. But the old painter belonged to another world. Before replying he smiled slowly and sadly, more with the eyes than the lips.

'Even death is not an insuperable barrier: it makes communion in the highest degree difficult, but perhaps that is the nature of life . . .'

He was taking his leave as he spoke; returning to his room, followed by the disciple. Clappique sat down.

'Sh! . . . Remarkable, old chap, r-remarkable! He slipped away like a well-behaved ghost. Young ghosts, I may say, are by no means well behaved these days: in fact the old ones have the greatest difficulty in teaching them to frighten people, for there's no language that they understand; all they can do is to cheep feebly! Which . . .'

He stopped; the door-knocker again. Through the silence came the resonant tinkle of a guitar. Soon the notes took definite shape, became a slow cascade of sound, growing in volume as they fell, until the long-drawn-out throbs faded away into the eternal background of silence.

'Playing the guitar is invariably his method of taking his mind off something which is worrying him: his protective mechanism, when he is away from Japan. When he came back from Europe, he told me: "Now I know that I can regain my peace of mind, no matter where I may be." '

'Is that more than a pretence?'

Clappique hardly realized that he had asked the question; he was listening. Coming at this moment, when his life was perhaps in danger (although it was seldom that he was sufficiently interested in himself to feel himself really in danger), those pure notes increased his distress, rekindling the love of music which had possessed him in his youth; then recalling the youth itself, and all its vanished happiness.

Once more the sound of a footstep; there was Kyo in the doorway.

He led Clappique into his room. Divan, chair, desk, and white walls: conscious asceticism. It was hot inside; Kyo threw his coat on to the divan, remaining in his pullover.

'Listen,' said Clappique. 'I've just received a l-little tip which you'd do well to take very seriously; unless we're out of here by tomorrow night, we are as good as dead.'

'Where did you get it from? The police?'

'Good guess. We'd better leave it at that, don't you think? But it's genuine right enough. The boat episode has been discovered. Don't lose your head, but clear out within the next forty-eight hours.'

It was on the tip of Kyo's tongue to say: 'There's nothing criminal in that now that we have come out on top.' But he remained silent. He was too well prepared for the repression of the workers' movement to feel any surprise. The break must have come, though Clappique couldn't guess that; and if they were after Clappique, it was because it was the Communists who had captured the *Shan Tung*, and he would be supposed to be working with them.

'What are you going to do, do you suppose?' Clappique went on.

'Before anything else, think it over.'

'A most perspicacious idea! And have you got any cash to get away with?'

Kyo smiled, and shrugged his shoulders.

'I don't intend to try and get away – not that your news isn't of the greatest importance for me,' he continued after a moment.

'You don't intend to go! You prefer to wait and have your throat cut?'

'Perhaps. But you must want to get away?'

'Why should I stay?'

'How much do you need?'

'Three or four hundred . . .'

'Perhaps I can give you part of it? I should like to be of some use to you. But don't imagine that this is my way of repaying you for what you've just done for me.'

Clappique smiled sadly. He was in no way deceived by Kyo's tactfulness, but he appreciated it.

'Where will you be tonight?' Kyo continued.

'Wherever you like.'

'Suggest somewhere.'

'Let's say the Black Cat. I must scrape something together, the b-best way I can.'

'All right: it's one of the "joints" inside the Concessions, so there won't be any Chinese police. And there's less danger of being kidnapped than here, even; too many people. I'll be there between eleven and half past. Not later. I've something else on hand then . . .'

Clappique looked away.

'. . . which I am not going to miss on any account. You're sure the Cat won't be shut?'

'Never heard anything so fantastic. It will be full of Chang Kai Shek's officers; whirling round the floor with their gorgeous uniforms twined around the bodies of their wantons, becomingly garlanded; am I not right? Very well then. I'll wait for you until eleven-thirty, giving this indispensable, if otiose spectacle my entire attention.'

'Do you think you could get more information by to-night?'

'I'll try.'

'It might be of the greatest service to me. Greater than you can imagine. And I am actually mentioned by name?'

'Yes.'

'And my father too?'

'No, or I would have warned him. He wasn't in any way involved in the *Shan-Tung* affair.'

Kyo knew that it wasn't the *Shan-Tung* which had to be considered, but the repression. May? She had played too unimportant a part to make it necessary to question Clappique. As for his companions, if *he* was threatened, so were they all.

'Thank you.'

They went back to the phoenix-room together. May was saying to Gisors:

'It's very difficult: if the Women's Union grants divorce to women who are ill-treated, the husbands will leave the revolutionary union; and if we don't, they will lose all confidence in us. And they'll be quite right.'

'As far as organizing goes,' said Kyo, 'I'm afraid it's either too early or too late.'

Clappique was on his way out, paying no attention.

'Display your characteristic generosity,' he said to Gisors: 'give me your cac-tuss.'

'I have a particular affection for the young man who sent it to me. Any of the others, with pleasure . . .'

It was a small, hairy one.

'Can't be helped, then.'.

'I'll see you again soon.'

'Yes . . . well, perhaps. Good-bye, old chap. Good-bye from the one man in Shanghai who doesn't exist; who just isn't real!'

He went out.

May and Gisors were looking at Kyo in dismay. He explained:

'He has learnt from the police that I'm on their list; he advises me not to show myself outside here in the meantime, and to clear out altogether within two days. And the repression may come any time. The last of the First Division have left the city now.'

That was the only division on which the Communists could

rely. Chang Kai Shek knew it, and he had ordered the general in command to take his men back to the front. The general had asked the communist Executive if he should arrest Chang Kai Shek. They had advised him to try and gain time, to pretend to be ill; but he had soon found himself faced with an ultimatum. Finally, not daring to fight without the consent of the party, he had left the town, contenting himself with trying to leave a few troops behind. They in their turn had just left.

'They haven't got very far yet,' Kyo continued; 'and the whole division may even return, if we hold the city long enough.'

The door opened again, a nose peered in, and a sepulchral voice said: 'Baron Clappique does not exist.'

The door shut.

'No news from Hankow?' asked Kyo.

'None.'

Since his return he had been organizing Shock Sections to fight Chang Kai Shek, just like those he had organized to fight the Northerners. The International had rejected any idea of actual hostilities, but approved of the retention of the Communist shock troops. In the new combatant detachments Kyo hoped to find a means of controlling the masses which poured into the Unions every day now. But the official Chinese Communist party completely tied his hands with their speeches, and their agitation for union with the Kuomintang. The Military Committee alone had supported him. All the arms hadn't been given up, but that very day Chang Kai Shek had insisted that the Communists surrender those still in their possession. Kyo and the Military Committee had sent a final appeal to Hankow.

Old Gisors was worried. (He was in no doubt – this time – as to what was going on.) Marxism seemed to his mind something too inevitable for him to do anything but mistrust attempts to force the issue. He was just as sure as Kyo that Chang Kai Shek would try and crush the Communists: and like Kyo he thought that the murder of the general would have struck at the reaction in its most vulnerable spot. But he detested the element of intrigue which for the moment characterized their activities. The death of Chang Kai Shek, even the seizure of the Shanghai Government, was a gamble. In common with other members of the International, he favoured the return to Canton of both the Iron Army and the small Communist element in the Kuomintang; there, with a genuinely revolutionary town behind them and a well-equipped arsenal at their disposal, the Reds could build up a really strong position and wait until the moment was ripe for a fresh attack on the north. A moment which would be brought very much nearer by the impending reaction. The Hankow generals were eager for lands to conquer, but by no means eager to enter southern China, where the Unions which remained faithful to the memory of Sun Yat Sen would force them into a long-drawn and utterly unprofitable guerrilla war. Instead of having to fight first the Northerners, then Chang Kai Shek, the Red army would in this way leave the two of them to fight each other. And whichever of them had to be faced subsequently as an enemy at Canton, would be greatly weakened.

'They are like so many donkeys,' said Gisors, referring to the generals, 'too fascinated by their carrot to bite us just now, unless we should stand between it and them.'

But the majority of the Chinese Communist party, and probably Moscow too, found this point of view rather too good to be true.

Like his father, Kyo thought that falling back on Canton was the best policy. He would have liked to go further, and start intensive propaganda for the mass emigration of the Shanghai workers to Canton. (They had nothing to leave behind them.) It would be very difficult, but not impossible: provided the southern provinces could be relied on for marketing their goods, the flood of new workers would industrialize Canton very rapidly. But it would prove a dangerous policy for Shanghai: workers in cotton mills are more or less skilled,

and training new ones would be producing new revolutionaries, unless wages were raised. A hypothesis, as Ferral would
have said, 'which cannot be entertained while the conditions
of Chinese industry remain as at present constituted'. Filling up
Canton at the expense of Shanghai, as had been done at Hong-
Kong's expense in 1925. But Hong-Kong is only five hours
from Canton, and Shanghai five days; it would be a difficult
undertaking, more difficult perhaps than letting themselves be
killed; but less stupid.

Since his return from Hankow, he was convinced that reaction was on the way; even without Clappique's warning he
realized that if the Communists were attacked by Chang Kai
Shek their situation would be so desperate that anything else
that could happen, even the murder of the general (whatever
its consequences), would tend to relieve it. If the Unions were
armed, they could try and give battle to a disorganized army
with some faint hope of success.

The bell again. Kyo ran to the door: an answer had come
from Hankow at last. His father and May watched him return.
They didn't speak.

'Orders to bury the arms,' he said.

He had torn the message up, and crumpled it into a ball in the
hollow of his hand. He took the fragments, spread them out on
the table, pieced them together, and shrugged his shoulders at
his childishness: the order was clear – to hide or bury the arms.

'I must go along at once.'

'Along' meant the Central Committee. So he would have
to leave the Concessions. Gisors knew that there was nothing
he could say. His son was risking death. Well, it was not the
first time: it was that which gave his life a meaning. It must be
his lot to suffer in silence. He took Clappique's warning very
seriously. In Pekin Clappique had once saved the life of
König, the German who was now in charge of Chang Kai
Shek's police force, by warning him of the impending massacre
of the cadet corps to which he belonged. Gisors didn't know

Chpilewski. As Kyo's eyes met his own, he tried to smile: Kyo did the same, and they remained staring at each other; they both knew that they were trying to deceive each other, and that this pretence was something very intimate and precious.

Kyo went back to his room, where he had left his coat. May started to put on hers.

'Where are you going?'

'With you, Kyo.'

'What for?'

There was no reply.

'We shall be more easily recognized together than separately,' he said.

'I don't see why. If you're on their list, nothing is going to make any difference. . . .'

'You can't do any good.'

'What good should I do waiting here? Men don't know what waiting is like.'

He walked a few steps, then stopped and turned towards her.

'Listen, May: when it was a question of your freedom, I gave it you.'

She knew what he was alluding to, and it frightened her: she had forgotten it. She was right, for he went on, dully this time:

'. . . and you took advantage of it all right. Now it's mine that is involved.'

'But, Kyo, what has that got to do with it?'

'To recognize some one else's right to liberty is to acknowledge that that is more important than one's own suffering: I know that from experience.'

'Am I just "some one else", Kyo?'

He remained silent. Yes, at that moment, she was. A change had taken place in their relations.

'You mean that because I . . . well, because of that, in future we can't even face danger together? Think, Kyo: one would almost imagine this was a kind of revenge.'

'Not to be able to any more and to try to when it's useless are quite different things.'

'But if it rankled as much as that, you could perfectly well have taken a mistress. At least, no: that's not true. Why do I say that? I didn't take a lover, I just went to bed with somebody. It's not the same thing, and you know quite well that you can sleep with any one you want.'

'I'm satisfied with you,' he answered bitterly.

May was rather puzzled by the way he looked at her. Every possible feeling seemed to enter into his expression. What made her feel really uneasy was the quite unconscious lust which was apparent in his face.

'As far as that goes,' he went on, 'my feelings are the same now as they were a fortnight ago: I just don't want to. I'm not saying that you are wrong, but that I want to go alone. You acknowledge my liberty; you possess the same degree of liberty yourself. Liberty to do what *you* please. Liberty isn't a bargain, it's just liberty.'

'It's a desertion.'

Silence.

'What is it that brings people who love each other to face death, unless it is that they can face it together?'

She guessed that he was going to leave without further argument, and placed herself in front of the door.

'You shouldn't have given me this liberty, if we have to be separated now as a result.'

'You certainly didn't ask for it.'

'You had already given it me.'

'You shouldn't have believed me,' he thought. It was true, he had always given it. But that she should discuss rights now, that widened the gulf between them.

'There are some rights which one only grants,' she said bitterly, 'so that they shall not be used.'

'If they had only been granted so that you could hang on to them at this moment, it wouldn't be so bad. . . .'

In that second they were drawing even farther apart than in death. Eyelids, mouth, temples, a dead woman's face still shows the site of every caress, whereas those high cheekbones and elongated eyelids which confronted him then belonged to a foreign world. The wounds of the deepest love suffice to create a thorough hatred. Was she so near death that she was recoiling from the animosity which she had seen preparing? She said:

'I'm not hanging on to anything, Kyo. Say I am making a mistake if you like, that I've already made one; say what you please, but just at this moment I want to go with you; now, at once. I beg you.'

He didn't answer.

'If you didn't love me,' she went on, 'you wouldn't think twice about letting me come. Well then? Why cause us unnecessary suffering?'

'As if this were a good time to choose,' she added wearily.

Kyo felt the old familiar devils beginning to stir within him, and was more than a little disgusted. He felt a desire to strike her, to strike right at her love for him. She was right: if he hadn't loved her, what would her death have mattered to him? Perhaps it was the way she forced him to realize this, at that particular moment, which was mainly responsible for his resentment.

Was she going to cry, looking like that? She had closed her eyes and the ceaseless, silent trembling of her shoulders, contrasted with the mask-like rigidity of her features, expressed utter misery. It was not only his intransigence which separated them now, but her grief. But if grief separates, the sight of grief unites, and as he watched her eyebrows slowly climbing – almost as though some marvel had aroused her admiration – he felt drawn to her again. The movement ceased and the tense face and lowered eyelids suddenly combined to give her the appearance of a corpse.

He knew her changes of expression so well that they often left him quite unmoved; he always had a slight feeling that she

188

was imitating herself. But this death mask was something he had never seen before – eyes heavy, not with sleep, but with pain – and death was so near that the illusion had almost the significance of a dire omen. She reopened her eyes, but did not look at him: she was staring blankly at the white walls of the room. Without a muscle moving, a tear trickled down the side of her nose and remained suspended at the corner of her mouth, a dumb symbol of the life within, poignant as pain in an animal, belying the inhumanity of that mask, again as dead as it had been a moment before.

'Open your eyes.'

She looked at him.

'They are open.'

'You made me think you were dead.'

'Well?'

She shrugged her shoulders; then, in a voice broken with utter weariness:

'If I were going to die, I should expect you to come with me.'

He understood now what it really was that he felt: he wanted to console her. But he could only console her by allowing her to accompany him. She had closed her eyes again. He took her in his arms and kissed her eyes. Then, when they separated:

'Are we going?' she asked.

'No.'

Too honest to hide her impulses, she reiterated her desires with a cat-like persistence which often exasperated Kyo. She had moved away from the door, but he realized that all the time he had wanted to pass through he had been sure that he wouldn't really do it.

'May, are we just going to leave each other quite suddenly like this?'

'Have I behaved like a woman who expects protection?'

They stood there face to face, not knowing what else to say, and not content to remain silent, conscious at once that that moment was one of the most solemn of their lives, and that it could not endure – that time was already corrupting it: Kyo's place was not there, but with the Committee, and a certain impatience lurked all the time at the back of his mind.

She nodded towards the door.

He looked at her, took her head between his hands and drew it gently towards him, without kissing her; as though in that firm embrace he had somehow projected all the mingled tenderness and ardour of which masculine love is capable. At last he withdrew his hands.

The doors shut, one after the other. May continued to listen, as if she were expecting to hear a third one close, brought into existence by her imagination. Her mouth hanging limply open, wild with grief, she was beginning to realize that if she had signed to him to leave, it was because she saw in that movement the one final hope of persuading him to take her with him.

*

Kyo had scarcely gone any distance when he met Katow.

'Isn't Chen there?'

He pointed towards Kyo's house.

'No.'

'You've abs'lutely no idea where he is?'

'No. Why?'

Katow seemed calm enough, but looked as though he had a headache.

'Chang Kai Shek has more than one car. Chen doesn't know that. Either the police have been warned or else they're s'picious. Unless he's warned he'll probably pick the wrong one and waste his bombs. I've been chasing him for a long while, you know. The bombs were to have been thrown at one o'clock. Nothing happened: we'd have known about it.

'He was supposed to do it in the Avenue des Deux-Républiques. The best thing to do would be to go and see Hemmelrich.'

Katow set off immediately.

'Got your cyanide?' Kyo asked him as he turned away.

'Yes.'

Like several of the other revolutionary leaders, they both carried cyanide in the flat buckle of their belts which opened like a box.

Parting had not relieved Kyo's distress. The reverse was the case: May seemed all the stronger in this deserted street – after yielding to him – than when she had been fighting him face to face. He entered the Chinese town, aware of the fact, but quite indifferent to it. 'Have I behaved like a woman who needs protection?' What right had he to extend his pitiable protection to this woman who had submitted even to his leaving her? *Why* was he leaving her? Was it perhaps a kind of vengeance? No doubt May was still sitting on the bed, broken by a despair which no reasoning could alleviate.

He turned and ran back.

The phoenix-room was empty: his father had gone out, May was still where he had left her. He stopped in front of the door, overwhelmed by a feeling of the friendliness of death, and yet conscious of how, despite its fascination, his body recoiled grimly before the unnaturalness of the contact. He understood now that to be willing to lead the woman he loved to her death was perhaps love in its most complete form, the love beyond which nothing can go.

He opened the door.

Without a word she hurriedly threw her cloak around her shoulders, and followed him out.

3.15 P.M.

Hemmelrich had been sitting looking at his records for a long while. No customers. There was a knock at the door: the secret knock.

He opened it. Katow.

'Have you seen Chen?'

'He's looking for his coffin!' groaned Hemmelrich.

'What?'

'Nothing. Yes, I've seen him. Between one and two o'clock. What's the idea?'

'I abs'lutely must see him. What did he say?'

From another room came the sound of the child crying, followed by the indistinguishable words of the mother attempting to calm him.

'He came with two other blokes. Friends of his. One of them's called Souen. Don't know the other. Chap with glasses, quite ordinary-looking. Looked a bit of a toff. All carrying little cases: you get me?'

'That's why I've got to get hold of him, you see.'

'He asked me, could he stay here for three hours?'

'Oh, good! Where is he?'

'Shut up! Listen to what's said to you. He asked me if he could stay here for three hours. I wasn't having any. D'you understand?'

Silence.

'I said I wasn't having any.'

'Where can he have gone?'

'He didn't say. Like you. There's a lot of silence about today. . . .'

Hemmelrich was standing in the middle of the room, all hunched up, looking almost baleful. Katow said quietly, without looking at him:

'Why all this abuse? I suppose you're trying to get some of it given back to you, so that you can stick up for yourself?'

'What do you know about it? And what the hell has it got to do with you, anyway? Don't stand there looking at me with your hair up on end like a cockscomb and your hands spread out like Christ waiting to be crucified.'

Katow placed the offending hand on Hemmelrich's shoulder.

'Are things any better upstairs?'

'Not much. Still quite bad enough. Poor kid! With his skinny body and big head he looks like a flayed rabbit. . . . Leave go.'

The Belgian wrenched himself roughly away, stood still for a moment, then moved towards the far end of the room: the effect was oddly childish, as if he were sulking.

'And that's not the worst of it,' he said. 'Don't look so self-conscious, and stop wriggling about as though you'd got lice all over you. It's all right, I haven't given Chen's name to the police. Not yet, at least.'

Katow shrugged his shoulders sadly.

'You'd better explain.'

'I wanted to go with him.'

'With Chen?'

Now Katow was sure that he wouldn't ever be able to find him. He spoke with the weary calm of some one who has met defeat. Chang Kai Shek wouldn't return before night, and Chen could attempt nothing before then.

Hemmelrich jerked his thumb over his shoulder in the direction from which the child's cry had come.

'And there you are. There you are. What the blazes do you expect me to do?'

'Wait. . . .'

'Wait till the kid dies, eh? Listen to me. Half the time, that's what I want. But if it really happens, I shall want to keep him; even sick, even an invalid, *I shan't want him to die.*'

'I know.'

'What,' said Hemmelrich, feeling his effect spoilt. 'What do you know about it? You aren't even married?'

'I used to be.'

'I should like to have seen it. The way you look. . . . No, that's not our line, all those grand little tarts you see on parade in the streets.'

He felt that Katow was thinking of the woman watching over the child upstairs.

'Devotion, yes. She does everything she can. The rest, all that she just hasn't got – that's what the rich get. When I see people looking as if they loved each other, I feel as if I'd like to smash their faces in.'

'D'votion means a good deal. . . . The one essential thing is not to be alone.'

'And is that why you're staying here? To help me out?'

'Yes.'

'Out of pity.'

'Not pity. Out of . . . '

Katow couldn't find the word. Maybe it didn't exist. He tried to find a way to explain.

'Something very like it. I've also felt your kind of . . . mad excitement. How can one ever understand anything unless one has experienced it oneself. That's why I put up with you, without getting annoyed.'

He had come close, his head sunk between his shoulders, and as he spoke he swallowed half his words, glancing at him out of the corner of his eye. With their heads lowered like that, one opposite the other, they looked as though they were about to start a fight – in the middle of the gramophone-records. But Katow knew that he was the stronger, even if he didn't know in what way. Perhaps it was his voice, his calmness, even his friendliness which was the deciding factor?

'When a man who doesn't give a damn about anything meets genuine d'votion or sacrifice, or something in that line, he's done for.'

'Just think of that! Then what is he to do?'

'Become a sadist,' replied Katow, looking at him quietly.

The cricket chirped. In the street, the sound of footsteps, growing gradually fainter.

'Sadism with actual pins,' he went on, 'is very rare; with words, common enough. But if the woman resigns herself abs'lutely, if she is capable of surmounting that. . . . I once knew a fellow who took all the money his woman had spent years saving up, so as she could get to a sanatorium, and gambled with it. A matter of life or death. He lost it. (One always loses on those occasions.) He came back abs'lutely shattered, all broken up like you now. She watched him from the bed as he came in. And she understood at once. And what do you think happened then? She tried to cheer him up.'

'It's easier to cheer up other people,' said Hemmelrich slowly, 'than oneself.' Then, suddenly looking up:

'Were you the fellow?'

'That'll do!' Katow crashed his fist on to the counter. 'I should say so if it was, and not pretend it was some one else.' But his anger quickly faded away. 'I haven't gone that far; there's no need to go that far. If one has no beliefs, just for that very reason real genuine feeling forces one to respect it, every time. That's only natural. And that's what you're doing. If it wasn't for the woman and the kid you wouldn't be here. I'm sure of that. Well, then?'

'And as those deep-felt emotions are what really make things worth while, you rub along somehow. Since you have to get your teeth into something, why not them? But that's all bunk, anyway. It's not a matter of being right or wrong. I can't bear the thought of having kicked Chen out, and I shouldn't have been able to bear having him here either.'

'None of us ought to be asked to do things we can't be expected to do. I want comrades, not saints. Don't trust saints.'

'Is it true that you once went with some of them to the lead mines, voluntarily?'

'I was in the camp,' said Katow constrainedly, 'mines or camp, it's much the same thing.'

'Much the same thing? Nonsense!'

'What do you know about it?'

'It's absurd. And so you'd have allowed Chen to stay?'

'*I've* no children.'

'I feel I shouldn't mind even the idea of his being killed quite so much, if only he wasn't ill. . . . I'm a fool. I'm a damned fool. And I'm not sure that I'm much good at work, even. How will it end? I'm a sort of lamp-post, with everything that's at a loose end coming and widdling over it.'

Once more he nodded towards the floor above, for the child was crying again. Katow didn't dare to say: 'Death will put it right.' It was death that had put it right for him. Since Hemmelrich had started to speak, the memory of his wife stood between them. When he returned from Siberia, hope gone, crushed, his medical studies disorganized beyond repair, fallen into the position of a factory-hand and convinced that he would die before seeing the revolution, he had realized dolefully that he was still vaguely attached to life by making existence miserable for a little working-girl who was in love with him. But no sooner had she grown inured to the suffering which he inflicted on her, than the realization of the amazing tenderness of the creature which suffers for the being by whom the suffering is imposed, had overwhelmed him. From that moment he had devoted himself to her completely, continuing his revolutionary activities as a matter of habit – but with his mind obsessed by the boundless devotion hidden in the heart of that simple-minded girl; he would stroke her hair for hours on end, and they would spend entire days in bed together. She had died, and since then. . . . But that was between himself and Hemmelrich.

He found words almost entirely ineffective; but in addition to words, there was all that could be conveyed by gestures, changes of expression, mere physical presence. He knew from experience that the hardest part of suffering to bear is the loneliness which accompanies it. Its communication brings relief, too; but there are few lacunae in the vocabulary of man so complete as that which profound grief brings to light. If he expressed himself badly, or if he lied, Hemmelrich would lacerate himself still further: his suffering was mainly due to himself.

Katow looked at him sadly, as discreetly as possible; and once more he was struck by the paucity and clumsiness of the ways by which the affection of one man for another expresses itself.

'I hope you'll understand without my trying to explain,' he said. 'There's nothing I can say.'

Hemmelrich raised his hand and then let it fall heavily, as if unable to decide between the misery and the absurdity of his life. But as he faced Katow there, he seemed overcome with emotion.

'Soon I shall be able to continue the search for Chen,' thought Katow.

6 P.M.

'The money was paid over yesterday,' said Ferral to the colonel, who was in uniform this time. 'What's the position now?'

'The Military Governor has sent General Chang Kai Shek a long memorandum asking what he should do in the case of a riot.'

'He wants to share the responsibility?'

The colonel peered at Ferral from behind his leucoma-filmed eyes and merely answered: 'Here is the translation.'

Ferral read the communication.

'I have also the reply,' said the colonel.

He handed him a photograph: two characters, with Chang Kai Shek's signature beneath.

'And that means?'

'*Shoot*.'

Ferral looked at the map of Shanghai on the wall, with large red patches indicating the masses of workers and utterly poverty-stricken areas (they were identical). 'Three thousand syndicalist guards,' he thought, 'with about three hundred thousand supporters; but will they dare to do anything definite? On the other side, Chang Kai Shek and the army.'

'He'll begin by having the Communist leaders shot, I suppose, whether an outbreak occurs or not?'

'Certainly. There won't be any outbreak: the Communists are practically disarmed and Chang Kai Shek has his troops behind him. The 1st Division is at the front, and that's the only dangerous one.'

'Thank you. Good-bye.'

Ferral was going to see Valerie. There was a 'boy' waiting beside the chauffeur with a blackbird in a large gilt cage on his knees. She had begged him to bring her one. As soon as the car began to move, he took a letter out of his pocket and read it over again. What he had been fearing for the last month was happening: America would give him no more credit.

The orders from the Indo-Chinese Government no longer sufficed to keep factories working which had been established to feed a market expected to go on expanding month by month, but actually shrinking from day to day: the concerns organized by the Consortium were on the verge of insolvency. The value of the shares had been kept up in Paris by the Ferral banks and the French financial syndicates which were linked up with them; and above all by the inflation. Since the stabilization of the franc they had steadily depreciated. But the Consortium banks drew their main income from profits made by the plantations – and especially by the rubber plantations. The Stevenson plan* had raised the price of rubber from 4¼d to 1s 5d. Ferral, who controlled rubber plantations in Indo-China, had benefited from the rise without having to restrict his production, as his estates were not in British territory. Accordingly the American banks, knowing from experience how much the Plan was costing America, had willingly accepted the plantations as security for loans. But increased native production in the Dutch East Indies, and the establishment of rival American

*A plan to restrict the production of rubber within the British Empire (the principal world producer), in order to raise the price of the commodity, which had fallen below the cost of production.

plantations in the Philippines, Brazil and Liberia, was now leading to a slump in the price, and they were now therefore withdrawing their credits for the same reasons as they had opened them. Ferral was thus hit by three disasters simultaneously: by the crash in the value of the one commodity which had enabled him to carry on – he had obtained credits by speculating, not on the value of the rubber he produced, but by mortgaging the actual estates; by the stabilization of the franc, which sent all his securities down (many of which belonged to his own banks who were determined to control the market); and finally by the withdrawal of his American credits. And he knew very well that as soon as this withdrawal was made public all the sharks in Paris and New York would 'bear' his securities; a manoeuvre only too likely to be successful. Active intervention, on moral grounds, was all that could save him: intervention, that is to say, by the French Government.

There is nothing like approaching bankruptcy for awakening a financier's consciousness of his nationality. Accustomed to seeing investors robbed, Governments nevertheless do not take kindly to the idea of their resources being depleted beyond all hope of recovery; an investor who can expect, with the obstinate faith of the gambler, to regain his losses in the future, is in a fair way to being consoled. It was therefore difficult for France, after leaving the Industrial Bank of China to its fate, to abandon the Corsortium also. But if Ferral's appeals for help were to stand any chance of success, he must be able to hold out some prospect of an improvement in his position; above everything, it was essential that Communism should be stamped out in China. With Chang Kai Shek master of the provinces, the construction of a Chinese railway system could be begun. He estimated the loan necessary to put that in hand at three thousand million gold francs, which meant an even larger number of paper ones. Not all the orders for materials to be used in the construction would come to him, to be sure, any more than he was alone at the moment in supporting

Chang Kai Shek: but he would get pickings. The American banks, moreover, also had reason to fear the triumph of Communism in China: its suppression would lead to modifications of their policy. As a Frenchman, Ferral enjoyed certain privileges in China; there was no question but that the Consortium would play some part in the construction of the railway. He could justifiably ask for a loan, in order to keep things going, and the Government would prefer that to a new crash: if his capital had been advanced to him from America, the deposits and the shares he held were French. He could not expect to pass through a period of acute crisis in China without *some* of his affairs going wrong; but the Stevenson Plan had come to the rescue of the Consortium in the past and the victory of the Kuomintang would do the same for it now. The stabilization of the franc had reacted unfavourably for him; the collapse of Chinese Communism would play into his hands.

Would he never, all his life, do other than stand and wait for the compelling pressure of a crisis in the world's affairs, stealing the energy from movements which began as innocently as if ordained by heaven, but which invariably developed a propensity for butting him in the stomach? Tonight, whether the struggle led to victory or defeat, he felt himself controlled by all the various forces which swayed the world. But at least he was independent of this woman; in a moment's time she would be dependent upon him. The complete submission in her face when she yielded to him, hid from him as completely as if a hand had been laid over his eyes, the maze of compulsions in obedience to which his life was arranged. He had seen her, since her return, in drawing-rooms (she had only returned from Kyoto three days before) and each time he had been thwarted and piqued by the complete refusal to surrender by which she stimulated his desire, though she had agreed to sleep with him that night. His desire for admiration was insatiable – it is from one sex to the other that admiration comes most readily and is most complete – and if her admiration wavered, he had recourse to erotic methods in order to rekindle it. That was why he had insisted on seeing Valerie's face while he was in bed with her: lips swollen with pleasure carry great conviction. He detested the coquetry without which she would have ceased to exist for him; the quality in her which irritated him above everything else at the same time was what most aroused his lust. But none of that was very clear, for it was his desire to imagine himself in her place, from the very first moment he touched her body, that gave him his keenest sensation of possession. For him, a body won by conquest had always had more savour than a body which resigned itself to him – more savour than any other body.

He left his car and went into the Astor, followed by the 'boy', who held out the cage solemnly in front of him. There were millions of souls in the world: the women whose love did not interest him – and one living adversary: the woman whose love he sought to win. The idea of complete possession had become rooted in his mind, and his pride evoked an equal pride, hostile to his, as the passionate gambler calls for another gambler to oppose him, foregoing peace of mind. Tonight, at least, the auspices were favourable, since they would begin by going to bed together.

Directly he entered the hall a European servant came up to him.

'Madame Serge left word for Monsieur Ferral that she will not be returning tonight and that this gentleman will explain.'

Dumbfounded, Ferral looked at 'this gentleman', sitting with his back to him, beside a screen. The man turned round: he was the director of one of the English banks, who had been paying his respects to Valerie for the last month. Just behind the screen stood a 'boy', no less dignified than Ferral's, also holding a cage containing a blackbird. The Englishman got up, bewildered, and shook Ferral by the hand, saying:

'You were to explain to me, sir.'

They realized simultaneously that they had been hoaxed. They looked at each other, while the boys sniggered and the white servants maintained an unnatural gravity. It was cocktail-time, and all Shanghai was there. Ferral felt the more ridiculous of the two: the Englishman was quite a young man.

Immediately a contempt as intense as the anger which filled him rescued him from his feeling of humiliation. He felt himself surrounded by human stupidity of the lowest kind, the kind which invades the senses and weighs upon the shoulders: the creatures who were looking at him were the most despicable morons that the world could show. Nevertheless, ignorant of how little they knew, he imagined them to be fully acquainted with the situation, and confronted by their mockery felt an overwhelming paroxysm of hate surge up within him, leaving him quite incapable of action.

'Is it for a show?' one 'boy' asked the other.

'Dunno.'

'Mine is a "he".'

'Yes. Mine's a "she".'

'That must be what they're for.'

The Englishman bowed to Ferral and walked over to the porter. The latter handed him a letter. He read it, pulled out a visiting-card from his pocket-book, fixed it on to the cage, told the porter: 'For Madame Serge,' and went out.

Ferral was trying to think, to find some excuse. She had struck him at his most sensitive point, as if she had put out his eyes while he was asleep: she was renouncing him. All that he could think or do or wish for seemed quite unreal. That ridiculous scene was real, and nothing could undo it now. He alone still existed in a world of ghosts, and he it was, and no other, who was being made a laughing-stock. Even worse – for he did not think of it as something over and done with, but as one of a series of mishaps, as if anger had made him a maso-chist – even worse, he wouldn't even be able to sleep with her. More and more eager to wreak vengeance upon that cynical body of his, he stood there alone, in front of all those dolts and those incurious 'boys' with their cages dangling beside them. Those birds prolonged the insult. But he must stay, at all costs. He ordered a cocktail and lit a cigarette, then stood there quite still, breaking the match in pieces between his fingers in his coat-pocket. A couple caught his eye. The man had the charm which comes from a combination of grey hair and a youngish face: the woman – quite nice, if somewhat loud – was looking at him with loving gratitude, springing either from real affection or from voluptuousness. 'She loves him,' thought Ferral enviously. 'And he's probably some dim half-wit who I dare-say is dependent on one of my concerns for a living. . . . ' He sent for the porter.

'You have a letter for me. Give it to me.'

Very surprised, but showing no sign of it, the porter gravely handed it to him.

Perhaps you know, my dear, that Persian women beat their husbands with their nailed babouches* when they are angry? They have no control over themselves. Afterwards, of course, they return to every-day life, when to shed tears with a man entails no obligation, but when sleeping with him – is it credible? – at once places them in the category of some one who has been 'had'. I am not a woman who can be 'had' in that way, a clod-like body which yields to your pleasure and which you placate with the little lies one tells to children and sick people. You know a great deal, my dear, but you will probably die without ever appreciating the fact that a woman is *also* a human being.

The men I have met (perhaps I shall never meet any other sort; so much the worse, you cannot imagine how much I shall regret it) have always been men who thought me 'charming', who have taken a pathetic amount of trouble to indulge my whims and caprices, but who turned to friends of their own sex only too readily, immediately there was any question of coming into contact with ordinary life. (Unless, naturally, they were on the look-out for sympathy.) My whims are an essential part of me, necessary not only for your pleasure but even to make you listen when I talk. What are they worth, my

*A kind of slipper.

charming caprices? They are worth just as much, or as little, as your affection. If your attempts to obtain a hold over me had made me in any way unhappy, you would not even have noticed it.

I have met enough men for me to know how to regard a passing affair. Nothing is unimportant to a man when his pride has become involved, and he gives the name of pleasure to the mechanism which enables him to satisfy his pride quickly and often. I refuse to be regarded merely as a body, just as you would refuse to be regarded merely as a cheque-book. You treat me as the prostitutes treat you: 'Talk, by all means, but pay up.' At the same time *I have* a body, the body to which you wish to confine me: I am fully aware of it. I do not always find it easy to defend myself against other people's ideas about me. You make me feel disgust for my body, just as spring makes me delight in it. But talking of spring, I hope you amuse yourself with the birds. And do please leave the electric light alone next time.

V.

He told himself that he had built roads, changed the appearance of a whole country, torn away thousands of peasants from their straw huts in the fields and lodged them in little corrugated-iron cabins around his factories – like the feudal lords, like the commissioners of imperial days: but the blackbird in its cage seemed to be mocking him. Ferral's energy, his capacity for clear thinking; the daring which had transformed Indo-China, the prodigious magnitude of which had just been brought home to him by the letter he had received from America: had all this been no more than a prelude to his being confronted by this ridiculous bird, which seemed to epitomize the whole universe, and which was quite definitely enjoying itself at his expense? Was a woman as important as all that?

It wasn't the woman who mattered. She was no more than a garment which he had torn off and thrown away: he came up with a shock against the confines of his will. The sudden thwarting of his sexual excitement increased his anger, producing a semi-hypnotized condition in which ridicule called for blood. It is only upon a living body that one can get instant satisfaction. Clappique had told him a wild story about an Afghan chief whose wife had been raped by a neighbouring chief, who had sent her back to him with the following letter: 'I am returning your wife, she is not as good as she is said to be'; and who had seized the ravisher, tied him up in front of the woman, who was quite naked, saying to him as he prepared to pluck out his eyes: 'You have seen her and scorned her; be sure that you will never see her again.'

He imagined himself in Valerie's room, with her tied to the bed, alternately crying with pleasure and sobbing with pain, so narrow was the borderline between the two; tightly bound, writhing under the pain of possession, since it was not of her own volition that she was aroused. The porter was waiting. 'I've got to keep calm, like that idiot there: what I'd really like to do is to clout him over the ear.' The idiot's face showed no trace of a smile. He would have his laugh afterwards. Ferral said: 'I shall be back in a moment,' and went out, leaving his hat behind and his cocktail bill unpaid.

'I want the largest bird-fancier in the town,' he said to the chauffeur.

It was quite near. But the shop was closed.

'In Chinese town,' said the chauffeur, 'plenty bird-dealers.'

'Go ahead.'

As the car drove along, Ferral's thoughts became fixed on a story he had read in some medical work, the confessions of a woman seized with an uncontrollable desire to be flagellated, who made arrangements by letter with an unknown man, and discovered to her terror that she wanted to run away at the very moment when she was lying on the hotel bed and the man, armed with the whip, had lifted up her skirts and reduced her to a state of complete paralysis. He could not see the face, but it was Valerie's. Should he stop at the first Chinese brothel they came to? No: no flesh and blood in the world would still the cravings of his outraged sexual pride.

The car was held up in front of the barbed-wire. Ahead was

the Chinese town, very black and unsafe. All the better. Ferral left the car, and slipped his revolver into his coat-pocket, rather hoping to be attacked: one takes opportunities to kill, when they occur.

The street of the animal-dealers was asleep; the 'boy' calmly knocked on the first shutter they came to, shouting 'Customer': the dealers were afraid of the soldiers. An interval of five minutes and the door opened; in the rich red-brown half-light, common in Chinese shops, which surrounded the lantern, the muffled thud of a monkey or a cat leaping from one place to another and a noise of beating wings announced the awakening of the animals. In the darkness beyond, long splodges of dull pink: parrots chained to their perches.

'How much for all these birds?'

'Just the birds? Eight hundred dollars.'

He was only a small dealer, and hadn't any rare ones. Ferral pulled out his cheque-book, then hesitated: the dealer would want cash. The 'boy' understood. 'It's Mr Ferral,' he said; 'the car's over there.' The dealer went outside; there were the car's headlights, streaked across with the wire in front of them.

'That's all right.'

This confidence, a proof of his authority, exasperated Ferral; his great power – evident in the fact that this shopkeeper knew his name – seemed ridiculous since he could make no use of it. But pride, helped by his absorption in the matter in hand and by the cold night air, came to the rescue: anger and sadistic visions were dwindling away into disgust, though he knew that they would recur.

'I have also a kangaroo,' said the dealer.

Ferral shrugged his shoulders. But already a lad, also awakened, was carrying it towards them in his arms. It was a small, furry creature, and looked at Ferral with the eyes of a terrified deer.

'Good.'

Another cheque.

Ferral went slowly back to the car. The essential thing was that if Valerie told the story of the cages – and she wouldn't fail to do that – he should be able to escape ridicule by capping it. Dealer, lad, 'boy', they all brought the little cages out, arranged them in the car, and returned for more; finally, last of all, came the kangaroo and the parrots, carried out in little round cages. From beyond the Chinese town came the sound of a few shots. Very well; the more they fought the better. The car drove off again, the sentries looking at it with amazement.

At the Astor, Ferral sent for the manager.

'Will you please come up to Madame Serge's room? She is away, and I want to give her a surprise.'

The manager contrived to hide his astonishment, and his still greater disapproval: the Astor was dependent upon the Consortium. The mere fact of his having some one white there, to talk to, released Ferral from the humiliation which had surrounded him, made it easier for him to face people again; the dealer and the night had done nothing to dispel his obsession; he wasn't completely freed from it even now, but at least he was no longer wholly dominated by it.

Five minutes later, he was arranging the cages in the room. Everything of value had been put away inside the cupboards, one of which had been left open. On the bed, a pair of silk pyjamas lay spread out. He was about to throw them into the cupboard, but almost the moment he touched them he seemed to feel the warmth of the silk creeping up his arms and invading his whole body, as though it had been in close contact with one of her breasts, exactly where he was holding it. There was something about the frocks and pyjamas hanging in the half-open cupboard that was perhaps even more sensual than Valerie herself. He could hardly prevent himself from burying his face in those pyjamas, squeezing or tearing them, in an attempt to project himself into those garments which were still redolent of her. If it had been possible for him to carry them away with him he would have done so. He threw them into the cupboard and the 'boy' closed it. The instant the pyjamas left his hand, the legend of Hercules and Omphale suddenly came into his mind – Hercules dressed as a woman, in warm flimsy material like this; humiliated, and content in his humiliation. He tried vainly to recall the scenes of sadism which had engrossed his imagination a moment before: the vision of the man beaten by Omphale and Dejanire refused to be dispelled, submerging him in an a basement that was at the same time an ecstasy. A step sounded outside. He put his hand to the revolver in his pocket: if she had come in at that instant, he would probably have killed her. It passed beyond the door, grew fainter; Ferral's hand moved to another pocket and he tugged nervously at his handkerchief. He must find some way, no matter what, of escaping from his present state of mind: he had the parrots released, but they were alarmed, and took refuge in the corners of the room, and the curtains. The kangaroo had hopped on to the bed, and looked like remaining there. Ferral switched off the main light, leaving only the one which could be left on all night: pink and white, with a superb beating of curved and gorgeous wings, which reminded him of the phoenixes of the East India Company, the parrots were beginning to fly, flapping clumsily and restlessly around.

Those boxes full of excited little birds, dumped down anyhow, all over the furniture, on the floor, in the fireplace, left him rather nonplussed. He tried to decide what to do with them, but couldn't think of anything. He went outside, came back again and at once realized; the room looked stricken. Would he get through that night without going off his head? Despite himself, he had left a flaring symbol of his anger behind him there.

'Open the cages,' he said to the 'boy'.

'It will dirty the room, Monsieur Ferral,' said the manager.

'Madame Serge will move to another one. But don't worry: it won't be necessary to bother about it tonight. Send the bill to me.'

'Any flowers, Monsieur Ferral?'

'Just the birds, nothing else. And see that no one comes in here, not even the servants.'

The window was protected against mosquitoes by a metal screen. The birds couldn't escape. The manager opened the casement, so that the room shouldn't smell foul.

The island birds were fluttering wildly around, on to the furniture and the curtains, and up to the corners of the ceiling, as colourless in that dim light as the birds in Chinese frescoes. The most charming present he had ever given Valerie had been inspired by hate. He put out the light, put it on again, put it out, put it on. He was using the switch at the head of the bed: he remembered the last night he had spent with Valerie, in his flat. In his desire to prevent her ever using that switch – with any one – he almost wrenched it from its socket. But he wanted to avoid leaving the least trace of anger.

'Take the empty cages away,' he said to the 'boy'. 'Have them burned.'

'If Madame Serge inquires who sent the birds,' asked the manager, looking admiringly at Ferral, 'is she to be informed?'

'She won't inquire. She will recognize the signature.'

He went out. He must find a woman tonight somewhere. But he didn't feel like going straight off to the Chinese restaurant. It was enough for him to know for sure that there were bodies obtainable – enough for the moment. Often, when a nightmare woke him up with a bump, he felt himself wanting to go on sleeping, despite the nightmare which sleep would bring back to him, and at the same time wanting to free himself from it by awakening completely: sleep meant the nightmare; awakening brought peace, but it brought the outside world with it. Tonight, the place of the nightmare had been taken by erotic excitement. At length he resolved to awaken himself from it, and had himself driven to the French Club: talking, re-establishing contact with a fellow-creature, even only through the medium of a conversation, that was the surest of methods.

The bar was full; it always was when there was trouble about. In the bay of the half-open window, with a brown cape of untrimmed wool over his shoulders and a sweet cocktail in front of him, sat Gisors: by himself, almost in isolation. Kyo had telephoned that all was going well and his father had come to the bar to hear what rumours were current: rumour was so often ridiculous, but at times significant; tonight was not one of those times. Ferral made his way over to him, every one greeting him as he did so. He knew the nature of his lectures, but attached no importance to them; and he didn't know whether Kyo was in Shanghai at present. He had felt that it was rather petty to question Martial about particular individuals and Kyo's part in affairs was in no way likely to bring him into the limelight.

All those imbeciles who were looking at him with a sort of timid disapproval imagined that it was opium which brought he and the old man together. Quite a mistaken idea. Ferral would pretend to smoke – one or two pipes only, never enough for him really to feel the action of the drug – because in the atmosphere surrounding the rite, the passing of the pipe from one mouth to another seemed to him a good way of getting into contact with women. He detested having to make advances, the bargain by which he was obliged to exaggerate a woman's importance in return for the pleasure which she accorded him, and accordingly accepted eagerly any opportunity of dispensing with this necessity.

The satisfaction which it had given him at times in Pekin, recently, to share old Gisors' couch with him was more complex in its origin. First, for the pleasure of the scandal. Secondly, a desire to be something more than just the President of the Consortium, a desire to dissociate himself from his activities in connexion with it – a method of convincing himself that he was worth more than that. His almost violent love of art, philosophy, and the cynicism which he called clear thinking was all a defence: Ferral didn't belong to any of the big families connected with banking or the revenue administration. The Ferral dynasty was too closely bound up with the history of the Republic for him to be considered a mere mountebank; but he remained an amateur, however influential a one. Too clever to try and fill in the ditch which cut him off, he set himself to widen it. Gisors' great culture and intelligence, always at the service of those who talked with him, his contempt for convention, his invariably original way of seeing things, which Ferral did not scruple to pass off as his own directly he left him; all this, tending to bring them together, far outweighed the causes of friction between them. When he was with Ferral, Gisors' political discussion took on a philosophical tone. Ferral declared that he needed intelligence around him, and as long as it didn't conflict with his own, this was true.

He looked about him; directly he sat down, heads were turned away. He would willingly have married his cook just then, if only in order to force that crowd to accept her. The thought of all those imbeciles criticizing him exasperated him; the less he saw of them the better: he suggested to Gisors that they should go and drink on the terrace outside, looking out on to the garden. Despite the coolness of the evening, the 'boys' had carried a few tables outside.

'Do you think it is possible really to get to know a living being?' he asked Gisors. They sat down near a little lamp, sending out a halo of light that gradually gave way again to the fog and the darkness.

Gisors looked at him. 'He wouldn't have this taste for psychology unless he found himself thwarted at times.'

'A woman?' he asked.

'What difference does it make?'

'Attempts to analyse a woman always have something erotic about them. . . . To try and unravel a woman's character is surely always a method of possessing or of taking one's revenge upon her. . . .'

A harlot sitting at a table close by was saying to another:

'She doesn't find it too easy to compete. She'd give a lot for my charm, that woman, let me tell you.'

'It is my opinion,' Gisors went on, 'that taking an intellectual view of things is an attempt to compensate: understanding a human being is a negative feeling; the positive feeling, the reality, is in the agony of always remaining cut off from what one loves.'

'Does one ever really love?'

'Time sometimes causes that feeling to disappear, just time alone. One never understands a human being, but there are times one ceases to be conscious of one's ignorance (I am thinking of my son, and of . . . another boy too). To arrive at understanding through intelligence is to make a vain attempt to anticipate time.'

'It isn't the function of intelligence to dispense with other things.'

Gisors looked at him.

'What do you mean by intelligence?'

'In a general sense?'

'Yes.'

Ferral thought for a minute.

'The possession of a method of imposing oneself upon people and things.'

An almost imperceptible smile appeared on Gisors' face. Every time he asked that question, the person he was conversing with, no matter who he was, would invariably answer in the light of his own desires. But Ferral suddenly seemed to grow more serious.

'Do you know what punishment was inflicted on women who were unfaithful to their masters, under the early emperors?' he asked.

'Well, there were several, weren't there? The principal one, it appears, consisted in tying them on to a raft, after first cutting off their hands, and putting out their eyes, as far as I remember, and then . . .'

Gisors noticed, as he spoke, the increasing attention and even satisfaction with which Ferral listened to him.

'. . . leaving them to float down those interminable rivers, until they died of hunger or exhaustion, with their lover attached to the same raft, just beside them. . . .'

'Their lover?'

How was it possible to reconcile the nonchalance of his question with his earnestness, his look of intensity? Gisors could not guess that Ferral's mind refused at present to recognize the conception of a lover: but he had already checked himself, perceiving his slip.

'The most curious feature,' Gisors continued, 'is that, until the fourth century, those ferocious penal codes seem to have been drawn up by men who, from what we know of their private lives, were in other respects enlightened, humane, and benevolent.'

'Yes, they seem to have been enlightened enough.'

Gisors looked at that sharp face with the eyes closed, lit up from underneath by the little lamp, the light playing upon his moustache. A sound of distant firing. How many lives were in jeopardy out there in the fog that night? The face was all tense and drawn, as though it had suffered some profound mental and physical humiliation, and was defending itself against it with all the sardonic energy which rancour produces in a man: the hatred of one sex for the other was at the back of it, as though the blood which was still trickling out over that land already saturated with it had perforce reopened ancient wounds. More firing, very near this time; it made the glasses on the table jump.

Gisors was used to the sound of shooting, which came across every day from the Chinese town. In spite of Kyo's telephone call, however, this last sudden outburst worried him. He had no idea to what extent Ferral was mixed up with politics, but whatever part he played he was certain to be a supporter of Chang Kai Shek. It seemed to him quite natural that they should be sitting next to each other – he never found that such a thing in any way compromised him, even in his own eyes – but he no longer wished to help him. More firing, farther off.

'What is happening?' he asked.

'I don't know. The Blue and Red leaders have made great play with a declaration of union. It seems to be working out all right.'

'He's lying,' thought Gisors. 'He must know at least as much as I do.'

'Reds or Blues,' Ferral was saying, 'coolies are none the less coolies; unless being coolies has been too much for them altogether. Doesn't it strike you as characteristic of the stupidity of the human race that a man who has only got one life to lose can throw it away for the sake of an idea?'

'It is only very rarely that man is able to endure his – how shall I say? – his human estate. . . .'

He thought of one of Kyo's theories: any ideal for which men are prepared to die, other than a purely selfish one, tends, more or less obscurely, to justify that state of affairs by investing it with a dignity all its own: Christianity for the slave, nationality for the citizen, Communism for the worker. But he had no desire to discuss Kyo's ideas with Ferral. He addressed him again:

'One always has to get drunk: here we take opium, in the Moslem world they use hashish, in the West, woman. Perhaps love is truly the Occidental's most favoured means of freeing himself from the burden of humanity. . . .'

Beneath his words there flowed a confused and hidden undercurrent of personal generalizations: Chen and murder, Clappique and his eccentricity, Katow and revolution. May and love's fidelity; opium and himself. . . . Kyo alone refused to be equated in this mental algebra.

'Many fewer women would go to bed with men,' Ferral replied, 'if, while still on their feet, they could be sure of hearing those expressions of admiration they so badly need – and which themselves really require a bed.'

'And of how many men is that not also true?'

'On the contrary, a man can, and should, dispense with women. Action – his actions alone fulfil his life and satisfy a white man. What should we think of a painter of whom we were told that he hadn't painted any pictures? A man is the sum-total of his actions, of the things he has *done*, and of the things he may do yet. Nothing more than that. I am not merely what such and such an embrace of a woman by a man has fashioned of my life: I am my roads, my work –'

'Those roads had to be built.'

Since the last burst of firing, Gisors had determined to play this role of justification no longer.

'If you did not, you know, some one else would. It's as if a general were to say: "With my soldiers I could sack that town." But if he himself were capable of sacking the town, he wouldn't be a general. . . . They make a general of you at Saint-Cyr; there's no other way of becoming one. . . . Besides, men are probably not interested in power. What attracts them about that notion is not the actual power itself, but the idea of doing what they damn well please. The might of kings consists in governing, doesn't it? But man has no desire to govern: his wish, as you said yourself, is to shackle, to constrain. . . . He wants, in a world of men, to be more than a man. As I say, to escape mortals' lot. To be not powerful, but all-powerful – that's his yearning. All this illusory sickness of the brain whose intellectual manifestation is the will to power, is a thirst for divinity. Every man dreams of being God. . . .'

What Gisors said disturbed Ferral, but he was not prepared in his mind to accept it. If the old man were to fail to find him a justification, his obsession would remain with him for ever after.

'Why then, in your opinion, do the gods take on human or animal shape in order to enjoy mortal women?'

As clearly as if he could actually see it, Gisors perceived that a shadow had settled beside them: Ferral had risen to his feet.

'You need to bring the essential part of your nature into play so as to be all the more fiercely conscious of its existence,' said Gisors, without looking at him.

Ferral could not guess that the perspicuous intelligence of Gisors' mind was due to the fact that he recognized in his interlocutor's fragments of his personality, and that the most subtle definition of his character would have been achieved by collating these examples of his responsive understanding.

'A god may enjoy,' the old man continued, with a knowing smile, 'but he cannot utterly possess. Surely the delight of a god is to become man and yet to know that he can always reassume the power of his godhead; whereas man's dream is suddenly to become a god and yet not lose his personality. . . .'

Ferral felt he really must find a woman to go to bed with. He took his leave.

*

'It's a curious case of intricate self-deception,' thought Gisors, 'you'd say that his erotic vision of himself tonight is the same as any romantic-minded clerk would have of him.' When, shortly after the war, Gisors had first come into contact with the financial powers in Shanghai, he had been not a little astonished to discover that his conception of what capitalists were like bore no resemblance to the truth. Almost all the capitalists he then met had arranged their emotional life according to some set form or other – more often than not, by marriage. An all-absorbing interest in money, which is what goes to make the business man, when wealth is not inherited and taken for granted, accords ill with a wastefully conducted love-life. 'Modern capitalism,' he would explain to his students, 'is based far more upon the strength of its organization than upon any inherent power.'

*

Ferral, in his car, reflected that his dealings with women were always identical and absurd. Perhaps he had known love in the past. Yes, in the past. What drunken sot of a psychologist had invented the term 'love' for this thing that was now poisoning his existence? Love of women is an exaltation, an obsession: he was himself certainly obsessed by women – as if by a desire for vengeance. He turned to women for judgement, he who brooked no one's judgement. No woman who had not expressed her admiration for him by giving herself to him, who had not struggled against him – meant anything to him. He had been restricted to whores and wantons. The body existed, which was fortunate. Otherwise. . . . 'Sweet, you will die without ever suspecting that a woman is a human being. . . .' Well, yes, that might be true for her – but not for him. A woman a human being! She's a respite, a port of call, a foe, an enemy. . . .

On his way he picked up a light of love in one of the houses in Nanking Road: a girl with a sweet and gentle face. By his side in the car, her hands demurely folded on her zither, she had the appearance of a Tang statuette. After a time they reached his house. He climbed the steps ahead of her, his usually long strides dragging slow. 'Let's sleep,' he thought. . . . Sleep, that meant peace. He had lived, fought, created; deep down behind all these outward seemings, that was the only reality he had found, that delight, an abandonment of self, a leaving of himself behind – lying there on the shore, like the drowned body of some other man, a friend, who was himself, the self for whom a life must each day be planned anew. 'Sleep – that is the one thing I have always longed for, truly longed for, all these years. . . .'

What could he wish for better than some soporific from the hands of this young woman whose slippers flapped behind him on the stairs? They entered the smoking-room: couches spread with Mongolian carpets in a den fashioned more for embraces than for dreaming. . . . A large tinted drawing dating from the first Kama period hung on the wall, and a Tibetan banner. The girl laid her zither on a divan. On a plate were old-fashioned opium-smoking appurtenances, with handles of jade, beautifully ornamented but not very practical – the property obviously of some one who never made use of them. She stretched her hand towards them: he stopped her with a gesture. A distant shot rang out, making the needles dance on the plate.

'Do you want me to sing?'

'Not now.'

He gazed at her body, which was at once defined and concealed by the sheath of mauve silk she wore. He knew that she was amazed: it is not customary to take a courtesan to bed with you without first having her sing, talk, serve at table, or prepare the opium pipes. Otherwise why not frequent ordinary prostitutes?

'Don't you want to smoke, either?'

'No. Get undressed.'

He was damaging her dignity, and he knew it. He would have liked to insist on her removing all her clothes, but that she would have refused to do. He had left only a night-light burning. 'The pleasures of love,' he thought, 'involve the humiliation of oneself, or of another – of both of you, maybe. An *idea*, that's evidently what it is.' Anyway, she was more alluring as she was now, in her clinging Chinese chemise; but she hardly attracted him at all, or perhaps he was attracted only by the submissiveness of this body that waited while he himself still made no move. His pleasure sprang from putting himself – clearly that was it – in the place of another, a creature in constraint, constrained by himself. In fact, he never achieved enjoyment of any one but himself – yet this was a joy that could only be attained in the presence of some one else. He understood now what Gisors had only suspected: yes, that was it, his thirst for power was never quenched, was kept alive by being renewed; but even if he had never in his life before possessed any woman, he *had* possessed, he would now, in this Chinese girl awaiting his embrace, possess the one and only thing he hungered for: himself. He needed the eyes of others with which to see himself, the senses of another by which to know his own touch. He looked at the Tibetan painting; there, he couldn't quite think why: travellers were depicted in it, wandering across a faded scene, in which two skeletons, identical, lay blissfully clasped in each other's arms.

He moved towards the girl.

10.30 P.M.

'If only the car isn't long in coming,' thought Chen. If the darkness were to become complete he would be less sure of his aim, and very soon the last street lamps would be extinguished. The desolate night of this China of ricefields and marshes had crept up over the almost deserted avenue. The shrouded lights of a city of fog, filtering through closed panes, past shutters left ajar, were being turned off one by one: weakening minute by minute, a few last rays glinted on the wet tramway lines, on the insulators of the telegraph poles; soon Chen saw their reflection nowhere but on the vertical Chinese signboards sprinkled with gold characters. This night of fog was his last night, and he was satisfied. He was going to be blown up with the car – head over heels in a flash which would illumine the hideous thoroughfare and splatter its walls with blood. The most ancient of the Chinese legends came into his mind: men were but vermin on the earth. Terrorism must be made a mystic faith. Solitude before the event: let the terrorist first take his resolve alone, and act alone. The best weapon of the police is a fellow-criminal's betrayal. The murderer who acts on his own is in no danger of accusing himself. Solitude, too, after the event – though it is hard for one living outside the world of men not to seek out his fellows. Chen was aware of the objections levelled against terrorism: police reprisals against the working classes and the counter-appeal of fascism. But as it was, police repression could not be more violent nor fascism more threatening. And perhaps Kyo and he were thinking for different sets of men. It was not a question of helping, in their own class, just for the sake of delivering that class, the best men, the best underdogs in it – the point was to lend significance to the very desperation of their plight: each should arraign and answer for the life of one of the masters. Each hopeless wretch must be given immediate guidance. The outrages ought to be more frequent; not by way of showing organization but for the cause: martyrs must be re-born. When Pei wrote, his writings would be heeded because he, Chen, was about to die: he knew what weight is lent to an idea by the blood spilled for its sake. All else beside his own resolute gesture melted away in this darkness covering the approach of a motor-car soon to pass this way. . . . Fed by the smoke of ships' funnels, far up the avenue, the fog obliterated pavements not yet entirely deserted. Here and there people passed along them still, one after the other, seldom catching each other up, as if the war had imposed a strict sense of discipline on the city. The general soundlessness of their footsteps made their movements weird. They carried no parcels, no baskets, pushed no little hand-carts; tonight their activity seemed aimless. Chen watched all these shadows flowing silently down towards the river, in a constant and inexplicable procession: surely Destiny itself was the force which urged them forward to the other end of the Avenue where an archway of light-signs, barely visible against the murk of the river, sank in a hazy perspective – like the very gates of death itself? This vast lettering vanished in a tragic, thistledown world, as if obscured by the march of time; and just as if it, too, hailed not from headquarters but from a long-past Buddhist age, the martial trump of Chang Kai Shek's car now echoed dully far away up the almost empty street. With a feeling of gratitude, Chen clasped the bomb more tightly beneath his arm. Only the headlights pierced the gloom. Almost at once, headed by an escorting Ford, the whole car leapt in sight; again it seemed to Chen to be moving extraordinarily fast. Suddenly three soldiers stood in the way; both cars slowed down. He tried to gain control over his breathing. Already his anxiety had vanished. The Ford passed him, the car was coming now – a large, American-made car, flanked by two police officers clinging to the running-boards: it loomed so powerful that Chen felt sure if he didn't step forward, if he waited, despite himself he would find he had jumped out of its way. He gripped the bomb by the nozzle, like a milk-bottle. The general's car was there, five yards away, a vast bulk. . . . He ran towards it, filled with ecstasy, and flung himself on it, eyes firmly shut.

He came to, some seconds later. He had not felt or heard the shattering of bone that he expected; but had gone under in a sheer flash of light. No jacket left. His right hand held a fragment of the car bonnet, dripping with blood and slime. A few yards away a mound of scarlet rubble, a heap of powdered glass reflecting one last gleam of light, and a . . . already he could distinguish nothing more. He was becoming aware of a pain which, in one quick flash, passed once more beyond feeling. He couldn't see clearly now, yet he felt that there was still no one about? were the police expecting a second bomb? His whole frame suffered agony, an agony he could not localize: he was all pain. Some one was coming. He remembered that he ought to get out his revolver. He tried to reach his trouser pocket. No pocket left, no trouser, no leg; mutilated flesh, that was all. The other revolver then, the one in his shirt. Its sight had gone. He seized the thing by the muzzle, turned it round he didn't know how, instinctively took off the safety-catch with his thumb. At last he opened his eyes. Everything was whirling slowly, invincibly, tracing the arc of a vast circle – yet nothing existed besides pain. A policeman stood close by. Chen wanted to ask if Chang Kai Shek were dead, but it was in some other world he wanted that; here in this world, even that death held no interest for him.

Letting fly with all his strength, the policeman rolled him over with a kick in the ribs. Chen screamed, fired straight ahead at random; the shock doubled this pain that he'd imagined fathomless. He was on the point of either fainting or dying. Making the most terrific effort of his life, he managed to push the muzzle of the revolver into his mouth. Awaiting this further shock, even more painful than the last, he lay stockstill. A violent jolt from another policeman's heel contracted every muscle in his body, and he pulled the trigger without knowing it.

Part 5

THROUGH the fog the car swung into the long sandy drive which led to a gaming-house. 'I've time to go in,' thought Clappique, 'before going on to the Black Cat'. He was determined not to miss Kyo, on account of the money he expected to get from him, and because he might perhaps, this time, be going not to warn him but to save him. He had procured the information Kyo wanted, without much difficulty; his informants knew that Chang Kai Shek's troops had been given a special order to parade at eleven o'clock that night, and that all the Communist gatherings were to be surrounded. It was no longer a question merely of 'Beware the police', but of 'Don't go to the meeting tonight'. He had not forgotten that Kyo would be leaving at eleven-thirty. So there must be some Communist meeting fixed for tonight which Chang Kai Shek intended to crush. Police information was often unfounded, but the coincidence was too marked. Kyo could perhaps call off the meeting or, if it was too late for that, he could just not go. 'If he gives me a hundred dollars, maybe I'll have enough money: a hundred plus a hundred and seventeen obtained this afternoon by pleasant and equally illegal means, that makes two hundred and seventeen. . . . Perhaps, though, he won't have any to spare; this time there are no rifles involved. Let's first try fending for ourselves.' The car stopped. Clappique was wearing a dinner-jacket; he handed the man two dollars. The hatless chauffeur thanked him with a broad smile: the fare was only a dollar.

'Such largesse is intended to enable you to buy yourself a little b-bowler hat.'

And, pointing his forefinger on high, for emphasis of this truth:

'I said a *bowler* hat.'

The taximan drove off.

'For, from the aesthetic point of view, which is that of all true men,' Clappique, in the midst of the gravel-walk, continued, 'that creature's face calls out for a bowler hat.'

The car had gone. He spoke only to the night: and, as if in answer to him, the scent of damp boxwood and spindle-trees rose up from the garden. For him this bitter scent spelt Europe. The baron felt his breast pocket and fingered his revolver, which was there in place of his pocketbook – that was in his other pocket. He looked up at the windows; there was no light in them, and they were barely distinguishable. 'Let's think. . . .' He knew he was only trying to prolong, before the gambling began, this moment in which flight was still possible. 'The day after tomorrow, if it has rained, there'll be this smell here still: and I may be dead. . . . Dead? What am I saying? That's crazy. Not a word. I'm immortal.' He went in, and up to the first floor. The croupier's voice and the noise of stakes cast on the tables seemed to rise and fall amid the curling wreaths of smoke. The Chinese attendants were asleep: but the Russian private detectives, fists plunged deep into the pockets of their coats, a Colt bulging in each right hand, leaned back against the window-sills and door-lintels or walked nonchalantly about; they weren't asleep. Clappique went through to the main salon: in a fog of tobacco smoke shrouding the gleaming grotto-effect of rock-studded walls, alternating smudges of black and white – dinner-jackets, bare shoulders – leant over the green of the table.

'Hullo, Toto!' cried several voices.

The Baron was often 'Toto' in Shanghai. He had only very occasionally been to this place before, when introducing friends to it; he himself didn't gamble. Arms outspread, like a father welcoming the kiddies home:

'Hurrah!' he cried. 'I'm so thrilled to be allowed to join your happy family – ' But the croupier spun: Clappique was no longer noticed. He was of little interest here: these people needed no other entertainment. Their eyes were all of them fixed, completely disciplined, on the ball.

He had a hundred and seventeen dollars. To play on the numbers would be too risky. He had already decided on *pair* or *impair*.

'Just a few little c-counters,' he said to the *changeur*.

'Of how much?'

'Twenty.'

He decided to lay one stake at a time: always on *pair*. He must win at least three hundred dollars.

He made his bet. The Five came out. He'd lost. That didn't matter, nor did it interest him. He bet again, still on *pair*. Two. He'd won. Again: Seven. He'd lost. After that, Nine; lost again. Four, a win. Three, lost. Seven; then One, lost. Eighty dollars gone. He had one bet left to make.

His last throw.

He laid it down with his right hand: his left never moved now, as if the motionless ball held it in check, as if this hand were bound to it. And yet his left hand reminded him of himself. He suddenly remembered; it wasn't the hand which worried him, it was the watch on his wrist. Eleven twenty-five. He had five minutes in which to catch Kyo. . . .

He had been certain of winning when he made his penultimate throw; even if he were going to lose, he couldn't have lost so fast. He had been wrong not to care the first time he lost; that had been a bad omen. But you almost always win on the last bet you make; and *impair* had come out three times running. All the same, ever since he arrived it must have turned up more often than *pair*, for he'd been losing. Should he change over? Should he play on *impair*? But something urged him now to do nothing about it, to stand his ground: it seemed to him that that was what he had come here for. Any move on his part would have been sacrilege. He let his stake lie – on *pair*.

The croupier set the ball rolling. It started, as always, at no great pace, seeming to hesitate. From the start, Clappique had not yet seen Red or Black appear. Theirs was the likeliest chance now. The ball sped on its wandering way. Why hadn't he backed Red? It was slowing up. It stopped on Two. He had won.

The thing to do was to put these forty dollars on Seven and play that. That was obvious; after which he'd have to quit. He made his two bets and won. When the croupier pushed his fourteen counters towards him, when his hands touched them, he discovered with amazement that it was possible for him to win; it wasn't all a figment of the imagination, a fantastic lottery at which the unknown always won. It seemed to him suddenly that the bank owed him money, not because he'd backed the winning number, nor because he had lost at first; but altogether, for all time, because of the freedom and the courage that was in him. This ball placed Chance at his disposal wherewith to pay all the debts of Fortune. Yet if he backed another number, he would lose. He left two hundred dollars on *impair* – and lost.

In disgust he left the table for a second and went over to the window. It was dark outside. Under the trees, the tail-lamps of cars showed red. Despite the thickness of the panes, he heard a great confusion of voices, laughter, and, all of a sudden, without being able to make out the words, some remark made in anger. Bitterness . . . Passion . . . All these creatures passing in the fog – what dim and idiotic force kept them alive? They weren't even shadows: merely voices in the night. It was within, here in this room, that blood coursed through living veins. Those who never gambled were not men at all. Had all his life been nothing but one long madness? He went back to the tables.

Again he put sixty dollars on *pair*. This little ball, with its failing motion, was Fate itself – his *own* Fate, moreover. He was

226

contending not against a living thing, but against some sort of god: and at the same time this god was his own self. The ball started off on yet another journey.

He experienced at once the passive sensation of collapse he was looking for: again he seemed to be taking hold of his whole life and suspending it above this derisive roulette-ball. With its aid he satisfied, both at once, and for the first time, the two Clappiques that went to make up himself: the one that wished to live and the other that longed for destruction. Why look at his watch? He was flinging Kyo into a world of ciphers. He felt that he was feeding this ball not simply with the bets he made, but with his own life – if he no longer saw Kyo, if he forgot Kyo, he lost all possibility of getting any more money. But also with the life of another; and that this other person should not know it gave the ball and its now waning, fainter motions the force of a conjunction of planets, of chronic illness, of all those things on which men believe their destinies depend. What connexion was there between money and this ball which hesitated nuzzling on the brink of its various little holes and by whose aid he clasped to himself his own true Destiny – the only means to self-knowledge he had ever yet discovered? He must carry on, risking more and more in order that the staking of the freedom he had won might make his gesture even more absurd! Leaning on his forearm, no longer watching the ball as now it spun slower and slower, and with a shudder in the muscles of his wrist and shoulders, he was discovering the real, the inner significance of games of chance – the frantic fun of losing.

Five!

Almost every one was losing; as well as with smoke, the room was filled with a desperate nervous tension and the rattle of counters gathered in by the croupier's rake. Clappique knew that he wasn't through yet. Why keep his seventeen dollars? He produced a ten-dollar bill and played on *pair*. He was so certain he would lose that he had not staked it all – as if to prolong this process of losing. As soon as the ball began to vacillate, his right hand followed its motions; but his left remained glued to the table. He now understood the intense life animating these very instruments of chance: this ball was unlike any other – not like balls not used for gambling. Its very hesitation lived. Its rhythm, at once both ineluctable and weak, had this tremulous quality because real lives were bound up with it. While it still turned, no gambler drew on his cigarette. It entered a Red niche, then came out again, wandered a little farther, fell into the Nine. Clappique's left hand lying on the table sketched an imperceptible gesture as if to snatch it away. Again he had lost.

Five dollars on *pair*: again he was making his last bid.

The ball, starting afresh, flew in wide circles; as yet it was not fully alive. But Clappique's attention was diverted by his watch. He wore it not on his wrist but underneath, where his pulse beat. He laid his hand flat on the table and now managed to concentrate entirely on the ball. He had found out that gambling is a form of deathless suicide: all he had to do was to put down his money, watch the ball and wait, as he'd have had to wait if he had just swallowed a poison; this was a poison endlessly renewed, plus a pride in losing. The ball stopped on the Four. He had won.

He almost didn't care he'd won. But on the other hand, if he had lost . . . He won once more, lost once. And now again he had forty dollars; but he wanted to rediscover the appalling sensation of a last throw. Counters were accumulating on the Red, which had not appeared for a long time. This Red square, on which most eyes were fixed, attracted him too; but to come off *pair* struck him as an admission of defeat. He stuck to *pair*, staking forty dollars. No other fling could ever equal that – maybe Kyo had not left yet; in ten minutes' time he would certainly not be able to catch him; but right away, now, perhaps he could. Yet now, at this minute, he was staking his last sou, his own life and the life of another – above all, that: the life of another. He knew that he was sacrificing Kyo. It was Kyo who was chained to this little ball, to this table; and it was he himself, Clappique, who was this very ball, stronger than all of them, stronger than himself – yet there he was watching it, living as he had never lived before; beside himself, worn out by a sensation of dizzy self-reproach.

*

He left at one in the morning: that was when the Casino shut. He had twenty-four dollars left. The air outside calmed him, like entering a wood. The fog was much less thick than it had been two hours ago. Maybe it had rained; everything was wet. Although in the dark he could not see either the boxwoods or the spindle-trees, he was made aware of their dark foliage by their bitter scent. 'It's remarkable,' he thought, 'that it should so often have been said that a gambler's thrill, at the tables, lies in the hope of winning! It's as though you said that men fight duels so as to become champion fencers. . . .' The serenity of the night seemed to have chased away, with the fog, all the troubles, all the sorrows of mankind. Yet a rattle of shots could be heard in the distance. 'They're shooting again. . . .'

He left the garden and, forcing himself not to think of Kyo, set out to walk. The trees were already few and far between. Suddenly, through what was left of the fog, the dull reflection of the moon gleamed on the surfaces of things. Clappique looked up. She had just appeared through a jagged tear in the leaden clouds and was slowly sailing along in a sombre, vast, transparent gap, like a lake with its depths full of stars. Her light, growing momentarily stronger, gave all these shuttered houses, and the total abandonment of the town, an other-wordly life – as if, with its beams, the very atmosphere of the moon had suddenly come to rest in this silent place. Yet behind this cold stage-setting from another planet, men were alive. Most of them were asleep, and such emptiness – as of a city sunk beneath the waves – suited their uneasy life in sleep as if it, too, were the life of some other planet. 'In the *Thousand and One Nights* you read of l-little villages full of sleeping people, villages abandoned centuries ago, their minarets glistening in the moonlit silence of the empty plains – veritable sleeping beauties of the desert. . . . Yes – but I may be going to die. . . .' Death, his own death, meant nothing very real to him in this atmosphere so inhuman that he felt himself to be an intruder. And what of those who were awake? 'There are those who read. . . . Those who ruminate. (Charming phrase!) And couples making love . . .' Life stretched into a future quivering beyond all this present silence! Ah, frenzied humanity, that no power could deliver from itself! The usual smell of corpses from the Chinese town wafted across on the wind, which was rising again. Clappique had to make an effort to breathe. His misery was returning to him. He could stand the idea of death better than the smell of it. And little by little the smell of death was beginning to pervade this décor which veiled the madness of the world with the peace of eternity, and while the wind blew on, yet made no sound, the moon of a sudden reached the opposite bank of cloud and all again was plunged into darkness. 'Is it a dream?' But the frightful stench dragged him back to life, to the uneasy night in which the recently lit street lamps cast wide circles of light on pavements whence rain had washed away all footprints. Where should he go? He hesitated. He would never be able to forget Kyo if he were to try to get to sleep. He was walking at the moment along a street full of little bars, brothels on a small scale, with signs hanging up in the languages of all seafaring nations. He entered the first of these.

He sat down by the window. The three serving girls – a half-caste and two whites – were sitting about the room with various clients, one of whom was preparing to leave. Clappique waited, looked outside; nothing there, not even a sailor. In the distance shots rang out. He gave a start – on purpose; a buxom blonde, now disengaged, had come and sat down by his side. 'A Rubens,' he thought, 'but not a perfect example of his style; probably by Jordaens, if one only knew. . . . Hush, not a word!' He spun his hat round on his forefinger, very fast, spun it right off, caught it neatly by the brim and placed it on the woman's lap. 'Take care of that leetle hat, dear girl. It's the only one in Shanghai. Besides, it's been broken in.' The young woman shrieked with laughter; here was a one – and her face, which until then had been a mask, became endowed with sudden life, thanks to this merriment.

'Shall we drink, or go upstairs?' she asked.

'Both.'

She brought some Schiedam. 'It's a speciality of the house,' she said.

'Is that so?' queried Clappique.

She shrugged. 'D'you think I give a damn?'

'Are you unhappy?'

She looked at him. You had to be careful with these funny fellows. Still, he was alone; there was no one for him to show off to; and actually he didn't seem to be trying to pull her leg.

'What else d'you imagine, in this life?'

'Do you smoke?'

'Opium's too dear. Of course you can kick the gong around, but I'm afraid to get some one to give me a scratch of the stuff – their needles are dirty and you can get an abscess that way, and if that happens to you, they shoot you out. There's always ten girls only too glad to take your place. Besides . . .'

'Flemish,' he thought. He cut her short. 'You can get opium fairly cheap. I pay two dollars and seventy five cents for this stuff.'

'You're from the north, too?'

He gave her a packet without answering. She was grateful to him for being a fellow-countryman – and for the gift.

'Even that's too dear for me. But this lot won't have cost me much. I'll chew some of it tonight.'

'You don't like smoking it?'

'D'you imagine I've a pipe? Who do you take me for?' She smiled bitterly, but all the same she was pleased. Then habitual distrust returned. 'Why did you give it to me?'

'Never mind. I just thought I would. I've been in the trade.'

Well, he certainly didn't look like a ponce. But then he obviously hadn't been connected with 'the trade' for some time now. He sometimes had felt the need to invent whole biographies for himself, but seldom where any matter of sex was concerned. She edged up close to him on the seat.

'Just try to be good to me, that's all; it'll be the last time I go to bed with a woman.'

'Oh; why?'

Slow on the uptake, but not actually stupid. After she had spoken, she understood.

'You mean you're going to kill yourself?'

It wasn't the first time she had met with this sort of thing. Clappique's hand was lying on the table. She took it in hers and kissed it – with a gauche and almost maternal gesture.

'It's a shame.'

'Do you want to go up now?'

She had heard it said that this desire came to men sometimes, before they died. But she didn't dare to be the first to get up; she'd have felt as if she was hastening his suicide. She still held his hand in hers. Slouched on the bench, legs crossed, arms tight against his side like an insect feeling the cold, nose jutting forward, he seemed to watch her from a long way off, despite the contact of their bodies. Although he had hardly drunk anything, he was intoxicated by this lie, this warmth, this make-believe world he had created. When he said he meant to kill himself, he didn't believe what he said; but since she believed it, he entered a world in which truth had ceased to exist. It wasn't true or false, it was a part of life. And as his past, which he had just made up, did not exist, and nor did the primitive and imaginary gesture so soon to take place, on which his whole relationship with this woman was based, nothing existed. The whole world had ceased to weigh on him. Delivered, he lived now only in a fictitious world which he himself had just created, strong in the bond forged by human pity in the face of Death. So drunk did he feel that his hand trembled. The woman felt it tremble. She took it for a shudder of misery.

'Isn't there anything you can do about it?'

'No.'

The hat, placed on the corner of the table, seemed to watch him ironically. He threw it on to the bench so as not to go on looking at it.

'A love affair?' she went on.

A salvo crackled in the distance. 'As if there weren't enough men who will have to die tonight,' she thought.

He got up without answering. She thought her question must have brought back memories. . . . Despite her curiosity, she felt she wanted to tell him she was sorry, but didn't dare. She got up too. Sliding a hand under the bar, she picked up a bundle (irrigator and towels) between two jugs. They went upstairs.

When he left – he didn't turn his head, but he knew she was watching him through the glass as he went – neither his mind nor his body was satisfied. The fog had returned. After a quarter of an hour's walk, the cool night air failed to calm him and he paused outside a Portuguese bar. Its windows weren't polished. Some distance apart from the customers a thin, scraggy brunette, with very large eyes, her hands over her breasts as if to protect them, sat gazing into the night. Clappique watched her without stirring. 'I feel like a woman must feel when she doesn't know what effect a new lover will have on her. . . . Let's go and commit suicide with this one, too.'

In the Black Cat dive, Kyo and May had waited.

Five minutes to go. They ought to have left already. That Clappique should not have put in an appearance surprised Kyo (he had collected close on two hundred dollars for him), but it didn't amaze him; each time Clappique behaved in this way he was acting so like he had on other occasions that those who knew him well hardly felt any surprise. Kyo had thought of him at first as eccentric and rather remarkable: but he was grateful to him for having warned him, and little by little he had grown really to like the man. However, he was beginning to doubt the validity of the information the baron had given him, and this meeting that wasn't coming off made him doubt it all the more.

Although a fox-trot was still being played, there was a rush to the door when one of Chang Kai Shek's officers entered: couples stopped dancing and gathered round him, and although Kyo could not hear what was being said he guessed that something of the greatest importance had occurred. May had gone over at once to join the group at the door: at the Black Cat a woman was suspect all the time, so nothing she did mattered. She came hurrying back. 'A bomb has been thrown at Chang Kai Shek's car.' She spoke very low. 'He wasn't in the car.'

'Who did it?'

She went over again to the crowd by the door, returning with a man who tried to insist on her dancing with him, but who went away when he saw she was not alone.

'He's escaped,' she said.

'Let's hope so. . . .'

Kyo knew how frequently such reports were incorrect. But it wasn't likely that Chang Kai Shek had been killed: his death would have been too important for the officer not to have known about it. 'The Military Committee will know,' Kyo said. 'Let's go along there at once.'

He hoped too much that Chen might have escaped, to be really doubtful about it. Whether Chang Kai Shek were still in Shanghai or whether he'd already left for Nankin, this frustrated attempt on his life lent paramount importance to the meeting of the Military Committee. Still, what could one hope for? That afternoon he had informed a sceptical – a deliberately sceptical – central committee of what Chang Kai Shek had said: this coup too closely corroborated Kyo's own point of view for its confirmation by him to be of much importance. Anyway, the Committee was aiming at playing a united hand, not a forceful one: a few days previously, the political chief of the Reds and one of the leaders of the Blues had made very moving speeches in Shanghai. And the fact that the masses had been thwarted in their siege of the Japanese Concession at Hankow was beginning to show that the Reds were powerless to make a move in central China itself. Manchurian troops were marching on Hankow and the Communists there would have to engage first them and then the army of Chang Kai Shek. Kyo walked on through the fog, May silent by his side, saying nothing. If the Communists were forced to fight tonight, they'd hardly be able to defend themselves. Whether their supply of arms had reached them or not, how could they face at odds of ten to one, and contrary to the official instructions of the Chinese Communist party, an army which would meet them in serried ranks of bourgeois volunteers, with up-to-date equipment and with the element of attack in their favour? Last month the whole town had called for a united revolutionary army: the Dictator had stood for foreign interests, Shanghai had been aggressively patriotic; the vast lower middle-classes were democratic in feeling, but not Communistic; the army that time had been there on the spot, and threatening, not retreating towards Nankin. Chang Kai Shek was no longer the villain of the piece he had been in February but a national hero to all but the Communists. Every hand against the police last month; the Communists against the army

235

now. The town itself was neutral; if anything, inclined toward the General. They would barely be able to defend the workers' quarters: Chapei, maybe. And then? If Clappique was mistaken, if a month were to elapse before the reaction set in, the Military Committee, Kyo, Katow, could marshal two hundred thousand men. The new storm-troops, recruited from the ranks of the more fiercely convinced Communists, would gain control of the unions: but a month at least would be needed before any adequate organization could be established for the handling of the masses.

And the arms problem remained unsolved. They would have to know not whether two or three thousand rifles would be delivered but how the masses would be armed if Chang Kai Shek were to spring a surprise attack. While all the discussion was taking place, the troops would have their arms taken from them. And even if the Military Committee were to demand armaments, whatever reasons it alleged, the Central Executive always took fright at any attitude that might, rightly or wrongly, seem to fall in with the views of the Opposition in Russia, because the Trotsky theories opposed a union with the Kuomintang.

Kyo, through the fog – it hadn't lifted yet so that one had to keep to the pavement for fear of oncoming cars – could now just see the dim light at the Military Committee headquarters. The night was dark, and there was thick fog: he had to strike a light to see the time. He was a few minutes late. He'd have to hurry. He slipped May's arm under his own; she pressed gently against him. They had only gone a few steps when he felt her give a jerk and her body suddenly go limp: she fell, slithering to the ground at his feet. 'May!' He stumbled, fell on all fours, and, just as he was getting up, a truncheon fetched him a vicious blow on the back of the head. He fell forward across her, full length.

Three policemen came out of a house and joined the one who had struck him. An empty car was drawn up a few yards ahead. They hauled him into it and drove off, starting to tie him up only when the car had begun to move.

*

When May came to (what Kyo had taken for a hiccup was a truncheon blow in the small of the back), a picket of Chang Kai Shek's soldiers had been posted at the entrance to the Military Committee headquarters: the fog prevented her from seeing them until she was almost on top of them. Walking straight on (she was breathing with difficulty and her side hurt), she hurried as fast as possible to Gisors' house.

As soon as he learned that a bomb had been thrown at Chang Kai Shek, Hemmelrich had dashed to get news. They told him that the general had been killed and the murderer had escaped; but there by the overturned car, with its bonnet torn off, he had seen Chen's body lying on the pavement – small and covered with blood, and already quite wet with the fog. A soldier squatted on guard beside it. Hemmelrich learned that the general had not been in the car. Unreasonably, he felt that his refusal to shelter Chen had been one of the causes of his death. In desperation he ran to the local Communist headquarters and spent an hour vainly discussing the attempted assassination. A comrade came in.

'The Weavers' Union in Chapei has just been shut by Chang Kai Shek's soldiers.'

'Did the comrades offer no resistance?'

'All who protested were instantly shot. They're shooting the active members of the party too at Chapei, or setting fire to their houses. . . . The Municipal Government has been broken up. . . . The unions are being closed.'

No instructions had come from the Central Committee. The married comrades left at once to convey their wives and children out of danger.

As soon as Hemmelrich went out, he heard more shooting. There was a risk he might be recognized, but first of all he had to get his wife and child out of the way. Through the fog he saw two armoured cars go by and lorries packed with Chang Kai Shek's soldiers. In the distance the shooting went on continuously; and there was shooting, too, nearer at hand. No uniforms in the Avenue des Deux-Républiques, nor in the street where his shop stood on the corner No; truer to say 'no longer' any uniforms The door of the shop was open. He ran across to it; gramophone records were scattered all over the floor, amid great pools of blood The shop had been 'cleaned up' like a trench, with Mills bombs. His wife lay huddled against the counter, almost in a squatting position, her breast a scarlet wound. In one corner, the arm of a child; its hand, thus isolated from the body, seemed even smaller. 'So long as they're dead!' thought Hemmelrich. He shrank above all else from a death agony he would have been impotent to tend; he would have had to stand there unable to do anything, able only to suffer, as always happened. . . . He dreaded that more than all these splintered music-stands covered with blood. Through his shoe, he could feel the floor; it was sticky. 'Their blood . . .' He stayed stock still, not daring to move, looking about him, looking. . . . At last he made out where the child's body lay, behind the door, which hid it from sight. Far away two hand-grenades went off. Hemmelrich hardly breathed, overcome by the smell of blood just spilt. 'Burying them's out of the question. . .' He locked the door, stood outside. 'If some one comes along and recognizes me, I'm a dead man.' But he could not go away.

He knew he was suffering but a halo of indifference encircled his misery – that indifference which follows illness or a blow on the head. No pain could have roused him: this time, in fact,

Fate had dealt him a shrewder blow than ever before. Death didn't stagger him; there was little to choose between it and life. The only thing that was shattering to him was the thought that there had been as much pain felt behind this door as there now was blood. All the same, this time destiny had made a mess of it: by snatching from him everything he had left, it had freed him.

He went in and shut the door. Despite his feeling of collapse, of having been hit with a club on the nape of the neck, despite the weakness in his shoulders, he could not rid his mind of a frightful, a weighty, a deep sense of relief. With mingled horror and contentment he felt it surging within him like an underground torrent, rising, coming nearer. . . . There the bodies lay, his feet were sticking to the ground and it was their blood which made them stick, nothing could be more point-less than these murders – especially the murder of his sick child – even less to blame, he reflected, than the dead woman – but now he was bound no longer. Now he too could kill. It had suddenly been revealed to him that living was not the only way of com-ing into contact with human beings, that it was not even the best way: that he could know them, feel for them, possess them more in vengeance than in giving them life. Once more he felt his soles stick to the floor, and staggered; the thought had at any rate not helped his muscles. But a fierce exaltation overcame him – the deepest sensation he had ever known; he gave him-self up to this awful intoxication, surrendering himself to it completely. 'You can kill – lovingly. Lovingly, good God!' he cried over and over again, hammering on the counter with his fist – seeming to hammer against all the world. . . . At once he drew back his hand, a spasm contracting his throat, beyond the power to sob: the counter, too, was soaked in blood. He looked at the stain already dark on his hand, a hand which shook as if stricken. Small flakes peeled off it. He must laugh, cry, he must escape from the tangled strain, the knot in his chest. . . . Noth-ing moved, the vast indifference of the world lay over all these broken records, the dead, the blood. The phrase: 'The limbs of the condemned were torn from them with red-hot pincers' swung in and out of his mind; he had forgotten it since his schooldays; but he felt that it meant in some vague way that he must leave, that he too must tear himself away.

Finally, he knew not how, departure became feasible. He managed to get outside, and as he started to walk in a sightless daze there stirred within him the germ of an infinite hatred. Thirty yards farther on, he stopped. 'I've left the door open, with them inside.' He went back. As he drew nearer and still nearer he felt the sobs coming, knotting far down his throat, deep in his chest, not rising, remaining there. He shut his eyes; heaved the door to. The lock clicked: shut now. He turned away. 'It's not over yet,' he groaned, as he walked. 'It's just beginning. Just beginning. . . .' With shoulders thrust forward, he lurched along, like a bargee plodding up a towing-path, towards a vague country of which he knew only that murder was done there, his shoulders and his brain dragging the weight of all these corpses which could now at last no longer hold him back.

With shaking hands, chattering teeth, carried along by this new frightful sense of liberty, ten minutes later he had reached headquarters. It was a single-storied house. No doubt mattresses had been propped up behind the windows: there were no blinds, but you could see no blocks of light through the fog, merely thin vertical streaks. The street, little more than an alley-way, was deathly quiet, and these thin streaks of light had here the pin-point, vivid clarity of dotted harbour signals. He rang the bell. The door half-opened: he was known. Inside, four active service men, Mausers in hand, watched him enter. Like an antheap, the broad passage-way within swarmed with confusion; everything flowed up from the cellar; the landing was empty. Away from the others, two workmen were emplacing a machine-gun at the top of the stairs, to cover the approach up the passage. It did not glint at all, but it caught the eye like an altar in a church. Students, workmen scurried about. He passed rolls of barbed wire (what would be the use of that?) edged past the machine-gun and reached the head of the stairs. Katow emerged from an office and glanced at him question-ingly. Without a word he held out his blood-bespattered hand.

'Wounded? The bandages are downstairs. Is the boy hidden?'

Hemmelrich could not speak. Obstinately, idiotically, he thrust out his hand. 'It's their blood,' he thought. But that couldn't be told.

'I've a knife,' he said at last. 'Give me a rifle.'

'There aren't many left.'

'Hand-grenades then.'

Katow hesitated.

'Damn your eyes, d'you think I'm afraid?'

'Go on down. There are grenades in the packing-cases. Not many. . . . Do you know where Kyo is?'

'Not seen him. I saw Chen: he's dead.'

'I know.'

Hemmelrich went downstairs. The men, arms buried to the shoulders, were rummaging in an open crate. Munitions were evidently running out. Comrades jostled here in the lamplight. There were no vent holes. To come upon this solid mass of heavy bodies round the crate, after the flitting shadows and veiled lights of the corridor, startled him: it was as if these men had suddenly gained the right to a life of greater reality than the others. He filled his pockets and went upstairs again. The others, the shadows, had finished fixing the machine-gun in position and had stretched the barbed wire behind the door, a short way back, so that it could be opened; the bell kept ring-ing every other minute. He looked through the peep-hole: the mist-laden street was still quiet and empty: Comrades came up, blurred shapes in the fog, like fish in muddy water, hugging the murky belt of shadow under the eaves. He turned back to look for Katow – as he did so, two hurried rings at the bell, a

ME–16   241

shot, and a gasp, were followed by the sound of a body falling.

'They're on us!' – a simultaneous cry from several of the guards at the door. There was silence again in the passage, broken by the sound of voices and the rattle of arms in the cellar. The men were taking up their battle positions.

1.30 A.M.

Clappique, recovering from his lie as others emerge from a hangover, walked along the corridor of his Chinese hotel where the native boys sprawling over a round table under the bell-board spat sunflower seeds about the spittoons. He knew he'd never get to sleep. Mournfully he opened his door, flung his coat on the familiar copy of *The Tales of Hoffman*, and poured himself out a whisky: alcohol assuaged the depression which sometimes descended on him. There was something odd about the room. He forced himself not to think about it: the inexplicable absence of certain objects in the room would have upset him too much. He had succeeded in escaping from almost all the things that men base their lives on: love, a family, work – but not from fear. Fear surged up in him, in a keen realization of his loneliness; ordinarily, to chase it away, he fled to the nearest Black Cat, took refuge with women who offer open arms and ready bodies, their minds elsewhere. That, tonight, was out of the question: overcome, stuffed with lies and momentary tenderness. . . . He saw himself in the glass, and walked over to it.

'All the same, old boy,' he said, addressing the Clappique in the mirror, 'why run away? How long can all this go on for, anyway? You've had a wife – all right, *all* right! Mistresses, money . . you can always think of them when you need ghosts to chase you out of yourself. Enough said! You've talent, as they say – imagination, all the qualities that are needed to make a good parasite. You can always be Ferral's valet when old age has mellowed you. Or one could be a gentleman-crook – the police, then suicide. Pimp? There you go again, crazy, ambitious. Suicide's what's left.... I keep telling you that. But you don't want to die. You don't want to die, you little bastard! Can't you see you've got just the sort of face that dead men have. ...'

He went closer still, till his nose almost touched the glass; he pulled a face, mouth open, grimacing like a gargoyle, and, as if his reflection had answered him back, exclaimed:

'Every one can't be dead? No, of course not: it takes all sorts to make a world. Bah, when you're dead you'll go to Paradise. You'd be such good company for the Almighty, wouldn't you now?'

He twisted his face into a different expression, his mouth closed and dragging down to his chin, eyes half-open like a samurai mask at a carnival. Then at once, as if the strain that words had not managed to convey were finding now its direct expression, he began to grimace, turning himself into an ape, an idiot, a man afraid, or in a trance, taking on every grotesque likeness that the human visage can assume. But that was no longer enough: he had recourse to his fingers, tugging at the corners of his eyes, widening his mouth into the frog-like expression of a comic mask, flattening his nose, pulling at his ears. Each of these faces meant something to him, explained a part of himself that life had concealed from him; this orgy of the grotesque in his solitary room, with the fog and the darkness massed thick at the window, took on the atrocious and terrifying comedy of madness. He heard himself laugh – a single note of his own voice, the same as his mother's; and suddenly recognizing that face, drew back in terror and sank gasping into a chair. There was a pad of writing-paper and a pencil near the chair. If he went on like this he would really go mad. To defend himself against the frightful power of the mirror, he began to write:

'You'll end up a king, my dear Toto – a real swaggering king, good and proper, in some cosy asylum, thanks to D.T.s, your only friend, if you don't stop drinking. Right now, are you drunk or sober? You who are so good at imagining things, why don't you start imagining you are happy? Don't you think . . .'

There was a knock at the door.

He slid back into reality: delivered, but in a daze. The knock was repeated.

'Come in.'

A woollen cloak, a black felt hat, white hair: Gisors' father.

'But I – I –' stammered Clappique.

'Kyo has just been arrested,' said Gisors. 'You know König, don't you?'

'I – there's nothing I can do, I –'

Gisors regarded him thoughtfully. 'So long as he's not too drunk,' he thought.

'You know König?' he repeated.

'Yes, I – I know him. I've – I've – done him a good turn before now. A very good turn.'

'Could you ask him to do the same for you?'

'Why not? But what is it you want him to do?'

'In his capacity as Chief of Chang Kai Shek's bodyguard, König can set Kyo free. Or at least prevent his being shot – that's the first consideration, is it not?'

'I under – I understand.'

All the same he had so little faith in König's sense of gratitude that he had thought it pointless, possibly rash, to go and see him, even after what Chpilewski had said. He sat down on the bed, gazing at the floor. He didn't dare speak. The tone of Gisors' voice showed him that he did not in the least suspect that Clappique had been in any way responsible for his arrest. Gisors saw in him only the friend who had come to warn Kyo that afternoon, not the man who had been gambling at the time of the rendezvous. But Clappique wasn't convinced. He didn't dare look at him, and could not calm his nerves. Gisors wondered from what drama or what mad fantasy Clappique had just emerged, not guessing that his own presence was one of the causes of this heavy breathing. It seemed to Clappique that Gisors was accusing him.

'You know, don't you, old man, that I'm not – well, I'm not as mad as all that. I – I – '

He couldn't stop babbling idiotically; it sometimes seemed to him that Gisors was the only man who understood him; and sometimes that he took him for a fool. The old man watched him silently.

'I – What is your opinion of me?'

Gisors would have preferred to take him by the scruff of the neck and drag him along to König rather than stay here talking to him. But such evident collapse was visible beneath the drunkenness he ascribed to him that he dared not fail to enter into the game.

'There are those who need to write, those who need to dream, those who need to talk. . . . It's all one. The theatre's not a serious matter; it's the bullfight that's really serious. Novels aren't serious either, but mythology is . . .'

Clappique got up.

'Have you hurt your arm?'

'A sprain. It is nothing.'

Clappique had just twisted his arm back with a clumsy gesture so as to hide his wrist-watch from Gisors; as if he would be betrayed by this watch, which had told him the time while he gambled. He realized from Gisors' next question that that was absurd.

'When will you go to see König?'

'Would tomorrow morning do?'

'Why not right away? The police are up tonight,' said Gisors bitterly. 'Anything might happen. . . .'

That suited Clappique perfectly. Not from any feeling of remorse – if he'd been at the tables now, he'd have stayed again a second time – but by way of compensation.

'Quick. Let's go, old boy,' he said.

The change he had noticed when he entered the room worried him anew. He looked more carefully and was amazed not to have seen it earlier: one of his Taoist pictures, that were his means of escape, and his two finest statues, had disappeared. A letter lay on the table: the writing was Chpilewski's. He guessed what it was. But he didn't dare read it: Chpilewski had warned him that Kyo was in danger. If he were fool enough to mention him, he would never be able to prevent himself blurting out the whole thing. He took the letter and slipped it into his pocket.

No sooner were they in the street than they met armoured cars and lorries full of soldiers.

Clappique was almost calm again; to hide the concern which he could not quite escape, he played the madman, as he always did.

'I'd like to be a magician; I'd send the Caliph a unicorn – yes, a unicorn. I tell you – which would appear in the palace, coloured like the sun, and cry: "Learn, Caliph, that the chief Sultana is unfaithful to you! Not a word!" I myself should make a gorgeous unicorn, with my nose! And the point is, of course, it wouldn't be true. You'd think no one knew how delicious it is to live in the eyes of some one else a life that is not one's own. Especially in a woman's eyes. . . . '

'What woman has not assumed a false personality for one at least of the men who have accosted her in the street?'

'You – believe that all human beings are mythomaniacs?'

Clappique's eyelids fluttered nervously; he walked slower.

'No, look here, tell me frankly,' he said. 'Why should you imagine they aren't?'

He suddenly experienced a wish, a wish that struck him as exceedingly odd and yet irresistibly strong, to ask Gisors what he thought of gambling; and yet without a doubt, if he mentioned gambling, he would confess everything. Was he going to speak? Silence would have forced him to; fortunately, Gisors spoke.

'I'm perhaps the person most unfitted to answer you,' he said. 'Opium teaches only one thing: which is that, except for physical suffering, there is no reality.'

'Pain, yes . . . And fear.'

'Fear?'

'You've never known fear, after t-taking opium?'

'No. Why?'

'Ah. . . .'

In point of fact, Gisors believed that although the world itself was unreal, men, even those who strove most against the world, possessed a very strong reality, and that Clappique, as it happened, was one of the very few human beings who were entirely devoid of reality. And it pained him to feel this, as it was into these uncertain hands that he was entrusting Kyo's fate. beneath the postures every man adopts is a foundation that can be reached, and to consider the sufferings he is capable of allows one a glimpse of what that foundation is like. Clappique's distress was independent of himself, like a child's; he was not responsible for it; it might have killed him – it would never be able to change him. He might cease to exist, he might disappear, thanks to some vice, some form of monomania – but he would never become a man. 'A heart of gold – but hollow.' Gisors realized that at bottom, Clappique was neither unhappy nor lonely, but merely a sensationalist. Gisors occasionally estimated people by imagining them in old age. Clappique would not age. Age could never bring him to man's experience only to an intoxication – either erotic or drugged – in which all forms of denying life might be combined.

'Perhaps,' thought the baron, 'if I were to tell him the whole story, he'd think it all quite natural. . . . ' Firing had become general now in the Chinese quarters of the town. Clappique begged Gisors to leave him on the outskirts of the Concession: König would not have received him. Gisors stopped and watched the other's lean, untidy silhouette fade into the fog.

*

A special section of Chang Kai Shek's police was installed in a
small villa built in about 1920: in suburban style but with
windows ornamented with extravagant Portuguese scrolls and
carvings painted blue and yellow. Two attendants and many
more pickets than necessary, all of them fully armed: that was
all. A secretary handed Clappique a form on which he wrote
'Toto', left the 'Object of visit' line blank, and waited. It was the
first lighted place he had been in since he left his room: he
pulled Chpilewski's letter out of his pocket:

MY DEAR FRIEND,
   I have given way because you were so insistent. My scruples were
well founded but now I have thought again: so you will please allow
me to seek peace and quiet. The profits that are at this time likely to
accrue from this business of mine are so considerable and so certain
that I shall surely be able to offer you before next year merchandise of
the same sort as well as certain even more beautiful pieces. The com-
missariat business in this town. . . .'

   There followed four pages of explanations.
   'That's not so good,' thought Clappique. 'Not so good at
all.' But an attendant came to fetch him.
   König was expecting him, seated at his desk, facing the
door. Squat and dark, his nose set aslant in his square face,
came over and gripped Clappique's hand in a quick, firm
grasp – which kept them apart more than it brought them
together.
   'You all right? Good. I knew I should be seeing you
today. I'm happy to have been able to be useful to you in my
turn.'
   'You are a powerful man,' said Clappique, half in jest. 'I only
wonder whether there hasn't been some mistake: as you know,
I'm no politician. . . .'

'There's no mistake.'

'His gratitude looks pretty like condescension,' thought Clappique.

'You've two days to clear out in. You did me a service once; I now warn you.'

'W-what? Was it you who warned me?'

'Do you think Chpilewski would have dared? You're up against the Chinese secret service, but it's no longer the Chinese who run it. We're having no more nonsense now.'

Clappique began to admire Chpilewski, but not without a certain feeling of irritation.

'Well, then,' he went on, 'since you are good enough to remember me, may I ask something else of you?'

'What?'

Clappique had no longer any great hope: every fresh answer König gave him made it clearer that the friendly feeling he had been counting on had ceased to exist. If König had warned him, he was no longer in his debt. It was more by way of salving his conscience than with any actual hope that he said:

'Couldn't something be done for the young Gisors? Only I suppose you don't give a damn for all that. . . . '

'What is he?'

'A Communist – a leading Communist, I gather.'

'Why is he a Communist, though, tell me? Because of his father? Is he an Eurasian? Couldn't he find a job? For a workman to be a Communist is idiotic enough, but this boy, really . . . Well, what's the point of it, anyway?'

'It's not very easy to say, in a word . . . '

Clappique thought for a moment.

'Maybe he's an Eurasian; but he could have got on all right. His mother was Japanese. He hasn't tried. He says something about the will to dignity. . . . '

'Dignity!'

Clappique was amazed. König was yelling at him. He hadn't expected the word to have this effect.

'Have I slipped up?' he wondered.

'What's that mean, dammit, anyway?' König demanded, wagging his forefinger as if he would have gone on talking even if there had been no one to hear him. 'Dignity!' he snorted. Clappique could not mistake the tone of his voice: there was hatred in it. He was standing on Clappique's right and his nose, which therefore seemed extremely beaky, strongly accentuated his face.

'Tell me, my dear Toto, do you believe in this dignity of yours?'

'Yes, in other people. ....'

'Really now?'

Clappique was silent.

'Do you know what the Reds did to the officers they took prisoner?'

Clappique still didn't answer. This was beginning to look very nasty. He felt that the last remark was a starting-point, an aid, a helping hand that König was giving himself: no answer was required or expected.

'In Siberia I was attached to a prison-camp as interpreter. I managed to get out of it by serving in the White Army, under Semenoff. Whites and Reds were all one to me; I didn't care, I wanted to get back to Germany. I was taken by the Reds. I was half-dead with cold. They beat me about with their fists, calling me "Captain" all the time (I was a lieutenant), until they knocked me down. Then they picked me up again. I wasn't wearing Semenoff's uniform, with those little death's heads on it. I had a star on each epaulette.'

He stopped short. 'He could just as well say "no" without making such a song and dance about it,' thought Clappique. Still, the huskiness and heaviness of König's voice seemed to imply some urge which Clappique tried to understand.

'They drove a nail into each of my shoulders, through those stars. A nail as long as your finger. Listen to what I'm telling you, my dear Toto ...'

He seized him by the arm, his eyes fixed on the eyes of the other, with the look of a man in love.

'I squealed like a woman, blubbered like a baby . . . I cried in front of them, with them looking on. You understand, don't you? Let's leave it at that. It will be just as well.'

This look of a man filled with desire enlightened Clappique. The confession he had just heard was not surprising now; it was not a confidence, it was a revenge. For a certainty he repeated this story – or told it over to himself – whenever a chance of killing some one came his way, as if the story itself could scratch and draw blood from the boundless humiliation that obsessed him.

'My friend, you would be well advised not to say too much to me about dignity. . . . My own dignity consists in killing them off. . . . What the hell do you think China matters to me? Eh? China – really, though! I'm not a member of the Kuomintang for any other purpose than to be able to stamp them out. I never live now as I lived once, like a man, like any one else in the world, like the least poor fool who passes by these windows— except when they're being killed. . . . I'm like an opium-smoker with his pipe. It's a mania. You came to ask me to save his skin? Even if you had saved my life three times over. . . .'

He shrugged his shoulders and went on, angrily:

'Have you any sort of idea, my good Toto, of what it means to see one's life taking on a shape, a definite shape; and to grow disgusted with oneself . . . ?'

The last words of his sentence were spoken through his teeth, but he did not move, his hands deep in his pockets, his untidy hair shaken by the fury of his words.

'One can forget . . .' said Clappique, almost inaudibly.

'It's more than a year since I bedded with a woman. Is that enough for you? And I . . .'

He stopped short, then went on in a lower tone:

'But see here, my dear Toto, young Gisors, young Gisors. . . . You mentioned a misunderstanding; do you still want to know why you're being punished? I'll tell you. It *was* you who handled the business of those rifles on the *Shan-Tung*, wasn't it? Do you know who they were for?'

'No questions are asked in this racket – not a word!'

He laid his forefinger to his lips, acting on his customary instincts. He immediately regretted it.

'For the Communists. And as you were risking your hide over it, they might at least have told you. Anyway, it was a swindle. They made use of you to gain time: that same night they rifled the ship. If I'm not mistaken, it was this present protégé of yours who got you into that business?'

Clappique was on the point of answering: 'All the same, I got my percentage.' But the information his interlocutor had just imparted to him had spread such an expression of content over his features that the baron wanted nothing better than to leave at once. Although Kyo had kept his promises, he had gambled with his, Clappique's, life without telling him. Would he himself have risked so much? No. Kyo had been right to give first thought to the interests of his cause; and he would be right to take no further thought of Kyo. All the more so, as there was really nothing he could do. He simply shrugged his shoulders.

'So I've forty-eight hours to clear out in, have I?'

'Yes. You don't keep on about it – and you're quite right. So-long.'

'He says it's a year since he slept with a woman,' thought Clappique, as he made his way downstairs. Was he impotent, or what? 'I should have thought that this sort of . . . melodrama gave you a morbid interest in sex, if anything. He probably makes a habit of such confidences to those who are about to die. . . . Anyway, I'd really better clear out.' He could not get over the tone in which König had said: 'If one's to live like a man, like any one at all . . . ' He felt fascinated by this utter intoxication, which only blood could satisfy: he had seen enough of the wreckage of civil war in China and Siberia to know what a negation of the world intense humiliation produced; only blood deliberately spilled, drugs, and neuroses, are nourishing to such loneliness; now he understood why König had so enjoyed his company, for he knew quite well how all reality faded away in his presence. He walked slowly, terrified of finding Gisors waiting for him there beyond the barbed wire. What should he say to him? . . . It was too late: in his impatience, Gisors, coming to meet him, appeared from out of the fog a yard or two away. He was staring at him with the haggard intensity of the madman. Clappique was afraid, stopped short. Gisors was already taking him by the arm.

'No good?' he said in a dull tone, showing no excitement.

Without a word, Clappique shook his head.

'All right. I must go and ask another friend to help me.'

As he watched Clappique appear through the fog, a realization of his own madness had been borne in on him. The whole conversation he had imagined taking place between them, on the baron's return, was absurd. Clappique wasn't an interpreter, or a go-between – he was just a playing-card. A card laid on the table – and lost. That much was clear from Clappique's face; the thing to do now was to find another. Choking with misery, in the utmost distress, he yet remained clearheaded in his despair. He had thought of Ferral; but Ferral wouldn't intervene in a conflict of this sort. He was going to try to get two of his friends to intercede.

*

König had called in his secretary:

'The younger Gisors: I want him here tomorrow, when the council meetings are over.'

Towards morning, Katow and Hemmelrich looked out from the first-floor windows, and watched the coming dawn lay streaks of lead-grey light on near-by roofs, up above the short, faintly yellow flashes of gunfire, while at the same time the outlines of houses began to take shape. With tousled hair falling across their white faces, each of the men once more recognized his next-door neighbour, and knew what he was thinking. Their last dawn. . . . Almost no ammunition left. No rising of the people had occurred to bring them succour. Shooting in the Chapei direction: their comrades besieged like themselves. Katow had explained to Hemmelrich why they were lost; at any moment Chang Kai Shek's men would bring up a small calibre field-gun – the general's guard had several guns of this type – and once they got it into the house opposite the Communist headquarters, walls and mattress bulwarks would collapse like an Aunt Sally. The Communists' machine-gun still covered the doorway of this house; as soon as their ammunition ran out it could cover it no longer. And it wouldn't be long now before that happened. For hours they had been firing furiously, taking their revenge in advance; themselves condemned to die, slaughter was the only aim they could give to their last hours of life. But they were beginning to tire of that too. The enemy, finding better and better cover, now very seldom appeared in the line of fire. It seemed that the skirmish was failing as the night failed – and, wildly, it seemed that this new day that was being born, bringing for them no threatening shadow, would set them free, just as the coming of the previous night had imprisoned them. The daylight on the roofs had turned now to a pale grey; above the checked battle in the street, the dawn light seemed to be swallowing up large slices of the night, leaving black oblong shapes before the houses.

Shadows were shortening little by little; to watch them shorten helped you to forget the men who were about to meet their deaths. The shadows shrank as they do every day throughout time, with that same eternal motion, yet today they had a savage majesty for these men who would never see them again. Suddenly all the windows opposite lit up and bullets spattered against the door like handfuls of pebbles: one of their number had held out a shirt on the end of a stick. The enemy had contented themselves with remaining on the watch.

'Eleven, twelve, thirteen, fourteen . . .' said Hemmelrich. He was counting the bodies which could now be seen in the room.

'It's all my eye, that,' replied Katow, almost *sotto voce*. 'They've only got to wait. They've the whole day ahead of them.'

There were only five wounded men lying in the room. They didn't groan: two of them lay smoking, watching the daylight creep between the wall and the mattress-bulwarks. Farther along, Souen and another fellow stood on guard at the second window. There were very few bursts of shooting to be heard now. Were Chang Kai Shek's troops biding their time all along the line? When, the month before, they had been winning, the Communists knew from hour to hour what progress they were making. Now, like their adversaries at that time, they knew nothing of what was happening.

As if to confirm Katow's last remark, the door of the enemy building opened slightly (the corridors exactly faced each other); the crackle of a machine-gun immediately put the Communists wise. 'They brought it along across the roofs,' thought Katow.

'This way!'

His machine-gunners were calling to him. Hemmelrich and he ran out at once and saw what had happened: the enemy machine-gun, no doubt protected by a steel shield, was firing steadily, continuously. There were no Communists in the corridor of headquarters because it lay in the line of fire of their own machine-gun which, from the top of the stairs, commanded, pointing downwards, their enemies' way into the house. But now the latter were protected by the gun-shield. Still, the all-important thing was to keep on firing. The gunner had fallen on his side – dead, no doubt. The loader was the one who had cried out. He was loading and firing, but he did it slowly. The bullets sent chips from the wooden steps flying, and plaster off the walls; also dull thuds in the short swift silences showed that some had struck flesh, either living flesh or dead. Hemmelrich and Katow flung themselves forward. 'Not you!' yelled the Belgian. With a punch on the jaw he sent Katow spinning down the corridor and himself jumped into the gunner's place. The enemy were firing rather less now. But that wouldn't last long. 'Are there any bandages left?' asked Hemmelrich. In lieu of answer the loader craned his head forward, taking in the whole staircase at a glance. Hemmelrich perceived that he had no idea of how to load a machine-gun.

He bounded upstairs again and felt his eye and calf scratched in the passage, beyond and above the enemy's range of fire; he stopped; his eye had only been touched by a flake of plaster knocked off the wall by a bullet: his calf was bleeding – another bullet. It was a surface wound. Before he knew where he was, he had gone back into the room with Katow, who, kneeling on all fours, was pulling the mattress towards himself – for concealment, not for protection – while in his left hand he grasped a handful of hand-grenades, the only thing that would have any effect against the gun-shield – if they burst close enough.

They had to be thrown through the window into the enemy corridor. Katow had another packet of them on the floor behind him; Hemmelrich seized it and threw them at the same time as Katow threw his over the top of the mattress. Katow found himself back on the floor riddled with bullets, as if his own hand-grenades had struck him: as soon as their heads and arms had shown above the mattress they had been shot at from every window. Was this crackle of match-sticks, that seemed so close, the sound of his own legs? wondered Hemmelrich, who had ducked down in time. Bullets still whistled into the room but, now that the two men were lying flat, the wall protected them; the window was set eighteen inches above the floor. Despite the volley of rifle-fire, Hemmelrich would have said that there was no sound, for the two machine-guns had fallen silent. He crawled across on his elbows to Katow, who did not stir. He tugged at his shoulder. Out of range of the shooting, the two of them looked at each other in silence; in spite of the mattress blocking the window, full daylight was now flooding the room. Katow fainted away; his thigh had been shot through and a red stain was spreading on the floor as if it had been blotting-paper. Hemmelrich again heard Souen shout: 'The gun!' and then there came a vast, dull explosion and, the moment he raised his head, a blow on the base of the nose: he fainted in his turn.

Hemmelrich returned to consciousness, floating gradually upwards from a deep place towards the surface of a silence so strange that it seemed to him to be that very consciousness itself, wakening within him: the gun was no longer firing. The wall had been smashed across. Katow and the others lay on the ground, covered with debris and plaster, either dead or unconscious. He was thirsty and feverish. The wound on his calf was not serious. He crawled to the door and, in the corridor, rose heavily to his feet, supporting himself against the wall. Except for the place which hurt in his head, where a flying fragment of masonry had struck him, he could not realize how much pain he felt. Clinging to the banisters, he went down not the stairs into the street, where no doubt the enemy still lay in wait, but the stairs into the yard. There was no shooting now. There were recesses in the walls of the entrance corridor, where there had once been tables. He flung himself into the first of these niches and stared at the courtyard.

To the right of a house, that looked as if it were deserted (though he knew that it was not), stood a corrugated-iron shed;

in the background, a house with pagoda-shaped eaves, and a row of wooden stakes which led away, one behind the other, towards a countryside which he would never see again. The barbed wire entangled about the doorway webbed in black wavering lines across this whole expanse of grey daylight, like faint cracks in china. A shadow loomed up beyond this desolate scene and the barbed wire: a sort of bear. It was a man, coming towards the house, bent completely double. He was beginning to get caught up on the barbed wire.

Hemmelrich had no bullets left. He watched this bulk moving forward from one tangle of wire to the next, without being able to foretell its movements; the wire stood out sharply against the light, but was entirely out of perspective. Like a huge insect, the man clutched, fell away, clung again. Hemmelrich drew closer, hugging the wall. It was obvious that his enemy was going to pass this way; at present, though, he was absorbed in freeing himself from the wire caught in his clothes, and was growling strangely. For a time Hemmelrich felt that this monstrous insect might stay there for ever, bent double and enormous, looming dark against the grey daylight. But a hand stretched out, in clear black silhouette, open, with fingers spread apart; it seized on another twist of wire and the body began to move forward again.

This was the end. Behind him were the street and the machine-gun. Above, Katow and his men, knocked out. The deserted-looking house opposite was no doubt stiff with machine-gunners – and *they* had no shortage of ammunition. If he ventured out of the house, they would fire at his knees, so as to take him prisoner (he suddenly realized how absurdly frail were these little bones in his knees, the patellae); but at least he might manage to kill this fellow.

The monster, part bear, part man, part spider, was still disentangling itself from its wires. Beside his black bulk, a glint of light marked the muzzle of the man's revolver. Hemmelrich felt as if he were helpless in a shell-hole, fascinated less by this creature approaching as gradually as death itself than by everything that was coming in its wake, all the horror that would once more come crushing down upon him, like the lid of a coffin closing over the face of a living man; it was the same horror that had choked all the days of his life, and it was returning now to crush him once and for all. 'They've pilloried me for the last thirty-seven years and now they're going to kill me. . . . ' It was not only his own past sufferings that were stalking him now, but his mutilated wife's sufferings, too, and those of his murdered sick child: all of it mingled in a haze of thirst, high fever and loathing. Once again, without looking at it, he was conscious of the bloodstain on his left calf – not as a burn or with any discomfort: he was merely conscious that it was there – and that the man was at last about to emerge from the barbed wire. This first arrival, this man who was coming to kill off those in whom life still lingered upstairs, was doing it not for money, but for the sake of an idea, a faith. He was now still a shadow checked by a barrier of twisted steel, but Hemmelrich hated the shadow, even for this motive behind it – it wasn't enough that the more fortunate of this world should do his people to death, they had to go so far as to believe themselves justified in doing so. The silhouette, now a body risen to its full height, seemed to fill the grey courtyard prodigiously, blotting out the telegraph wires swinging away into the limitless peace of a rainy spring morning. A voice called out from a window, and the man answered, his answer echoing along the corridor round Hemmelrich. The glint of the revolver vanished into its holster, and a broad flat gleam took its place, showing almost white in the darkness; the man had drawn his bayonet. He was no longer a man, though, he was everything that had hurt Hemmelrich until that day, time and place. In this black corridor, with the machine-gunners across the road crouching behind their door, and with this enemy advancing, the Belgian went mad with rage. 'They'll have smashed every one of us all our lives, but this one shall pay for it, pay for it. . . . ' The man came nearer, his bayonet thrust forward. Hemmelrich squatted down and at once the shadow seemed to grow larger, the torso lessening in proportion above legs as strong as girders. Just as the bayonet came level with the top of his head, he sprang up, seized the man's throat in his right hand, and squeezed. . . . With the jerk the bayonet fell to the ground. The neck was too thick for one hand; his thumb and the tips of his fingers dug convulsively into flesh, without choking the breath in it; but his other hand had gone mad now and jabbed fiercely at the man's snorting face. 'You'll pay for it all!' screamed Hemmelrich. 'You'll pay for it.' The figure was swaying on its feet. Instinctively it clutched at the wall. Hemmelrich beat its head against the wall with all his strength, and stooped for a second; the Chinaman felt an enormous object rip into him, tearing his entrails – his own bayonet. He opened both his hands, pressed them to his stomach with a sharp groan and fell between Hemmelrich's legs, shoulders hunched forward – then suddenly jerked out flat. A drop of blood, then another, splashed from the bayonet on to his open hand. As if this hand, darkening every moment with blood, were the symbol of his revenge, Hemmelrich at last brought himself to look at his own hand and realized that the bloodstain on it had dried hours before. He discovered, too, that perhaps after all he was not going to die. Hurriedly he stripped the officer's clothes from him, loving this man who had come to this place to bring him his freedom, while at the same time he loathed him because the uniform could not be dragged off his body quickly enough, as if confined by it. He shook his saviour's corpse as if to jerk the clothes off him. Finally, having put on the uniform, he showed himself at the window looking into the street, his head bent so that the peak of the cap hid his face. On the other side windows were thrown open and men shouted to him. 'I'll have to clear out before they get here,' he thought. He walked out into the street and turned left as the man he had just killed would have done to rejoin his own people.

'Any prisoners?' called the men at the windows.

He made a vague gesture in the direction of those he was supposed to be rejoining. It was natural yet absurd that they should not be firing at him; he had lost all sense of surprise. He turned left again and started off in the direction of the Concessions; they were under guard, but he knew all the houses with secret entrances along the length of the Rue des Deux-Républiques.

The Kuomintang filed out, one man behind the other.

Part 6

'PROVISIONALLY,' said the guard.

Kyo realized that he was being lodged in the common gaol.

As soon as he entered the prison building, even before he had time to take a look round, its appalling stench had assailed him: a mixture of slaughter-house, dog-show and dung-heap. The door he had come through opened on to a corridor exactly like the one he had just come along: to right and left, the whole way up to the ceiling, two lines of vast wooden bars. Men were inside these wooden cages. In the middle sat the warder at a small table, on which lay a whip: short in the handle, its lash was long, flat, as broad as your hand, as thick as a finger – a lethal weapon.

'Stay there, you bastard,' the warder said.

In the darkness – he was accustomed to it – the man entered Kyo's name and particulars in his book. Kyo's head still hurt and standing still made him feel he was going to faint; he leant against the bars.

'How, how, how do you do?' some one called out behind.

The voice quavered like a parrot's, but it was the voice of a man. It was too dark for Kyo to make out his face; all he could see was an enormous hand clasping the bars – not far from his neck. Farther back, lying on narrow benches or standing up, a cluster of elongated shadows: men, like worms.

'Not so well as might be,' he answered, stepping away from the bars.

'Shut your mouth, you filth, if you don't want me to shut it for you,' said the guard.

Kyo had several times heard the word 'provisional'; so he

262

knew he would not be staying here long. He was determined to pay no attention to insults, to bear all that could possibly be borne; the important thing was to get out again, to carry on with the fighting. Nevertheless, he felt humiliated to the point of nausea, as every man does, in the presence of another human being to whom he is entirely subservient: there was nothing he could do against this obscene shadow with its whip. His self, his personality, had been taken away from him.

'How, how, how do you do?' cried the voice again.

The warder unlocked a door leading, fortunately, into a cage on the left. Kyo entered this horse-box. At the back, lying on a bench, there was only one man. The door closed behind him.

'Political prisoner?' asked the man.

'Yes. Are you?'

'No. Under the Empire, I was a mandarin.'

Kyo was growing accustomed to the dark. The speaker proved to be an old man, almost without a nose, like an old white cat; he had a straggly moustache and pointed ears.

'My trade is women. When business is good, I give the police money and they leave me alone. When business is bad, they think I'm hoarding the money, so they throw me into gaol. But anyway, when times are bad I'd rather be fed in prison than be free and die of hunger. . . .'

'What? In this place!'

'You know, one gets used to it. . . . Things aren't too easy outside either, when one's old, as I am, and not as strong as one was. . . .'

'Why aren't you with the others?'

'I sometimes slip some money to the clerk of the court on the way in. So that whenever I come to this place, I'm put in the "provisional" section.'

The warder brought round the rations; he pushed through the bars two little bowls containing a mud-coloured paste, which gave off a vapour as fetid as the surrounding atmosphere.

He dipped a ladle into a pot and poured broth into each little bowl, where it landed with a *plop*, and then handed them along one by one to the prisoners in the next cage.

'Not worth it,' said a voice. 'Fixed for tomorrow.' (His execution, the mandarin explained to Kyo.)

'Me too,' said another voice. 'So you might give me a double dose, damn it. Thinking of tomorrow makes me hungry.'

'D'you want my fist in your face?' the warder asked.

A soldier came in and asked him a question. He went into the cage on the right and prodded a body lying there.

'He still moves. I expect he's alive . . . ' he said. The soldier departed.

Kyo strained his eyes to see which of the shadows owned these voices that were on the verge of death – as he was, too, perhaps. He could not make them out: they were men who would die without ever being for him anything more than voices.

'Aren't you eating your stuff?' his companion asked.

'No.'

'It's always like that, just at first. . . . '

He took Kyo's bowl. The warder came in, fetched the man a terrific slap across the face and went out again, taking away the bowl, without saying a word.

'Why didn't he hit me?' demanded Kyo in a whisper.

'I was the only one to blame, but that's not really why. You're a political prisoner, here only temporarily, and you're well-dressed. He'll try to get some money out of you, or your family. Not that that'd stop him, either. You wait . . . '

'Money dogs me even here, even to this filthy hole,' thought Kyo. As if a part of some legend, the depredations of the warder seemed to him not wholly real; and at the same time struck him as dire and fateful, as though a position of authority were enough to change any man into a beast. And these dim creatures swarming behind the bars, as dreadful as the huge

264

crabs and spiders he had seen in dreams as a child, were not men either. Utter loneliness, complete humiliation. 'Be careful,' he thought, for he felt himself weakening already. It occurred to him that, had he not overcome the idea of death, panic would have seized him at this point. He unbuckled the clasp of his belt and slipped the cyanide into his pocket.

'How, how, how do you do?' the voice cried out again.

'Shut up!' the prisoners in the next cage shouted, together to a man. Kyo by now was accustomed to the gloom and so was not surprised by the number of voices: more than ten figures lay on the benches, behind the bars.

'How, how, how do you do?'

The warder got up.

'What is this chap – a buffoon or a lout?' Kyo asked in a low tone.

'He's neither,' said the mandarin. 'He's mad.'

'But why . . .'

Kyo asked no further questions; his cell-mate had clapped his hands to his ears. A shrill, raucous cry – a cry both of anguish and fright – burst forth in the darkness. While Kyo had been looking at the mandarin, the warder had gone into the next-door cage with his whip. The lash cracked, and the same cry echoed out again. Kyo didn't dare stop up his ears, so he waited, clinging to the bars, for the frightful cry to tingle through him again to his finger-tips.

'Give it to him good and proper this time,' said a voice, 'then maybe he'll let us have some peace!'

'Have it out with him once and for all,' five or six voices exclaimed. 'Let's get some sleep!'

The mandarin, his hands still covering his ears, leant towards Kyo.

'That's the eleventh time he's beaten him in a week, apparently. I've only been here a couple of days – and this is the fourth time already. You can just hear, even like this. . . . You know, I can't shut my eyes. I feel that if I look at him, I somehow come to his help, I'm not leaving him quite entirely alone.'

Kyo also watched, almost without seeing anything. 'What makes me look – pity or cruelty?' he asked himself, terrified. . . . All that is lowest in a human being, that part of him that can be attracted, spellbound, was being appealed to here savagely, overwhelmingly, and Kyo's whole brain was struggling against human ignominy. He remembered what an effort it had always needed for him to escape from the chance spectacle of human flesh in pain; he had had, literally, to tear himself away. That men could watch the thrashing of a madman who was actually harmless – and old, probably, judging by his voice – produced in him the same terror as Chen had called forth in him that night in Hankow: 'the octopus . . . ' Katow had spoken to him of the effort a medical student has to make in order to control his nerves the first time he glimpses living organs in a stomach cut open on an operating-table. This was the same numbing horror, so different from fear itself, a horror all-powerful even before the conscious mind could register it and all the more devastating because Kyo sensed, to the point of nausea, his own submission to it. Yet his eyes, which were far less accustomed to the darkness than the other man's, could make out only the streak of the lash which tore these screams from the victim, like a boat-hook. After the first stroke he had not moved: he stayed there, clinging to the bars, his hands level with his face.

'Warder!' he yelled.

'D'you want it too?'

'I've something to say to you.'

'Oh, have you?'

While the warder slammed-to the enormous lock, the prisoners he was leaving behind him in the other cage danced up and down. They loathed 'political prisoners' who were kept apart from themselves.

'Go to it, Boss, go to it!' they squealed.

The man stood face to face with Kyo, halved vertically down the middle by a bar of the cage. His face expressed the most despicable of all forms of anger: the anger of the moron who believes his authority is being questioned. Yet his features weren't degraded, merely anonymous, ordinary. . . .

'Listen,' said Kyo.

They looked into each other's eyes. The warder was slightly taller than Kyo, whose hands he saw, still clinging to the bars, one on each side of his head. Before Kyo could realize what had happened, he felt his left hand torn to ribbons. With full force the whip, held behind the warder's back, had cut through the air on to his hand. Kyo had not been able to prevent himself screaming.

'That's right!' yelled the prisoners opposite. 'Now it's their turn!'

Kyo's two hands had fallen to his sides, subconsciously reflexing in terror.

'Have you still got anything to say?' asked the warder.

There was the whip between them now.

Kyo clenched his teeth with all the strength he had in him and, with all the effort required to lift an enormous weight, never taking his eyes off the warder, he again raised his hands to the bars. As he slowly lifted his hands, the fellow stepped back to give himself room to swing. The whip cracked – this time on wood alone. The reflex had been stronger than Kyo's will: he had removed his hands. But already he was putting them back; there was a dragging strain in his shoulders, and the warder knew from his look that this time he would leave them there. He spat in his face and slowly raised the whip.

'If you'll . . . stop beating . . . that madman,' said Kyo, 'when I come out, I'll . . . give you fifty dollars.'

The warder hesitated.

'O.K.,' he finally agreed.

He looked away and Kyo was relieved of so fierce a tension that he expected to faint. His left hand was so painful that he

267

could not close it. He had lifted it, with his right, to the level of his shoulders and there it stayed, stretched out. Renewed howls of laughter.

'Are you holding out your hand to me?' asked the warder, joining in the guffaw.

He shook it. Kyo felt that never, as long as he lived, would he forget that handshake, not because it hurt so hideously, but because never before had life put him through so ghastly an experience. He drew back his hand and sat down all of a heap on the pallet. The warder faltered, wagged his head, and scratched it with the whip-handle. Then he went back to his desk. The madman was sobbing.

Hours of abject monotony followed. Eventually soldiers came to fetch Kyo and take him to the headquarters of the secret police. No doubt he was going to his death, and yet he left that place filled with a joy the violence of which surprised him; he felt as though he were leaving behind him some obscene part of himself.

*

'Come in!'

One of the Chinese guards gave Kyo a push on the shoulder. But not hard: when dealing with foreigners (to a Chinese, Kyo was either Japanese or European; in any case, a foreigner) the guards were afraid of the brutality they normally took to be their prerogative. At a sign from König, they stepped back out of the room. Kyo walked forward to the desk, hiding his swollen left hand in his pocket, carefully observing this man who, in his turn, also stared into his eyes: an angular, shaven face, nose on the slant, hair anyhow. 'Obviously a man who is almost certainly going to order your execution looks just like any other.' König stretched a hand towards his revolver lying on the table: no, he picked up a cigarette-box. He held it out to Kyo.

'Thanks. I don't smoke.'

'The prison ration is revolting, which is just as it should be. Would you like to share my meal with me?'

On the table were coffee, milk, two cups, slices of bread.

'Just some bread. Thank you.'

König smiled.

'It's the same coffee-pot for you and for me, you know. . . .'

Kyo was determined to be careful; anyway, König did not press the point. Kyo remained standing in front of the desk (there was nowhere to sit) and gnawed at his bread like a child. Following on the abject horror of the prison, everything seemed to him airy and unreal. He knew that his life was at stake, but even death was easy for one returning from the place where he had been. The kindliness of a police-chief inspired very little confidence in him, and König remained a good distance away from him, as if separate from his own benevolence: friendliness to the fore, himself hanging back. Nevertheless, it was possible that this man was being kind through sheer indifference. He was a white man; perhaps his present position was due either to chance, or to greed. So Kyo hoped; he had no liking for the man, but would have preferred to be relieved of the tension that had so worn him down in gaol – he had just made the discovery that to be forced to seek refuge entirely within oneself is wellnigh unendurable.

The telephone-bell rang.

'Hullo,' said König. 'Yes, Gisors, Kyoshi. Certainly. He's here with me.'

'They're asking whether you are still alive,' he told Kyo.

'Why have you had me brought here?'

'I believe we can come to an understanding.'

The telephone rang again.

'Hullo? No. I was just telling him that we should no doubt understand each other. Shot? Call me back. We shall see.'

Ever since Kyo had come into the room, König's eyes had not left his.

'What d'you think about that?' he asked, hanging up the receiver.

'I don't think anything.'

König lowered his glance, then looked up.

'Do you want to go on living?'

'It depends on how.'

'There are also several ways of dying.'

'Still, as one can't choose between them. . . .'

'You think then that one can always choose one's way of living?'

König was thinking of his own case. Kyo was determined not to give way on any essential point, but he did not want to irritate the man.

'I don't know. Do you?'

'They tell me you became a Communist for the sake of dignity. Is that true?'

At first Kyo did not understand. Waiting tensely for the telephone to ring again, he wondered what could be the meaning of this singular catechism. Finally:

'Would it really interest you to know?' he asked.

'More than you can imagine.'

The tone was threatening, even though the words were simple enough. Kyo replied:

'I think that Communism will make dignity possible for those who are fighting with me. In any case, the forces that are opposed to Communism oblige them to have none, unless they happen to possess a wisdom which is as rare in them as in the others – more rare, maybe, by very reason of the fact that they are poor and that their work separates them from their true lives. Why ask me this question, if you're not listening to my answer?'

'What do you call "dignity"? It means nothing.'

The telephone-bell rang. 'My life,' thought Kyo. König did not lift the receiver.

'The opposite of humiliation,' said Kyo. 'When you

come from where I've just come from, it has some meaning.'

The telephone went on ringing unanswered. König laid his hand on it. He merely asked:

'Where is your hidden armoury?'

'You can leave the telephone alone. I've tumbled to it at last. All these calls are a stage-set rigged up for my benefit.'

Kyo ducked instantly: König had been within an ace of throwing one of the two revolvers at his head. Probably it wasn't loaded. He put it back on the table.

'I can do better than that,' he said. 'As for the telephone, you'll soon see whether we're fooling with it or not, my young friend. Have you seen torture yet?'

Kyo, in his pocket, tried to close his swollen fingers together. The cyanide was in this same left pocket and he was afraid of dropping it if it came to lifting it to his mouth.

'I've seen the after-effects, anyway. I've fought in civil war. What amazes me is why you should ask me where the arms are. You know where they are – or will know soon. So why ask me?'

'The Communists have been defeated all along the line.'

'Maybe.'

'It is so. Think it over carefully; if you work for us, you're saved, and nobody'll be any the wiser. I'll let you escape. . . . '

'He might very well begin with that,' thought Kyo. Nervousness was sharpening his sense of the humorous, though there was no need for that. But he knew that the police weren't ever satisfied with anything but absolute certainty. All the same, the proposal surprised him, as if, because it was the usual thing, it couldn't be genuine.

'Only I shall know about it,' König went on. 'That's all that's needed. . . . '

Why such smacking of the lips, Kyo wondered, over the phrase: 'That's all that's needed'?

'I won't enter your service,' he said, almost casually.

'Take care: I could bundle you off to the Secret Police

together with a dozen innocent men, telling them that their fate depends on you, and that they won't come out of prison until you talk, and can employ what means they like . . .'

'An execution's easier.'

'But alternating supplications and cruelty, that's worse. Don't talk of what you know nothing about – so far, at least.'

'I've just been seeing what was to all intents and purposes the torturing of a madman. A madman – do you understand?'

'Have you a clear idea of what you are risking?'

'I have fought in civil war, I tell you. I know, all right. Our people did some torturing too. Humanity will have to be very well compensated for that. Never mind. I won't serve you.'

König was sure that, in spite of what he had told Kyo, his threat had not been understood. 'His youth helps him,' he reflected. Two hours before he had questioned a prisoner who was a member of the Tcheka; within ten minutes he had made friends with him: they both belonged to a world which was not the ordinary world of men; and from then on they had left it behind them. Well, if Kyo was too unimaginative to be susceptible to fear, he could wait. . . .

'Don't you wonder why I still haven't flung this revolver at your face?'

'I realize that I may be on the point of dying. That does away with curiosity. Besides, you told me: "I can do better than that. . . ." '

König rang the bell.

'I may come and see you tonight to ask you what you feel about human dignity,' and, as the door opened and the guards entered, 'Prison-yard, Section A,' he said.

4 P.M.

Clappique mingled in the crowd from the Concessions streaming towards the barbed-wire entanglements. As he went along

272

the Avenue des Deux-Républiques the public executioner passed by, his curved sword on his shoulder, followed by a police escort armed with revolvers. Clappique turned back at once and entered the Concession. Kyo had been arrested, the Communist stand overcome, many of their sympathizers murdered there in the European quarter itself. König had given him until the evening; he would not be safeguarded much longer. Isolated shots could still be heard at intervals. Borne on the wind, the sound seemed to be chasing him, bringing death with it. 'I don't want to die,' he muttered between his teeth; 'I don't want to die.' He discovered he was running. Running, he reached the docks.

He had no passport. And not enough money left to buy a ticket.

There were three passenger-steamers, one of them French. Clappique slackened his pace to a walk. Could he stow himself away under the tarpaulin cover of one of the lifeboats? He'd have to go on deck to do that, and the man on the bridge would never let him pass. It was foolish, anyhow. What about the bunkers? Idiotic, quite idiotic. Should he go and see the captain, brazen it out? He had got himself out of jams in this way before now – but on this occasion the captain would take him for a Communist and would refuse to have him on board. The boat was sailing in two hours' time: not a good moment to choose to start pestering the captain. If he were found when once they were out at sea, he'd fix things all right, but he'd have first to get aboard somehow.

He pictured himself hidden away in a corner, crouching in a crate or something; but this time his imagination didn't help him. He felt as if he were offering himself up to these vast, bustling steamers lying there, loaded with other fates than his, indifferent to his sufferings to the point of hatred; as though he were begging them to intercede for him before some unknown God. He had halted opposite the French boat. His mind a blank, fascinated by the gangway, he watched the men tramping up and down it, not one of them giving him a thought or guessing at his agony of mind – he'd have liked to kill them all for that. Each showed his ticket as he came to the head of the gangway. Should he fake a ticket in some way? That too was absurd.

A mosquito stung him. He struck at it and stroked his cheek: his beard was beginning to grow. As if tidying oneself up were an essential part of going away, he decided to go and get shaved, though not too far from the boat. Beyond the warehouses, among the American bars and junk stores he found a Chinese barber's shop. The proprietor also ran a third-rate café and the two establishments were divided only by a screen of rope-matting. Awaiting his turn, Clappique sat himself down close to this curtain and kept an eye on the ship's gangway. On the other side of the matting, he could hear voices.

'That's the third,' a man was saying.

'None of them will take us in with the kid. What if we tried one of the swagger hotels, maybe?'

It was a woman who answered.

'Dressed as we are? The braided gent at the door would throw us out before we even looked like getting in.'

'Kids have a right to cry in places like that though, anyway. . . . Let's try again, no matter where.'

'As soon as the managers see the child, they'll say "no". Only the Chink hotels would agree to take us, but their filthy food would make the kid ill.'

'If we could only smuggle the child into one of the cheaper European hotels, once we were there perhaps they wouldn't dare to turn us out again. At any rate, it would be a night gained. We'd have to wrap him up in a bundle, so they'd think it was just clothes. . . .'

'Clothes don't squeal.'

'Put his dummy in his mouth and he wouldn't squeal. . . .'

'Maybe. I'll fix it up with the fellow at the desk and you come along later. He won't see you for more than a second.'

Silence ensued. Clappique watched the gang-plank. There was a sound of rustling paper.

'You've no idea how it upsets me to have to carry him this way. . . . I feel it'll be a bad omen for the rest of his life. . . . And I'm afraid it may harm him.'

Silence once more. Had they gone away? The man whose turn was before Clappique's rose from his chair. The barber motioned to Clappique, who went and installed himself in the man's place, never taking his eyes off the packet-boat. The gangway was clear at the moment, but no sooner was Clappique's face covered with soap than a sailor climbed up it carrying in his hand a couple of new saws (which he had no doubt just bought) and several bundles over his shoulders. Clappique watched him closely, step by step. He would willingly have been a dog, if only that had meant he could scamper up the gang-plank and go away. The sailor passed the man at the head of the ladder without a word.

Clappique paid, throwing some money into the basin, tore the towels from round his neck and went outside, his face covered with soap. He knew where to find a slop-shop. He got himself a sailor's rig-out from the first old-clothes dealer he came across. Then he hurried back to his hotel and changed into his new garments. 'I need a bundle, or something.' Should he buy an old kitbag off one of the boys at the hotel? That would be stupid; would a sailor coming on shore for a spree carry a kitbag? So as to make more of a hit? Quite absurd. If he went on board with some sort of bundle it would mean he'd bought it on shore. It had better be new then. . . . He went off to buy one.

He went into the shop with his usual Clappique air. Fixed by the English salesman's scornful eye, he cried: 'In my very arms!', slung the bundle on to his shoulder and turned, knocking over a copper lamp as he went out. The phrase 'In my very arms!', despite a deliberate attempt at exaggeration, did exactly express what he was feeling: up to that point he had been playing an uneasy comedy, partly to salve his conscience and partly out of fear, but without escaping subconscious conviction that he would be unsuccessful. The salesman's disdainful attitude – despite the fact that Clappique, forgetful of his dress, had not adopted a sailor's bearing – had shown him that success might be his. With his bundle over his shoulder, he walked off towards the boat, searching the eyes of every one he passed for confirmation of his new personality. Just as, a little while before, when he had first reached the quay, he had been stupefied to discover how little any one cared what happened to him – passengers had then walked up without even noticing this bystander on the dock, maybe about to meet his death – so now passers-by were utterly indifferent to the sight of a mere sailor; not one of them came forward in surprise or recognition; no face showed even the slightest curiosity.... Not that a fictitious personality was in the least calculated to surprise him, but this time it had been forced upon him and his very life depended on it. He felt thirsty; stopped at the first Chinese bar he came to, laid his kitbag on the ground. No sooner had he drunk than he realized he was not in the least thirsty; it was simply that he wanted to put himself through one more test. The way the bartender gave him his change was a sufficiently good indication. As soon as he had changed his clothes, the whole world had altered round him. He tried to think exactly how it had changed: it was the way people looked at him that was different. The single person he had always before chosen as an audience for his make-belief had become everybody in general. At the same time – the instinct was either one of self-defence or of pleasure – he was swamped with joy at this general acceptance of himself in his new role. He had suddenly stumbled on the most brilliant success of a lifetime. Human beings had, in fact, no real existence, since in the eyes of all these people a suit of clothes was all that he needed for escape. It was, fundamentally, the same translation, the same happiness as he had experienced on first coming into contact with the Chinese crowd. 'And to think that when you say "spin a yarn" you mean write it, not live it?' Carrying his bundle as if it were a rifle, he climbed the gang-plank, strode past the man at the top, his legs giving beneath him, and found himself on deck. He went for'ard with the steerage passengers and dropped his kitbag on a coil of rope. There was nothing for him to fear now until the first port of call. Nevertheless he was very far from feeling easy in his mind. A steerage passenger, a Russian with a wild shock of hair, came up to him:

'You belong to the boat?'

And without waiting for an answer, added:

'Is life pleasant on board?'

'Good Lord, man, you've no idea! Your Frenchman's a great traveller, make no mistake about that. Sure thing. The officers are bastards, but no worse than any other employer, and sleep's impossible (can't stand hammocks myself; it's a question of taste) but the grub's good. And you come in for the most extraordinary sights now and again. When I was down in Rio the missionaries had made the natives learn little Latin chants by heart. Taken them days and days to do it. One day the bishop comes along and the head missionary starts to conduct: but there's complete silence – the natives are so shy they can't utter. Then – hey presto! – the canticle suddenly strikes up as if by magic; the jungle parrots, you see, old boy, who'd never heard anything but that, piped up with great feeling.... One time, too, ten years ago, right out in the open sea, way down in the Celebes, I came across Arab caravels, all whittled and notched like coco-nuts and stiff with stinking dead men whose arms hung down over the bulwarks amidst a swarm of seagulls. Absolutely....'

'You've had luck then. I've been travelling for the last seven years and I never saw anything like that.'

'One has to introduce a certain artistry into one's life, my dear sir, not for the sake of art – ah no, not that, certainly not that – but for the sake of life itself. That's it, you know, in a nutshell.'

He poked the Russian in the ribs and cautiously turned aside: a car he knew had drawn up at the foot of the gang-plank; Ferral was going back to France.

A steward made his way along the first-class deck, ringing the 'All ashore!' bell. Each clank of the bell echoed in Clappique's heart.

'Europe!' he thought. 'The party's over. Now for Europe.' It was as if France itself materialized in front of him with the approach of the clanking bell, which seemed to be sounding, not for his release, but for his captivity. Had it not been for the threat of death hanging over him, he would have gone ashore.

'Is the bar in the third class open?' he asked the Russian.

'They've been serving drinks there for the last hour. Anybody can get one until the ship puts out to sea.'

Clappique took him by the arm. 'Let's go and get drunk,' he said.

6 P.M.

In the great hall of the prison – once a school courtyard, covered in – two hundred wounded Communists waited for some one to come and finish them off. Katow, who had been brought along with the last batch, looked around him, leaning on his elbow. They all lay flat on the floor. Many groaned, and there was an extraordinary regularity about their groaning. Some, like the wounded at the Depôt, were smoking and the swirls of smoke were lost in the roof, dark already despite the large European windows showing the fog and the failing evening light outside. It seemed a long way off, high above all these reclining men. Although daylight had not yet entirely faded, in the hall it seemed as though night had fallen. 'Is that because

278

every one's wounded,' Katow wondered, 'or because we're all lying down, like in a railway-station? A railway-station – that's what this place really is; we shall leave it and yet go nowhere, but that's what it is. . . . '

Four Chinese regulars marched up and down among the wounded with bayonets fixed; sticking up hard and distinct above so many indeterminate bodies, their bayonets weirdly reflected the failing daylight. Outside, pale yellow flares gleaming in the depths of the fog – no doubt they were gas-lamps – seemed also to keep watch over them. And, as if it came from them (because it, too, issued from the further depths of the fog), a whistle shrilled, drowning the whispers and the groans: the whistle of a locomotive. They were close to Chapei station. There was in the room some hideous sense of strain, which was not expectancy of death. His own throat told Katow what it was: thirst – and hunger. Propped against the wall, he looked to right and left: a good number of the faces were known to him, for many of the wounded had fought in the *tchons*. All along one of the two narrower sides of the hall, an open space had been kept, three yards broad. 'Why,' he asked out loud, 'do the wounded lie one on top of the other instead of moving over into that space?' He was among the last arrivals. Clinging to the wall he helped himself on to his feet; although his wounds hurt terribly he believed he could stand – but he paused, bent double; for, although no word had been spoken, he felt a wave of such complete terror surge up all round him that he stopped short. Was it in the way eyes looked at him? No, he could hardly make them out. Was it their gestures? Their gestures were, above all else, the gestures of wounded men occupied with their own sufferings. Yet, whatever its means of communication to him, the fear was there – not fright, but terror, the terror of dumb animals, of men face to face with something unhuman. Still supporting himself against the wall, Katow stepped over the prone body of his next door neighbour.

279

'Are you mad?' asked a voice from the ground.

'Why?'

His question was peremptory. But no one answered. And one of the guards, five yards away, instead of hurling him back into his place, gazed at him in stupefaction.

'Why?' he asked again, even more roughly.

'He doesn't know why,' declared another voice, again from floor-level, and at the same time still another voice, in a lower tone, said:

'It'll come in time. . . .'

He had asked his second question in a very loud voice. There was something of itself essentially horrible in the hesitancy of this crowd, furthermore, since he was known to most of these men, the threat that hung on the wall opposite weighed on them all and on him in particular.

'Lie down,' some one said.

Why did not a single one of them call him by his name? And why didn't the guard step in and intervene? Only a few minutes before he had seen him fell a man, who had wanted to change places, with the butt of his rifle. . . . He stooped over towards the man who had spoken last, and lay down by his side.

'That's where they put the ones who are going to be tortured,' the man explained under his breath.

Now Katow understood. They were all of them aware of it, but they hadn't dared tell him; either because they were too frightened to speak of it, or because they were afraid to tell *him*—no, they couldn't tell him. A voice had said: 'It'll come. . . .'

The door opened. Soldiers with torches entered, wheeling in trolleys on which wounded men lay like luggage, and tipped them off quite close to Katow. Night came in with them, came up from the floor – amid the most appalling stench: the sound of groaning was like the scurrying of rats. Most of the men could not move. The door closed.

Time passed. Only the sentinels paced to and fro; overhead the last gleam of light glinted on their bayonets; below seethed the myriad sounds of anguish. Suddenly, as though the darkness had added to the impenetrability of the fog, from afar came the deadened shriek of the locomotive's whistle. One of the last batch of prisoners, lying on his face, pressed his hands over his ears, and screamed. None of the others cried out, but again the terror was in their midst, low on the ground.

The man lifted up his head, raised himself on his elbows.

'The swine!' he yelled. 'The murderers!'

One of the sentries came across and turned him over with a jab of his boot. The man shut his mouth. The sentry moved away. The wounded man began to mumble and rave. It was too dark for Katow to see how he looked, but he could hear the sound of his voice; soon, no doubt, he would become coherent. Sure enough: 'They don't shoot them, they fling them alive into the furnace of the locomotive,' he was saying. 'Then that's that – they blow the whistle. . . . ' The sentry was coming back. Silence, except for the sounds of the suffering.

The door again opened. More bayonets – this time lit from below by the torch-flares; but no wounded. A Kuomintang officer came in alone. Although now he could distinguish nothing in all this mass of bodies, Katow was aware that each man stiffened. The officer, over in the distance, a shadow thrown up dimly by the torchlight against a background of the dying day, was giving orders to a sentry. The sentry came over in Katow's direction, looked for him; found him. Without laying hands on him, respectfully and without a word, he merely signed to him to get up. Katow with difficulty followed him, to where, by the door, the officer was still busy issuing orders. The soldier, with rifle in one hand, torch in the other, took up his position on his left. On his right there was nothing but the open space and the white wall. The soldier jerked his rifle to indicate the open space. Bitterly Katow smiled, with desperate pride, but no one saw his face: the sentry was careful not to look at it, and all the wounded who were not on the point of death raised on an arm, a leg, or rested heads on chins, to watch his shadow, still faint, loom larger on the wall reserved for those awaiting torture.

The officer went out. The door remained open.

The sentries presented arms: a civilian entered. 'Section A,' cried a voice outside, and the door immediately closed again. One of the sentries marched the civilian towards the wall, mumbling all the time as he went: Katow, to his amazement, recognized Kyo. As he was not wounded, seeing him arrive escorted by two officers, the sentries had taken him for one of Chang Kai Shek's foreign advisers. Now, realizing their mistake, they swore at him from a distance. He sank down into the shadows by Katow's side.

'D'you know what's in store for us?' asked the latter.

'They took care to let me know. I don't give a damn. I've my cyanide. Have you got yours?'

'Yes.'

'Are you wounded?'

'In the legs. But I can walk.'

'Have you been here long?'

'No. When were you taken?'

'Yesterday evening. Any way out?'

'Not a hope. Almost all of them are badly hurt. Outside, the whole place is swarming with soldiers. You saw the machine-guns at the gates?'

'Yes. Where were you caught?'

Both of them needed to escape from this mournful vigil, they wanted to talk, to talk a great deal: Katow about the siege of headquarters; Kyo about the prison, about his interview with König, and what he'd heard, even before going to gaol: he had known then that May had not been arrested.

Katow lay on his side, quite close to him, separated from him, nevertheless, by the whole width of his suffering. Mouth half-open, puffed lips beneath that merry nose, eyes almost

282

shut – yet this man was bound to him by that sense of ultimate friendship, unrestrained, unquestioning, which only death can give. This life that was fated to end had landed up here side by side with his own in a gloom choked with threats and wounds, among so many of their brothers in the wretched rank and file of Revolution. Each of these men had furiously seized, seized in passing, the only distinction that could ever come within his reach.

The guards brought in three Chinese. They were placed apart from the press of wounded, but apart also from the men against the wall. They had been arrested before the fighting began; they had been judged vaguely in off hand fashion, and now were waiting to be shot.

'Katow!' One of them called his name.

It was Lou You Shen, Hemmelrich's partner.

'Yes?'

'Do you know if the shooting's done near here, or some distance away?'

'I don't know. You don't hear it where we are, at any rate.'

A voice somewhat farther off said: 'It seems that afterwards the executioner nabs your gold teeth.'

Another remarked: 'That doesn't matter a damn to me; I haven't any.'

Very deliberately the three Chinese smoked cigarettes, puff after rapid puff.

'Got more than one box of matches?' asked a wounded man, a little farther off.

'Yes.'

'Throw me one.'

Lou threw him his.

'I'd like it if some one could tell my son that I died bravely,' he said, half under his breath. Then added, softer still: 'It isn't easy to die.'

Katow discovered a cause of blind joy for himself: he had no wife, no children.

The door opened.

'Shove one along!' called the sentry.

The three men stood bunched together.

'Well, dammit,' said the guard, 'make up your minds. . . . '

He wouldn't pick one out himself. Suddenly one of the two Chinamen who were unknown to Katow took a step forward, threw away his half-smoked cigarette, lit another – breaking two matches in doing so – and strode rapidly across to the door, buttoning all the buttons of his jacket one after the other. The door closed behind him.

One of the men on the ground picked up the broken bits of match. He and those near him had broken the matches from the box Lou You Shen had given them into little pieces, and were using them as counters in a game. Less than five minutes later the door was again opened.

'One more!'

Lou and his companion stepped forward together, arm in arm. Lou was reciting, in a loud, timbreless voice, the death of a hero in a famous stage-classic, but the ancient Chinese sense of community had completely died out: no one listened to him.

'Which of you?' the soldier queried.

They made no reply.

'Well, come on, what about it?'

He forced them apart with a dig of his rifle. Lou was the nearer: he seized him by the shoulder.

Lou shook himself free. Then stepped forward. The other man went back to his place and lay down.

Kyo realized how much harder it would be for this man to die than for the other two who had preceded him: he, now, was alone. As brave a man as Lou, seeing that he had stepped forward too, at the same time. But now his posture on the ground, as he lay, crouching, quivering like a game-dog, his arms clasping his body, made it horribly clear that he was frightened. And so it was, for when the sentry laid his hand on him, he collapsed entirely. The soldiers seized him, one by the feet, the other by the neck, and carried him out.

Lying on his back, his arms folded on his chest, Kyo shut his eyes: becoming the exact effigy of a corpse laid out for burial. He imagined himself lying there, straight and stiff, eyes closed and features set in that expression of serenity which is vouchsafed by death, for at least a day, to almost all its corpses, as if to show that there is, in even the most wretched of creatures, an innate dignity which must be given expression. He had witnessed death on many occasions and, aided in this by his Japanese upbringing, he had always felt that it would be beautiful to die a death that is one's own, a death appropriate to the life it closes. And to die is passive, but to kill oneself is to turn passivity into action. As soon as they came to fetch the first of his lot, he would kill himself in full consciousness of what he was doing. He remembered the gramophone records – and his heart dropped a beat: in those days hope still had meaning. He would never see May again, and the only hurt he felt was the hurt that she would feel – as if he were doing something unkind, and wrong, in dying. 'Death brings remorse,' he thought, with a twinge of irony. He felt no such qualms for his father, who had always given him an impression not of weakness, but of strength. For more than a year now May had protected him from all loneliness, though not from every sorrow. There sprang into his mind, alas, as soon as he thought of her, the remembrance of that swift refuge in tenderness of body joined to body. Now that he was no longer to be numbered among the living . . . 'She will have to forget me now.' Could he have written to tell her so, he would only have been torturing her and tying her closer to him. 'And it would mean telling her to love another . . .' Oh, this prison – a place where time stops still, while elsewhere it runs on. . . . No. Not so. It was here in this prison-yard, hedged from the outer world by a cordon of machine-guns, that the Revolution, whether or wheresoever it might spring to life again, had received consecration; in every place where men laboured in misery, absurdity or humiliation, condemned men such as they were remembered as in the prayers of the faithful; outside these walls people had begun to vouchsafe them, dying, the reverence that is a tribute reserved only for the dead. Of all the surface of the world that this last night covered, this place of groans was surely the most charged with love and manhood. Ah, to moan in concert with this prostrate crowd, to be united even in its mumbling cries with the sacrifice of its suffering! An unheard wailing was prolonged far into the outward night with the mutterings of present pain: like Hemmelrich, most of these men were fathers. . . . Nevertheless, their acceptance of fate wafted up, like the peace of evening, mingled with their murmurings of wounded men. It shrouded Kyo, as he lay, eyes closed, hands clasped across his limp, lost body, with all the grandeur of a funeral chant. He would die having fought for what in his own day would have possessed the strongest meaning and inspired the most splendid hope; die, too, among those whom he would wish to have seen live; die, like each of these recumbent forms, so as to give significance to his own life. What would have been the value of a life for which he would not have accepted death? It is less hard to die when one is not alone in dying. This death of his was hallowed by a touch of common brotherhood, by contact with a gathering of broken men whom future multitudes would recognize as martyrs, whose bloody memory would bring forth a golden hope! How, already staring into the eyes of death, should he fail to hear the murmur of human sacrifice calling aloud to him that the heart of man is a resting-place for the dead, well worth the loss of life itself?

He had unclasped the buckle of his belt and held the cyanide in his hand. He had often wondered whether death would come to him easily. He knew that if he decided to kill himself, he would do so; but, knowing too with what savage indifference life snatches our masks from us, he had had misgivings as to the precise instant when death should crush the thoughts out of his brain with the full impact of its immovable weight.

No, dying could become an action, an exalted deed, the supreme expression of a life to which this death was itself so similar; it meant, too, escape from these two soldiers who now uncertainly approached him. He jerked the poison between his teeth, as he would have barked an order, heard anguished Katow still asking him something, felt him stir and touch him; then just as, gasping for breath, he tried to clutch at him, he felt his whole strength slip, fading from him, giving way before the inrush of an overwhelming convulsion.

Soldiers were among the crowd picking out two of the prisoners unable to stand up. Evidently to be burned alive entitled one to special, though limited, privileges: they were trundled along on a single trolly, one on top, or almost on top, of the other and then tipped off on Katow's left; Kyo, dead, lay to his right. In the empty space separating these men from those condemned merely to death, the soldiers squatted down beside their torches. Little by little heads and watching eyes sank back into the gloom, glancing only rarely now at this light which, at the end of the hall, marked where the condemned men lay.

After Kyo's death – he had lain gasping for at least a minute – Katow had felt himself again thrown back into a loneliness all the deeper and more desperate because he was surrounded by men he knew. He could not get the Chinaman whom they had had to carry to his death, struggling and screaming, out of his mind. And yet he was discovering in his total abandonment a certain sense of peace, as if for years he had been waiting for just this: a restfulness stumbled upon and encountered anew at all the darkest moments of his life. Where had he read: 'It was not the discoveries explorers made, but the tribulations they endured, that caused my envy. . . . '? As if in answer to his thought, for the third time a distant whistle made itself heard in the hall. The two men on his left gave a start. They were very young Chinese; one was Souen, whom he knew only because he had fought beside him at headquarters; the other he did not know – it wasn't Pei. Why were they here, aside from the others?

'Organizing groups for armed resistance?' he asked.

'Attempt on the life of Chang Kai Shek,' answered the one who wasn't Pei.

'Was Chen with you?'

'No. He wanted to throw his bomb alone. Chang wasn't in the car. I was waiting for it farther along. I was taken with the bomb on me.'

So strangled was the voice that had answered his question that Katow peered into both their faces: the young men were weeping, soundlessly. 'There's not much help in words,' thought Katow. Souen tried to shift his shoulder and his face contorted with pain – he was wounded in the arm.

'Burned,' he said. 'To be burned alive! One's eyes too, even one's eyes – can you realize . . .'

The other man, his friend, was sobbing now.

'It could happen in an accident, a fire . . .' Katow said.

It was as though they were talking not to each other, but to some invisible third person.

'That's not the same.'

'No. It is less good.'

'Even one's eyes.' The young man spoke, lower still. 'Eyes as well . . . Every finger and then one's stomach . . . the stomach. . . .'

'Shut up!' the other said; his voice was broken.

He would have cried out, but he couldn't. His hands gripped tight on Souen's wounded arm; Souen went rigid with pain.

'Human dignity,' Katow murmured, thinking of Kyo's interview with König. Neither of the young men spoke now. Beyond the torch, in the now complete darkness, the voices of pain still mumbled. . . . He edged over closer to Souen and his companion. One of the guards was telling the others a story; all their heads were together, they crouched between the torch and the condemned men, who could now no longer see each other. Despite the sound of voices, despite the presence of all these men who had fought side by side with him, Katow was alone, alone between the body of his dead friend and his two frightened comrades, lost between this wall at his back and the locomotive-whistle far away in the darkness. But a man could rise superior to this solitude, possibly even superior to that ghastly screech of the whistle. Within him fear battled against the most terrible temptation he had ever known. He, in his turn, unclasped his belt. Finally:

'You there, listen,' he said, in what was barely a whisper. 'Souen, put your hand on my chest and shut your fingers when I touch them: I'm going to give you my cyanide. There's just – only just – enough for two.'

He was renouncing, giving up everything, save this admission that there was only enough for two. Lying on his side, he broke the cyanide in half. The guards screened the light, which cast a hazy aureole about them – but wouldn't they be sure to move? However, it was far too dark to see. Katow was making this gift of more than his life to a warm hand upturned on his chest – not even to an actual body, not even to a voice. As if it were an animal, the hand snatched and was immediately withdrawn. He waited, his whole body tense. Then suddenly he heard one of the voices say:

'I've dropped it. It's lost.'

It was a voice in which there was almost no trace of horror, as if so vast, so tragic a catastrophe could not have happened, as if everything would have to be all right. For Katow, too, the thing was beyond possibility. A boundless fury mounted within him, then subsided, powerless in the face of this impossibility. And yet – ! To have given *that*, and then for this blundering maniac to lose it!

'Where?' he asked.

289

'By me. Couldn't hold it when Souen passed it to me: I'm wounded in the hand.'

'He's dropped both pieces,' Souen said.

They were, of course, searching the space between them. Then they felt between Katow and Souen – on whom, probably, the other man was almost lying, for Katow, unable to see anything, was conscious that both the bodies were at his elbow. He searched, too, forcing himself to control his nerves, making sure to place his hand flat on the ground, moving it sideways its own width, groping to the full length of his arm. Their hands brushed against his. Then suddenly one of these hands seized his hand, clutched it, held it fast.

'Even if we don't find anything,' said one of the voices, 'still . . .'

He, Katow, too, pressed the hand – he was beyond the meaning of tears, overcome by the sadness of this unseen and barely heard gratitude (all murmurings here were alike) that was being offered to him, blindly, in the surrounding darkness, in return for the greatest gift he had ever made – made, perhaps, in vain. Although Souen went on searching, the hand that held his stayed where it was. Its grip, all of a sudden, tightened madly

'Here it is!'

Oh, triumphant release! But –

'You sure it's not just a pebble?' the other asked. The ground was covered with fallen plaster.

'Give it me!' said Katow.

With the tips of his fingers he recognized the shape of the pieces.

He gave them back – gave them back! – more fiercely held the hand that again sought his, and waited, his shoulders shuddering, teeth rattling in his head. 'If only the cyanide hasn't spoiled, even through its silver paper,' he thought. The hand he held suddenly wrenched at his and, as if he were joined by it to this other body lost in the darkness, he felt the body stiffen. This convulsion of asphyxia filled him with envy. Almost in the same moment, there broke from the other a strangled cry which no one heeded. Then silence.

Katow felt himself alone, deserted. He rolled over on to his stomach and waited. The quaking in his shoulders would not stop.

In the middle of the night, the officer returned. Amid a clatter of unslung rifles, a squad of six soldiers marched up to the condemned men. All the prisoners were awake. The new torch, too, lit up only dimly a few long vague shapes – graves in the loose earth already – and the reflection of here and there a pair of eyes. Katow had managed to scramble to his feet. The sergeant in command of the squad seized Kyo's arm, found it rigid, then immediately took hold of Souen: he, too, was stiff. The first rows of prisoners began to mutter, and the muttering spread through the hall. The sergeant picked up first one leg, then the next: they fell back, stiff. He called the officer. The officer did likewise. The rumour among the prisoners grew louder. The officer stared at Katow.

'Dead?'

Why answer?

'Isolate the six prisoners nearest to them.'

'No point in that,' Katow remarked. 'It was I who gave them the cyanide.'

The officer hesitated.

'How about yourself?' he asked at last.

Exultant, overjoyed, 'There was only enough for two,' said Katow. 'I'll get a rifle-butt in my face,' he thought.

The murmuring among the prisoners was now almost a clamour.

'Quick march.' The officer said no more.

Katow had not forgotten that he had already been condemned to death, that he had seen machine-guns pointing at him, had heard them fire. . . . 'As soon as I get outside, I shall try to strangle one of them, and I'll manage to keep my hands on his throat long enough for them to be forced to kill me. They may burn me, but I'll die first.' At that same second, one of the escort flung his arm round him, while another dragged Katow's arms behind his back and tied them. 'The other boys are well out of this,' he thought. 'Hell! Let's suppose that a fire broke out and I was among the casualties. . . .' He started to walk. Despite the groans, again there was silence. Just as a little while before it had cast his shadow on the white-washed wall, the torch-flare now showed him in even blacker silhouette against the windows that looked out on to the night. He walked heavily, slumping first on one leg, then the other, hampered by his wounds; as he staggered towards the glare of the torch, the shadowed outline of his head merged into the roof. The entire darkness of the hall had come to life and watched him step by step. The silence now was such that the ground rang at each heavy tread of his foot. Nodding up and down, every head followed the rhythm of his walk, tenderly, in terror, in resignation, as if, although all the movements were the same, each man would himself have struggled to follow these faltering footsteps. No head fell back as the door closed.

A sound of deep breathing, like the sound of sleep, came up from the ground; breathing through the nose, jaws clenched in anguish, not stirring now, quite still, all those who were not yet dead waited to hear the shriek of a distant whistle. . . .

THE NEXT DAY

For more than five minutes Gisors had sat gazing at his pipe. There, before him, the little opium-box lay open, the lamp lit – that doesn't commit one, though – and the clean implements. Outside was the night: indoors the beam of this little lamp and a great rectangle of bright light – the open door leading to the next room, into which Kyo's body had been brought. The prison-yard had been emptied to make room for new prisoners and no one had objected to the bodies thrown outside being taken away. Katow's corpse had not been retrieved. May had brought Kyo's body home with her as carefully as if he were desperately badly wounded. There he lay, stretched out. Not serene, as he had imagined he would be before he killed himself, but distorted by asphyxia, already something other than a man. May was combing his hair for burial, in her thoughts talking to this last presence of a dead face in appalling, motherly phrases which she did not dare to utter aloud for fear of hearing them herself. 'My darling,' she murmured, as she might have said 'My own,' knowing full well that it was a part of herself, not something distinct from her, that was being wrenched away: 'My treasure. . . .' She was startled to realize that it was a corpse she was thus addressing. But she had long passed beyond the reach of tears.

'All grief that leads nowhere is absurd,' thought Gisors, hypnotized by the lamp, taking refuge in this obsession. 'There I could find peace . . . peace . . .' But he did not dare to stretch out his hand. He had no belief in life after death, stood in no awe of the dead; but he did not dare stretch out his hand.

She came into the room, went over to him. Her mouth, weak with suffering, was sunken in a face whose eyes regarded him sightlessly. . . . She gently laid her fingers on his wrist.

'Come,' she said, faltering, in a whisper. 'I believe he's not quite cold, after all. . . .'

He looked into the eyes of this tender, this pitiful but perfectly sane face. She was gazing at him calmly, less in hope than in supplication. The effects of poison are doubtful: and she was a doctor. He got up and followed her, steeling himself against a hope so tremendous that, were he to give way to it, to have it then removed would prove too much for him. He touched Kyo's bluish forehead, that forehead which would never now grow wrinkled: it was cold, with the particular coldness of

death. He did not dare to draw back his hand, to find May looking at him. He continued to gaze at Kyo's open palm, from
which the lines were already fading.

'No,' he said, reverting to his misery. Had he known any
escape from it? He realized that he had put no faith in what May
had said.

'Alas,' was all she said.

She watched him go slowly back into the other room. He
was thinking – what was he thinking? While Kyo was still
here in this room, she owed him her every thought. His death
called for some response from her, some answer which she did
not know but which must all the same exist. How lucky were
those who, though wretched, find solace in wreaths and
prayers! Some answer there must be beyond this tragedy that
wrung from her hands motherly caresses which no child had
ever drawn from her, beyond this frightful urge to use life's
tenderest endearments in speaking to the dead. These very lips
which but yesterday had framed the words: 'I was afraid you
were dead,' would never speak again; and it was not with this
poor vestige, this caricature, but with death itself that she had
come into contact. There she stayed, stock-still, tearing from
her memory pang after pang, tense, in a passive, open-armed
deliverance of herself to an aching void.

Gisors had lain down on the couch again. 'Then, later,' he
thought, 'I'll have to face waking up. . . . For how many days
would each morning bring his son's death back to him? There
lay the pipe: it spelt forgetfulness. If he were to put out his hand,
prepare the pellet of opium . . . a quarter of an hour later he
could have looked upon death itself with infinite unconcern, as
though it were some harmless paralytic who wished him ill: no
longer able to reach him, it would then lose all hold on him,
would sink gently back into a general beatitude. Immunity was
there, for the taking. Nothing can be done to help the dead.
Why suffer further? Is sorrow a sacrifice to love – or to fear? . . .
Still he did not dare touch the plate, and his misery was choking

him along with this overwhelming desire to smoke and the sobs gulping in his throat. He picked up, at random, the first paper that came to his hand (he never touched Kyo's things, but of course Kyo would never read it now). It was a copy of the *Pekin Political Journal*, which had fallen there when Kyo's body was brought in, and it contained the speech for which Gisors had been expelled from the University. On the margin, he saw, in Kyo's writing: 'This speech was made by my father.' Never had he said that he thought anything of it. Gisors closed the pamphlet, very gently, and pictured the destruction of all his hopes.

He opened the door, flung the opium far into the darkness, then came back and sat down, his shoulders sagging – to await the dawn, to wait until, by dint of self-communion, the pain within him should be silenced. . . . Despite the mental agony twisting his mouth, transforming the grave expression of his face into a wild-eyed parody of idiocy, he retained a certain control. Tonight his life was being changed: thought itself has little power to check the remodelling process of death. From now on he was flung back into himself. The world no longer had any meaning: it no longer existed. Such immobility there beside that body never to return again, that body that had been his link with earth, was like the suicide of God Himself. He had not expected success, or even happiness, for Kyo; but that there should be no Kyo in the world. . . . 'I have been cast out from Time': his child had been his link with Time, his link with the course of things. No doubt, in his innermost heart, hope dwelt in Gisors, no less than misery, a rejection of all hope, a waiting – and perhaps love had to be crushed out of him for this hope to be revealed: yet his mind eagerly seized on anything that would destroy such a hope. 'There's something beautiful about being dead,' he thought. He felt stirring within him that fundamental sadness which is not the misery of individuals nor of things, but which wells up from within, and which life seeks to hide from us. He might escape from it but only by ceasing to think of it –

and so he submerged himself deeper and deeper into it, as though this fearful introspection were the only voice that death could find intelligible, as if this agony in being man that filled his heart were the only prayer that could affect the mind of his murdered son.

Part 7

FERRAL, fanning himself with the paper which had been the most violent in its attack on the Consortium, was the last to arrive in the Finance Minister's waiting-room. There were already present, sitting about in groups, the Vice-President of the General Funds Corporation – Ferral's brother had wisely fallen ill the week before – the representative of the Bank of France, the manager of the leading French private banks, and managers of various public ones. Ferral knew them all: a son, a son-in-law and several erstwhile officials of the Finance Board and Funds Corporation; the link between the State and the Banking Houses was too close for the latter not to see an advantage in attaching to themselves men who had been the trusted servants of the former. Ferral noticed their astonishment; it would have looked better if he had got there before them. As he wasn't there when they arrived, they had assumed he had not been asked to appear. That he should take the liberty to arrive last amazed them. Everything separated them from him: what he thought of them, what they thought of him; even their difference of attire. Almost all of them were turned out with impersonal carelessness, whereas Ferral wore a rough and variegated tweed suit, and a grey silk shirt with a soft collar, bought in Shanghai. They and he were two distinct races.

They were ushered into the presence of the Minister almost immediately.

Ferral knew the Minister only slightly. Was the 'period' expression of his face due to that white hair of his – as white as a Regency wig? The aristocratic face, with its fair eyes, its welcoming smile – the man was a parliamentarian of the old school – agreed with the reputation for courtesy the Minister enjoyed: a reputation parallel to that of his gruffness when in Napoleonic mood. Ferral, while every one took a seat, remembered a well-known anecdote about the Minister: at that time in charge of Foreign Affairs, he had tugged at the coat-tails of the French envoy to Morocco and the seam down the back of the man's jacket had suddenly split – with a loud, rending sound. 'Bring the gentleman one of my coats,' he had said; then rang again just as the servant was hurrying away. 'The oldest!' he had added. 'Anything better would be too good for him!' His expression would have been extremely engaging but for a look about the eyes which seemed to countermand what the mouth promised: he had been injured in an accident and had one glass eye.

They were all seated: the Director of the General Funds Corporation on the Minister's right, Ferral on his left. The banks' representatives sat at the other end of the room, on a sofa.

'You know, gentlemen,' the Minister observed, 'why I have assembled you here today. You have no doubt already considered the situation. I will call upon M. Ferral to outline it for you and to expound his own point of view.'

The banking world waited patiently for Ferral to deliver himself of the usual rigmarole.

'Gentlemen,' Ferral began, 'it is customary at such a meeting as this to present an optimistic statement. You have before you the report of the Finance inspectors. The Consortium's position is, speaking practically, worse than would appear from that report. I am not submitting for your approval either swollen assets or doubtful credits. You are all perfectly familiar with the Consortium's liabilities, I realize that. But I should like to draw your attention to two points on the assets side, which no balance-sheet could show and on the strength of which your support is now requested.

'In the first place, the Consortium can claim to be the only French concern of its kind in the Far East. Even if run at a loss, even if on the verge of bankruptcy, its structural organization remains unimpaired. Its network of agencies, its trading-branches, both import and export, in the Chinese interior, the connexions established between its Chinese customers and the manufacturing firms in Indo-China – all that is being, and can be, maintained. It is no exaggeration for me to assert that to half the merchants on the Yang-Tse, France *is* the Consortium, just as Japan is Mitsubishi and Co. Our organization can, as you know, be compared, in its extent, to Standard Oil. Furthermore, the present revolutionary state of affairs in China cannot last for ever.

'Secondly: by virtue of the Consortium's connexions with a large section of the Chinese business world, I have been enabled to take an active and effective part in General Chang Kai Shek's assumption of power. We have, in this way, made certain that the whole of that part of the building-contracts for the Chinese railways that has been promised, by treaty, to France, shall be undertaken by the Consortium. You will realize the importance of this. It is in view of our advantages in this matter that I ask you to combine in affording the Consortium the help that it asks you to give. It is this consideration which prompts me to hope that the only large firm which represents our country in Asia may not be forced to close down – even were it to pass into other hands than those that founded it.'

His audience carefully scrutinized the balance-sheet, though they were already perfectly aware of its contents and could hope to glean no further information from it. They were all waiting for the Minister to speak.

'It is not to the interest of the State alone,' the latter gentleman remarked, 'but also to the interest of the Banks that French credit should suffer no detriment. The failure of important institutions – such as, for instance, the Chinese Industrial Bank and the Consortium – would, of course, have an adverse effect on all of us. . . .'

He spoke carelessly, lounging back in his chair, gazing abstractedly round the room, tapping the point of his pencil on the blotter before him. The banks' representatives waited for him to express himself rather more definitely.

'Will you allow me, sir,' said the representative of the Bank of France, 'to put forward a somewhat different point of view? I alone, of those present, am not here on behalf of a credit establishment, and am therefore entirely impartial. For several months, it is true, business crashes have been diminishing deposits, but at the end of six months, the monies that have been withdrawn flow back automatically and reappear in the books of the leading firms – the firms whose sureties are the soundest. It might well be that the collapse of the Consortium, far from being prejudicial to the public banks these gentlemen represent, would, on the contrary, be to their advantage. . . .'

'Except that it is always dangerous to play about with credits: the failure of a dozen provincial banks would be not at all to the advantage of the public banks – if for no other reason, because of the political measures it would entail.'

'All of which is merely talk for the sake of talking,' thought Ferral, 'except that what he means is that the Bank of France is afraid of becoming involved and having to shell out if the other banks do the same.' No one spoke. The Minister's questioning glance encountered that of one of the other delegates. The man had the look of a cavalry-subaltern – eyes on the alert, ready to reprove, a clear, clipped voice:

'I ought, perhaps, to say that, contrary to what usually occurs at such meetings as this, I am somewhat more sanguine than M. Ferral with regard to the sum-total of the items that figure on this balance-sheet. The position of the banks affiliated to the Consortium is admittedly deplorable: but certain companies could be kept going even in their present form.'

'The whole body of the organization is what I am asking you

to preserve,' said Ferral. 'If the Consortium comes to an end, its business will be lost to France.'

'I, on the other hand,' observed another, a banker with clear-cut features, 'am of the opinion that M. Ferral is, if anything, unduly optimistic with regard to the Consortium's assets. The loan has not yet been floated.'

While he was speaking he looked at the lapel of Ferral's jacket; this intrigued Ferral, who followed the man's line of vision and then, suddenly, understood. He wore no decoration. On purpose, as a matter of fact. His interlocutor, on the other hand, was commander of the Legion of Honour, and scrutinized so bare a buttonhole with disdain. Ferral had never looked for respect other than that due to his own strength of character.

'You know that it will be floated,' he said. 'And covered,' he added. 'The American banks will see to that–not their clients, who will take what they are told to take.'

'All right – let us say it will, then. And once the loan is taken up, who will guarantee that the railroads will be built?'

'But, after all,' Ferral exclaimed, in some surprise – the man could not fail to know perfectly well what his answer to that would be – 'but, after all, it's not a question of the greater part of the money being made over to the Chinese Government. It will pass direct from the American banks to the manufacturers of material – that's obvious. Otherwise do you imagine the Americans would consider the loan for one moment?'

'Quite so. But Chang Kai Shek may be killed or over-thrown: if a Bolshevik régime were to supplant him, the loan would not be floated. Personally I do not believe that Chang Kai Shek can hold out. We have information which would suggest that his fall is imminent.'

'The Communists have been routed everywhere,' Ferral replied. 'Borodin has evacuated Hankow and is returning to Moscow.'

'The Communists may have been crushed, but Communism hasn't. China will never be the same as she once was, and, following Chang Kai Shek's successful *coup*, there is a danger of renewed Communist risings. . . .'

'My own view is that he will still be in power in ten years' time. But there can be no business deal without certain risks.'

('That's right,' he thought, 'pay no attention to anything but your own intuitions – which never tell you a darned thing. Didn't Turkey fail to return one sou of your money while all the time she was using it to buy guns with? You wouldn't have scored much of a point, if you'd been left to your own devices, in that affair. When you're through coddling and tickling the State you mistake your cowardice for canniness, and you think that because you've no arms you may be the Venus of Milo – which is taking rather too much for granted.')

'If Chang Kai Shek remains in power,' put in the gentle voice of a young banker with curly hair, 'China will turn protectionist again. How are we to know that, even if we accept everything that M. Ferral has said, all the value of his work in China may not at any moment be knocked on the head by Chinese law? Of course I realize there are several answers he can make to that. . . .'

'Several,' said Ferral.

'Nevertheless,' retorted the man who looked like an officer, 'it doesn't alter the fact that uncertainty attaches to the whole affair and, even granting that there may not be any actual risk, in any case it involves a long-term investment and practically means tying up money for a life-time. . . . We all know how near M. Germain came in ruining the Crédit Lyonnais by the active interest he took in Aniline Colours Ltd., although that, too, was one of the most famous of French business concerns. It is not for us to embark on business deals: our job is to lend money on good surety and for short terms. Anything outside that is not our affair but the province of the commercial banks.'

Again there was silence. A long silence.

Ferral wondered what reasons the Minister might have for

not stepping in. They all – and he, too – spoke an elaborate and conventional language, like an Asiatic ritual tongue: it was therefore not to be surprised at that the whole thing should be somewhat Chinese. That the Consortium had insufficient sureties to offer was obvious – otherwise how should he be there? Since the war, the losses sustained by the thrifty French investor (as blackmailing financial journals put it, he thought: irritation had a rousing effect on him), in subscribing to the stocks and shares of foreign commercial loans recommended by the larger public banks, have amounted to close on forty thousand million francs – distinctly more than the Treaty of Frankfort. A bad investment rendered better commission than a good one; that's all there was to it. But even at that, the public banks must have their bad investments put up to them by one of their own people. They would never dream of producing this money unless the Minister formerly intervened. Besides, Ferral was not their sort. Not married; and there had been stories about well-known women. . . . Suspected of smoking opium, too. He had turned down the Legion of Honour. Too proud to be either easy to deal with, or a hypocrite. It may be that great individualism can only flourish to the full on the dung-hill of hypocrisy. It wasn't just by chance that the Borgia was a Pope. . . . Not in the France of the late eighteenth century, among revolutionaries intoxicated with the idea of virtue, did you find your great individualists strutting about, but in Renaissance times, when the structure of society was, of course, so essentially Christian. . . .

'Sir,' the eldest member of the bankers' delegation addressed the Minister, gnawing both his syllables and a little moustache, which was as white as his wavy hair: 'it goes without saying that we are ready to be of assistance to the State. No question about it. You know that.'

He removed his monocle and the slight spread of his fingers when he moved his hands made it obvious that he was half-blind without it.

'But after all . . . even so . . . the thing is: to what extent? I'm not saying that each of us here could produce five millions – what?'

There was an almost imperceptible shrug of the ministerial shoulders.

'But that's simply not the point; the Consortium has to refund deposits to the tune of two hundred and fifty millions. So what then? If the State feels that a crash on such a scale is to be avoided, it will find the money itself. After all, what about the Bank of France and the Government of Indo-China? It's more their business than ours to protect the interests of French and Annamite shareholders. We have our own depositors, our own interests, to consider. Each of us is here on behalf of his Company. . . .'

('Though, of course,' thought Ferral, 'if the Minister were to make it quite clear that he insists on their supporting the Consortium, why, the dear depositors and their interests would cease to exist.')

'. . . Which of us could claim that the depositors he represents would welcome the idea of a loan for the purpose of keeping a tottering concern on its feet? We know very well, sir, what they think – and are not alone in thinking. They are of the opinion that the stock market ought to be put on a sounder basis and all unpracticable enterprises abandoned; that to bolster them up artificially is to do a good turn to no one. What is the use of free competition, the keystone of all French trade, if unsound businesses are sustained automatically?'

('My good sir,' Ferral thought, 'only last month your firm asked the State for a thirty-two-per-cent increase on tariffs – presumably for the benefit of free competition.')

'. . . Am I not right? Our business is the lending of money against security, as our friend here has so rightly pointed out. The security offered to us by M. Ferral . . . why, you have heard M. Ferral himself on that subject. Does the State intend to take the place of M. Ferral in this matter and provide us with such securities as would justify us in advancing the Consortium the sum it needs? In a word, is the State offering no compensation and does it appeal to our devotion to its interests or are we being asked – by the State, not by M. Ferral – to facilitate a Treasury transaction, as a long-term investment? If the first of these alternatives is correct, let me say that we are ready to do our duty by the State, though, of course, our share-holders would have to be considered: if the second, what guarantees are we offered?'

('There's symbolism for you,' thought Ferral. 'If we weren't so busy play-acting, the Minister would reply: "I am charmed by your so humorous use of the word 'devotion'. By far the greater part of your profits derives from your dealings with the State. You live off commissions, which are the stock-in-trade of your house, not by hard work or any trade-efficiency. The State has this year paid you, in one way and another, a hundred millions; it is taking back twenty; be duly grateful and clear out." But there's no danger of that happening.')

The Minister drew a box of marshmallows from a drawer in his desk and handed it round. They all took one, except Ferral. He knew by now what the Banks wanted: they were ready to lend the money, since it was going to be impossible to leave this room without, to some extent, letting the Minister have his way, but they would part with as little as possible. As for the Minister himself . . . Ferral waited, certain that he was thinking: 'What would Choiseul have looked like doing in my place?' 'Looked like': the Minister did not hope to be taught strength of will by the example of great men – merely deportment and polish.

'The Vice-President of the General Funds Corporation can tell you as well as I can,' he said, lightly tapping the table with his pencil, 'that I cannot give you these guarantees without a vote of Parliament. I have called you together, gentlemen, because the business in hand affects the prestige of France: do

305

you imagine that a good way to uphold that prestige would be to have the whole question debated in public?'

'No doupbt, no doupbt, but neverdless adlow me, sir . . .'

A hush ensued. The bankers, chawing their marshmallows, took refuge, in a pensive solemnity, against the provincial accent which they now realized suddenly threatened them if they opened their mouths. Without the trace of a smile, the Minister glanced from one to the other, and Ferral, presented with the glass-eyed rather than the other profile, likened him in his mind to a great white roc perched, disdainful and un-stirring, among a flock of lesser birds.

'In that case, gentlemen,' he went on, 'I see that we are agreed on this point. . . . From whatever angle we envisage the problem it is essential that the deposits be cleared. The Government of Indo-China will help to put the Consortium on its feet again to the extent of one-fifth of its liabilities. What are you gentlemen willing to contribute?'

Every one now relied on his marshmallow for protection. 'A neat little whimsey,' Ferral told himself. 'He must have his little joke – but the upshot would have been the same without the marshmallow. . . .' He knew just how much weight the Minister's suggestion would carry. It was his own brother who had answered, when the Funds Corporation was asked for a loan unsupported by vote of Parliament: 'Yes, and after that I might go and give my lady-friend two hundred million, don't you think?'

Silence. Longer than the previous silence. The delegates, were whispering among themselves.

'Sir,' said Ferral, 'if, in one way or another, the sounder part of the Consortium's business is taken over; and if the deposits must, whatever the circumstances, be paid back; do you not think that we are entitled to hope for a greater effort which would enable the Consortium to be maintained? Does not the State regard the continued existence of so widespread a concern in French hands as being quite as important as a few hundred million francs' worth of deposits?'

'Five millions is no sort of sum, gentlemen,' the Minister remarked. 'Must I make a more urgent appeal to the sense of devotion you mentioned? I know that you are particularly eager, that your Boards of Directors are particularly eager, to obviate State-control of the Banks. Have you no fear that the downfall of such an undertaking as the Consortium may incline public opinion to demand, nay, urgently to insist, that such a control be established?'

'More and more Chinese,' thought Ferral. 'All that means is: "Stop putting up idiotic bids of five millions to me." State-control of the banks is a ludicrous bogey since the Government that threatens it follows a policy that is in direct opposition to the adoption of such measures. And the Minister has no more real need to call it into play than the gentleman present who controls the Havas News Agency needs to lead a press-campaign against the Ministry. The State could no more tackle the banks than the banks could take on the State. They've everything in common: the same personnel, identical interests, similar psychology. It would be like a squabble between the heads of departments in one store – who run the place between them, anyhow. And run it badly.' As at that time at the Astor, he was only saved by the necessity of not weakening, of not showing he was angry. But he had lost: he had made efficiency his fundamental claim to respect and nothing could compensate him now for finding himself in a position of inferiority before these men whose personalities and methods he had always despised. He was weaker than they, and so, by the terms of his own system of life, his every impulse was now deprived of meaning.

'Sir,' said the eldest delegate, 'we are only too eager to give yet another proof of the excellence of our intentions towards the State; but if we are to have no guarantees, we cannot, out of consideration to our shareholders, see our way to allowing the

307

Consortium credit over and above the sum entailed by the deposits to be repaid and covered by the control that we may assume over the more solid business transacted by that company. God knows that we have no desire to take over the responsibility of this control, but we will do so in view of the higher interest of the State. . . .'

'Really, this creature's incredible,' thought Ferral. 'Like a retired don – a blind Oedipus of a don. And all these fools, the whole, hoodwinked country, running to the stockbrokers for advice and having gilt-edged Government stocks tossed to them when it's advisable, from a strategic point of view, to build a railway in Russia or Poland or at the North Pole! During the war that stick on the sofa deprived French investors of eighteen millions in Government bonds alone! Serve them right – as he said himself ten years ago: "Any man who asks the advice of some one he doesn't know before investing his capital, deserves to lose it." Eighteen million francs! Not to mention the forty milliard that went on commercial shares. And not mentioning me, either. . . .'

'Monsieur Damiral?' queried the Minister.

'I cannot but associate myself with that last observation. I too, like M. de Morelles, cannot pledge the institution I serve to this affair without the guarantees he mentioned. Were I to do so, I should be running counter to the principles and traditions which have made that house one of the strongest in Europe: principles and traditions often, I know, combated, but which, nevertheless, enable it to stand by the Government when called upon, as it was five months ago, is today and will be, perhaps, again tomorrow. It is the frequency of these appeals, sir, and our own determination not to say them "nay" which constrains me to ask for the guarantees which I am required, by these very principles, these traditions of my house, to offer our shareholders; and in exchange for which – if you will allow me to say so, sir – we place ourselves entirely at your service. No doubt we could provide twenty millions.'

The delegates stared at one another in consternation: the shareholders would be reimbursed. Ferral now understood what it was the Minister had been aiming at: he had wished to satisfy his brother without becoming entangled himself; also to indemnify the depositors and to make the banks pay – but as little as possible; and to be able to draw up a satisfactory report. Trading would continue. The Consortium would be done away with; but its destruction would not much matter if the deposits could be refunded. The banks would get the guarantee they had asked for (they'd lose all the same, but not very much). A few branches of the business would be kept going and they would be dependent on the banks; the rest didn't matter. Everything that had been achieved in Shanghai was being robbed, here and now, of all meaning. He would far rather have seen himself despoiled and the living work of his hands won, or snatched, from him. But the Minister would consider nothing but his fear of the Chamber: he was in no coat-tail tugging mood today. Ferral, in his shoes, would have begun by relieving the Consortium of his own presence and would then have kept it alive at all costs. As for the public banks, he had always maintained that their avarice was incurable. He recalled with pride a remark once made about himself by one of his antagonists: 'He can't tell the difference between a Bank and a gambling-den.'

A telephone-bell rang, close by. One of the attachés entered.

'Sir, the Prime Minister has come through on the private line.'

'Say that it's all being fixed up all right. . . . No, I'll go myself.'

He went out, to return a minute later. He glanced at the spokesman of the leading commercial bank in the country, the only one of its kind represented at this gathering. The man's moustache made a straight line, parallel to his pince-nez; a bald dome, a look of utter weariness. Until now he had not spoken a word.

'We have no interest whatsoever in keeping the Consortium on its feet,' he remarked slowly. 'A share in the building of the railways is assured to France by the terms of the Treaty. If the Consortium goes into liquidation, some other company will be formed, or come into being, and the gap will be filled. . . .'

'And this new company,' Ferral observed, 'instead of industrializing Indo-China, will pay dividends. But as it won't have done anything for Chang Kai Shek it will find itself in exactly the position you would find yourselves in here, if you had never been of service to our Government: and the contracts will fall into the hands of any American or British firm sheltering behind a French name – that's quite obvious. Then of course you'll be lending them the money you won't lend me. We formed the Consortium because the French banks in Asia were so set on a policy of guarantees that they ended up by lending money to the British so as not to lend it to the Chinese. We have always taken risks, that's –'

'I did not like to say so.'

' – quite true. It's only natural that we should reap the consequences of that policy. Your investors will be safeguarded' – he smiled with one corner of his mouth – 'up to a loss of fifty-eight milliards, instead of fifty-eight milliards and an additional few hundred millions. And so, gentlemen, let us, if it please you, proceed to arrange the details of the Consortium's demise.'

KOBE

With all the sunlight of spring blazing down on her, May, too poor to afford a cab, climbed up towards Kama's place. If Gisors' luggage were heavy, they'd have to borrow some money off the old painter to get back to the ship. When he left Shanghai, Gisors had told her he was taking refuge with Kama;

and on arrival, he sent her his address. No word, after that. Not even when she wrote to tell him of his appointment to a professorship at the Sun Yat Sen Institute in Moscow. Was it that he was afraid of the Japanese police?

As she walked, she read a letter from Pei which had been handed to her, when the boat dropped anchor at Kobe, as she was having her passport visa-ed.

. . . and all those who escaped from Shanghai await you. The pamphlets arrived safely. . . .

He had published, anonymously, two accounts of Chen's death; one straight from his heart: 'The destruction of a dictator is the individual's duty towards himself and should be unrelated to politics, which are the expression of a collective consciousness'; the other written for the traditionalists: 'Just as filial obligation – the trust our ancestors have in us – requires us to seek the highest perfection in our lives, even so it calls to each of us for the death of the usurper.' The secret printing-presses were already reissuing these pamphlets.

. . . I saw Hemmelrich yesterday. You are often in his thoughts. He is a fitter at the power-station. His words to me were: 'Before, I began to live when I left the works; now I start to live when I go there in the morning. It's the first time in my life that I work with a knowledge of why I am working – not merely while waiting patiently for death. . . .' Tell Gisors that we expect him. I have thought, since I've been here, of that lecture in which he once said: 'A civilization becomes transformed, surely, when its most painful aspect – the slave's humiliation, the toil of the modern workman – suddenly attains its value, when the victim no longer seeks to escape this humiliation but to find in it his salvation, no longer seeks relief from work but discovers in it a reason for his existence. It is essential that our factories, which are still so like Christian churches in the catacombs, should become what the medieval cathedrals were; and men must come to see therein, not gods, but the strength of the human will battling against Earth itself. . . .'

Yes; no doubt men were only worth what they themselves had transmuted. The revolution had recently undergone a terrible malady, but had come through it alive. And it was Kyo and others like him who, living or dead, defeated or not, had brought it into the world. . . .

I am going back to China as an agitator. I shall never be a pure Communist. Nothing's at an end there yet. We may some day meet again; they tell me your request has been granted. . . .

A newspaper cutting slipped from the folds of the letter. She picked it up.

> 'Work must become the chief weapon of class-warfare. The most tremendous industrialization plan in the world is at present under consideration. Its object is in the course of five years to transform the entire U.S.S.R. and make it a leading industrial power in Europe; next to overtake and surpass the United States. This gigantic enterprise. . . .'

Gisors was awaiting her, framed in the doorway, wearing a kimono. There was no luggage in the hall.

'Did you get the letters I wrote?' she asked, as she entered a bare room – matting and paper were all it contained, and the window-panels were thrown back, revealing the whole sweep of the bay.

'Yes.'

'We'll have to hurry. The boat sails again in a couple of hours.'

'I shan't be going, May.'

She looked at him. 'No use questioning him,' she thought; 'he'll explain on his own.' But it was he who queried.

'What are you going to do?'

'I shall try to serve as an agitator in one of the female squads.

It's almost fixed up already, apparently. I shall get to Vladivostok the day after tomorrow and leave at once for Moscow. If it doesn't work out, I'll serve as a doctor in Moscow or Siberia. I hope it does, though. I'm so tired of nursing. . . . To be always among sick people – when it's not because you're fighting – needs a special kind of grace – and there is no grace left in me of any sort. Besides, to watch people dying is almost more than I can stand now. . . . Well, I suppose if I must. . . . It's a way of avenging Kyo, even so.'

'I am too old for revenge, May.'

There was indeed something that had changed in him. He seemed far away, isolated from her, as though only a part of himself were there in the room with her. He lay down on the floor: there was nothing to sit on. She too sank down beside a tray of opium.

'What are you going to do yourself?' she asked.

He shrugged his shoulders, indifferently.

'Thanks to Kama, I'm Professor of Western Art here. . . . I've gone back to my old job, you see. . . .'

She sought his glance, amazed.

'Even at this point,' she said, 'when we have been defeated politically and our hospitals are closed, secret groups are forming again in all provinces. Our people will never forget that they are suffering on account of other men, and not owing to any fault in their own lives. You used to say: "They have awakened with a start from a sleep thirty centuries' long to which they will never return." You also said those who have given a consciousness of their revolt to three hundred million wretches are not like the shadows of men that slip by – even if they have been beaten, even if they were tortured, even if they died. . . .'

She was silent for a moment.

At last: 'They are dead now,' she said.

'I have not forgotten that, May. It's something else. . . . Kyo's death isn't only pain, it isn't only that things are changed.

. . . It's – a metamorphosis. I have never loved the world over-much: Kyo kept me in touch with mankind, it was through him that men existed for me. . . . I have no wish to go to Moscow. I should teach wretchedly there. Marxism no longer lives in me. Kyo looked upon it as a form of will – that's true, don't you think? But I see in it a fate, and I adhered to it so that my fear of death might have a link with fate. There is almost no fear left in me now, May: since Kyo died, I haven't minded dying. I have been freed – freed! – at one and the same time from death and from life. What should I do there?'

'Change anew, perhaps.'

'I have no other son to lose.'

He drew the opium tray towards him, began to prepare a pipe. Without a word, she pointed to a near-by slope: tied by the shoulders, a hundred or so coolies were dragging uphill some massive load which was out of sight; they strained – a living vision of slavery down the ages.

'Yes,' he said, 'I know – yes.'

'And yet,' he went on, after a moment, 'don't be deceived: these men are ready to let themselves be killed for Japan.'

'How long will that go on for?'

'Longer than I shall live.'

Gisors had smoked his pipe straight off. He opened his eyes once more.

'You can go on tricking life for a long time, but in the end it converts you into what you were intended to be. Every old man is an admission of defeat, believe me, and if old age is often so empty, it is because so many of the elderly are themselves empty and have concealed the fact. But that in itself is un-important. Men should be able to comprehend that there is no reality, but that worlds of contemplation exist – either with or without opium – where all is vain. . . .'

'And what is there to contemplate in these worlds?'

'Perhaps nothing other than this same vanity. . . . That in itself is a great deal.'

Kyo had told May: 'Opium plays an important part in my father's life, but I sometimes wonder whether opium determines his life for him or if it bears out certain forces that cause him uneasiness. . . .'

'If Chen,' Gisors went on, 'had lived outside the revolution, you may be quite certain that he would have forgotten all about the murders he committed. He'd have forgotten –'

'The others haven't forgotten: there have been two terrorist attempts since his death. He had no use for women, so I knew him hardly at all; but I don't believe he would have lived even for a year, outside the revolution. There is no dignity that is not founded on suffering.'

He had scarcely listened to what she said.

'Forgotten . . .' he continued. 'Since Kyo died, I have discovered music. Music alone can speak to us of death. Now I listen to Kama whenever he plays. And yet' – he was talking to himself as much as to May – 'when I make no effort to remember, what is it I still recall? My longings and my wretchedness, the very weight of my fate upon me, my life itself. . . .'

('But while you are sloughing the husk of your life,' she reflected, 'other Katows are burned alive in furnaces, other Kyos. . . .') Gisors' glance, as though in the wake of his forgetting, lost itself in the landscape outside. Beyond the road, the thousand sounds of toil in the harbour seemed to flow back in waves across the glistening sea, countering the dazzling brilliance of the Japanese springtime with all man's activity, ships, cranes, cars, and scurrying crowds. May thought of Pei's letter: it was in this avalanche of work – as desperate as war – that had swept down over Russia, in the will of the multitudes for whom this work had become life itself, that her dead had found their refuge. The blue sky sparkled like the sun, in gaps between the pine-trees; the breeze which gently stirred the branches caressed their two bodies as they lay. To Gisors it seemed that the wind swept through him like a flood, like Time itself; no longer now was he further isolated from the world by the idea that Time, slipping through him, was bringing him closer to death. It drew him thither in serene acceptance. His eyes took in the tangle of cranes on the edge of the town, the sailing-ships and the liners in the harbour, and human dots on the distant road. 'They all suffer,' he thought, 'and each man suffers because he thinks. Fundamentally the mind only conceives of man as eternal, and so all consciousness of this life can be nothing but an agony. Life should be envisaged not by human thought, but in an opium dream. How many of the sorrows that stalk abroad this bright, sunlit day, would disappear, if thought itself were banished? . . .' Relieved of every burden, even of the burden of being man, he stroked in gratitude the stem of his pipe, as he contemplated the hurrying movements of all these unknowns striding towards death in the blazing sunlight, each nursing his deadly parasite in the innermost recesses of his being. 'Every one of us is mad,' he reflected, 'but what is each individual fate if not a lifetime of efforts designed to couple fool and universe together?' He remembered how Ferral had looked with the lamplight shining up from below, and behind him the fog and the darkness. 'Every man dreams of being God. . . .'

Fifty sirens screeched together; it was the eve of a holiday, and work was over. Before any change became visible on the quayside, tiny figures of men, like reconnoitring scouts, appeared on the road leading straight into the town, and soon after that the masses swarmed over it, dark and distant, amid a great hooting of klaxons; employers and employees were coming away from work together. The crowd rolled forward as to the attack, swinging along with that uneasy motion typical of all crowds seen from a distance. Gisors had seen animals hastening down to drink at nightfall: first one, then several, soon the whole herd would rush towards a stream, impelled by some force that seemed to have been brought into play with the coming of darkness. In his memory opium gave their universal onrush a sense of savage harmony, and these men moving along in a distant clatter of clogs seemed to him, every one of them, mad, and far removed from a system of things universal, whose throbbing heart, somewhere high up in that blaze of light above, gleaned them and cast them back like grains of an untold harvest. Light, infinitely remote clouds sailed above the sombre pine-woods and little by little faded back into the sky; and it seemed to him that one of these clumps of cloud – that one in particular – symbolized the men that he had known or loved, men who were now no more. Humanity was squat and heavy, heavy with the weight of flesh and blood and suffering; like everything that must needs die, preoccupied eternally with its own existence. But even flesh, even blood, even pain and death vanished in the upper brightness of the air, like music dying away in the silence of the night. He thought of the music Kama made, and human suffering seemed to him to sail away and be lost like the hubbub of the world below; deliverance trembled within him as deeply hidden as his heart itself, and over it there slowly closed in an inhuman embrace, the grief he had mastered.

'Do you smoke much?' she asked again.

She had asked the question once already, but he had not heard her. He focused his eyes on the room once more.

'Do you imagine I don't know what you are thinking? And do you imagine I don't realize all that better than you do yourself? Can you not see that it would be easy for me to ask you by what right you presume to judge me?'

He looked hard at her.

'Have you no wish to bear a child?'

She returned no answer to his question; her always passionate desire to bear a child now seemed to her a betrayal. Yet she gazed at the serene expression on his face in terror. Truly he had come back to her from the far domain of death and was as much a stranger to her as any corpse in a common grave. The deeds of Kyo had made their mark on the repression that had beaten down an exhausted China; they remained engraved on the hopes and sufferings of the masses, as the inscriptions of the early empires remained for ever emblazoned on the slopes of river gorges. Yet not even this ancient China, which these men had catapulted back irrevocably into the darkness of the past, with a roar like that of a landslide, was as effaced from the living world as was the meaning of Kyo's life from the face of his father.

'The only thing I loved has been torn from me, you realize that, and yet you expect me to remain the same. Do you imagine my love was not as great as yours – you, whose life has not even changed?'

'It has changed no more than the body of a living person changes when life fades from it. . . .'

He took her hand in his.

'You know what they say: "It takes nine months to create a man, and only a single day to destroy him." We both of us have known the truth of this as well as any one could ever know it. . . . Listen, May: it does not take nine months to make a man, it takes fifty years – fifty years of sacrifice, of determination, of – so many other things! And when that man has been achieved, when there is no childishness left in him, nor any adolescence, when he is truly, utterly, a man – the only thing he is good for is to die.'

She looked at him, petrified; but his eyes were on the clouds.

'I loved Kyo as few men love their children. You know that.'

He still held her hand in his; he drew it towards him and closed his other hand upon it.

'Listen, though. One should love the living, not the dead. . . .'

'Love is not the reason for my going to Moscow.'

He gazed down at the splendid vision of the bay sparkling in the sunlight. She had withdrawn her hand.

'One starts out on the road to vengeance, May, my dear, and one meets life by the way. . . .'

'That is no reason for seeking it.'

318

She got up, gave him her hand again to say good-bye. But he took her face between his two hands and kissed her. Kyo had kissed her like that on their last day together, just like that. And never since then had a hand caressed her face.

'I hardly ever weep now, any more,' she said, with bitter pride.